Harry Pond Looks Homeward

THE SPIRITUAL ADVENTURES
OF
AN OHIO FARM BOY

.

Jay Allan Luboff

CHAPTER ONE
COMING HOME

No name is no-thing ... learn your name and learn your destiny

I ran to the house that day expecting to see Mom and Dad alive, even though I knew that this could not be. The year was 1967 and I had just returned from Vietnam. I knew that they were dead, but I reasoned that Mom and Dad would somehow still be around, that somehow some part of them would be, well, home when I arrived.

I was wrong.

The day, I remember, was hot, very hot, and I was tired. I'd been wounded in the hip and now I was almost healed. Only Becky, my older sister, was there to greet me at the Columbus airport. I hadn't seen her in three years and she was as I had remembered her before enlisting, as beautiful as ever: brown hair and eyes, slender aquiline nose, and "six feet tall in bare feet" as she often joked, and very full of body, mind, and spirit.

In a way, her greeting saved my life, for I had been forlorn for weeks at the news that Mom and Dad had passed on in a car accident. "This can't be," I thought out loud upon hearing the news. "Surely, God is greater than this?" These were good people. "Why them?" But my lament, sadness, and anger did nothing to change the fact that they were gone.

I hadn't really thought myself close to them, but lying in a hospital bed in Saigon and hearing the news brought such a jolt to my being that I knew this wasn't so. Now, nearly four months later, the shock still remained. Driving home from the airport through the Ohio countryside, Becky's usual jovial manner gave way to somberness as she spoke of the accident. No one really knew what had happened—two cars on a rainy night, a narrow country road, both drivers perhaps shocked by the glare of oncoming lights. Dad and Mom's car went out of control and, in the end, no one survived.

I listened as we drove, a part of me present and a part wrapped within myself, full of those feelings of rage and despair, depression and loss that I had experienced upon hearing the news. In the midst of these emotions, I found myself searching for that place of strength within me that I knew I'd need to face my return home. Now, as Becky drove us on, I felt an inkling of that familiar place within. I had called upon it often in Nam to bring me through the worst of the war. It had served me well then, been my protector, my advisor, my guardian, and even, I thought at times, my own personal angel. Yes, that's what I felt most about it. It had been, indeed, my guardian angel!

Now, being home, I wondered. I wasn't at all certain that I'd be able to really touch that place inside me, away from the ceaseless rain, mud, gore and pain of Vietnam. Yet, as we turned the car into the familiar, long and dusty driveway leading to the farmhouse, I knew that that strength was with me.

CHAPTER TWO
FRIENDS MEETING

Love takes many forms, most of all it comes from the heart of Light

I sat with Becky in the living room. Four months isn't a long time to register the passing of people who lived in this house for more than a quarter century. Familiar objects, vibrating with their presence, rested everywhere: the picture of the family outing to the summer place at the lake, Mom's hand crocheted throw at the back of the couch, the old black and white TV that Dad had refused to throw away even after we'd bought a new color one.

"Memories, I said as I turned to Becky, make up so much of our lives and our thoughts. I sit here remembering and I feel sad, yet Mom and Dad were happy people, and we'd a happy life here with them. All that's left, though, are the memories."

For a moment Becky's eyes filled with tears, and then lit again as if the sun shone through her cloud filled eyes. "Do you remember," she said, "how Dad used to take us pony riding at the circus? I liked that. Those are the times I won't forget."

I did remember, fondly, and responded with my own remembrance. We talked this way on into the night about having been raised in this house, about Mom's cooking and Dad's attempts at being strict, and about our lives growing up in this ever-so-familiar place, sharing past times that were no more.

I couldn't remember the last time Becky and I talked like this. As children we'd played together, but Becky became more aloof as we grew older, interested in different things, a girl with her own ideas and friends. Now, in the midst of this tragedy, she seemed to want to make contact with me, as if by doing so we'd bring back Mom and Dad.

Eventually the conversation came around to the war. I said sadly, "it wasn't any fun, none at all … what with my injury and all that I witnessed there, and still there were things that happened to me there in Vietnam that I … I can't explain, mysterious and magical things that I can only call Godlike interventions. I'm still trying to sort it all out, but I can say this: I met a part of me … a quieter and, well, more spiritual part of me there, and I want to find out more about it."

As I spoke, I watched Becky's eyes. I could always tell how she reacted by the look in her eyes. She could never hide a thing, and now, as I talked, a glow of shiny light began to sparkle there.

"Harry," she said, "you're my little brother, but I've never once considered you less than me. I want to know all that you went through.

Some strange and wonderful things have happened to me as well these past months, over the last year or so. Things that have led me to ask some serious questions about what I call spirit. Maybe we can help each other?

"Becky," I said, "I don't really know how to explain it, but," and I reached deep inside myself for the right words to say, "I hear a voice in my head that talks to me, gives me direction and advice. It's strange. I hope you don't think I've lost it or something, but I trust that voice."

Becky looked at me in a way that I had never seen before, as if she were seeing me for the first time. She said, "No, it doesn't sound strange at all, not with the kind of things that have been happening in my life. But, please, tell me more."

"Well, it started while on patrol in Nam. One night, I found myself cut off from the rest of my platoon. I guess I turned right when they turned left. As I walked on, I realized my situation … all alone in hostile territory. My knees actually started to shake. I'd been in several tight situations before, but nothing like this. As night came, I knew that the sounds I heard in the jungle didn't come from just night birds. The North Vietnamese were everywhere and it took all my will power to keep from making noise as I lay motionless on the ground. Then it happened, from somewhere within me I heard a voice … a voice different from my own, and this voice told me to get up and begin to walk in a certain direction. At first I felt skeptical, but the gravity of my situation left me open to advice. If I stayed, I knew that I would be caught. The moonlit night made my position very vulnerable, and there were just too many enemy soldiers roaming around the area for them to continually miss me. So, I did it! I just got up, held my breath, and as quietly as I could I walked in the direction the voice told me to walk.

"My guess is that if any of the North Vietnamese did hear me, they mistook me for one of their own, because as I walked I heard the familiar Vietnamese language all around. I held my breath and continued to walk. The voice guided me "turn left here … right there …" and before I knew it the jungle became quiet around me and I soon found myself walking in what felt like familiar territory. I was right, just around the bend of a stand of trees I came into our camp.

"I didn't tell anybody about the voice, but it came back to me a lot during my time in Nam. Every time I found myself in a dangerous situation, I found it there with me. After awhile, I got used to it and expected it to be there to help me out. It never failed me and I didn't even question where it came from. I only knew that it came to me as a friend and meant me well."

Becky looked at me once again with that same look she had before, as if she were listening to someone who couldn't possibly be her little brother. "Harry," she said, "I know this'll sound strange to you, but the same thing has happened to me. Well, not exactly the same, but similar. It started happening just before Christmas. I was on my way to visit a friend in the city when a huge snowstorm hit. I was driving on the back road from our place to her home and the snowstorm came so fast and furious that I didn't even know what was happening. As I turned around a bend, the car started to skid. My instinct was to put my foot on the brake, but this voice, very calm, yet very firm, came inside me, and told me to just relax and turn the wheel in a certain direction, and all would be okay. It happened so fast. I just instinctively listened and everything worked out fine. I got to my friend's that evening and stayed over.

"The thing is, it has spooked me ever since. That voice keeps coming back. It says that I've asked for it to come. Well, I tell you, if I asked for it I'm sure not aware of it. It's not that it's so bad. It tells me things about life, about Mom and Dad and me, about, well, a lot of things. It's scary. People around here would think I'm crazy, so I haven't told anyone else, either. As I think about it, I'd have to say, like you, that the voice is a friend of mine. It offers help and knows how to give just the right advice at the right time."

We both fell silent. Surely, Becky's voice couldn't be the same as mine, and what were these voices, anyway? Had we inherited some kind of "hearing voices disease" from our parents? I wondered, and then said, "I can't answer all these questions tonight, but I do know that it's been a long day and we're both tired and need to get some sleep. Let's talk tomorrow. Maybe we can help each other."

We hugged goodnight and went off to our rooms, the same rooms that we'd slept in since childhood.

CHAPTER THREE
FOREST WALK AND ANGELS' VOICES

No one can know but you, and you can know all if you want

The next afternoon Becky and I took a long walk in the forest that bordered our farm on the northern and partially eastern sides of the property. The scent of evergreen fronds greeted us as we walked along the central forest path. Everywhere, tightly grouped stands of hemlocks, Austrian and Canadian pines, some standing a tall as seventy feet high and forty feet wide, filled the forest, creating a Christmas-like feeling no matter the time of year.

Massive old growth American Sycamores with their spotted gray-white bark, and equally large Cottonwoods spread across the forest floor. They rose above the evergreens to create a green and golden leaf umbrella across the rooftop of the forest, providing much needed relief from the often brutal heat of the Ohio summer. As children, Becky and I had marveled at these giants some with canopies sixty feet across at their widest point. On hot summer days like this one, we would often come into the forest to escape the blistering heat of the day. We never tired of our visits, for they always brought with them gifts of adventure, watching tadpoles grow into crocking frogs, picking wildflowers for Mom's dinner vase, or eating our fill of the berries abounding everywhere.

In autumn, old growth stands of White Oak and White Ash bordering the forest along its edge treated us to fireworks displays of changing leave colors of yellow, orange and reddish-purple showing the dance towards winter. The sycamore's bark turned pure white, signaling a time when the freezing cold kept us from visiting this magical place of childhood mirth and fancy.

Walking lightly on the carpet of moss resulting from the giant shade trees, speckles of sunlight filtered through the forest's ceiling, sprinkling our faces and the path on which we walked with rays of golden light. We knew this path well. Growing up, it had been our pathway to adventure, our playground. Both of our memories were rich with days spent here roaming by the summer streams, together or with friends, seeding our days with bullfrogs, flowers, purple-berried hands, insects, and any other object that caught our fancy.

But today we simply walked in this place and Becky spoke, "Last night we spoke about voices that came to you. It's been happening to me, too. I don't know, what they say is okay, but it makes me feel that I'm somehow going crazy. What do you think? Have you found out anymore about them since the first time they came to you?"

"No, I haven't, except one thing I know is to trust them—as strange as it sounds. Like right now, I hear a voice that wants us both to know that the voices we hear are like guardian angels that have come to help. They think that that's the best way we'll understand all this. I feel a little scared, myself, but they tell me that the truth is that both you and I've asked them to come, and that they're here to help us awaken to what they call our true nature.

"You know," I continued, "Somehow, for me, I know it's true. Ever since I got hurt and had all that time to be with my thoughts in the hospital bed in Saigon, I've been thinking more and more about who I am and about what life is all about. I mean, if these voices are real, then where do they come from and what do we really know about the nature of life, anyway, and really about the nature of our own selves? "Something inside me thirsts to know the answers to these questions," I continued, "and I can't think of anything more important to do with my life than to find them out."

At this point, I stopped speaking, for I could see that, big sister or no, Becky felt stretched beyond her normal composed self by all this talk of voices and the "nature of things." She needed a comforting hand. I gently put my arm around her shoulder and we walked in silence for a while. As we went on, I thought of all the other times I'd spent in this forest.

With a little more than five hundred acres of land, it had been part of a much larger forest from which our farm, and the four other surrounding farms, had been cutout in the early part of the century. Now, these five farms held the forest in joint ownership.

We walked on, and as we did I began to hum a tune that came into my head. Then words came, and as if in a dream, I chanted them out loud:

On the path as I walk
Lightly footed, lightly footed
On the path as I walk
I deliver my song
To the spirits of the forest
Who are here as our friends
To the spirits of the forest
I've come to give my song
Like a lovers' embrace
We're all on in the Light
Like a lovers' embrace
We are One says my song

Never fear, says the forest
For the days are drawing near
Never fear, says the forest
That our voices come so clear
Soon you'll see the blue light
of the angels
Soon they will sing
in realms long forgotten
Soon they will dance in the
places of yore.

Becky looked at me in surprise, and in that moment I felt just as surprised as she, for surely I had never heard this chant before this day.

"Where did you learn that song?" she asked.

"I don't know," I said. "It just came." She looked at me strangely. I felt startled myself, but said, as if singing such a song were second nature to me, "Perhaps those who've been speaking to us want us know something new about the forest … something we don't already know."

Becky looked scared. I could see that in this moment, this whole thing went way beyond anything she could accept. I guessed it felt okay for her to hear voices in her own head, and even hear that I had been "receiving" the same, but now, with this chant, I could tell that it all seemed too much for her.

I said, "I know this is difficult to believe, but the feeling I keep coming up with about these voices, and I sort of said it last night, is that somehow these are angels speaking to us. Perhaps if we ask them who they are they'll tell us."

Though shaken, Becky stood tall and said, "Okay, all right, go ahead and ask." So I did. I asked the voice within my mind, "Are you an angel, or what?" As we walked alongside each other, I waited to hear something back, but nothing came. Becky just stared straight ahead; her eyes had a funny look as if she were in deep thought. As for me, I tried to relax and see what I could find out. We soon came to a place along the trail were an old fallen oak log rested across a narrow, almost dry creek bed that ran alongside the main forest path. As if choreographed, Becky and I moved in unison toward it, both sitting down at the same time.

Becky spoke. "I know you've been trying to get answers for us about the voices, but instead, the voices have been speaking to me just now and they told me I'm the one who will get the answers for us, at least for now."

I realized that even though Becky had spoken about *her* hearing voices, I had somehow still wanted to be the only one able to receive the answers to our questions. I'd gotten used to be the one who could "hear" and I wasn't at all sure that I liked the idea of sharing the knowledge imparted by the voices.

Becky went on. "I'm told that we're to come to the forest regularly, in this spot, and we'll receive all the information we need to know. The voice says that the forest holds a secret that can help many people if discovered, and that they'll help us discover that secret."

"They," I asked. "Who are *they*?"

So far I had been the one that heard voices and I knew, or thought I knew them to be angelic messengers. Now that Becky received the answer to the question we asked, everything seemed different. I began to wonder exactly who these voices were. I knew my "guardian angel's" voice, but now with Becky involved and hearing her own voices, I experienced fear about the whole situation. What had started out to be a unique event in my life, felt to me now to be out of control as Becky came to hear the voices as well. I felt a little frightened ... and upset, and I told her so. A broad smile crossed her face.

"When we were young," she said, "you were always getting us involved in some exciting hunt on the trail of some wild animal or other. I often felt scared and reluctant. Then, when we'd finally followed its footprints right up to the door of its den, you'd get scared and start talking about turning back. Fortunately for us now, I know you well, and even then, though scared, you'd still go on with the adventure until we found what we were looking for."

Her brown eyes sparkled with love and friendship as she spoke, and I could feel only the same towards her as I smiled myself at these cherished childhood memories. I knew Becky was right. I'd lead us into the wildest situations, but she would always be there to encourage us to complete the adventure, even when my knees started to shake.

"Yeah," I said. "I remember, and it was your courage that led us on."

I took a deep breath.

"Okay," I said, calming myself. "So, what now, what do they say?"

"That we should go back to the house now and wait for a sign that they'll send as to when to come to the forest again. Events outside of their control are unfolding," they say, "and we'll need to find the secret and use it well in order for it to help the many who will benefit from it."

"I don't understand all," I said, "but it sounds very serious—even a bit ominous."

"Yes," Becky said, "it worries me. The images I saw in my mind as they spoke were very unsettling."

"What did you see?"

"I saw a large horse, a beautiful horse, black as night, strong and powerful, but it was stuck in a bog somewhere and strange animals that

I'd never seen before threatened it. I hope it's okay. It felt to me like a friend and one that I would do almost anything to help."

"I hope we *can* help," I said, "and that everything works out well for that horse and for us. This whole thing is a little scary, and a lot more complicated than the days when were tracking possum in the forest."

Becky said, "You assured me when I felt scared about the voices. Now, I can soothe your concerns. Just as you said to me that time that you trusted the voices, I, too, know that they're friends and they need our help. I know they'll let us know more about them as we go along."

"Okay," I said, as I smiled again at the strength and wisdom of my older sister, "we need to *go forward!*"

Becky smiled at my use of the childhood motto that led us on when we were kids as I added, "So, let's continue on now, big sister."

With that we both got up and began the walk home.

The forest became cooler as the evening began to set in. What had begun as a short walk and a chat on the oak log had actually taken several hours, and now we felt famished as we approached the farmhouse.

CHAPTER FOUR
MEETING WITH UNCLE JULIUS

Many try to comprehend the other side ... few succeed ... better to follow your own light back home

When we got back to our farm, we were surprised to find our Uncle Julius waiting for us. Uncle Julius was in his late seventies when I left for the war, but I remembered him as being as fit and sharp as any thirty-year-old that I knew. That's the way I remembered him before I left three years ago. A tall man, six-feet-five or so, Julius wore an imposing, Santa Claus white beard that flowed down to his chest. As Dad told it, his older brother had traveled a lot before moving to Ohio to a little town about fifty miles down the road from us. There he married a local woman, my Aunt Lucy, and together they raised Aunt Lucy's three girls from a previous marriage and the two boys they had together. All told, Uncle Julius had been married four or five times, not even Dad knew for certain the exact number, and had fathered eight or ten children, all cousins of mine, spread across the country. Most of them were out of touch with Julius and he had a slew of grandchildren who didn't even know Uncle Julius.

Neither Becky nor I knew much about Uncle Julius' past or why he'd moved to Ohio, yet we did know that something serious had happened in the past between the two brothers, our father and our uncle, that had strained their relationship, a strain that had lasted their entire lives.

I hadn't seen Uncle Julius for some time and was pleased to see him now. Becky was not. As we approached the house she whispered to me that she'd a feeling that he was somehow involved in Mom and Dad's death. I looked sideways at her, surprised that she would say this about an Uncle she'd adored for the better part of our life. Now, she bristled at his presence as we approached the house, and couldn't hide her disdain as she spoke to him.

"Julius, what're you doing here? Mom and Dad didn't want to see you anymore, and neither do I."

Her words shocked me. I'd never heard Becky speak to anyone this way and now she spoke to our Uncle Julius with venom in her voice that I'd have reserved only for an enemy.

Uncle Julius stuttered, "Why, why Becky you know that just because your parents and I had a falling out doesn't mean that we shouldn't be friends ... like in the old days."

"I don't want to be your friend, so please leave," she insisted.

But now, instead of being hurt as I'd expected, Uncle Julius' large body shook in anger as he responded to Becky. "You know, your ma and pa had refused our offer on the farm back in the fall. But if you have any sense you'll take me up on it." Julius stopped for a moment, looking confused, as though he'd lost the thread of whatever it was that he was going to say, and then, a moment later, he seemed to catch it again, and said, "That's why I've come, to welcome Harry back home, and to talk about you two sellin' us the farm."

Now, Julius turned to me for the first time. "You should ask Becky about my offer. It's fair and it will set the two of you up for life, what with the price we're offering being way above market value. Talk it over with her Harry and maybe we can then get together."

With that Uncle Julius turned his huge body, walked to his old Chevy pickup truck, got in, and drove away.

I felt dumbfounded. All this had moved way too fast for me. I'd remembered Uncle Julius as somewhat eccentric, but not as mean man. Now, something had changed in him since the last time I'd seen him. He seemed to have lost something, something in his eyes, and in his heart had hardened. He seemed a man lost, with no laughter left in him. My mind whirled in confusion as Becky invited me to sit on the porch with her to answer my question as to how things had gotten so bad between Uncle Julius and our family.

She said, "Uncle Julius started acting strange, oh, about three years ago, right after Aunt Lucy died. "Mom wrote you about it, remember?"

"Yes, I got the letter," I said. "I remember."

"He had always been my favorite," Becky went on, "but something happened to him about that time, he just seemed to lose it and started acting stranger and stranger. At first, we thought it pretty natural and we all tried to comfort him, but it didn't seem to do any good. It just got worse and worse."

I shook my head in wonder at the downturn of events in Uncle Julius' life since my leaving for the war, and felt sad about Aunt Lucy's passing for I knew her as a kind woman.

"Well," Becky continued, "after awhile he started hanging out at the Dexter tavern with some very strange people over by Belecroft, near the river. I never met any of them, but Dad said that they were the kind of people that would make you shiver up and down your spine if you met them on a dark night. Dad didn't know for sure where they were from, but as far as he was concerned, the farther away he and the rest of the family stayed from those people the better. He'd told Uncle Julius this himself. But Julius only got furious at him, actually called Dad a thief for some reason or another, and from that time on things got even worse between us all."

"Boy," I said, shaking my head "I'm sorry to hear that, Uncle Julius was always nice to me and when I saw him just now I assumed we'd have a great reunion. I can see now how wrong I was about that!"

Still, even as I acknowledged the change in Uncle Julius, I wondered what could have happened. Julius was not, as I knew him, a bad man. The man who'd just been here acted like no one I would wish to know. He had a mean edge about him, something … well … dark about the way he looked at Becky and me. His mind seemed clouded. I knew something was wrong. Nobody would change so completely in only three years. Yes, Julius was up there in years, but something else had happened to him, something having nothing to do with age. And, no matter how alienated we all were from each other in this moment, I felt a certain sense of duty to help Uncle Julius. The words came rushing into my mind, "help him come back to himself."

I expressed this sentiment to Becky, but her anger with him left her far from wanting any parts of it. Then, I remembered what she'd said about her suspicion that Uncle Julius had actually played some part in our parent's death. I asked her about it.

"Well, Julius said, he and his friends had made Mom and Dad an offer on the farm. I don't know where they got the money, but they had a lot of it. Ours wasn't the first farm they offered on. They first wanted the Henley place, but old man Henley wouldn't budge. Do you know what happened next? Henley's farm 'accidentally' caught fire one night and Henley himself barely escaped with his life. He's still holding onto the farm, living in the old log cabin on the land, but he's scared and is sure Julius and his friends have something to do with the fire.

"Those slime have made offers on the other three farms that border the forest as well, besides the offers they made on ours and Henley's. So far, none of the families have sold, but the Hayes family is talking about it. They say the money is good and they don't want to end up," she hesitated, "well, like our parents did."

"I can tell you," she continued, "I feel scared all the time. I sensed from the beginning that Mom and Dad's death wasn't just an accident, and I, too, have a feeling, like old man Henley, that Julius and his friends had something to do with the Henley farm fire as well."

Becky paused, and then as if held back like a log jam freeing itself, all of the tension and fear Becky'd been feeling swelled up in her and tears came rolling down her cheeks.

"Oh, I'm so glad you're back," she said, wiping the tears. "I can't stand the thought that Julius had something to do with Mom and Dad's death, but I don't know what else to think. We were best friends, Uncle Julius and I. He, he was my favorite, but now," she shook her head, and said, "maybe together we can figure out what's going on, why so much interest in our farm, and the others'."

"Perhaps," I muttered, "perhaps." But I was beginning to wonder. Thoughts whirled around my mind as I tried to comprehend the meaning of all of this: the offers on the farms, not only ours but the others as well, the fire at the Henley farm, and Mom and Dad's death.

Anger and sadness swelled within me. What was going on? It all seemed like a bad dream and I turned to Becky and told her so. But she would have none of such talk, and responded strongly. "Whatever it seems like to you, it's real. Mom and Dad are gone, and Uncle Julius has turned bad, and all the rest is true. We can't just turn this off like a dream we can wake up from, we've got to deal with it, and I need your help, now!"

I nodded my head. I would help. The sadness wouldn't stop me. We said nothing more about it that evening as we prepared dinner and settled in for a quiet night at home.

CHAPTER FIVE
GOING TO VIETNAM, BACK AT HOME

We dance together and make friendship our partner

Since my growing up and teen years, I had changed a lot. In my last year in high school, I had traded TV for Sartre and Camus, athletics for photography and art, and spent the rest of my time studying to get into college. These were the beginning of years of great turmoil in the country as opposition to the war began showing up on college campuses, at first in a scattered way, and then on TVs across America. Even in our small community the debate couldn't be avoided. Henry Flugg had gone and "done the right thing" by signing up; Jack Rabin put himself "on the wrong side of the issue" when he declared to all, including the draft board, his position as a "conscientious objector."

While our community, like most farm communities, considered itself conservative, more and more people were becoming concerned about the war. For every Jack Rabin detractor, some supporters popped up who at least echoed their own misgivings, in the bingo parlor, or the old 1950s style soda shop on Main Street.

I had gone around a lot in my mind about the war, debating what I really felt about it. On the one hand, I felt frightened and didn't want to go. But, as an American, I felt that if the country needed men then I should give it support. Sure, I understood Jack Rabin and his stance. I even respected him for it. War is bad."I thought to myself. Death stinks, whether it comes on your side or the other. No one deserves the pain. And yet I knew that if I didn't go it would be to appease my fear, not my conviction, and I knew I needed to do what felt right to me.

So, the day I graduated high school, instead of reading letters of acceptance from colleges, I went down to the local Marine recruiting station and signed up to go to Vietnam.

***

Now, I wonder about it all. I missed Mom and Dad. Their death hit me hard. The war had been tragic, yet here at home I found only sadness and more tragedy. In my mind I struggled to know what best to do. Clearly, something had gone very wrong in our town since I'd left. Uncle Julius' behavior echoed the whole of it. On the drive in from the airport with Becky, I could feel it, too.

The town had lost its sparkle. When I left, the town had energy about it. I'd even spoken about it with one of my buddies in Vietnam as "A lively town with lots of hope." Annual Labor Day and Memorial Day parades gave the town an air of friendship, patriotism and care. People's homes showed that care, as proud homeowners waved at passersby and proudly showed the new flowers in their garden to their neighbors. By all means, I wouldn't call Placerville a perfect place. We'd our share of corruption, even on the police force, embezzlement of a trusted employee, and other such problems. But we were still a community.

Yet, as Becky drove us through town on the day of my arrival back home, I could feel that things had changed. Houses went unpainted, gardens untended and instead of a parade atmosphere, I saw hung heads and clouded looks on people's faces.

I asked Becky about it. She said, "so many things have changed since you've been gone. It's as if some dark force has come to take over people's minds. They don't laugh anymore. Maybe it's the war. I don't understand it, but I know it's not good."

I nodded and said nothing.

CHAPTER SIX
VISIT TO MIKE'S PLACE

No path is easy ... but the right one will take you home

The next day I awoke refreshed and ready to go. I wanted to visit town and catch up with old friends. An air of expectancy filled me as I dressed and went down stairs.

I found Becky waiting for me in the kitchen. "Well, how did it feel sleeping in your own bed for a change?" she said with a smile. I could say nothing at first, for in just that moment a ray of sunlight burst through the kitchen window casting a burst of light across Becky's face and hair and gave a sparkle to her brown eyes that made her look just like Mom. It took me a moment to get over the shock. I answered, "I loved it. I can't remember when I've had such a good night's sleep. It's been a long, long time."

We ate together, talked about the day ahead, and my plans to visit town. Becky, I knew, would be going to work, so I would be on my own. Neither of us spoke about the voices, nor about our meeting with Uncle Julius, but I could tell that we both had these things on our minds. Yet, we spoke no further about them, as if an unspoken pact of silence existed between us. In the end, I waved goodbye and wished her a happy day as she drove down the driveway and off to work.

Now, alone in the house and with myself, I came in touch with how much the incident with Uncle Julius had troubled me. What could have happened to him? Eighty-year-old men don't just change their stripes overnight. Becky seemed certain about his involvement with our parents' death. I couldn't help but feel disturbed by the situation, and I wanted to find the answer, for myself, for Becky, and even for Uncle Julius.

My concern soon faded as Frisky, our family's calico cat, came into the kitchen and jumped onto my lap as I sat drinking a final cup of tea before heading into town. I'd never enjoyed Frisky as much as I did at that moment. Up until her playful leap on my lap, all that I'd come home to seemed pretty desolate, confusing and, well, just down, except for Frisky. Playful and friendly, Frisky's one consistent demand was to be touched. Now, amidst all the events going on, her presence brought a much needed smile to my lips. I stayed like this for some time, a smile on my face and Frisky in my lap, purring away, and then I knew it was time to go to town.

Dad's 1961 Chevy truck cruised along the road just as well as I had remembered it, as I drove the five miles of country road from our farm into town. Placerville had grown little since my leaving. As I pulled onto

Main Street, the familiar sign listing the town's population, 6,500, beneath the Rotary, Elks, Chamber of Commerce, and Knights of Columbus logos welcomed the new visitor to "our fair city."

The town looked the same. However, the same feeling of gloom that I'd felt before as I drove through town with Becky on our way home from the airport permeated the place. What was it? I couldn't find the right words for it within myself, yet I could feel "it" in the buildings, in the dirty streets that used to be sparkling clean, and yes, sadly, in the gloomy faces of the people themselves.

I parked in front of Mike's Place across from the Old Vic movie house. Mike's was my high school hangout, a place that I had spent many, many hours in during those years. I hoped to connect with some of my old buddies here, but I couldn't have been more wrong. New owners from out of town had bought the place and they definitely weren't into letting high school students hang out there. As soon as I walked in I felt the difference.

Mike's had had a festive atmosphere about it. Helium filled balloons covered the ceiling as local children brought their birthday party friends for hot fudge sundaes and hamburgers. Now, the balloons were gone, and where there had once been pictures of flowers on the wall, pictures of half naked women stood. What had once been a family place, now seemed to cater more to a very rough type of truck driver crowd.

When I asked about friends, no one knew any of those that I mentioned. I wondered what could have happened in the short time since I had left. I shook my head at the strangeness of it all.

As I came out of what was now called Henry's Grill, I saw Uncle Julius across the street with several men I didn't recognize. I walked across the street intent on speaking with him, for I still couldn't believe that he had changed so much.

But he had. As I approached, the two men with Uncle Julius looked my way, both with a look that could only say, "What're you doing here? We're having an important talk and you presence isn't welcome!" One of the two, the shorter one with a thin, almost skinny face, turned to his companions and whispered something as I neared. About five-feet six inches or so tall with balding grayish hair and a quick and nervous look about him, this man reminded me of several of the shoe salesmen I'd seen at the city shopping mall—decent enough, but always harried and in a hurry as if the time they'd to make their daily sales goals but never really got there. The other man with Uncle Julius, the taller of the two, also a man in his middle years, stood over six feet tall with the bulky frame of an ex-football player whose weight had gotten out of control since his playing days many years before. I didn't like the feel of either of them.

"Hi, Uncle Julius," I said, "do you have a minute?"

"Sure" he said, "just give me a moment." Uncle Julius mumbled a few words to his associates about meeting them later.

"Come," said Julius, and he led me to the bench at the front of the movie theatre. I can't remember how many times I'd sat on that bench before, and now with my favorite Uncle, it all felt so familiar. And yet, something about him was different. I couldn't put my finger on it, but that same instinct that I had had in Nam about the enemy being near came back now.

"Uncle Julius, "I said, in the same comfortable way that I'd always talked with him before going to Nam, "what's going on? Becky tells me that you and Mom and Dad had a falling out, and now the only thing you can find to say to me yesterday at the farm is something about some offer to buy our farm. I don't get it. You and Dad weren't always so close, but at least you talked to each other."

To my surprise, as I spoke to him, his face became redder and redder, his eyes angrier and angrier. Finally, with my last words he could hold back no longer, and it wasn't the Uncle Julius I'd known at all who spoke to me.

"You listen here, you stupid youngster," he said, "I never did care for your father or mother, but I put up with them all those years until I realized that the farm should have been mine and that your father stole it from me. Now me and my friends are looking to buy it back and I'll get back what was rightfully mine in the first place. We made your pa and ma a good and fair offer on the place," he went on. "They should've taken it, that's all I can say, they should've taken it."

As he spoke these last words, Uncle Julius' voice faded and a confused look came into his eyes, as if some distant memory from the past got in the way of his train of thought. Yet, this didn't last for long. Something inside him seemed to grab him and bring him back to his anger. He stopped speaking and without another word, simply got up to go to join his friends. Before he left, though, he turned back to me and said, "And you'd be wise now to take the same offer, Harry. No telling what could happen if you don't."

Uncle Julius' open threat hit me hard. He was my Uncle, and yet, he wasn't. I looked hard at him in amazement. This was not the man I'd grown up with, known, and loved.

From that moment forward I could no longer regard him as simply "my beloved Uncle," but rather as a likely enemy, and a dangerous one at that, to be watched at all times.

***

On the ride home I wondered about all the changes. The summer's heat rose from the blacktop in waves, giving the road an air of mystery and unfocused reality as I tried to figure it all out, but I couldn't. Instead, as I drove down the road, I found solace in listening to my favorite country station on the car radio. The music took my mind off the seemingly inexplicable darkness that had come to permeate our world. For the rest of the ride, the sounds of Hank Williams blasting "your cheatin' heart," along with the sights, sounds and smells of the beautiful Ohio countryside that I knew so very well, comforted me as I relaxed and enjoyed the drive home.

CHAPTER SEVEN
JULIUS AGAIN

We know who we are, if we look to the right places to find ourselves

Becky and I both went to bed early that evening, but the next morning I awoke to the sound of a loud, clacking engine noise. The sound so permeated my brain that at first I thought the noise to be part of a dream. I was wrong. I turned and looked at the clock. I wondered about Becky. But she'd gone to work. If not her, then who—or what?

A bit groggy, I roused myself and went to the window to find out the source of the racket, only to find Uncle Julius sitting in his noisy old pickup and waiting for his two friends who'd been in town with him., They were just pulling up to the house in a late model convertible.

Uncle Julius saw me and waved. It felt like a dream. One minute he was a friend, the next an enemy. I steadied myself and remembered my instinct the day before at our meeting in town. The thought sobered me as I dressed and headed downstairs to answer the ringing doorbell.

On the stairs, a familiar voice, one I had heard often in Vietnam, stopped me. "Beloved one," it said, "understand that Julius is no longer the Uncle you knew. He is controlled by forces other than of the Light. For now, let the die be cast as it will. Do not sell the land, it's sacred and in need of your protection!" These words rang in my ear as I opened the door to face Uncle Julius and his two friends.

Julius introduced me to his friends, John Freed, the smaller of the two men, and the bulky man Robert Frosten. I didn't invite them in, but met them outside the door. Julius spoke first, "We're here Harry to make you a fair offer on the farm, please hear us out." He spoke as if yesterday's threat had never happened, as if we were the buddies of old. I knew that the warning that had just come was real. What could it mean, "... controlled by the forces other than of the Light?" As confused as I still felt about what had happened to my Uncle, I knew to trust the voice.

I held myself in check as I spoke, "Julius," I said, "we don't want to sell the house and we don't want any more offers from you." As I spoke, he began to turn red as he had the other day, as if every *wrong* answer he might hear became an affront to his very being. I went on. "Becky and I've spoken about it and we're just not interested." Before I could say more he reached to put his hands around my neck. Instinctively, I blocked his grip and even though taller than I, I soon enough held him in a pressure lock around his head and neck.

Surprisingly, his friends jumped in to stop Julius. Trying to grab him by the arm, the shorter of the two men, John Freed, apologized, "We're sorry this happened. We're here to make a legitimate offer. If it isn't acceptable, perhaps we can make one more attractive to you?"

My hold on Julius was strong, but not strong enough to bring forth the reaction that came. He simply collapsed into my arms, and as I let go of the hold and looked into his eyes I saw a look of familiarity that I knew well. It was the old Uncle Julius and the look was one of friendship and pleading. He said nothing, but his eyes said it all. I was looking into the eyes of a man in a prison and begging to be let out, and I knew in that moment that I had to help him, no matter what he'd gotten himself involved in. I let Uncle Julius' body gently go to the ground and turned to the others.

"I don't know what it will take for you to let go of the idea of buying our farm and land," I said, "but it isn't going to happen. Now, get off my land." As I said this, Julius rose from his place at my feet, dusted himself off, and began to go along with the others. But now, sadly, the look in his eyes had changed again from one of recognition and need, back to one filled with anger and hatred. He walked away listening to the tune of a different drummer. One, I knew not.

Even free spirits still need to free their hearts to learn to fly

Becky came home around five that evening. I told her the story as we walked in the late afternoon glow of the forest. She listened intently, and then said, "You realize that the more desperate they become, the more desperate they may act to get us to agree. I feel scared, but the voices have been talking to me again. They say that we're protected and the angels of the forest will work with us to ensure that the farm itself is safe."

At Becky's words, I looked at our surroundings. Angels of the Forest, where are they? As we walked, the late day sun shone through the huge stands of cottonwoods and sycamores. I had been raised to believe in a Higher Being, creator of the All-In-All, the Oneness of all life, God. But, recent events that raised the specter of angels being real and tangible put me into a different frame mind. Sure, I'd come to believe in my guardian angel speaking to me in Nam, and even that Becky had heard voices that seemed to be the from the same source, but my mind whirled with the prospect of angels right here in the forest, in the physical.

I reached back to remember when people had seen angels before on Earth. Certainly, angels were spoken of as real in bible times, being prophetic signs of great things to come, and more. But in modern times, the thought of angels on Earth seemed to be a matter of faith. Those who said they'd seen them could never prove it; those who believed and even confirmed seeing angels did so based on a prior deep spiritual conviction that they did, in fact, exist and would physically come to Earth at times of crisis to help out.

Now, as we walked, I turned my head in every direction. Becky noticed me peering into the trees and laughed a laugh that rang like the sweet sound of a bell through the forest.

A huge smile on her face, "You look so funny, as if you expect an angel to pop out of every bush and from behind every tree."

"That's not far off," I said. "With what you've been saying, *I am* looking for angels at every turn and around every corner." We both laughed at my "angel hunt." We continued our walk, broad grins lightening our faces, and our spirits high, as we arrived at the fallen oak log; the "special place" the Guardian had called it, and the one he advised us to return to often. We sat down and Becky spoke, "Yeah, I suppose you're right to look. It all sounds pretty weird, but, you know, I believe the voices when they say we're safe. I feel the truth of it deep inside me, and in a strange kind of way, I'm looking forward to meeting the forest angels."

As I sat there and as strange as it seemed to my everyday mind, I had to admit that I, too, looked forward to the meeting. Amidst all confusing happenings taking place in my and our life since my return home, I had to admit that the presence of the voices was giving us both a sense of reassurance that everything would be fine.

As we sat together in the cool of the evening, a breeze gently rolled through the leaves of the tall trees of the forest. In the rustle of the leaves I heard, at first what seemed like a whisper of words, and then the words became a full song. Becky looked to the trees, letting me know that she could hear the song as well. We glanced at each other with surprise and a questioning look on our faces in confirmation that we both heard the same melody.

> Today's the day we speak our song
> of love
> and pure delight,
>
> We ask your help in saving all the secrets here so light
> Yes, we know that man has fallen
> from the grace of pure divine light
> Yet, now is the time for the raising of the flag
> of Spirit's purpose …
> … here enshrined
>
> You've come so far to be here now
> and this we ask of you
> Allow no man to buy this land
> that serves the deep and new
> We tell you both the secret lies
> within the doors of light,
> Which are found in groves of peace
> beyond the human sight
>
> Together you'll find this song
> so long put to rest
> To wait for a time when man can hear
> again the truth of peace
> … and happiness
>
> Hear these words
> and be at rest

seek no place
for there is
no test
Soon enough
we'll show the way
and you'll find the answer
to humanities' deep abiding need
for each to become
the divine dancer
of their own forgotten seed

My eyes wondered through the trees as the beauteous song faded in the rustle of the breeze. As it did, a bird that I'd never seen ever before in the forest landed on the highest branch of the large cottonwood tree that stood next to the fallen log: a white snowy owl.

As quickly as it alighted, it flew away, up and over the top of the tree into the rising moonlight. I said nothing for a moment and then looked over at Becky who'd also watched the owl's unexpected arrival and rapid departure.

I spoke first. "I know that no one would believe us, but the song we just heard is real, and its words are important. This forest, our forest, hides a secret that has been placed here to help humanity," I searched for the right words and then calmly, with knowingness beyond my own understanding, said, "*regain its grace,* and we need to protect that secret until it's time for it to be found."

Becky nodded and then said, "This is so exciting, the song, the white owl." And then her face darkened and tears welled up. "If only Mom and Dad could be here, but that's how really real this is. They're not here, and their deaths might very well have been caused by their wanting to protect the forest and its secrets."

I nodded and then, as had become my habit of late, retreated into that quiet space within me that always gives me comfort, and is sometimes a precursor to the voices within speaking to me.

***

This time though, the ringing boom of a familiar male voice abruptly interrupted the silence. I looked to my left down the path at the tall, bearded, heavyset man, who called our names, waving to us as he approached from around the turn of the path.

It was Frank Pond, Uncle Julius' oldest son.

Frank grabbed my hand and gave it a big shake, "It's been a long time" he said. "I'm happy as can be that you're back safe and sound."

Frank and I had been more like uncle and nephew than cousins. Ten years older than I, Frank was the one who'd take me fishing as a young boy when pa couldn't set aside his farm chores. And it was Frank who'd been there for me to answer my questions about "girls" as I entered my teen years. Not long after that, Frank left to join the marines, and I hadn't seen him since.

Now, it had been nine years since we'd seen each other and as much as I still felt the love that I felt then, I also looked at him with a questioning eye. I felt myself a different person after the war, and as Frank stood before us now, I wondered what I truly felt about this man who'd been like a God to me, my childhood hero. On the outside, he hadn't changed very much, but something, I felt, on the inside had. He had put on weight and his six foot two inch or so frame showed it with signs of bulging around the waist. Yet, even with the beard, he was still the Frank that Becky and I had known as we grew up. Friendly, jovial at times, and yet always secretive as a youth, I remembered asking often what he "really" thought about this or that. At the time, it was just instinct to ask, for somehow this man, who'd been such a good friend, also felt to me to be a mystery. Frank never seemed to reveal his true feelings, and with the events of recent days with Uncle Julius, I wasn't all that sure whether I should trust Frank or not.

"Sorry about your mom and dad," he said to me, "it was a real shock to us all." I nodded. Then Frank turned to Becky who stood to meet Frank's outstretched arms that promptly wrapped around her in a big bear hug. "Oh, you're my favorite. Gosh, it's been a long time since I've seen you as well." Becky couldn't hide her pleasure at seeing Frank. They'd always been close, and his presence brought a much needed broad smile to her face.

As much as I admired him as a young boy, the times were such that I had to wonder what he was doing here in the forest at this particular time. After all, he was Uncle Julius' son and I couldn't help but wonder if he'd come to make us yet another offer? I said nothing though, for me, too, felt the glow of seeing an old friend after such a long time.

Releasing Becky, Frank sat down on the log and spoke. As he did, the smile that had brightened his face a moment before left him, to be replaced by a seriousness that I had never seen before in him.

"I've come to talk to you both" he said, "because I heard something the other night that made me think that you two might be in danger. I don't know whether to go to the police with it, or what to do. It was something I heard my pa say that got me worried and that's why I've come. You know, after I got out of the marines about six years back, I lived in the big city for a while. Then, I moved back here about three years ago, after my pa started acting so strange and my ma passed away. He's changed. He's simply not been the same man.

"It scares me to think that he had such a falling out with your family, and then your ma and pa's accident, and the fire at Henley farm. I don't know what to do about it, but I wanted to talk to you about it. The other night I was visiting pa at the place where he rents a room when he got a phone call. He took the phone into the bathroom, thinking I couldn't hear, but because he's been acting the way he has, I decided to listen as best I could. I didn't hear all of the conversation, but I heard him repeating something that the other person said to him on the other side, and what I heard wasn't good.

"He was obviously talking to someone he's involved with in wanting to buy the farms around here, including yours. He told the person that you two haven't wanted to sell the farm any more than your parents did. His voice rose as he spoke and it seemed to me I heard him agree with the person he was talking to that they might have to 'do something drastic.'"

Frank continued, "I'm not clear what my pa's gotten himself into, but I'm certain that he was talking about the two of you. It scared me. He hung up the phone before saying too much more, except that they would meet soon to discuss it."

I looked at him in amazement. For all that Becky had said and I myself had seen Uncle Julius do with my own eyes, I still had trouble believing what had happened to him. Before I could speak, Becky joined in.

"Frank," she said, "you and I haven't spoken since the funeral, but I do want to let you know that it's been on my mind a lot that your father may have had something to do with our parents' death. I know it's horrible to have to think about someone we love going bad, but I think that's just the case. What you're saying now, Frank, just confirms my suspicions and also raises an issue about our safety that Harry and I have been talking about. I think it's time to call the police."

CHAPTER NINE
POLICE TALK ... REMINISCING

Know that on the journey of self-awakening, you will find more courage within you than ere you thought possible

Two days later we were together again as Frank came to our farm for the meeting with the police. Frank arrived an hour early. As we made small talk, I remembered Uncle Julius and Frank from my days as a youth. Even though Julius and his wife Lucy farmed a bit, he made his living as a carpenter and a good one at that. In later years he focused his work on his little cabinet shop, and I remembered the happy time that Dad and I had had the last time we went to visit the shop.

Uncle Julius was there alone, but he looked excited as he greeted us as we entered his shop. "Hello, you two. God, it's nice to see you. Come on in," he said, as he hurried us into the back room, "I want to show you something I just finished."

The light wasn't that great in the room as Uncle Julius went to a large maple cabinet on the far wall of his work area and took something out. Whatever it was, it must have been heavy, for even with his height and strength, he nearly bent over with the weight of the thing. Then he turned and in his hands he carried the most exquisite jewel encrusted chest that I had ever, ever seen. About fifteen to eighteen inches high and about two feet long and about a foot or so wide, it wasn't so large, but something about it made it seem much larger than that. Even though Uncle Julius had just made it, it "felt" very big, and very old, as if crafted thousands of years ago. But the thing most remarkable about it was the glowing light that radiated from the jewels set around the chest. So bright was their glow that Dad and I both had to squint to get used to it.

Uncle Julius couldn't hide his pride in making the chest as he told us that he'd just crafted it for a Catholic priest who'd recently returned from many years of living in South America. Julius said he'd built the chest to the exact specifications of a drawing the priest had brought to him. He told us that the priest's drawing showed the precise placement and spacing for insetting each jewel into the face of the chest, and that he'd been perfectly true to the drawing in doing the work.

"The best thing I've ever made. The very best," he kept saying, "the very best." But more than this, as he showed the chest, Julius' gray-blue eyes had a sparkle that almost equaled that of the jeweled chest itself. From their positions around the chest, pearls, ruby-red gems, sapphires, and a variety of smaller precious gems radiated a remarkable light as if filled with the light of the sun itself. Made of shiny, dark, almost black ebony-like wood with an inlay of ivory and lighter wood that intermingled with the glowing jewels, the chest presented an intricate maze of carved forms creating a series of shapes that looked like what I could only think of as writing or lettering from some ancient language. The priest, Uncle Julius said, had called these designs "runes."

I'd never seen anything like it before and I know that Dad hadn't either. We marveled at the workmanship and the strange light emanating from the jewels on the chest. Though Dad didn't say much, I could tell he was proud and a little in awe of his older brother as he starred at the chest and then at Julius in admiration.

Now, sitting with Frank, three years or more after the visit, I wondered, what had happened to the chest. As far as I knew, Julius had presented it to the priest who'd commissioned it.

***

Still, now, as I remembered this last visit, I recalled also that Dad and his older brother had not always gotten along. Dad's birth had been a "surprise" to his parents as they'd had him when Grandma was in her late forties when they still lived in Pennsylvania before moving to the farm in Ohio. Uncle Julius, their only other child, was a grown man in his late twenties by then and off living on his own in one of the big east coast cities. Grandma and Grandpa bought the farm in 1930 when Dad was fifteen years old. The three of them moved to Ohio together, with Uncle Julius still somewhere in the east. When Grandpa suddenly died of a heart attack shortly after the move, Grandma and Dad ran the farm alone. But Grandma died only a few years after that, and when she did, she left the farm to Dad.

I remembered Dad telling me the rest of the story. After Grandma died, he said, his brother Julius moved to Ohio. Uncle Julius, who'd already been married and divorced three or four times by then, stayed initially with Dad at our farm. But he left shortly after coming to the farm after he and Dad argued over which one of them should have been the rightful heir. Julius moved on over to Centerville, then, about fifty miles down the road, eventually met Aunt Lucy and married. They bought a small farm themselves and raised the three girls that Aunt Lucy had had from a previous marriage, and Frank and George, their two boys.

Dad told me once that didn't think Uncle Julius had ever really ever gotten over the fact that he hadn't gotten the farm when Grandma passed on. In any case, Dad said that Julius and he never were that close. Dad didn't say much about this, but it was something I always wondered about. The official family explanation for the lack of contact was that the difference in age made it difficult for them. I had a feeling it had more to do with the farm situation than with age.

Even though not close, there was still some affection between the two of them. So, when Dad and Mom married and had Becky and me, things changed a bit between them. For a while they became warmer as the families spent time together on occasion at holiday dinners and other events. For our part, Becky and I visited often at Uncle Julius' and Aunt Lucy's farm at times of school vacations. During these visits Frank took us to the swimming hole, and on "creepy" night explorations of the forest around their farm. Becky and I always looked forward to the vacations with Frank at Aunt Lucy's and Uncle Julius' farm.

I thought, now, about how wonderful those memories were.

***

As we waited for the police to come, I also thought about the changes in our town. The town had grown since we were young, and with it, the police department. Newer, younger looking faces of men and women in police cars now rode around town replacing the old familiar faces of those who used to walk their beats on Main Street. It was one of these young policewomen, Sergeant Annie Gerhig, who came to speak with us two days after our meeting Frank.

As she drove up to the farm in a police car with "special investigations" written on the side, we waited as a young woman, calm in demeanor and petite in stature emerged. I wondered whether she would be able to help. She had a pretty face, young, thin, with light brown hair and brown eyes.

As I answered the door to greet her, my doubts disappeared. Perhaps it was the look in her eye, the bent of her jaw, I wasn't sure, but as I let her in I had a feeling we'd found a friend who could help.

We sat in the living room facing out onto the now overgrown fields of the farm as we told Sergeant Gerhig our story. At first, she took no notes and only listened. Then, she spoke and we heard more, much more than we'd expected to hear about Uncle Julius and his friends. Apparently, they'd made themselves well known to the police over the past six months.

Julius had become a constant nuisance to the police as he had tried time and again to get them to look for some object he claimed that his brother, my father, had stolen from him and hidden on the farm. Some kind of "box or chest," Sergeant Gerhig said. The police hadn't put much effort into following up on the complaint, thinking the whole situation a family affair and one that they could or would do nothing more about.

But Julius had insisted and continued going around town calling his brother and sister-in-law thieves. When John Freed and Robert Frosten arrived in town a little while after Julius himself had showed up in Placerville, he seemingly found allies in his quest to "get back what was his." Only this time, Sergeant Gerhig said, he teamed with Freed and Frosten not to find his object, but to become an agent working with them to help them convince the Pond family and other four farm families to sell their land and the forest that sat at the center of it.

Julius' two new partners, it seemed, had come to town to buy farmland in the area for a shopping mall that they, or the principals the two represented, wanted to build.

"At first," Sergeant Gerhig continued in her soft voice, "we believed that Frosten and Freed were legitimate businessmen and we, at the department, tried to be helpful. But, when these tragic incidents took place on the farms that they were interested in buying, we began to wonder. We just recently began an investigation of the two men and your Uncle Julius, but so far have found nothing to link them to the farm incidents. Now, though, with your concern that Julius Pond might be involved somehow in a homicide, we can't just let this sit any longer."

She turned to Frank and asked him what he knew about this. With a low voice of one obviously pained to have to relay his story, Frank spoke. "It all started several years back," he said, turning to me, "right about the time you left, and about the time I moved back to the area. "For some reason, nobody knew exactly why my pa started actin' strange. He became more and more irritable and angry. He wouldn't tell any of us what it was he was so upset about. He just started mutterin' about the fact that he'd been cheated of what was his. He'd never been like that before. Oh, he could be a little ornery at times, but never anything like that. He simply wouldn't listen to anybody. He started drinkin', too, and hangin' out in Belecroft with some pretty sleazy folks, folks you really wouldn't want to know. Pa'd never been a drinker before either, it just wasn't like him.

"You can imagine that we all had a hard time with him. It just wasn't easy for any of us to be around pa, but we all loved him, so we did our best to be with whatever it was he was goin' through, and then, a few months after pa started actin' strange, my ma passed away.

"Well, you can image what that did to our family. We were all really sad, but it hit pa really hard. He got super down after that and something in him changed. He just sat around the farm for days starin' outside the window. Then one day he got up and started roamin' around our Centerville farm looking for something he said he'd lost. When we asked him about it, he only muttered somethin' about a 'treasure' that he couldn't find, but no one really knew what he could be talkin' about. For days he looked all over the farm house, then the barn, and finally he started diggin' holes around the property after deciding that he must have hidden whatever it was he was looking for and forgotten where he hid it. He even went down to his shop to look, but he never did find whatever it was that was looking for.

"Then, one day, about a month after Ma's passin', Pa came to my younger brother George and me and told us that he was leaving the farm to us, and the next day, we found him gone."

"He disappeared for nearly two years." Frank recounted, "We tried to track him, me and George, but couldn't find were he'd gone. Then, about six months ago he showed up here in Placerville. I heard pa came back and came to talk to him."

At this point, Frank's voice lowered, and his eyes dropped. He said that his meeting with his pa turned out very sad and that his pa had changed greatly over the time he was away. Instead of having returned to his old self, he was hardly coherent, a man who could barely put together a sentence without anger and bitterness. The focus of his anger and bitterness was our father who he called the thief "who first stole my farm and now my treasure," and he told Frank, that he was "going to get it back!"

Frank still didn't know what the treasure could be, or where his father had been these past two years, but he did know that Julius' obsession with it had grown greatly.

"Now," Frank continued, "with all that's happened, I'm feeling scared that the threat that my pa made to you, Harry and the words he spoke in that conversation I heard the other night are something we should all be concerned about."

Sergeant Gerhig listened intently, took some notes, and then sitting on the edge of her chair spoke. "First, I'd like the three of you to know that what I'm going to say is confidential. For some time now, as a department, we've been concerned with an influx of people into the town who don't seem to have a, what we call, a neighborly view of life. Your father, Frank, seems to be part of this crew. It's funny, they all seem to know each other and they've all arrived over the past six to eight months."

She sipped the tea I'd prepared and went on. "We don't know exactly how it all fits together, but there have been a series of strange crimes. I say strange, because the object of these crimes is unclear to us. Someone will feel threatened by another, but without any sense of why. Cars will be stolen, but then show up a block away without anything missing. Cats are stolen, and then returned two weeks later on their doorstep in a box. Lawn signs are missing only to show up glued to people's license plates. Of course, we've looked to all the usual suspects like teen pranksters, drifters, and others whose names appear in our files, but none of it connects with any modus operandi that we know of. We can't tell what motivates these actions and frankly, they baffle us.

"But one thing we do know is that these incidents have added a sense of menace and insecurity to the lives of our ordinary citizens and a lot of the old timers have begun talking about moving on to another, quieter, town." She stopped there and looked at the floor as if a new thought had come to mind. "Perhaps," she said, "that that's the goal, to destabilize people's sense of safety in living here." Then, looking directly at each of us, she said, "We want you to know that we're working on these incidents and the information you're telling me adds to the puzzle. What we'd before was a series of what looked like pranks, but with what's happened to your parents, and at the Henley farm, this is much more serious than that. We're very concerned at the department and are doing all we can to get to the bottom of this. After listening to you, we'll be working on this even harder to make sure that all of you folks living out here on these farms are safe and well."

Sergeant Gehrig stayed only a little while longer to tell us about the status of the Placerville Police Department's investigation, and what next steps the department planned to take. She said she would need to go back to the station, but wanted the three of us to come there in the morning to sign a written deposition of all that we had seen or heard. We all nodded, and agreed to be at the station together in the morning.

***

Becky saw the sergeant to the door and then we spoke, not at all about this terrible situation, but about the old days, our childhood, the farm visits that we'd all loved so well and of our lives. Becky's words touched me as she recalled her life over these last three years that I'd been gone. She'd had a hard time. Her high school sweetheart, Fred, had joined the army after they both graduated from the State college. They'd planned on marrying, but decided to wait until he returned. She said she was nervous about his going, but hoped all would be well. She felt now that it had been a mistake not to marry. "Had we married," she said, "I just know that he would have somehow been protected."

Sadly, her fears came true. All went well for the first six months after his leaving. They corresponded and he had even found ways to call her several times. But in the seventh month of his tour, he was killed on night patrol.

For almost a year after his death, she said she wanted only to "crawl into a hole, hold herself tightly, and cry." Then, something within her "shifted" and she found herself wanting to go out again, laugh, dance and have fun. Though she didn't say it outright with Frank there, I knew this was when the voices began speaking with her. She told us that as part this shift she'd begun to meditate. "You know," she said, "like they do in India." The meditation, she said, had helped her find a calmer place inside her, and to get over the tragic loss of her love.

Since then she'd dated several men, but none had found a way into her heart. She missed Fred greatly, but knew she needed to keep dating to "heal herself." Most recently, she'd begun thinking about going back to graduate school and had applied to several schools in the west. "But," she concluded, "with all the trouble here at home I'm not certain what I'll do."

I listened intently, watched Frank and saw the love that he had in his eyes for Becky, and for me, and I knew to let go of any misgivings that I may have had about him.

Then Frank spoke. "As for me," he said, "my life has been pretty uneventful these past three years. With my mother passin' and Dad having problems, I just decided to stay around here and got a job working at the high school as the assistant football coach. My love life," he said with a shy smile, "has been pretty sparse. I've had a few girlfriends, but nothing serious to speak of."

But then Frank's voice rose and became, well, almost electric. "I don't know if you two know this about me, but I've a great love of the theater and acting. I've kind of kept it to myself, but I've been talking with an acting school in New York. It hasn't all been worked out yet, but my plans were to leave for New York in the next six months or so. But now that Dad is back and he's in such a bad state, I don't know. I think it's best to stay around here and help. My brother George is wrapped up with the farm and really couldn't help anyway being so far away."

"I don't know what's happened to my pa. But if I can help him find himself again, I'd sure like that. I miss him, his smile, and words of encouragement. Whatever has happened is bad and only God can tell how we will get him home again." Tears welled in Frank's eyes as he spoke.

"Uncle Julius is dear to me, and to Becky, too," I said. "When I saw him the other day I got the feeling that he was somehow, well, possessed by something or someone that was controlling his actions. I hope we can get him back, too."

CHAPTER TEN
FOREST MORNING

Dance a dance of Light … and know yourself in it

As I walked alone in the forest this July morning, the forest's early morning mist gave way to rays of rising sunlight streaming through the umbrella of the giant cottonwoods and sycamores. Sparkles of dewdrops created a unreal Christmas-like effect overhead as the sun's reflection captured one drop, then another, and yet another, until the entire roof of the forest came alight with cascading bulbs of white against the deep green of the leaves.

These ancient and noble trees created a sanctuary of shade as they nestled the forest in a cocoon-like ambiance within which one couldn't help but feel whole and secure. Here and there the giant trees gave way to sky and the new morning, but in the heart of the forest, quiet and shade reigned as fairies played their eternal melodies amidst the ferns and other plants of the forest floor.

My eyes caught the miracles of life all around: a ladybug waddling along atop a newly fallen branch, small yellow flowers springing up from the ruins of a log on the ancient forest floor, ferns clustering at the foot of trees, moss clinging to fallen logs, ants on their eternal march of survival, and the ever present dance of the birds whose songs played a note counter to their little dramas of chasing one another from tree to tree across the rooftop of the forest.

Each element of life, I thought, in its own way is struggling to survive amidst the rapture and beauty of life itself. How could so much pain be allowed on an earth of such depth and beauty? I thought of the Bible stories of Adam and Eve and of the fall and of *good* and of the rise of *evil*. Could it be that simple? Could a fallen angel and a tempted woman have set the stage for the violence and pain of the world of the war that I had just left behind? I thought not. I needed another explanation. Surely God had more to say about what's happened here on Earth than to merely let "dark" angels have their way, and surely God wouldn't have created woman with all the love and sensibility she has for life, to bring her to "ruin" paradise for her mate and herself. No, these explanations didn't work for me, there had to be better ones for this existence of light and darkness.

As I thought about it, I felt a familiar feeling within as the voice of the one I had come to call the Guardian spoke to me in my mind.

"We will tell you," he said, "God is the one great creative force, the one great Consciousness in all existence and fills the universes with

Beingness and *Light*. These two fundamental forces exist in all creation and are reflected in the essence and expression of God's purest qualities of *Unity, Love, Joy, Creativity*, and an ever present *Quest for Self knowledge*. And yet, these qualities exist in their perfection only at the higher levels of Beingness and Light within the All-In-All.

Unfortunately," he continued, "the perfection of the expression of God's purest qualities has become limited at the lower levels of God's consciousness, and it is the job of those such as I to help humanity in its own search for its path back home.

All things exist in the omnipresent One Mind of God, existing everywhere as Beingness and Light—and expressing everywhere in a vast field of ever present, ever vibrating energy—energy that is continually resonating at different frequencies throughout the infinity of the One. Understanding the movement of the Creator's consciousness within its own energies through time and space is the key to understanding not only the answer to your questions, but also to understanding humanity's journey on Earth.

"Do not try to comprehend this now in all its totality. We will say more in the days ahead. What you can know now is that every man and woman on Earth, as well as those Beings living in higher realms of the Oneness such as we, are part of the essence of a unified God Mind that ventured in its ever expanding quest for self knowledge farther and farther from the center of creation into deepening and expanding realms of its own energies or existence.

At its highest vibrational energies, God Mind reaches beyond to realms that are so vast as to be beyond comprehension. At its lower levels, the actual nature of God's own existence changes—as the vibratory frequencies within God Mind slow in a way that one would say is consistent with the vibratory frequency needed to birth or create the material plane of existence as you know it. The "Big Bang" theory of creation approximates well that moment in time when God's own journey within its own Consciousness slowed to such a degree that it created material life.

I struggled in my mind to understand. Yes, I could see that God was everywhere and that even God Mind was everything within which I and all else existed. But it still was not clear to me how it all fit together and in particular what it had to do directly with me, Becky and our life.

The Guardian continued, as if reading my thoughts. "With the creation of the material world came the creation of duality as the essence of God Mind ventured into lower frequency vibration on its continued journey of self exploration and self knowledge. And with the creation of duality, came limitation. Where notions of light and darkness, good and evil, and above and below did not exist before at higher realms, they now came into being. Universes, galaxies, solar systems and planets birthed in this duality, including the creation of this glorious planet, Earth.

"Where the pure qualities of God's love, unity, creativity, quest for self knowledge and joy find unlimited expression at higher and higher frequencies of the One, on Earth these qualities have become clouded. Rather than maintaining its connection with the highest realms of God Mind, for many reasons humanity has come to act mostly from 'survival consciousness' and not from a day to day awareness of its unity within God's presence and consciousness.

"So," the Guardian continued, "while access to the fullness and purity of God's expression is the norm in higher energy realms of existence, at lower levels where the world exists in duality—such as here on Earth—access to the purity of the One mind isn't as full and complete.

"This is why human beings both *know* that they're connected to the Great Spirit, the One, the All-In-All, and yet also feel at a loss and oft times abandoned by God, not really knowing what their innate connection really is or means in their lives on a day to day basis."

The Guardian continued, "Great Spirit exists in its purest unity of *Beingness* and *Light* above and beyond all human concepts of light and darkness. Each and every part of life on Earth—with all its contradictions and dualities—has within it the very essence of God's purer or higher vibrations and it's in the conscious seeking within humanity for union with these higher frequencies of the Oneness that progress is made.

"'Light' and 'darkness' do exist on Earth, and yet it's a great truth that one of these, the light of Earth, connects with the grander *Light of God* and illumines the other, the darkness. This great Light creates the momentum for progress as it shines its rays on the dark side and fills the darkness with more and more of the purity of the Light of the One. The evening comes and no one doubts its benefits for the sleeping forest or for humankind as it sleeps. But just as the morning sun brightens the forest awakening from its nighttime slumber, just so the Light of the God existence *beyond earthly light and darkness* illumines the consciousness of a sleeping humanity. This omnipresent Light brings revelation and awareness, releasing forever the held energies within the shadows of darkness.

"As for the story of Adam and Eve, we will, indeed, save this story for another time. For now, we will say that sacred man and woman were never meant to be caught in the play of struggle between light and darkness on the earth plane. The drama of man and woman not knowing their true nature came not from ill intent, and certainly not from any 'fault' of woman, but from a movement of consciousness itself within in the mind of God.

"Of these things more will be revealed. For now, Harry, it is vital for you to focus your attention on this sacred forest and the lessons you will be taught here. It is your place and your sister's place of learning about the Divine. You might call it a school for angels, for we will teach you, indeed, the ways of Light. Not since olden days have the angels and other Beings of Light come to prepare the way for humanity to awaken. We've always been here, but at this sacred hour we've come to do what we can to illumine humanity's path.

"So listen well now, Harry Pond. We wish for you to work with us to save the one you call Uncle Julius. He has indeed been 'taken' and it's ours to free him from the bondage of that which is called 'the darkness'. Will you help?"

I felt surprised. In the past when I had heard the voices they simply gave me hints about the best thing to do, what trail in the jungle to take and which to stay away from, but now I was being asked to help. And my answer came so easily.

"Yes," I said in my mind, "I'll help in whatever way I can. I've seen what's happened to Uncle Julius. If we can help save him, then I wish to try."

As I said this, my own burgeoning curiosity remained tremendously strong within me as my desire to know more about humankind's origins in the *Light* of the One, and about the nature of light and the darkness on Earth, and about the truth of the story of Adam and Eve, and, well, about *everything*. I felt impatient and I asked the Guardian for help.

In my mind I received his firm reply, "There's much to learn. Be patient and we will get there in due time." Something about the way the Guardian spoke, a tone, perhaps a special resonance I felt, made me know that from that time onward I would need to simply listen and wait for the right time for the answers to come to my many, many questions.

Then, just as I turned onto an old deer trail that led to one of the two clearings in this part of the forest, I knew that the Guardian's presence was gone. In Nam, I'd gotten used to knowing when he came and went, and now, in this forest of my youth, I discovered that I had the same faculty of knowing when he'd come and when he'd gone.

I walked down the trail until I came to the clearing. I stopped to listen to the forest. Majestic sycamores gave way here to oversized evergreens that provided luscious scents and backdrops of green fronds as hemlock and Australian pines combined with ancient stands of white ash to encircle this small clearing within the forest. Here, in its depths, this ancient land gave up to the listening ear lyrical notes from the trickle of a branch of the creek that meandered along the forest's northern edge and then split off into tiny rivulets running throughout the forest. The water's sound now blended with the gentle murmur of the wind and rustling leaves, the caw of a blackbird, and the ever present croak of the forest frogs, all combining to tell the story of this land untouched by time. Like a fundamental language, these elemental notes told of times past, of animals and people who'd roamed these lands, of the floods and of the dry periods, all part of the evolution of this glorious land.

I remembered Dad talking about the Native Americans who lived nearby more than a thousand years ago. Mound builders who built great turtle-like ceremonial mounds that still stand today, built in honor of their dead and the land itself, he'd said. He spoke, too, of more recent natives to these central Ohio lands, the Shawnee and others. An old timer had once told Dad a story about the forest that had come down from his grandfather, about how the land was sacred to the local tribes, a special meeting place that withstood the strains and hostilities between the tribes, where union and agreement took precedence over conflict and strife.

I looked around and felt that familiar feeling of safety and awe that I had often felt when coming to the forest as a youth. I took a deep sigh as I rested on a large stone near the center of the clearing. This was our forest. It had been here with us as I grew up and I knew that I would do all that I could to maintain it.

With its five hundred acres of old growth virgin forest, the land itself remained one of the few privately held places of its kind in this part of the county, a place where nature had gone untouched. Shaped somewhat like the broad rectangular outline of the United States, only with rounded corners, here old growth trees shared the land with young sprouts able to survive in the limited sunlight that sprinkled the forest's floor. I felt calmness here in this place passed over by modern times, a protected sanctuary of a time long forgotten.

I walked on now, back towards the main trail, stopping occasionally to admire the varieties of fern and wild berry stands that danced together along the forest floor, all part of the well-orchestrated symphony that played for me its favorite melodies of color, sound, and smell against the backdrop of the inner forest silence that merged on occasion with the gentle water song of one of the nearby streams.

I smiled as I walked, thinking now of our summer rains, and how fortunate we were in this part of the country to have plenty of water for all of our needs. Ohio's summer rains filled the streams, and then, as if never there, the water rushed away, returning the creek beds to quiet.

Not too long back, earlier in the century, the forest had been part of a larger sixteen hundred acre parcel of land that had since been divided into its current configuration that included this central forest land and the five adjacent farms surrounding it. My grandparents had been the first of the five farm families to come buy the land in the early 1930s. The others came perhaps a decade later, but all the landowners had migrated to central Ohio from the same Pennsylvania Dutch region of the neighboring state and now all held the forestland in common. By the grace of these five families, the forest had been kept safe and taken care of these last three decades through a common covenant, signed by all, to protect the land.

I didn't know much about the covenant, nor, for that matter, about the origins of the other four farm families who'd signed it. I only knew that the families had lived not far from each other in Pennsylvania before moving to Ohio and had agreed to come together to buy the land here. I recall once asking Dad about it and all he said was, "It just happened, son. It just happened." After that, I asked no further, for I knew Dad would say no more about it so I decided to leave well enough alone.

In fact, our family and the other's did just that: leave each other alone. Even though we lived near to the others, we rarely, if ever, had interactions with them. Mom and Dad seldom mentioned them, and, except for an occasional visit from Mr. Blakely, who owned one of the northern farms and was close with Mom and Dad, the other farm family owners didn't play a role in our life. One thing I did know about them all is that they all held the same strong beliefs about taking care of the forest and the land.

Throughout the area, progress went on. Old stands of forest gave way to shopping malls, new neighborhoods, highways, and even new towns, but these three hundred and twenty acres of land remained untouched. The families farmed their land around it, but the gentle forest remained, holding its quiet like a treasure. One could almost feel the mystical presence of fairies and elves dancing and laughing in the wood.

The forest's main walking path ran from east to west across the broad southern belt and directly connected to our farm in the southwestern corner and the Bates family farm at the southeastern most corner. On this path, Becky and I filled the days of our youth with the miracles of seasons changing, birds, deer, and squirrels giving birth to their young ones, and the scents and tracks of unknown, mysterious nocturnal animals that lived their lives in the depths of the forest.

The creek branches flowed from north to south and cut their way across the main path after leaving their source in Olden Creek, a larger stream running parallel to the path along the forest's northernmost border. Olden Creek, sometimes quiet, sometimes raging, ran across the width of the forest from east to west and provided abundant recreational opportunities for members of the three northern farm families. In summer and fall the creek flowed gently along its way. But in spring it inevitably overflowed its banks, making it impossible for those families to cross the small footbridges that led from each of their properties to the path. Perhaps that was why they rarely ventured south to our part of the forest and why Becky and I hardly ever saw other people there.

Along the main path, the tiny streams from the north created natural gullies two or three feet wide which, in summer and early fall, became our "watering holes" where we frolicked barefoot in enjoyment of the coolness of the forest waters. At spring runoff season, this all changed as even these little creek branches swelled and overflowed their boundaries, making it impossible for us to go very far into the forest.

Together, the five farms surrounded the forest, fanning out from their individual borders along its edges to encompass acre upon acre of some of the most fertile farmland in central Ohio. Our family's farm wrapped around the southwestern-most border, running north towards the Blakely farm and east to the Bates family's farm.

The three farms to the north sat side by side along the northern border, with the Henley family farm directly opposite ours at the northeastern edge where it stretched across the forest's northern edge to meet the Hayes family farm. The Hayes farm sat between the Blakely and Henley farms along the forest's northern border. With the largest acreage of the northern farms, its wedge shape contained one of the richest pieces of farmland in the area.

CHAPTER ELEVEN
MEETING WITH FRIENDS *DANS LA FORÊT*

Songs of old to come to those who listen. Listen well for the call to come home

The next day we met Frank at the police station and gave our depositions. Afterwards, outside, Frank announced that he was going to be leaving for a few days to visit his brother George on their old family farm. He wanted to see if he could find out anything more about where Julius had been while he was away. He said that his father had pretty much disappeared during those years, but he wanted to check to see if George or other family members might know have some clues or even know something about where Julius had been.

Becky and I left Frank and drove back to the house, deciding that our best approach now was to actively try to contact the Guardian and other angelic voices to seek their help.

***

We arrived in the forest at midday. The air felt hot and sticky, but a gentle breeze blowing across the forest floor as we entered the shade of the forest soon cooled us off.

Walking side by side down the main path, Becky turned to me and told me that she had been receiving information and wanted to share it with me. "The voice that spoke to me still wouldn't identify itself," she said, "but it wanted us both to know that we're safe."

She stopped for a moment on the path and said, "You know, I had a strong sense that while I only heard one voice speaking to me, somehow many spoke, as if the words came from a group, not just the one."

We walked on and Becky continued, "It felt very strange. The voice said that they will help us soon to be able to receive these messages together. At first, I didn't know what that meant, but just then I found out I was actually able to listen in to the conversation that you had with the Guardian. I mean, I could hear every word that was spoken to you, exactly what you relayed to me just now, as if, well, as if … as if you and I were tuned in to the same channel."

Chills ran down my spine at her words, for I had had the strange experience myself of the Guardian speaking to me in my mind and of *feeling* someone inside me at the same time. Now Becky's words propelled my mind back to those moments a few minutes before when I could keenly feel the Guardian's presence. I had listened to the Guardian's words in my mind, but somehow my awareness of myself felt grander, less limited, and more open than I'd ever experienced myself before. I had trouble even explaining it to myself. I could hear the words, but I felt my consciousness to be, well, enlarged, expanded in a new way. The normal boundaries of myself, the one I called *I*, felt stretched and extended, and in this extended state *I could feel the presence of another within me*!

I struggled to keep my mind clear as I projected back to that moment when the Guardian had been present, and there in my own being I *saw* Becky's presence in my mind's eye. I didn't know how I was seeing her, or what mechanism within me made it possible, for I didn't see her as much as felt her energy. Yes, that's what it was. I felt Becky's energy within me.

I did my best to describe to her that somehow I had been aware of her listening in to our conversation.

Birds chirped their noontime songs as we looked into each other's eyes. Nothing during our growing up together years had prepared us for what had just happened.

Then the Guardian spoke again. "You will both see, as we go along," he said "that it's easier than you might think for you to receive our messages at the same time. We're speaking with you together so that you may move as one in the days ahead. Your own energies in this life, and your history together in past lives, make you compatible and, as you might say, make this a thing that's doable.

"Don't be afraid, for the two of you have indeed been able to do this in the past, so it's a process familiar to you both."

As the Guardian spoke I heard and felt his energy within me, but I also felt the familiar energy of Becky as well. We looked at each other in amazement as we shared the strange experience of hearing the voice speaking to us as if we were one person.

The Guardian went on, "Yes, we're aligning the two of you to learn together that which we have to teach. You'll get used to this as we come more often to visit with you.

"Our visits will bring you much knowledge about yourselves. We will be available to help you in whatever ways we can with the challenge of protecting the forest and its secrets. For a very, very long time this has been a place of sanctuary for those who work with the Brotherhood of Light, an organization of Light Beings dedicated to helping humankind awaken from its state of sleep to full conscious memory of its source in the Light. Membership in our organization is by self-invitation of those who have reached a certain place in their own personal evolution that allows them to make a choice to help humanity.

"The Brotherhood is comprised of those of us still working in the physical, both male and female beings, and those of us working from the higher frequency vibrations of the angelic and other realms. For a long time we've worked to help those who so chose to do the work of Light. Much needs to be healed as wars ravage humanity, prejudice and avarice control far too much, and the feminine energies of Earth are treated without the respect and honor which they were meant to be given.

"Our goal is clear: the expansion of the consciousness of the One Light, the One Great Spirit, God, on Earth and in all the universe. And our means of doing this is to help humanity enlighten itself to its own true nature in the One Light.

"You had a sense of the specialness of this forest even as a child. You came here often, played in the streams and listened to the ever present sound of the bird's call. Now, you'll begin a training in which you can learn exactly what the calls of the birds mean, what story the oak tells the sycamore as they whisper to each other in the wind. The result of your training will be the mastery of the forest, the experience of knowing the living things in the forest in the same way as you know yourself."

The Guardian's voice paused then, for just a moment, "Are you willing to undertake this training?" he said.

I heard Becky's affirmative "Yes!" in my mind as if I had spoken it myself.

"You, Harry, have a different task". The Brotherhood has shared knowledge with humankind for millennia. This knowledge allows those who are on the path of Light to accelerate the pace of their journey. Your job, Harry Pond, will be to follow the course of these teachings. As with your sister's work, the process won't always be easy. To succeed you'll both need to give up ideas you've held, and ones you've both even cherished, for a long, long time. The teaching will accelerate your movement forward on a different track than the ones you've been on.

"Are you willing to undergo the training? We cannot promise that it will be easy. You must choose."

The answer, "Yes," came immediately within me, as if the Guardian's question were one that had already been answered by me long, long ago and now only needed the word "Yes" to be spoken. Yet, as the word echoed in my mind, I felt a funny feeling at the pit of my stomach, as if I knew that the decision I'd just made would somehow change my life forever. As I looked back many years later, I saw that my instinct at that moment was correct.

"Good," the Guardian said, "then we will meet again here tomorrow to begin our course. Harry, we will meet with you during the day, and Becky, with you when you return home from your job."

CHAPTER TWELVE
BROTHERHOOD REVEALED

The light shining through reveals the lack of clouds in the sky

We left the woods that day, walking side by side, but said nothing. The "Brotherhood of the Light"? Was it real, or some mutual illusion or fantasy in which both Becky and I were participating? Honestly, I didn't know for certain at that point, but my faith held strong as I remembered the help the Guardian had given me on those horrid, hot jungle nights on patrol. I had survived then with his help, and now I would trust him again to help me right here at home, my home, the home I had grown up in, which had changed so very much since I went away.

As for Becky, she couldn't have been more jovial. Overall, her heart seemed to have lightened in the days since my arrival home, and now, with the visit to the forest and the meeting with the Brotherhood, her spirit continued to rise.

Becky and I didn't see each other much the rest of the day, but got together that evening. As we sat together in the living room, she spoke of leaving her job, of the savings she'd gathered, and of her desire to find a "center," as she called it, a place within herself were she "knew who she was and where she was going!"

From Becky's point of view, the existence of the Brotherhood of Light was taken for granted, as if they'd been around the whole of her life. And, in fact, they had been according to some of the things she said that evening.

"You know," she said, "as we both sat on the couch, "I feel so good about what happened today. It's, it's as though I've been waiting for some hidden treasure that I've know about my whole life to be found, and now, at last, I've found it.

"I remember when I was about seven I was in the forest by myself. Mom had walked over to the Blakely farm to borrow some flour and told me to stay around the house. Well, I wasn't much for listening even then and instead of staying I went to play in the forest.

"I remember seeing an old robin's nest high up in a tree and deciding that I wanted to reach it. Well, I got pretty high up, for a seven year old, and I was feeling pretty proud of myself when suddenly I slipped and started to fall.

"I was lucky, my overalls caught on a branch and instead of falling, I hung their like a flying bird swinging back and forth ten feet or more above the ground. I remember being terrified, and even though I shouted, no one could hear me.

"Then a funny thing happened. I heard a voice in my head and it told me to be calm. All I could do was listen. It told me exactly, step by step, how to get myself untangled from that branch and down from the tree.

"I was seven, but I remember it like yesterday. And you know, Harry," she concluded, "I swear that the voice I heard feels just like the Guardian's voice when he speaks to us. I've heard it at other times in my life, so this whole thing in some ways is like 'old home week' to me. I'm excited about the school and the lessons!"

***

The next day, Becky went to work vowing to leave her job, the only one she could find in our small town. "Being a secretary isn't much fun, anyway," she said.

I stayed around the farm all morning, and as I did, my excitement grew. Being offered the opportunity to learn the lessons of the Brotherhood filled me with anticipation. Was I worthy? Was it right to do this? After all, my parents had taken us to church "to learn about Jesus Christ, the man" they'd said, and I believed in the Christ, yet something of the total picture escaped me. It wasn't that I didn't feel Jesus was divine and had come to show us the way, because I did believe that. But I wondered whether he could have been the *only* one who'd come with such a mission. Over all these many millennium that man has been on Earth, couldn't there have been others who'd also come with similar gifts and messages to share?

Throughout my life I've had incidents happen that convinced me of God's presence right by my side, helping out when my need was greatest. In my youth, I prayed a lot, and I prayed to a Higher Power who answered my prayers. In Southeast Asia, the war convinced me even more that God was with me, always helping out. But all along, I considered Jesus a good friend rather than one who'd "died for my sins."

God was important to me, but I believed in my own view of God, my own relationship to the One Great Spirit, as the Guardian had called it.

So the Brotherhood's offer intrigued me. How could the Guardian exist? Where did he live? Who or what supported him? Guided him? Who were the others I had felt? Who had been talking to Becky, and what was the secret of the forest? Why was it so important to those other men? These questions and more flooded my mind as I waited for the time of our meeting.

CHAPTER THIRTEEN
SYMBOL OF THE BROTHERHOOD OF LIGHT

Often we reach to know something … yet fail to grasp it … keep reaching … the answers are always there

I arrived in the forest at the appointed time, my excitement mounting. As I walked down the path to the oak log, I heard the voice of the Guardian welcoming me.

"We're here, Harry," he said directly into my mind, "and we want to get to work right away.

"The first thing we want you to know is that your involvement with us is not something, as you might say, out of the blue. We've been with you for many, many lifetimes, watching over you, guiding you, and conferring with your soul in the between times when you'd not yet selected another body.

"We know that you're unfamiliar with the concept of reincarnation, but it is a reality that you'll become more and more in touch with as the teaching progresses. Do you have any questions before we go further?'

I sat down on the oak log. "No," I said. "I've heard that people in India and other places believe in past lives, but I've never given it much thought. I guess I always assumed that this life was all I had, here and now, so the past didn't much matter."

"We've heard you ask questions, though, in your dreams and even in your daydreams about the nature of life."

"That's true," I said. "I've had such questions."

The Guardian went on, "We're here to help you. Please be patient with yourself during the teachings."

Then, almost without warning, I found myself transported in my mind to a place and time that I didn't recognize, at least at first. It looked like a Greek temple with some sort of central, roofless courtyard, and a terrace from which I could look out at the strange world.

I felt younger. I wore robes of white. The sky didn't look the same as I was used to. It was bluish with a tint of red and simply didn't have the look or feel of our earthly sky. Instead of the familiar yellow-gold sun sitting high in Earth's blue horizon, the sky in this place pulsated with colors that danced to the rhythm of a song I couldn't hear, and I saw a white-gold glow radiating from the horizon.

In my mind's eye I watched as a man and a woman entered the temple courtyard. The man wore a white toga-like robe, but the woman's robes differed, reminding me of a very old, very beautiful, large tortoise shell. An oval motif plate that looked like the underside that creature decorated the front of her golden dress. As the plate reached her waist it narrowed to meet a belt made of what looked to be a similar substance. A swath of cotton-like material, arranged in a crisscrossed fashion across the front of the dress, held her well-rounded breasts. Two turtle designs on separate plates adorned the back of the full-length gown and rounded out the overall reptilian appearance of her attire.

I didn't recognize the two people standing before me at first, but then I realized that they looked very much like my father and mother, only younger than my memory of them.

The strength of the vision wavered, seemingly far away in one moment and then in the next, very close and clear. The Guardian's familiar voice came to me. "We bring you this image to remind you of your roots. Watch and listen."

My emotions were mixed: exhilaration on the one hand, and confusion on the other. I felt myself fully participating within the scene, and yet I watched it as well, as though observing a long-forgotten dream. As I looked on, the scene became clearer, less far away, as if the intensity and focus of my own attention moderated its clarity.

The three of us were speaking to each other, and I soon realized as I listened that the conversation was about me. My parents were saying that they wouldn't be seeing me for some time, but that in the *sacred days* we'd meet again.

They then turned to a viewing screen set in one wall of the courtyard. In the vision, the three of us turned to watch as scene upon scene, all having something to do with me, unfolded. In some, I saw myself a younger man; in others, older. Each represented, it seemed, a different time, and showed me interacting with others, wearing different outfits for each of the cultures I found myself in.

I heard the man who looked like my father say, "We will meet again. Your job is to keep the sacred memory of the Light awake within you at all times."

My mother hugged me. Then, as the screen went blank and I turned back to the two of them, they weren't there. I looked over to where they had been standing. They were gone and I sensed, rather than knew for sure, that in this strange and beautiful place, departing in this fashion was normal.

I watched for several seconds longer. Looking out from the portal of the temple, I saw a plain of orange-brown-tinted hills stretching in every direction. The moving sky's blue-red hue played upon the hills, giving the appearance of a moving ocean of land, at first appearing solid, but then flowing into waves of color. The beauty of the surrounding terrain, breathtaking as it was, was exceeded by the elegance of the temple's courtyard and interior rooms. Marble walls shimmered with gold flecked with specks of lapis blue. The same material covered the floors, only there the builders had laid multi-colored gemstones and jewels into patterns and symbols, most of which I didn't recognize.

But now, as I looked more closely, one symbol jumped out. I recognized it immediately. A modified purple fleur-de-lys, imbedded into a background of pink within a heart also bordered in purple. It occupied a place of grandeur in the center of the temple courtyard floor. My mind whirled at the sight it, for it exactly matched the symbol I'd seen the whole of my youth—hanging on a wall of my parents' bedroom. I remembered asking Mom one day about it, and all she said was, "One day you'll learn all about it, but for now, just enjoy how pretty it is."

Yes, I found it pretty, but it also held, I knew, some strange secret. As very young children, Becky and I would sometimes run into Mom and Dad's bedroom and find them sitting in their easy chairs by the floor to ceiling windows that overlooked the forest. A painting of a fleur-de-lys symbol in a heart—just like this one—hung on the wall alongside the windows, and Mom and Dad would inevitably be looking at the symbol, as if in silent prayer, almost as if in a trance. We knew that they liked to relax that way with the symbol, but we never really understood why.

In my teenage years, we heard more and more talk of the far east, India, and meditation, and it had crossed my mind that that was what Dad and Mom had been doing all those years.

But now, as I saw it here in the temple, I realized that the symbol meant more, much more, than I had imagined. For as I gazed into it, I saw in my mind's eye a group of men and women, all dressed in robes of gold, encircled in an arc of light. They looked at first to be holding hands, but instead of touching, a glow of golden light radiated from each one's hand, touching the next, until the entire circle pulsated. In the center, on the floor, sat the symbol of the hearted fleur-de-lys, radiating the same golden light.

The vision faded and I found myself back in the temple courtyard where I had met my parents.

The Guardian came to me and spoke. "Harry, we will be returning to the wood now. Remember all you saw. As the lessons continue, your questions will be answered. For today, your work is to go back to the house and find the symbol, sit in the chair your parents sat in, and allow the energy of the symbol to comfort you."

The Guardian was gone.

I opened my eyes, and as I did, a lark flew very near my head and landed in an ash tree. Its evening song fit my mood entirely, resonating joy and the coming quiet of evening time. I sat listening for a while before heading back to the farm. As I walked home, I thought of the lesson, of what I had seen. I knew that the symbol was that of the Brotherhood of Light.

CHAPTER FOURTEEN
BECKY'S FOREST DANCE

Loving the One leads in directions unknown … beyond comprehension to those who choose to remain asleep!

Becky arrived in the forest just before dusk. Walking down the main path she admired the rhythmic swaying of tall trees as a gentle evening breeze came to wash the heat from their great expanse. Work had been tiring for her, but for now she wanted to get started with her lessons as soon as possible rather than resting at home. She'd been anticipating this moment all day and now it was here.

As she arrived at the spot where she was to meet the Guardian, she thought of the events of the day. Yes, she'd quit her job, just as she'd told Harry she would. But it wasn't that simple, for her new boss, Will Taker simply wouldn't hear of it.

Mr. Taker had recently moved to Placerville. She didn't know where he'd come from, but when he came to the outlet store as her boss, Becky had had an uneasy feeling about him. He seemed to be one of those newer people moving to the area who, she'd thought, didn't always bring with them "the Light." She'd surprised herself in saying this, as it was not her usual way of speaking about people. But now, Becky mused, many of the new faces in town felt that way. They carried something of a cloud around them, and sadly, the more she thought about it, Uncle Julius came to mind. He, too, carried the same cloud about him.

And now, one of these newcomers, Will Taker, wanted her to stay. He became almost obsessed with her leaving from the moment she announced it to him. He had come back to her time and time again to ask her to change her mind, and even offered to find her different work at a higher pay. Yet she knew deep within herself that no matter what this man would offer, she would leave the job.

***

The pleasant voice of a woman within her mind startled her from her thoughts. "My name is Katran," the voice said, "and I will guide you today in your lessons. We've much to do and I'm honored to be with you on this day. Let's begin the lesson."

With that, Becky immediately became aware of a sensation within her body that she'd never felt before. She felt warm and tingled all over, as if it were being filled with a gentle charge of electrical energy. Every one of her cells felt lifted, made lighter and yet all the while feeling the presence of Katran.

As Katran went on speaking, Becky found herself walking down the main path of the woods and turning at one of the minor trails that had been channeled out, perhaps by deer."This evening," said Katran, "we will visit with several forest creatures to see if we can listen in on their conversation."

The trail led deeper in the forest to an area that Becky had not been to before. As a child, she'd stayed close to the main path with its overhanging trees high above. She loved playing along the creek branches that ran nearby, and had ventured some way along the deer trails, but this area was new to her.

The electric feeling in her body grew stronger as she walked on. Her arms and legs tingled as if in anticipation of flight. Her feet stayed on the ground, but it felt that the ground itself moved beneath them with its own anticipation of the excitement of Becky's visit.

"The forest elementals know you're here to visit with them," Katran said. "They loved watching over you as you came to this forest as a child, and now are excited that you come in this manner." With each word Katran spoke, Becky had the strong sensation that she was actually becoming more like Katran. A sense of elation and trepidation filled her as her logical mind tried to understand these new feelings and emotions.

Katran's soothing voice comforted her. "The Brotherhood of Light is an association of those of us who have been through the rigors of life on Earth," she said. "We say rigors," she went on" because the time on Earth was not always easy. Earth itself was meant to be a shining star, a place where conscious beings of the One God Mind could grow in stature, consciousness, and love. But the duality of this plane caused this to change. The thought of 'unified Oneness' faded for the mass of people as forces loyal only to their own illusions of power took more and more control of this sacred place. Until now, a darkened consciousness rather than Light consciousness dominates the land.

"All members of the Brotherhood who have spent time on Earth have had to awaken from the shadow of illusion cast by those who wanted to pretend that they were grander than the One God. We all had to awaken from this dream, and now we work with those like you and Harry who have a special destiny — along with many others at this time — to awaken in this life.

"We choose not to stand by, arms crossed, doing nothing, but we cannot assist on Earth either unless we're called by souls like you and your brother who are willing to learn the next steps of awareness to wake from the 'great blanket of sleep' that has been cast over Earth. For now, know that you've chosen within your soul to be part of this awakening, and we of the Brotherhood thank you and honor you for your courage."

And then Katran spoke words that Becky felt she'd heard before, but couldn't remember where. "Remember this always, Becky," she said, "the Light of God *always prevails!*"

Becky suddenly stopped. She and Katran had come to the edge of a small clearing and here, in this intimate place, Becky found herself facing an animal that she'd thought only existed in fairy tales. As the evening light began to deepen into dusk, she saw a large silvery white horse-like animal. On its forehead was an unmistakable white horn.

The animal turned towards her and made a gentle but strong neighing sound, as if to beckon her to come further into the clearing. Startled and not knowing what to do or say, Becky went forward. As she did, the beautiful white beast came to her to caress her cheek with its own.

Within her mind Becky heard the Unicorn speak. "I've come to be with you, as I've been with you in the past. When the call went out to help with the lessons, I came, for you and I are true friends of old, and I came to thank you for your presence in my life."

Becky didn't know what to say, but as the Unicorn's final words rang within, she saw in her mind's eye a scene of herself as a young girl in a woods that looked much like this one. With her was a silver-white Unicorn. As she watched the scene, she realized that the Unicorn of her vision was the very same one standing next to her.

"The time on Earth is near for the walls to be broken down," said the Unicorn. "The lesson today is for you to learn that the animal kingdom has its own voice, often a very wise and kind voice, worthy, indeed, of man's listening." With that, the Unicorn turned and gently beckoned Becky to follow it to the edge of the clearing and there, to her surprise, waited a family of deer.

As Becky approached with the Unicorn, she could feel their excitement. Deer had lived in the forest for as long as she could remember, but they'd always shied away from humans, self-protective and aloof. But this was not the case now, for as Becky came near the group of four, she had the distinct impression that their excitement came not from fear of her, but due to their happy anticipation of the meeting with her!

The electrical feeling in her body transformed, and her every sense began to "feel" the forest land, its trees, the animals, and surroundings in a way she'd never felt before. Becky bathed in these heightened sensations of connectedness.

Rather than feeling the ground under her feet, she now experienced every step as a gentle interaction with the earth itself, as if her walk were part of a grand dance, choreographed long ago and still being played.

The closer she came, the more she could "feel" their very beings, actually sense all that *they* were feeling! The largest of the clan, a male with a full eight-point set of antlers, raised his head. At another time, she would have felt fear at this gesture, but not now.

The buck moved to her to in the clearing alongside the Unicorn. To her own surprise, she also took steps towards it. They met a few feet from where the Unicorn stood and it was as if they'd known each other for a long, long time. Later, she would have trouble describing the experience in words, but now, she *knew* that she and the deer were friends and that she'd nothing to fear.

The deer bent its antlers in what Becky took as a gesture of greeting, and in her turn Becky reached and touched the smooth ivory antlers, gently rubbed the deer's light brown fur just above the eyes. As she did, Becky knew that she wouldn't be able to "speak" with the deer in the same way she could with the Unicorn. Even though she could feel its intelligence and kindness, she sensed the intelligence was less than that of the Unicorn—limited in a way she didn't understand.

She stood touching the stag's forehead a few moments before the others members of the family moved toward her. A beautiful doe, with deep and grand brown eyes so filled with gentle pools of light that she could feel their kindness touch her deep within her soul. The two remaining smaller does followed.

Tears came to her eyes as she realized the power of the gift they'd come to give her. For the first time in her life, she knew what it was like to be in the presence of pure love. Her heart overflowed with it. The deer came to grace her with their presence, and Becky knew that she would never forget this moment.

The family gathered around her as she stroked the fur on each of their backs. The mamma doe nudged Becky with its nose as if to say, "Come, I want to show you something." Becky followed along as the doe led her deeper and deeper into the forest on a narrow track that she hadn't noticed before. The others stayed behind.

The path opened to a second clearing, a much smaller one this time. As she entered it, a heightened sense of calm and peace filled her. But Becky sensed something different here. The light in this part of the forest seemed brighter than in other parts. Her deer guide stopped as Becky's eyes took in the small clearing. A feeling of pure enchantment came over her. She marveled at this secret place, its coziness, its quiet, a blessed retreat in the heart of her beloved forest.

Then, as she turned to her right, pure delight filled her. Sitting on a tree stump at the edge of the small clearing, she saw the most beautiful and remarkable bejeweled chest she'd ever seen.

The chest, encrusted with red rubies, dark green sapphires, and other precious stones, radiated a glowing light that lifted her heart to joy. She started towards the chest … to touch it, to be near it … but stopped, for she knew that she must not.

She stood for several seconds longer admiring the intricacy of the chest's design, and then it was time to go as the doe nudged her side and Becky followed her back to the clearing. When they returned, the other deer were gone, and the doe nudged her with affection one more time, and then ran off.

The Unicorn stood where Becky had left it. As she approached, a smile crossed her face, for she, too, felt a tremendous sense of familiarity and comfort with this magical animal. She knew, without really knowing how she knew, the Unicorn's name: Egedine.

"Becky," Egedine spoke within her mind, "you are correct, for you remember well my name from days gone by. Much is to be learned in this place of wonder that you roamed so freely in your youth. Believe in what you saw and felt this night. Our lesson will continue a week from now. Don't speak of the chest, nor try to come this way again. Neither this trail, nor the chest will be where you saw them this evening.

"Trust that the gifts of the lesson will increase during the week and we will have much more to learn as we go forward. We are very pleased to be with you and look forward to our next visit." Egedine then came to Becky and gently touched her forehead with the tip of his horn. Immediately, Becky's eyes closed and images of pure golden light raced across her mind, accompanied by a tender feeling of love and kindness in her heart that she'd rarely, if ever, felt before.

A smile crossed her lips as the touch of the Unicorn faded. With eyes closed, Becky sensed the gentle movement of Egedine, and knew that he would be leaving her soon. And so it was, for she opened her eyes just in time to see Egedine turn away from her and walk towards the edge of the clearing. Then, in awe, she watched as the mythical being took a gentle step, leaped, and disappeared into the air above the place where it had stood only a moment before.

Her eyes blinked in wonder at what she'd just seen. She wanted to speak, to say more, feel more of Egedine, but could not. She stood in silence. A feeling of connection to the soil beneath her feet filled her with a sense of contentment. Surely, she thought, I'm blessed to be alive on this beautiful Planet Earth. And, as this thought ran through her mind, she once again experienced the feeling of lightness she'd experienced earlier. The combination of earthly intimacy and lightness exhilarated her, filling her with strength and hope for the future.

Katran's voice came to her, "We will be returning to the oak log and, as we do, I would be pleased to answer any questions you might have."

Becky thought for a moment, then within herself asked, "How does it all work? I mean, am I dreaming or something? Unicorns aren't real. Are they?"

Katran's gentle laughter rang out within her.

"Yes, Unicorns are real. You've spent much time with them in days past. Egedine came to be with you because of this. As the lessons go forward, you'll remember more of the past and all will come clear. As to how it works, we will only say *that time and space are*, and Katran hesitated as if looking for the right word ... *fluid*. They exist in this dimension as the fixed entities, *time*, and *space*, but in reality are on an endless continuum that exists within the all that is."

"This, too," Katran concluded, "you'll learn more about, for your lessons will take you far without ever leaving this woods." Then Katran stopped as if this were all that she had to say. Becky waited, curious at the abrupt interruption of her conversation with Katran. Then something remarkable happened.

As she walked along the path she felt the lightness that filled her when Katran was present begin to leave her. But rather than feeling regret at the loss, a sense of warmth radiated from her heart, and immediately, a beautiful blue-white opalescent oval of light appeared alongside her.

The feeling of warmth in her heart grew, and she knew unmistakably that a connection existed between it and the incredible oval of Light that now stood beside her. Becky stopped walking and just stared in amazement at the Light. Its beauty touched her beyond anything she'd experienced before, and yet, she couldn't ignore the *feeling* of familiarity that she felt in her heart in the presence of this Light.

Katran's voice resonated once again within Becky. "I'm honored to be with you, Becky. It has been very long since I brought my energies to Earth in this way. I thank you for the opportunity to serve." As she spoke, the silhouette of a rather petite woman began to form within the circle of light.

"We will meet this way and I will do my best to teach you all that you'll need to know for the journey ahead."

Without Becky consciously knowing it, they'd moved forward along the path and now stood in front of the oak log. As they reached the log, Katran's image faded into evening light, and Becky stood in the forest alone.

She waited for some time, pregnant with expectancy of some "magical" happening. Her senses felt super heightened in a way new to her as she heard evening creatures moving about the forest and birds making their final preparation for sleep. She stayed listening this way for some time before moving, took a deep breath and said out loud, "How wonderful life is!" as she strolled gently back along the path to the farm.

CHAPTER FIFTEEN
JULIUS RIDES IN

No one can know how to turn the tides back, but asking shows the way

The next day Becky and I were awakened early to the distinctly loud sound of a motorcycle coming down the farm road and arriving in front of the farmhouse. In our robes, we both rushed to the sitting room window to see who could be making such a racket. We were surprised to see Uncle Julius sitting astride a brand new Harley Davidson.

I think Becky must have felt the same mixed emotions as I about the scene. On the one hand, here was our eighty-year-old uncle with his long white beard sitting atop a brand new, very fancy and expensive motorcycle. My first instinct was one of excitement to see this beloved old friend with such a racy vehicle. On the other hand, the current circumstances were such that we felt immediately pulled out of these childhood sentiments into the harsh reality of how Uncle Julius had changed during these past few years.

We headed downstairs to see what this six o'clock in the morning visit might mean, Becky giving voice to my own thoughts.

"I know that Julius has come to bring us another offer," she said, "or try to trick us in some way into giving up the farm. The thing is," she said," I'm scared about his persistence. Shouldn't we just call Sergeant Gerhig?"

"No, not yet," I said. "I have a feeling we can help Uncle Julius, if we only stick with him, at least for a while longer. If every time he comes around, we call the police … well, I think we'll never have a chance to help him."

I knew Becky wasn't happy about what I said, but she nodded her assent as we went outside.

Something about Julius had changed. He no longer had that angry look in his eye that I'd seen several days back, but instead, came off the bike with a kind of sly smile and a hello.

Yes, he was here to make us one more offer, but that wasn't the core reason for his visit. He wanted to know if he could visit the forest with us. "You see," he said, "before your parents died, they told me that they'd left something for me there, and I … well, I just wanted to search for it."

He wouldn't say what it was that he was searching for, except to indicate that it was a gift that he and Dad had made arrangements long ago to transfer to him should our father pass on before Julius.

The look in Becky's eyes couldn't have been sharper. Her words matched her look. She told Uncle Julius that he couldn't go into the woods at all, that there was nothing there to see or to find. She went on to say that she knew that Dad wouldn't have willed him anything, given the way he had treated the family before our father and mother died.

Uncle Julius said nothing for a moment, and I watched as he seemed to flinch at Becky's words, as if hurt by her remarks. But this only lasted a second or so before the emotion in his eyes changed from hurt-filled to pure hatred radiating pure anger, violence, almost more than I had ever seen before, even in my days in Vietnam. His face turned red and I felt him wanting to attack Becky, to take revenge for the simple truth she'd spoken to him.

As Uncle Julius took a threatening step towards Becky, my own protective instincts rose sharply. I wouldn't let him harm Becky in any way, even though a part of me still looked for an opening in Uncle Julius, still looked for a way to reach him, I couldn't take the chance that he would hurt her.

With mixed feelings, I acted. I grabbed Uncle Julius as gently as I could by the shoulders, and threw him to the ground. I wanted to stop his movement towards Becky, and I wanted to shock him, to awaken another part of him, a kinder part, that he didn't seem to be in touch with.

My movements were calculated not to harm him. Still, he fought hard to keep me from my goal of pinning him to the ground. It took all the skills I'd learned in the Marines to maintain my position and control as the rage that captured him fueled his will to fight. Finally, I held him and the struggle was over as I felt something inside of him let go, as if the anger had lost its grip.

Now, as I looked into Uncle Julius' eyes, I saw not the fires of rage that had been there only a moment before, but the eyes of a weary old man. This was what I had hoped would happen and I was just about to speak to him, to make contact with the Julius we'd known as a child, when Becky jumped in and began pulling me off him. Immediately, Julius' strength and rage returned as he took advantage of the break in my attention to free himself from my grip.

"What're you doing, Harry? I told him we weren't going to sell and we could have just asked him to leave," she said. "Why on Earth did you do that?"

I didn't answer Becky immediately, for my eyes were fixed on Julius. His anger had returned, and I wasn't sure what he would do. He stood there, his cheeks bristling red, his chest heaving. He said, "Listen, this is the last time I'm going to talk to you this way. I used to know you two pretty well, but now, well, you're just like your father and mother. They didn't see what they had to do anymore than you." And then with a finger pointing as he moved back to his motorcycle, he said, "You'll see, I won't have to do a thing and you'll still want to sell the farm. You're on the wrong side, but you'll see, you won't be able to resist and I'll be the one with the last laugh." With that he started his motorcycle and raced down the driveway.

Becky continued her questioning. "What was that all about?"

I wanted to explain to her my motive for taking Julius to the ground, my desire to find a way to break through to him, my instinct that he could still be reached, but before I could, the voice of the Guardian came to me and I knew that Becky could hear it as well.

"The desire to turn the darkness back to the Light is a noble one, but for now," he said, "we need you and Becky to focus on your lessons. Let that one be. If you see him again, call on the angels to help out and all will be well. In the meantime, give your all to the lessons." Then, he was gone.

The confusion of knowing that Julius could be reached, but then being told not to try to help him, weighed heavy within me. No matter what he had done, I still had a warm place in my heart for that old man. Yet, something else was also at play. I felt that saving Uncle Julius from the forces that had "captured" him was part of a greater scheme to support the work of the Brotherhood of Light. I knew that if the Guardian wanted me to focus on the lessons rather than on Julius, that I should do just that. But, I also knew, without a doubt, that helping Julius was on my map at some time in the future.

CHAPTER SIXTEEN
FOREST PASSAGE WITH THE GUARDIAN

*Searching and searching to find ourselves; one day it happens and we **know** we are home*

With Becky home from work, we spent our days over the next few months visiting the forest and doing the homework given to us by our teachers.

Becky spent more and more time in the forest alone, and though she didn't speak very much about her lessons, I knew they were changing her. Her body, for one, was becoming more lean as she changed her eating habits. She was interested in vegetable meals and gradually gave up meat in her diet. Her spirit remained as strong as ever, but she became more inward and silent, as if her visits to the forest were somehow helping her become strong and quiet, like the forest itself.

As for me, the Guardian came often. However, shortly after Uncle Julius' visit, something changed in our lessons. I'd now adopted a habit to go to the forest each morning for daily walks with the Guardian. This morning, he'd been speaking about the origins of separate thought from God and wanted to show me the results of the separation from the "Oneness". We walked deep into the forest, eventually walking along a small deer trail that ran off the main forest path, to arrive at a clearing encircled by trees.

I knew this clearing well, as I'd come here often as a boy. My father would bring me to this place, and together we'd spend nights camping. In the middle of the clearing lay the charred rock remains of the campsite that Dad and I had made so many, many years back.

I felt so engrossed with the Guardian's story of creation, at first I didn't notice the path we were on, at least not until we arrived at the old campsite. It had been so long since I'd been here, but I knew this place very well. A smile of joy crossed my face as I remembered the nights Dad and I spent here under the stars.

The Guardian stopped talking as we arrived, giving me a moment to reminisce about the past, but soon continued, "Here we will stay for awhile. Today is a special day. It's the anniversary of the day your grandparents came to this area and bought the farm and their share of the forest. Your remembrance of this place is important. It's here that your father chose to bring you to initiate you to the forest mysteries. Many of these have been lost to your memory, but now together we will revive them.

And then, as if by magic, I found myself literally transported back to my youth, to the first time my father and I ever came to sleep here. I saw myself at the age of five as if a watcher of the scenes of my own life. We were just arriving at the clearing. This open part of the forest felt very new, as if it had only recently been cleared. No campsite or charred rocks remained at the site. The forest was thick with young evergreen shoots. A little creek ran across the lower edge of the clearing.

As we arrived, Dad put us immediately to work gathering rocks for the campsite. I couldn't really carry any of the big ones, but what I could, I did, while Dad gathered the heavier rocks. These are the rocks that are still present to this very day. As I watched us, I noticed that we weren't building a round fire pit, but that Dad had a different idea. With my little stones and his larger ones, he had us make a common pile. When we'd gathered all he thought we'd need, he sat down with me and explained what we were going to do.

The scene stirred deep memories within, for I had no recollection of it in my conscious mind … until now. Still, as I watched, I had the eerie experience of watching a scene that I had participated in as a child, and at the same time of consciously remembering, in the present, the actual events of the scene. Dad's words rang in my mind. "Harry," he said, "we will be coming here for a few years and then we will stop. Our purpose is for you to know this area of the forest. One day you'll be brought back here and it will start a process of remembering that will be very important."

With that he began to explain to me how we were going to build the campfire that we'd use at this spot—on that evening and on the other evenings that we came here.

"First," he said, "what we're building is an altar, a symbol to the Light, that we will use to keep us warm at night in body and spirit. Though you may not remember this time as you grow up, it will come back to you."

We started to build the campfire, rock by rock. Dad had a plan. He knew exactly where each rock went, and he also seemed to know which rocks he should put down and which ones that I would place. I watched my little hands as they struggled to lift the sometimes too heavy rocks that Dad had me carry, and yet all the while I rejoiced at the effort, for just being with him was enough for me, as I loved him dearly.

The little five-year-old boy that I was saw it all as fun. I lifted little rocks and bigger ones and alternately ran and stumbled over to the area of the campfire, but eventually the pile of rocks that Dad had us collect was gone. In its place was what looked at first appearance to be a normal campfire, but upon closer inspection, it was shaped like a large round heart and in the middle was a rough image of the same *fleur-de-lys* pattern that I had seen on my first journey with the Guardian, and on the wall of my parents' bedroom.

The leaves of the *fleur-de-lys* crossed in the middle of the heart, and as I watched I saw Dad begin to build the first fire of this fledgling campsite's life directly over the point where the *fleur-de-lys* crossed. I watched the little boy and how exciting it was for me to be there with my father. And yet, I also saw the tears that came to my little eyes as the first sparks of the fledgling fire caught. Somehow, even then, I knew the importance of this place and that Dad wouldn't always be with me when I returned to it.

The Guardian's voice interrupted my private thoughts about that moment. "We have come," he said, "to stir your memory about this place, for it's here that your father told you of the mysteries of Light that are the Brotherhood's secrets.

"We know that you're wondering why you have no memory of this time, and even why your father didn't speak of these things when you were ever so young.

"The answer to this question resides in the rules of the Brotherhood that were given to your father at the time of your birth, and before. Each person, or life stream, has many contracts with others to help them on their way regarding awakening their consciousness to their own unique Light. Our job in the Brotherhood is to work with both those who are awakening and with those others who've made agreements with them to lend a hand on their journey of awakening.

"Your father knew of your awakening in this life. But it is a strong tenet of the Brotherhood to allow each individual to choose his or her own pace and time. Had your father raised you to be a *child of the Brotherhood of Light*, you would have found yourself with a great deal of knowledge of the form of our order, but you may still not have made the choice to pass along the road to our house to learn the essence." He stopped for a moment, as if in thought himself, and said quietly, "To the House of the Light of God."

Then he continued, "So you were left to grow on your own after only a short introduction to us. Your father brought you here, but as you know, he only rarely mentioned the symbol or the elements of knowledge that encompass our work.

"You're here now and, by your faith, you've come to study our life, and be taught what it is you'll need to know to freely join us. The illusion of separation of man from his own Creator has damaged the very fabric of life itself. It was never meant to be. Our task is to help correct that which went wrong and strengthen the order of things in the service of the Light. The challenge is to help a sleeping "God-Man" and "God-Woman" trust that reawakening a desire within them to regain a conscious connection to the unity of the *Light* will be not only be safe for them, but will also result in a more joyful and sacred life here on this plane of duality.

"The movement of God mind from higher to the lower and denser vibrations of Earth affected humanity's thoughts and consciousness in ways predictable and unpredictable. The day to day realities of being in human form—needing to feed, clothe and shelter the body—began to take precedence over man's direct connection to 'God Mind.' Instead, humanity's *Survival mind* came to dominate life on Earth and with it, humankind began to lose its conscious connection to the whole.

"And yet, it is a great truth that the struggle to survive within Survival consciousness can never displace the fundamental reality known somewhere deep within each person's being, either consciously or not, that they are part of the One—capable of re-accessing and experiencing a purer expression of the qualities of God Mind of joy, light, creativity, love and expanded self knowledge that are currently available at the higher reaches of the One mind. Still, conscious knowledge of this truth varies within each person depending on their own personal evolution and growth in re-awakening their connection to their Source. The Guardian then paused, as if conferring with others as to the next thing that I would be shown, or taught. "We must go now," he said. "You're needed in town to visit with a certain man named Bill Bates. He is the owner of the farm to the southeast of yours, one of the five farms that also surround this sacred land, and he is in need of your help to confirm his own instincts that he must maintain hold of his part of the land.

"We will return to the forest again, soon," he added. "For now, we thank you deeply for your interest and desire to learn." With that he was gone. By the tone of this last communication I knew that this was not the Guardian's preferred order of things. I had learned to listen well in Nam, so I moved rapidly jogging through the forest's main path back to our farm and to an important meeting with Bill Bates.

***

When I returned to the farm, Becky was there. She'd been meditating upstairs, she said, but had a strong sense that she needed to come out of her meditation to speak with me. I told her of my pending journey to town to visit with Bill Bates, the owner of one of the other nearby farms. For a moment, she got pensive, closed her eyes, opened them again, and then declared her intent to come along to the meeting with me.

As we readied to go, I told her about the campsite and the symbol. "You mean," she said, "all those nights that you and Dad would have an outing, as Mom used to call it, you spent in the forest? You know, I never knew that. I was only a child myself and all she would tell me was that the boys needed to spend some time together. On those nights, we'd spend special girl time together.

"Mom had a quilt that she was working on and I helped her with it. I tell you," she continued, "the more I remember and find out about our own parents, the more they become a mystery to me. It's not like they told us anything about the *fleur-de-lys* symbol in the heart, or the Brotherhood, or anything. I wonder why they didn't. It feels like it would certainly have made life easier for us now, had they initiated us into what they were doing."

Then, taking a deep breath, she got quiet for a second and said softly, "I feel like I really didn't know them for all they were, and that's the saddest part of all.

"Had they told us about their life with the Brotherhood, we could have joined them and felt closer to them. As it was, we both felt them distant." Then she added, "Warm, but distant."

Becky said, "I'm beginning to understand, at least a little bit, their distance. They had a huge secret that they felt they needed to keep from us, about the Brotherhood and the forest. I wish they were here now, so that we could talk with them about all that's going on. Oh, Harry, I miss them so."

I held my arms out offering her a shoulder to lean on and Becky came, just for a moment. It wasn't our usual way, but the visits with the Brotherhood were changing us. We were growing more like friends than big sister and little brother! So, here in the living room where we'd both played and grown as children, I comforted my big sister, and in doing so, comforted myself as well. In truth, I, too, missed them greatly.

But Becky's words rang true for me as well. As a child, I remembered how I often wondered why they were so different. I remembered thinking with a bit of regret that they certainly weren't your normal parents. They didn't come to the school dances and chaperone and Dad didn't encourage me to be a hotshot on the football team. I'd go to friend's houses and everything always appeared topsy-turvy compared to our life: TV always on, brothers and sisters fighting over who should play with which toy, and a general atmosphere of chaos.

In our house, things were different. We seldom watched TV, and Becky and I got along well. Mom always seemed calm and collected. She cooked for us all, but so did Dad, and they shared the work on the farm. At night they would sit and read to us when we were little, or we'd all partake in an art project of one sort or another, or sing a few songs together. As we got older, they expected us to create this atmosphere ourselves, and for the most part we did, reading, doing art, or creating some other project on our own.

It was then, after we got old enough to direct our own evening activities, that Dad and Mom required what they called their quiet time. Three or four times a week in the early evening, after we'd had supper and cleaned the dishes and the kitchen, they would go into their room and sit quietly, their eyes closed, under the painting of the *fleur-de-lys* in the heart symbol that hung on their bedroom wall. We weren't allowed to bother them at these times. They became so quiet, so still, that once Becky even thought that they'd fallen asleep in their chairs.

She was wrong about that. One evening she tiptoed into their room to retrieve a book from their bedroom bookshelf, and they both turned immediately asking her what it was that she needed. Becky told me all about it later on, and from that day onward, we both knew never to go into their room during their quiet time that usually lasted an hour or two.

As teenagers, we both found them respectful of our privacy and our own personal integrity. We both believed ourselves fortunate in our early years to have their caring kindness around us. Yet there existed this mystery about them. They kept to themselves, loving each other greatly, yet were still friendly enough with all the people they met or knew. But, fundamentally, they didn't seem to need others around. And though they'd both come from large families, they never seemed to care to connect with any of them.

I asked Dad about it once, why we didn't connect with others of the family. He said, "Son, we journey with God, and that's enough for us," and I never asked him again to explain what he meant, to go deeper. Now that they were gone, my heart ached to have known them better. It was almost as if they did their job, left, and now it was our turn.

As if reading my mind, Becky interrupted my thoughts, "I guess no matter how much we miss them and wish that they were here, it's our work now to carry on and protect the forest, just as they did."

I nodded, and for the moment, put aside my own thoughts and childhood hurt feelings about how they'd been so caring to us on the one hand, and yet at the same time so distant and secretive … especially about their connection to the Brotherhood of Light.

And now, as we drove to town to talk to Bill Bates, I thought of the vision I had seen that very first time in the forest with the Guardian. The one in which my parents spoke of us all being together in the *sacred days*. Deep inside me I knew that these were the sacred days. For though Dad and Mom weren't physically with us, I felt their presence more and more as the lessons deepened and their own connection to the Brotherhood became clearer.

CHAPTER SEVENTEEN
ON OUR WAY TO MEET BILL BATES

Though we may KNOW what we know, we confuse ourselves often with "kind" words thinking this is a better way to "see it all." Listening is more important!

This time of year, the drive through the Ohio countryside to town presented a marvel of contrasts and contradictions. The oak lined roads, with the gently flowing river shimmering alongside, radiated a sense of tranquility and safety. By contrast, Becky and I couldn't ignore the steaming heat of late August. Its ever-present near one hundred percent humidity created an intense feeling of oppression. We chatted about this as we drove to our prearranged meeting with Bill Bates. Becky had called his law offices that morning and fortunately he had time to see us. As we drove, Becky and I shared what we knew about the man we were about to meet.

Bill Bates was several years older than Becky, and though we all went to the same high school, neither Becky nor I knew him. His grandparents had been part of the group that had bought the five farms and agreed to the forest covenant. They moved to Ohio several years after our grandparent's settled our farm. But the "farm families", weren't prone to meet or spend social time together. They quietly stayed to themselves. Bill's grandparents lived on the farm for many years before passing on.

Bill's father and his brother moved to Ohio from Pennsylvania with Bill's grandparents. Both brothers stayed on the farm and worked it for several years after the purchase of the land and forest, but both eventually left the area to make their lives elsewhere. No one in the area seemed to know much about what had happened to the older of the two Bates boys, but it was known that the younger of the two, Bill's dad, had married and had settled in Arkansas.

From what little Becky or I could piece together, or remember from what Mom, Dad or others around town had said about the Bates family, Bill had grown up in Arkansas. But, as a teenager, he returned to his grandparent's Ohio farm with his mother after his dad died. Bill attended the local high school, living on the farm with his grandparents and mother at first, then left the area to go to college and then to law school. Becky remembered Mom saying that the older Bates couple passed on not long after he left and that Bill's mother had stayed on to live and work the farm, and that she "… did a fine job, what with all the work she had to do to keep the place up and goin'."

Now, with law school finished, Bill had returned to the area and established his practice here in Placerville. Becky said she heard once at the office that Mrs. Bates had been become ill and couldn't run the farm any longer, and that that was the reason for Bill Bates' return to the area. As we drove to meet him at his law offices, I wondered aloud about what his plans might be for the farm.

"You know, he must be thinking about selling or the Guardian wouldn't have sent us to talk to him. I can just imagine who'd be putting pressure on him to sell. I'll bet Uncle Julius and his partners are right there looking for an opening. My guess is that each of the farm families is being pressured by that crew.

"I wish I knew more about them and their motivation. I don't really believe their story about any mall, or anything like that." I said, "Next time I'm with the Guardian, I'll ask him to help me better understand what they're after."

"Yes," said Becky, "that's a good idea. You know, the way that Katran works with me doesn't give me much chance to ask questions. I spend so much time communing with the forest creatures and elements that my lessons don't really lend themselves to asking questions.

"Still," she concluded, "I'd like to know more about that crew myself. I think I'd feel a little more comfortable if I knew exactly what they wanted and why."

***

We pulled onto Main Street a few minutes before our appointed meeting time. As we drove down the street, a great well of affection filled me. I had spent my youth here and the memories of times past flooded my mind as we drove to our meeting. Becky and I looked at each other and smiled all the way down Main Street as we passed one 1930's vintage red brick building after another, for she, too, loved this place.

The town's buildings and the central plaza, which sat right in front of the old City Hall, had held up well these many years. Even with all the new people and changes happening in the town, it was something of a miracle that it still had held the integrity of its past. It was as if no one could take away its history of good people living and raising their families in a good place no matter how negative the impacts of the many newcomers might be.

The people may change, I thought, but the place itself still holds to its old dignity. As we drove down the street to the Conklin Building, where Bill Bates had his law offices, we passed a café that hadn't been there before I'd left to join the marines. It had a different feeling than the rest of Main Street. A dozen or more motorcycles sat in front of the building that housed the café. Alongside these stood a group of men dressed in black leather with the symbol of a skull and crossbones painted on the back of their jackets. The words "Alcaz Motorcycle Club" scrolled beneath the symbol in letters ablaze with fire.

Our passing raised a few heads as not many cars were on the street at this time of day. As we drove past the café, one of the men, a tall blonde man with a raw, angry-looking scar across his left cheek, gazed intently at me, as if he knew me or who I was. For just a second I looked into his icy blue eyes, then I heard the Guardian voice say, "Do not take this one on, we will need to address him and the others later, for now, your job is to talk with Bill Bates. Tell Bill he is not alone in his decision to keep the farm and forest." With that, the Guardian left.

We continued to drive down the street and parked across the road from Bill Bates' law offices. As I got out of the car, though, I could still feel those icy eyes looking at me. My instinct was to turn and fight. I had felt this emotion often in the war. If someone had malevolent emotions towards me, I immediately felt it, as if the person were right in front of me ready to attack. I learned to trust this feeling and act on it, and it had saved my life several times. Now, I stopped. For instead of turning back to defend myself from the "coming attack," I heeded the Guardian's call not to act and to keep focused on the reason of our visit.

I found this one of the hardest things I had ever had to do: to not look around and not take on the man with the icy blue eyes. Trained for action, the action I needed to take now was to do nothing. Without looking back I went around to the other side of the car and joined Becky, as we walked across Main Street and entered Bill Bates' office.

CHAPTER EIGHTEEN
MEETING WITH A FRIEND

Dance the dance of Light with the other and you may learn your own name

We found ourselves meeting a tall man with dark hair, an open smile, and kindness in his medium dark brown eyes. Becky introduced us both after the receptionist led us into the office where Bill Bates greeted us.

"Please," he said, "have a seat," as he pointed to the two burgundy leather chairs across from his somewhat imposing oak desk.

"We have never really met," he said, "but I've known who the two of you are ever since high school. It's nice to see you. What is it that I can do for you?"

Becky took the lead in telling him our story. She was precise on every detail: about our concern that he might be interested in selling the farm; about wanting to persuade him to keep the farm; about our understanding of the importance of the farm, and the little understood agreement that had existed between the "farm families" who'd originally purchased and divided the land, keeping the forest in common ownership; and about the offers to buy our farm and our suspicions about the negative intent of those wanting buy the land. She omitted only the facts of the Guardian's words and the Brotherhood of the Light's involvement in encouraging our visit.

He listened carefully to Becky with a look of wonder and surprise in his eyes. When Becky completed what she had to say, he sat back in his chair with a pensive frown on his face for several seconds before responding.

"Well," he said, "this is a lot of information you bring me, and were it not for one thing that you just said, I probably would simply play lawyer with you, keep my own cards close to my chest, and not say too much. But you mentioned something that I've heard about since childhood, and that makes what you're talking about very, very important to me. So, please, listen carefully and I'll tell you all I know about this, and where I am in the matter.

"The thing that I've heard so much of, and yet know nothing really at all about, is something my father called the farm families compact. Unlike the two of you, I didn't grow up here. But when I did come to Ohio as a teenager, I became very close with my grandparents.

"The subject of the farm families buying the land and holding the forest in common interested me even then, and I asked my grandparents often about it. And, you know, the only thing they would tell me is that it was a sacred trust and that one day I would know more about it. Well, I guess today may be that day, for I haven't heard the words farm families in years, and your bringing it up now stirs all the old questions that I used to have about it."

As he spoke, Bill looked from one to the other of us with questioning eyes, as if to ask, "If I don't know about this, maybe you two do?" For our part, Becky and I listened intently, as if the speaker, full of doubts as he was, still might have some new insights for us.

He went on, "So, my grandparents wouldn't answer and I went away to school forgetting all about it. But now that I've returned to the area, the old questions about the farm are beginning to come up. "Yes," he said, "I've had several offers on the farm. They come from different sources, but my suspicion is they're generated from a single source.

"I've not met your Uncle Julius, but I have met the other two, Freed and Frosten. They came the first time to visit me about six months ago and made me and offer on the farm. I told them I'd think about it and get back to them. My mother and I talked about it and decided that we weren't interested in selling. They came back several times after that to try to convince me to change my mind.

"In truth, the story of the compact had something to do with our choice. But, at least when I was around, my grandparents wouldn't say much about the farm ... or the forest. But one thing they were firm on and spoke of often was that the farm must never be sold, no matter what. They would say, 'its value is far greater than you know.' I remember asking them about it, and all they would say is that it was very important to hold the farm. So, you can see that even though I told them I'd think about it, I had no inclination to sell when approached by those two.

"That was about six months ago, but only yesterday, I got a second offer. It came from the new operator of the café down the street, the one that has all the motorcycles out in front of it. The guy's name is Felix Butezz. I don't know where he came from, but he opened the café about the same time as I got the first offer on the farm. Those fellows Freed and Frosten seem to spend a great deal of time there. I've seen them coming out of the place pretty regularly over these past months. Frankly, though I may not like those two, this guy Butezz really gives me the creeps. Something about how he looks at me makes me feel like getting an iron bar and defending myself. I've never had that experience before, not even in criminal court when I served as an assistant DA intern during law school. I don't know, but if you meet him, you may have the same response. I'd like to know what you think about him if you ever do meet."

"From what you told us," I said, "it doesn't sound like either Becky or I would want to meet him!" We both smiled and laughed at that.

"Yes," Bill joked, "I can understand that."

Though we'd never met before, I usually have a pretty good sense about people, and in the few minutes we'd been together, I decided that I liked Bill, a lot. I found myself responding to him with a sense of camaraderie and friendship, as if I'd known him well all my life. This surprised me, but still brought a smile to my face. He had a strength about him, and yet a kindness at the same time.

While Bill smiled at my making light of the situation, Becky didn't, and her attitude sobered me. Even though it was my habit to joke in the face of danger, Becky's stern demeanor reminded me of the seriousness of the business at hand. Sadly, as I looked over at her unsmiling face, I remembered Mom and Dad and the reality of what had happened to them. At that point, I made a promise to myself never to make light of the situation again.

"I can understand that," Bill continued, "but still, I'd like your opinions about him. At any rate, my suspicion is that those two men who are working with your Uncle are also working with Butezz. As I've said, I've seen them at his café often, but I've also seen the three of them around town together. To be frank, I get the chills when I see them," he went on. "The town sure has changed in the last few years and I don't think it's for the better."

Both Becky and I nodded in agreement. "I'd like to say that you're wrong about that," said Becky, "but I can't. The town has changed and those who've come, I fear, have come with some plan in mind, I believe, that includes those of us in the farm families. It doesn't feel good, and it doesn't feel safe.

"As for the rest of what you said, Harry and I, too, were raised with the idea that the farm families had some kind of an agreement or compact before they all purchased the land. When our parents died, I had the opportunity to look at the legal papers for the farm. The deed of ownership is pretty normal except for the fact that it refers to a trust that has been set up for the forest that doesn't allow any of the owners of the five farms, or their descendants to sell the forest. It also refers to certain standards of stewardship for the forest that all the five families are obliged to maintain. I couldn't find the land trust papers, but if there's such a written document, it does seem to keep all of us pretty much sworn to uphold the safety of the forest."

Bill sat forward, almost leaning across his desk as Becky spoke, as he became more and more excited at what he heard. Then, before Becky finished speaking he could contain himself no longer. "Yes, yes, Becky," he almost stammered, "I've been looking at the same issue. I just reviewed my grandparent's deed of trust and it, too, refers to the land trust. I don't have the document either, but it must be registered at the county seat. It's too late today, but we can go over there tomorrow to check it out.

"I can tell you, just so you know, that neither I nor my mother has plans to sell the farm. I'm not clear about all the particulars as to why the forest is so important, but our family will keep to its part of the compact. We're not selling." Then, lowering his eyes for just a moment in thought, as if checking something within himself that might not comport well with his legal training, he said, "Not now, nor ever!"

I didn't see Becky's face as he said this, but I know mine must have relaxed as if a ray of pure sunshine crossed my brow. I smiled and said, "You know, Bill, all of us aren't exactly sure what this land holds, but it does have treasures that I'm certain we'll all discover as we go along."

Then, as if the Guardian himself were speaking, I said, "I would like to invite you to walk in the forest with me one day. Becky and I go there often for our own, meditation, you might call it, and I want to share the specialness of the place with you."

Bill nodded, "Yes, that would be fine. You know, I've not spent time on the land since moving here from Arkansas. My grandparents had it fenced off with a high gate from their farm's entrance so that no one, not even me or my mother could go out onto the land without being invited." Bill smiled. As you know, the forest itself is surrounded with that high dense blackberry hedge with thorns the size of crochet needles. So, I've just stayed away.

"I'll have to find the key to open the fence." A strange look came over Bill's face then, as if something more than the high hedge and locked gate had kept him out of the forest. Then, as if remembering our presence in the room, he said, "If I can't find it, would it be okay for me to come over to your farm to take you up on the offer?"

"Yes," I said, "that would be fine." I looked at Becky as she wondered why I had not included her in the invitation. Then I realized that though I had spoken the words, the Guardian had been the one who'd invited Bill for the walk in the forest. I wondered about the intent of the invitation and why Becky's exclusion, when Becky looked over at me and smiled, and with that smile I knew that she understood that the invitation came from the Brotherhood and that all was well.

The meeting ended with a smile and friendly handshakes all around. Even Becky, who seemed a bit tight during the meeting, smiled. As we left, we all decided to meet the next day at the law office to take the thirty minute ride together over to the county seat to research the land trust.

As Becky and I drove back to our farm we spoke of our impressions of Bill and the relief that we felt at his response to our visit. "He's a nice man, isn't he, Harry?" she said. I looked at her and responded positively to her query. "I'm so pleased that he's on our side. After all, can you imagine what it would be like if he wasn't?"

"I don't even want to think about it," I said. "The fact of his being a lawyer should help us understand the ramifications of the land trust document tomorrow when we go to the Courthouse."

"Yes," she said emphatically, "We're lucky that he's here!"

I looked over at Becky again as she spoke. She was an attractive woman and something in her voice made me know that she was happy to meet Bill for more than the reason of our mutual interest in holding onto the farms and forest.

CHAPTER NINETEEN
BECKY LISTENS WELL

Nobody has a better way to see than you; nobody can ask but you

The next day we drove to the County Recorder's office, which was on the fourth floor of the old Courthouse; a stately three story building replete with Grecian columns and elegant white wood siding. Constructed in the 1850's, it had served as the administrative center for the county ever since. Our search was rewarded as the clerk's records showed that the land trust had been recorded and put on microfiche. As we waited for the clerk to find the document and make copies, I had the sudden urge to go outside, and I told Bill and Becky that I would meet them on the front lawn of the Courthouse.

The building felt old and musty, like one that hadn't been cleaned for a very long time. I decided to take the eastern stairwell to the street rather than take the old rickety elevator, probably installed in the nineteen forties.

As I started down the steps, however, my senses snapped alert to the faint aroma of burning wood. I hurried down the old stairwell as if guided by an invisible hand leading me to the second floor landing. There could be no mistaking the fact that a fire had caught in the lower floors of the stairwell. Flames were beginning to leap rapidly from the lowest level of, the basement and to the upper levels.

I began choking on the smoke as the fire licked the stairwell beneath the level where I stood. I looked down to see if I could help still the flames in some way, but soon realized that the fire's own momentum had built to such a rapid speed I would have to use all my wits just to save myself.

I ran back up the steps to reenter the building at the level of the Recorder's office. The stairwell acted as a flue, pulling the heat and smoke up the stairwell to the building's roof. I felt the almost unbearable heat of the flames grab at me, and as I reached for the door, I realized that it had locked behind me. I could go nowhere further in this four story building … the stairwell ended right here. I pounded on the door in hopes that someone would hear me. But no one came.

Apparently, the fire had just begun at the base of this stairwell and had not yet tripped any fire alarms in the rest of the building. My instincts for survival had been tested many times in Vietnam, but now, I couldn't imagine how I would get out of the stairwell before the flames and smoke made it impossible for me to breathe.

In that moment, I heard a familiar voice inside me say, "Trust, all is well." Then, "fall to the floor and wait." Without hesitation, I did so, for that voice had been with me too often before to doubt. Pulling my shirt over my head to filter the rising smoke, I curled against the farthest wall of the stairwell, directly alongside the door. I stayed like this for what seemed like a very long time, until I felt the burning smoke that filled my lungs would soon make it impossible for me to take another breath. My mind whirled, my lungs burned, breathing became harder and harder. I banged once more meekly on the door, hoping upon hope that someone would hear, but no one came. Then, nearly unconscious, I heard my name, and in that moment the door opened as I heard Becky's familiar voice call my name, again and again.

Through the fog of smoke and fire that filled my consciousness, I staggered to my feet and through the doorway to the temporary safety of the fourth floor hallway. Becky and Bill helped me walk as we crossed the now crowded fourth floor corridor to the western stairwell. By this time, alarms sounded as the buildings old fashioned sprinkler system strained to still the flames as they poured through the wooden fibers of the Courthouse.

We hurried down the crowded stairwell to the safety of the lawn. Looking back, we saw an afternoon sky filled with smoke and flames rising from the Courthouse as fire consumed the old building.

***

We all stayed silent for most of the ride home. I felt shaken by the experience, and could see the worry and concern on both Becky and Bill's faces. Still, the quiet oak lined country road, the warmth of the summer's day, and the calm of the stream alongside the road lent an air of unreality to what had just happened. Yes, I had almost died in that fire, and, yes, the reason of our visit went up in flames with the rest of the Courthouse and its records, and still my life went on.

As we neared home, I thanked Becky for coming to find me. I didn't wonder about how she knew where I could be found, for I felt certain in the knowledge that the "Guardian" or another of the Brotherhood of Light had guided her to the right place. Bill, though, wanted to know more. As we neared home, the shock of what had just happened was wearing off, and Bill could no longer hold back his natural curiosity.

"We were already heading to the outside," he said to her. "How on Earth did you know to go backup and look for Harry in that other stairwell?"

His demeanor, only a few minutes ago somber and calm, changed now to excitement as if he had witness some new form of magic. Now that we were safe, he wanted to know what the trick was, what the "sleight of hand" might be that led to such an extraordinary event.

As he pressed Becky on this, she responded only that she had an instinct to go to the stairwell door. Bill's questions persisted for a while longer, before he finally accepted her pat answer, "Instinct, Bill, that's all, just instinct."

Our conversion turned to the fire. It had greatly frightened us all with its tremendous heat and the rapid spread of flames and smoke. But, we all agreed that even more frightening was the fact that deep down, we all knew that this fire was no accident. "You know," Bill said, "with all my lawyer's training, I'd like to wait to pass judgment on a thing likes this. Arson is a pretty serious crime. Still, I'd have to say there's a bit too much of a coincidence what with the fire starting just as we were about to get the land trust papers."

Becky and I agreed. "It's really scary," she said, tears welling in her eyes. "You almost died back there. I've already lost Mom and Dad, and now this. I wish we knew more about why they want the forest land and who's behind all this."

I sat listening intently before speaking. "I feel that the path for us to get the answer is through Uncle Julius. He's up to his teeth in this thing, but I still feel we can reach him. The question is how?" Then I thought better of what I had just said, "Maybe we need to just take one thing at a time and figure out first how we're going get our hands on a copy of the land trust document. It's that that we need to understand right now."

Bill responded, "You know, when Becky and I were waiting for the clerk, I remembered that it's a law in this state that all county microfiche records related to land ownership are kept as copies at the state capitol. If I'm not mistaken, I think we'll have no problem getting copies of the papers, even with what just happened at the Courthouse."

Becky took a deep sigh of relief as she listened to Bill's words. A look of admiration filled her eyes as she listened and I knew that I had not been wrong about her attraction to him. And, by the way he looked back at her, I could see that the feeling was mutual.

My strength had returned completely by the time we pulled into the farm. But I knew Becky wanted to return do some errands in town.

With a concerned look on her face, she asked, "Will you be okay, Harry? I don't want to leave alone if you're not feeling right." I reassured her, so she decided to do the grocery shopping she'd planned. Bill chimed in saying that he would pleased to give Becky a ride back to town and then back home later that day as it was on his way home. Becky smiled at Bill's suggestion, and then gave me a look so pregnant with meaning that said, "Harry Pond, you'd better say okay!"

The agreement amongst the three of us was that Bill would take the lead in tracking down the land trust documents. I felt excited to be home, for the "Guardian" had invited me to join him in the forest for our next lesson.

CHAPTER TWENTY
MY FOREST DANCE; MEETING SAKYA

It's good to know what man and woman are capable of if aligned with all the elements of God and nature!

The forest breezes blew across my face as the day's heat receded into the coolness of the late afternoon. As I walked through the forest, I reveled in its silence. Even though our farm was in the country, sounds of human activity invaded the ear throughout the day: backhoes digging their straight ditches, tractors carrying farmers to their crops, and the general din of country roads that had become more and more crowded as city dwellers bought and built newer homes farther and farther from the downtown area.

Here, in the forest, a silence filled me as never before. Though I had been here as a youngster with Dad, he had stopped our camping trips after several years in favor of family outings to the nearby mountains in Pennsylvania. Becky and I had come often in our childhood as well.

Since that time and during my teenage years, I hadn't really spent much time here. Coming now to meet the "Guardian" brought back memories of my boyhood, and an acute awareness of the quiet calm that I felt all around. As I walked slowly along the path, a feeling of rapture overtook me. Perhaps it was the silence, perhaps the perfect tempo of the forest breeze, perhaps … I didn't know, but it didn't matter, for as I walked this feeling carried me, and I started to dance.

Slowly I moved to my right, and to my left, and then around in circles—in a way that would have made me dizzy had I not set a gentle pace of lifting my feet—dancing to the rhythm of a music my mind didn't consciously hear, but my body knew well. Around and around I spun, turned and rhythmically moved my feet. All at once, I became a Greek in an Athens taverna, a Russian dancing at a wedding, a Gypsy dancing at a campfire. My mind had no bounds as I laughed a laugh that came from deep within and my heart sang its own silent, yet joyous song.

I was Harry Pond, *the* Harry Pond, the *only* Harry Pond, and I felt my uniqueness in every movement, yet I felt my unity as well with the earth beneath my feet, the trees, and the invisible animals of the forest.

My dance lasted only several minutes, but those were not minutes that I could count in Earth time, for my consciousness merged with the all in those moments, and time had no meaning. When I stopped my dance, I felt stunned at these moments of bliss that I'd just experienced. Surely, life should feel like this all the time!

Jay Allan Luboff

The Guardian came to me. "Harry," he said in my mind, "it's good to know what man, any man is capable of, if aligned with all the elements of God and nature. Your dance belongs to you. The forest holds many secrets, and your dance is one of these. It's a place where the primordial elements of life have not been stilled. In truth, what humankind calls magic can happen here. But it isn't magic; it's the true nature of things uninhibited. The pledge to save the forest from those who'd destroy it is a pledge to defend the purity of God's kingdom here on Earth.

"The work that you and the others do is vital to this mission of protecting the primordial consciousness of the elements that have survived here. We of the Brotherhood thank you for your efforts and for joining us in holding sacred that which has the potential to bring humankind back to its senses."

I walked further on into the forest as the Guardian spoke. My own experience of the forest changed from one of visitor to the place, to one of inhabitant of the land. I don't know how Native Americans experienced their world, but I suspect, at their highest consciousness of spiritual unity, their religious experiences matched my own when it came to being at one with this land.

I walked down the path, not sure what to do next. This was my lesson time with the Brotherhood, but without specific direction from the Guardian, I simply continued on down main path. As I walked on I passed the little trail to the clearing that Dad and I had visited so often in our camping days, the one I visited just recently with the Guardian, and went on until I reached the fallen oak log—the place where Becky and I came to meet the teachers of the Brotherhood for our lessons.

I sat and waited, still filled with the exhilarating sense of unity with the forest and all life within it. And then I saw him! Not far from me, coming down the path from the opposite direction from which I had arrived at the log, came a huge man, perhaps seven feet tall, dressed in an outfit that unmistakably came from somewhere on the Indian continent.

With head wrapped in a turban of white, he wore a white silk shirt with puffy sleeves and a white vest adorned with embroidered symbols of red and white down the front. The pants he wore, if that's what they would be called, came to just below the knees of his massive legs and were held there by a button of white ivory. The pants were of silk as well. The delicate carved features of his face belied the tremendous girth of the man. Brown skin shone bronze-like in the afternoon light of the forest and his dark, dark brown eyes sparkled, amidst high cheekbones, giving an air of both elegance, and kindness to his face. Still, his strong chin let me know that this was a man very much used to making decisions.

As he approached the log, I rose to meet this tall stranger, wondering how he had gotten here. To my surprise he spoke to me, not out loud, but directly within my mind.

"Please, sit down, Harry, I'll come to be with you." he said. My name is Sakya, and for a time I will be your teacher." He continued to walk towards were I sat, and proceeded to sit his huge body beside me. He looked over at me and then reached his broad hand to mine as we shook hands. Then, as if communication through thought and word were equally easy for him, he spoke aloud, looking straight into my surprised eyes.

"It's good to meet you, Harry," he said with a broad smile. "Yes, we're aware of the emotions of shock you're experiencing, for we aren't, as you'd say, your normal person on the street. But do bear with us, for despite this unusual format for a teacher to meet his student, you'll find that all will work out quite to your satisfaction. Still," he said with a serious look on his face, we have much to do and not that much time in which to learn it. We must move forward and you must listen carefully and learn."

I nodded my ascent. This giant of a man held such a demeanor of kindness that though I felt a little intimidated by his size, I knew no fear in his presence. Rather, his eyes penetrated my own, and looking into them felt like diving into a pool of clear water. They called to me. As my eyes met his, I found a deep sparkle opening before me into a luminous sea of pearly mist, glowing as brilliant and bright as the nacre inside the shell of an abalone. I felt safe, but even more, in that instant, I knew this man to be kinder than any I had ever met before on Earth, and I suspected, wiser as well.

"Well, shall we begin," he said, his unmistakable Indian accent now became obvious as we settled into a mode of communicating with words rather than through direct mind contact. "As I said, my name is Sakya, and I do, as you've noticed, have some background in India where I've spent most of my time on Earth.

"As you're wondering how I got here in your forest, I'll allow an answer to this question before moving into today's lesson. I have what you may call the ability to transport myself from place to place on Earth, through a spiritual mechanism called *frequency adjustment.*

"Yes, you're right," he said, as if reading my own thoughts, "frequency adjustment allows one who's able to practice this discipline to fundamentally alter the vibration and speed of the molecules of his or her body. As the frequency of the body's molecular structure increases, the body loses it solid physical form. In my case, for instance, my ability to practice this discipline allows me to maintain my consciousness in a sort of invisible light body, which has been called by some a Merkabah vehicle, through which I'm able to transport myself to any place I will the vehicle to go."

He stopped and looked at me with a smile said, "We know that you have many questions. For now, we will walk together, if that's all right with you."

Yes, he had read my mind, I did have many questions, but I honored his request, nodding my agreement as we stood to walk together. This giant of a man dwarfed my own six-foot-one-inch frame. As we traversed the path in the direction from which he had come, I kept having the sense of the physical form of his body slightly fading in and out of view at the edges.

"We're here in this forest because it's one of the few places on Earth that we can be together and talk without being overheard. Yes, we understand your confusion, but please listen. There was a time on Earth when those of us of the Brotherhood roamed freely, helping out as we could with the struggles of humankind. But the rules of religion and society closed in on humanity, and only those with special religious views and beliefs were allowed to roam the earth. This was the time of the change from the religions that honored the earth, to those which honored the sky, instead.

"The vision of Mastery of Self and Light that we shared with Earth before that time became a vision outside the standards of consciousness on Earth.

"Indeed, Jesus the Christ came to show a path to a humanity that had gotten tangled up in rules and circles of information about what God is and isn't. He wanted to show that individuals, not religious societies or deities, if well focused and practiced in the consciousness of the One, could indeed find their way back to their Father-Mother Creator, and source of all that is. As it turned out, his message became known as one of sin, and the salvation of the soul from wrongdoing. Yet what is wrongdoing, but to not know who one really is?

"The tragedy of Earth is the tragedy of a humanity gone so far away from its own true pulse, its own true heart … a humanity that wanders around perpetually afraid to look at its true nature and relationship to the One. For what we have now is a humanity with so much guilt, so much violence, so much pain, and so much confusion that it has caused incredible harm not only daily to itself, but also to Earth, for as humankind lost its sense of itself, it short circuited Earth's own sense of herself.

"You'd be surprised, my friend, how few places on Earth are held sacred for the truth of unity to be spoken. This is one of those places, and as it has been spoken of before, we thank you for your help in maintaining this sanctuary for the light. For from this place, and several others, the Brotherhood continues to share the lessons of light learned over the ages by its members."

Then he stopped speaking and looked at me and said, "I've spoken much, perhaps it's best if we walk a bit in silence and then I will answer your questions."

I had listened carefully and now, as my feet stepped upon the soft earth of the forest trail, I felt honored that I was receiving this knowledge. Still, a question kept nagging at me, one that had been there since the first time the "Guardian" came to me in Vietnam: Why me? Why have I been chosen to receive these teachings? Surely, I thought, others are equal or even more worthy than me.

"The truth, Harry," I heard Sakya say out loud, "is that you've not been chosen so much as you've chosen yourself to make the journey home. Each of us choosing the Master's Path has chosen to come home to our true nature, our true self, what some call, our true name or true identity within the One … Sat Nam!

"The practices or disciplines associated with this journey are many. Some of us have come through traditional paths of the Far East, while others through spiritual disciplines associated more with occidental religions, both ancient and modern, and still others have made the journey on their own. Yet we are all students on the same journey.

"For now you've chosen a work on Earth that will help preserve this forest as a safe haven for the Light. Others along this path chose other works that focuses their energies on supporting the Light on this sweet planet, all the time learning more and more of the secrets of self mastery, and eventual mastery of Light itself. This is the journey and the path that you've chosen to be on and we of the Brotherhood, who are also on this same journey, though a bit more advanced along the path than you, welcome your help, your commitment, and your courage."

Sakya stopped walking and looked directly into my eyes as he spoke these last few words. Never before had I felt so wanted, so accepted, so "home". My heart pounded as he went on speaking.

"So, to be clear, Harry, you've not been chosen by us, but your soul has chosen to join us. This is the answer to your question. Have you others?" he smiled, as if to say, "Please ask, I'm enjoying answering you."

I had only one about the circumstances surrounding my parent's death, but decided that this was not the best time to ask it. I was starting to get used to the fact that Sakya could tell what I was thinking before the words came out of my mouth. So, instead of speaking out loud, as I thought about the question, I also gently suggested to Sakya in my mind that this was not the time that I wished to deal with it.

We walked on as we approached the small trail that led to the southeast end of the forest and to the Bates farm and we stopped there.

Sakya's gentle manner, friendly way of speaking, and kind smile, made it easy to be with him. I had no desire for the lesson to end, yet, as we neared the little trail I knew that this day's lesson was over.

The unusualness of the situation had thrown me into a kind of frenzy of silence. I didn't know what to say, and in a certain way, didn't even know how to say whatever it was that I wanted to say. Without thinking about it, I found myself looking up at Sakya, asking with my eyes, almost as a child would, for surely I felt like one, when, or even if, we would meet again.

He looked at me, and a smile broad as his face beamed as Sakya placed his both hands on my shoulders and answered without words, "Yes, my friend, we will meet again. The "'Guardian' will tell you when I'll be here."

With that he stepped a few steps back from me and his body faded into thin air! Where was he? Where did he go? Sakya's demonstration of what he called frequency adjustment right in front of me filled me with awe as I looked around the forest near me, at first disbelieving that such a thing could happen.

I took a deep breath, feeling all the sense of calm and amazement I felt at the events of the lesson. Then, without warning, my whole body filled with a great surge of energy and excitement as I found myself running full speed along the path, laughing all the way, back home.

***

I arrived at the farmhouse, huffing and puffing from the experience, with a big smile on my face, just as Bill and Becky pulled up in his late model Chevy sedan. Seeing me, Bill reached his head out of the car and said, "Boy, you look like you just won a foot race or something. I don't know what you just did, but it sure must have been fun!" And he was right. How could I describe what had just happened to me? It was the stuff of magic, and miracles, and science fiction, and yet, by God, it was real!

I laughed as I huffed, still out of breath "Oh, I was just enjoying a good jog and sprinted home, what fun!"

Becky now came around the car with a questioning look in her eye. She knew that I hadn't jogged or even run since coming back home. She waited until later on, after Bill left, to ask me about it. When she finally did ask, it was as if she knew the answer before she even finished asking the question. This pattern was beginning to happen more and more with Becky and me. As we went forth in our learning over the following months, she was able to know when I had had my lesson and even, in some cases, what it was that I had learned.

For now, she and Bill unloaded the groceries and took them in the house. Bill stayed for dinner. We spoke of many things, and especially about how different it was for us to have grown up here in Ohio, rather than in Arkansas where Bill spent most of his youth. In the end, he invited us to visit him and his mother at their farm for dinner several days later.

CHAPTER TWENTY-ONE
VISIT TO THE BATES FAMILY FARM

Knowing the Light, seeking the Light, is the right of every living being; Light belongs to all

A comfortable early evening breeze flowed through the car's windows as Becky and I drove up the hill to the Bates family farm. Slightly larger than our own, the Bates farm sat atop the crest of a hill with the majority of its land spreading to the east into the valley below. A major county road sliced through the farm's fields, dividing them into two, as the road led on to the east and then into town. The fields themselves, once verdant and full of life at this time of the year, lay fallow in recognition of the fact that Bill's lawyer's income supported the farm's survival, not its cash crops.

A sturdy two story white clapboard home with gabled roof, the farmhouse reigned over the land like a castle, its windows overlooking the rolling hills and farmlands to the east, north and south. To the west and southwest, the lush foliage of the forest swayed in the breeze as greenery rolled like a carpet to the west and southwest where it ended its journey at the border of our farm.

The architecture of the building stood out as unusual in an area of traditional farmhouses. A cross between a Victorian mansion and an Ohio farmhouse, I thought to myself. Oak trees dotted the hill like sentinels, watching and protecting the land. A large lawn, brown now with lack of care, encircled the home with overgrown gardens encroaching on stone patios on every side.

This was a home that had once been very important, I thought, even stately, yet, one left to age now without much care. Still, this was not all. Something else struck me about it. Something I couldn't quite put my finger on, for the house carried an air of calm, as if some special essence of the place had been kept from the ravages of time. I couldn't explain it at the time, but later I came to think of the Bates house as I would a church or cathedral that had never lost that special spiritual something about it, even though left untended.

The locked entrance gate to the forest stood west of the farmhouse at the bottom of the hill. A broad porch surrounded the house on three sides. From the back porch, one could look out across the tops of the trees that rose into the hills to the west where the green foliage of tall sycamores and elms now faded into the horizon of the still early evening blue sky.

Bill greeted us with a smile at the door. "Hi you two," he said, "I'm so pleased you've come. My mother is in the living room. I know she'll like you just as much as I do."

With that, he led us through a well-lit hallway into a living room. Late afternoon light flooded into it through a series of floor to ceiling windows running along the south and southwest corner of the wall. The large room felt cozy with an oak mantled fireplace at the center of the west wall, and light wood bookshelves packed with books from floor to ceiling, on the north wall. Two large puffy couches and an easy chair in a U-shaped arrangement faced the fireplace. Bill's mother sat on one of the couches.

As we entered the room, Mrs. Bates struggled to her feet to greet us. A tall woman with an air of dignity about her, her illness had obviously taken its toll.

"Please," said Becky, "don't get up."

But Mrs. Bates would hear nothing of it. She might be sick, she said, but she still could get up to greet visitors. This, indeed, she did as we chatted for quite awhile. Bill went to the kitchen to see about dinner.

Mrs. Bates loved the farm and loved Ohio. She had been raised and married in Arkansas but came home to the Bates family farm when her husband died. She wanted, she said, to continue to raise her son in a decent and good atmosphere. For her, this place was heaven.

"I'll tell you," she told Becky and me with a twinkle in her eye, "there's no place on Earth more calming to the nerves than right here. Oh, I know, a lot of people think the city is more exciting. Lots more to do. But for me, sitting on the back porch, feeling the cool breeze and listening to the songbirds is just about all I need to be happy.

"That's why I brought Bill back here when my husband died," she went on, "because there's something magical about this place, something that resonates of, well," she thought for a moment, "goodness. Yes, that's it, the place resonates of goodness and of times past when people cared about each other and about living a good and decent life with their neighbors."

Becky smiled, "You know, Mrs. Bates, Harry and I where both raised here and we feel the same. I can remember as a child being so happy to come home from school. We played in the forest and it felt magical to us, too."

"Isn't it glorious just to be near that forest," said Mrs. Bates "it's the reason that I don't really want to go anyplace else. I feel so content here. Just sitting outside at night, gives me a feeling of safety, and belonging. That might sound silly to you, but it's what I feel!" she concluded.

"No, not at all," Becky reassured her, "we both understand."

We spent a few minutes more chatting before Bill came to call us to dinner in a room off to the side of the living room. Becky held Mrs. Bates' arm as we followed Bill through a set of French doors into the dining room. As we entered, Becky must have been just as surprised as I. The Bates dining room was so unusual, so filled with a sense of elegance and mystery, that I could hardly hide the look of astonishment that came across my face.

In truth, it felt less like the dining room of Twentieth Century farmhouse, and more like one belonging to a wealthy oil baron of the late Nineteenth Century. Fully thirty feet long and about twenty feet wide, the room, an obvious addition to the house, nearly as big as the rest of the downstairs of the house. A huge walnut dining table ran down the middle of the room. Able to sit twenty-five to thirty people, the table reminded me more of a table that would fit in a corporate board room than one suitable for a small family farm. Dimly lit, the walls, clad in red and white velvet-like wallpaper adorned with various floral designs, seemed to vibrate and dance in the light of a series of converted oil lamps on the wall.

Bill led us through the room to the far end of the table where a dinner setting for four occupied that end of the table. The settings of porcelain and silver gave the impression of an elegant hotel, rather than one of a country farmhouse.

After helping his mother to her chair, Bill excused himself and slipped through a door that gave opened to the kitchen to make final preparations for dinner. Bill's mother had been watching us closely as we crossed the room with her. Now, as Bill left the room, a broad smile beamed across her face.

"You know, you two, your reaction to this room isn't unlike others who've been here for the first time." Then, as if remembering something important, she laughed and said with a broad smile, "Not at all unlike my own on my first visit to the farm with Bill's father. Of course, we'd all be surprised! After all, who'd ever expect to see a room such as this in an old Ohio farmhouse? And yet," she went on, "it's here, this marvelous, mysterious, and strange room!"

"What was it used for?" Becky asked, echoing my own thoughts.

At this, Mrs. Bates became more serious, at first saying nothing. Then, she spoke, telling us that she would like to wait until after dinner to answer that question, if we didn't mind. Both Becky and I nodded at the same time. Just then, Bill came into the room to serve the first course of what proved to be a wonderful dinner.

Our conversation focused on the town's changes, and on the fire at the courthouse. Mrs. Bates was pleased to find out that that the records of the farm "compact" were safe and secure at the state capital. After dinner, as Bill served us a freshly brewed pot of tea, Mrs. Bates began to speak. She smiled at first, a curious look on her face, as if what she was about to say came from a long forgotten, but very sweet, memory. Then, she asked Bill to sit down, as she wanted to share something with the three of us. Bill sat at the large dinner table across from Becky and me. With eyes fixed on her son, she spoke to him directly from her seat at head of the table.

"I've been waiting a long time to talk about this room and what it is that I know about it," she said. "Bill, I can remember us coming here for visits when you were young and you always asking how come this room was so big, and so different. Now that these two young people have come to be here with you, my son, I want to tell you and them the meaning and purpose of this room, as I know it."

Then, turning to speak directly to Becky and me in that serious fashion she had adopted earlier, she said, "Your presence here, you two, isn't outside the bounds of the unusual. In a very real way, I've been waiting a long time for you to come."

At this Mrs. Bates' eyes filled with tears, and she began …

CHAPTER TWENTY-TWO
MRS. BATES MEETS THE BROTHERHOOD

Not all have the opportunity to go home in any one life, but all can choose to step bravely on the Path

"The farm families are very dear to me and have been since I first found out the meaning of this place and the forest," she said. "Bill, you haven't heard this story before, and I guess that you, Becky and Harry, have only heard parts of it, if any of it at all.

"I met your father, Bill," she continued, "when he was very young and I already believing myself an old maid ... at least by Arkansas standards. We fell in love, really at first sight, and married soon after. Before our wedding in Arkansas, however, my husband-to-be brought me back to the farm to meet his parents, your grandparents.

"I'll never forget that meeting for it happened in a most unusual fashion," Mrs. Bates said, now settling into the story. "We'd arrived from our journey from Arkansas early on a Saturday evening with plans to stay until the following Wednesday or Thursday, as this was all the time we could take off from our jobs. To our surprise, no one was home.

"We brought our travel bags, which were pretty shabby and slim in those days," she said, "into the house, and then my fiancé proceeded to show me around the house. We toured the whole place, and then, when we'd visited the rest of the farmhouse, he brought me to this room.

"Well, as you can image, the surprise on my face equaled that of your own. After all, growing up on a small farm myself in Arkansas didn't prepare me for the grandeur, and yes, mystery, of this room ... and yet, beyond the grandeur and mystery, something else happened here that night, something *very* unusual.

"We came into the room and the lights were on just as they are now, dim, yet still on. My eyes needed time to adjust to the light, and as they did, I slowly marveled at the room's elegance, and then, at the end of the table, I saw him!

"Sitting just where I'm sitting now, sat a man so huge that I could only think of him as a giant. I can tell you, I nearly jumped out of my skin! At first I didn't believe my eyes, but here he was and he was real. I held my husband's hand tight as I felt the urge to run rushing through me. After all, here we were in Ohio, ready to meet my future in-laws, and instead of them being here to greet us, here sat this huge man, with shining brown eyes sitting at the end of the family dining room table, and to top it off, he had a big white turban wrapped around his head.

"Well, in spite of being frightened half out of our wits, we didn't run. Somehow, we both knew, your father and me," she said looking at Bill, "that we were safe, and so we stayed.

"I didn't know what to say, or do for that matter, and neither did my husband. I think we just stood at the end of the room where we'd entered, our mouths wide open in astonishment until he spoke. To this day, I remember his exact words. In an accent that I had never heard before, he said, 'Please don't be frightened. Come in and sit down. Mr. and Mrs. Bates asked me to greet you. So, please, do sit down.' I can tell you this, this must have been the strangest visit any future daughter-in-law ever could have had when taken home to meet her in-laws!"

She stopped to sip her tea, taking a break in a story that she took obvious pleasure in relaying to us. Then she continued, "Well, we both walked to the end of the room with my husband, John, taking the lead. John was so brave; I admired him even more than before for that. As we came near to this end of the table, the large man rose to greet us, and his head, turban and all, nearly touched the ceiling.

"But something strange happened, instead of any greeting that I was used to, the man placed his hands together in front of his face and bowed his head, and to my surprise, John did the same back to him.

"Well, you can imagine, at this point I didn't know what to think. I imagined all sorts of things. John seemed, if not to know that man, at least to know his way of greeting. So, I felt myself to be the only one in the room who didn't have an idea about what was happening. But I was wrong. As it turned out, John told me later that he and his brother had grown up greeting his parents' friends with this gesture, but in this case, was just as baffled as I about who this giant was, and what he was doing here greeting us in place of his parents.

"We did eventually sit down, John and I, in the seats you two young people are sitting in right now," she said, nodding at me and Becky. "Then he spoke. As I said, his accent was unfamiliar to me then, but later I realized that it originated in the Indian subcontinent.

"We want you to know," he said, "that your presence here is very much appreciated. John, your parents raised you on this farm without you really knowing the significance of this land. But now it's time for you to learn about the farm and its true value. Your parents have gone on an errand in the city and should return within the hour. For now, I've been asked to greet you and explain some things about the visit and your upcoming marriage that may influence your life together.

"But first, please, ask whatever questions you will of me."

"John responded first. 'I know that my parents have a special feeling for this farm, and that the place has a special significance of some sort. This idea has been around our family's life all along. So, I'm interested in knowing more. But for me,' John went on, 'the thing I want to know most of all is that my parents are okay. Your being here, when we expected to be greeted by them is very strange, and both of us are shaken by it.'

"'I assure you,' responded the tall man, his bronze skin glowing and eyes that said *all is well*, 'I am here because it has been prearranged for me to meet the two of you, explain the importance of the farm, and seek your aid in a time when your own personal commitment is required.'

"Somehow," Mrs. Bates continued, "though the strangest situation I'd ever been in, I was not surprised or frightened. Instead, I found myself speaking to him with words that came out of me from a place deep within, as if speaking something that I had committed to saying a long, very long time before, and now needed saying at the right time.

"Even though it felt strange, I said, 'We are very honored that you've come and we will, I assure you, fulfill our part.'

"Well," she continued, "you can imagine my surprise at me saying that. After all, I'd just arrived from Arkansas, just met the man, and wasn't even married to your father yet, Bill. What a shock! And yet … and yet I *knew* that it was right that I had said what I had said. I remember John looking over at me with a surprised look on his face, but his response to the man echoed my own as he said, 'Yes, I agree, we will do our part.'

"'Good,' said the tall man. 'Thank you for your faith and listening ear. My name is Sakya, and you'll not be meeting me again in this lifetime. I've come to explain the forest's significance and the importance of the family *compact* that has maintained the safety of the forest.'"

With this, Mrs. Bates stopped and looked directly at Becky and me, and said, "You two, I know, have been privileged to receive some of the information that I received that day. I believe you'll find what I have to say interesting."

Then, turning to Bill, she said. "From here on out, son, what I say is for your ears, and I know that you'll know what to do with the information when the time comes." She continued her story, "Sakya went on to explain that the farm and its lands—especially the forest—were sacred and needed always to be protected. He said that the forces of Light needed places on Earth where they could maintain the purity of the original intent for Earth. The forest, he said, had never been touched by negative thoughts of darkness. But, rather, it had been maintained by what he called the Brotherhood so that it could be used as a kind of base for training, education, and recruitment for those members of humanity who had it in their soul's design to awaken from their sleep and support the forces of Light.

"This huge man then turned to John as he said, 'Your parents' special role has been to maintain what might be called a school for students to come and be initiated into the teachings of Light.' Sakya went on to say that he wanted John especially to know about this," Mrs. Bates said, "and that this was the reason my fiancé and his brother, Harold, had been sent to summer camp each year, beginning with John's fifth and his brother's seventh birthday."

"Sitting next to John," Mrs. Bates continued, "I felt a sense of tension, first, at the mention of the summer camp, and then, strangely, a sense of relief run through my husband-to-be. John had spoken to me often of his resentment at his parents for, as he said, 'just wanting to get rid of me and Harold for two months each year as soon as school let out.' He didn't know why, but both he and his brother had surmised, as children sometimes do, that it was because their parents didn't care enough about them.

"Now that Sakya had spoken the truth about his summer exile, John's entire body relaxed. His face changed right before my eyes from one of a stern young man listening to a lecture that he wasn't at all certain that he wanted to hear, to the face of a man who'd come to this table," and Mrs. Bates made a broad sweep of her hand to indicate the dining table at which we sat, "to hear important information conveyed to him by someone that he respected.

"What a remarkable change. For as long as I had known John, he seemed always angry at something. But as this kind giant spoke to him, something inside him seemed to calm and he became a man not at all angry, but one ever so gentle. I could see it in his eyes.

"Frankly," Mrs. Bates said with a smile as she turned to Bill, "I rejoiced at Sakya's revelation, for it released something in your father, a kind of tension that never, ever returned all the years of our marriage."

Mrs. Bates continued, "I saw that Sakya, too, was delighted at the impact his words had on John. He said nothing more about the school. Instead, Sakya spoke about the farm itself. He wanted us to know the details of the farm's history, and told us it was important that we hear these so that at the right time we could share them with others."

Mrs. Bates stopped, thinking for a moment, before speaking, and then said excitedly, "And you know, children, I think he was talking about us right here, right now. I mean, I know that he told John and me the story so that both of us, or at least one of us, could share it at this very dinner table, at this very moment!"

Her eyes glowed bright with the sparkle of memory and she shook her head, as if amazed at her own revelation, and continued. "Sakya told us about the farm and the forest. He said that that part of the forest still remaining here had been a portion of a larger forest that had spread north and eastward from here. Native people who populated the land for centuries before the arrival of settlers from across the ocean, held the forest to be sacred as a matter of course. Thus, he said, the work of Light that went on even in those times, continued unhindered. As settlers moved west, however, the land became part of a very large estate owned by a wealthy landowner from Scotland, who left the forest and the lands untended. In the eighteen hundreds, the Scotsman sold the land to a family that began the practice of farming the land. The new owners developed the fields that still exist today and also cut down large portions of the forest."

Mrs. Bates paused for a moment, as if thinking back to that exact time of her meeting with Sakya, to remember, and, I thought, savor those moments so very long ago. Then, she continued, "As Sakya told us about the early farming time and the cutting of the forest, his voice lowered, obviously pained to share this information. Still, he continued to tell us the history of the land, all the way into the late nineteenth hundreds, when small farm holders came into possession of the land.

"John and I both got the impression that the Brotherhood was happy with the small farm ownership of the land surrounding the remaining five hundred or so acres of forest. But, Sakya said, the coming of the great depression made it less and less likely that the small farm holders would be able to protect the land and keep the remaining forest from misuse, or even destruction.

"It was at this point, early in the 1930s that the farm families came together in Pennsylvania to plan for the future protection of the land. The Pond family, your grandparents," she said, nodding at Becky and me, "and the boys came first, and then the others came later on in the 1930s."

Mrs. Bates stopped to sip her tea, looking pensively into her cup as if reading the tealeaves. Then, she looked up, remembering we were all here and said, "Well, that's my story." Then, turning to Bill, she said, "I wish I weren't alone to tell it. Your father would have loved to be here with me if he could have been."

Then, as if in an afterthought, she turned to Becky and me. "You two have come here, I know, to share a simple dinner with another of the farm families. Perhaps, it would all be easier if that were all that we were. But there's more to it, much more! As you know, the Brotherhood of Light is ever present in our lives. Although, since that first meeting, I've not had the privilege of meeting Sakya again, I've in my own way become a student of the Light."

Bill, who'd been listening intently the whole time to his mother, became more and more agitated as she spoke, and now as she continued, he seemed unable to control himself any longer as he jumped in at this point, and said, "Wait a minute, mother please! This is all going too fast for me. Are you telling me that Grandma and Grandpa were part of some cult and that Becky and Harry here, and you, are also part of it. Because if you are, I want nothing to do with it! I love you, and I'm enjoying getting to know Becky and Harry, but, cults, and strange rituals, well, that just turns me off!"

I watched Mrs. Bates as she responded to Bill. Becky and I both decided to remain silent.

"My dear son," Mrs. Bates said, "please understand that you've not been asked to join anything. After all, I'm simply relaying a story to you about what actually happened to me the first time I entered this house. Remarkable as it seems, the story is true, Bill. You're asked only to check inside yourself as to the truth of my words to see what you feel about it. If you believe me, then I would think that you'd be curious about all this. But if you aren't, I'll speak no further to you about these things."

The look on Bill's face changed from one of smug self assurance at his own utterance to one of shock and amazement at his mother's words. When Becky and I later spoke about the events of the evening on the drive home, we both agreed that this might very likely be the first time Mrs. Bates had ever spoken to her son in such a forthright manner. "She seems mild mannered," Becky said, as we drove home "but inside is a woman of great faith and strength. I respect her a lot!"

Watching Bill, I saw a man in a quandary as to what to do or believe. On the one hand, all his education and teaching focused on using his logical mind to understand life. The law was the law! And yet, here he was obviously touched by his mother's words, words that were by no means logical, seven-foot-tall giant and all!

Somewhat softer now, Bill said, "Listen mother, I've not been around this stuff for a long time. Even though you and Grandma and Grandpa never spoke about it, I watched and I saw some strange things around the farm. Visitors to the farm late at night, meetings in this very room that started after everyone thought I was asleep. I even heard Grandpa talk once over the phone to someone about the sacred forest. So, I'm not unfamiliar with how unusual this place is. But your story about a so-called Brotherhood scares me. There's enough madness in the world as it is," he concluded, "without some group from God knows where, recruiting and teaching members to serve another cause, no matter how well intended it is."

Mrs. Bates said nothing to her son. She only looked at him pensively, then as if she knew that it was best for her not to speak directly to his words, she simply said, "My son, you have your choices, as we all do, choose well."

Once again, I could see by his reaction that his mother speaking to him with such self assurance likely didn't happen very often, if at all. A man trained in words, he seemed speechless.

Becky spoke, breaking the silence. "Bill," she said, "what your mother is talking about isn't unfamiliar to Harry and me. Since our parents' death, we, too, have been, well," and she struggled for the right words, "introduced to some of the secrets of the forest and to some of the ideas that your mother is speaking about. If you'd like," she said with a smile, "we can spend some time together tomorrow. Harry and I can tell you what we know, and maybe that would be a good time as well for you to take Harry up on his offer for a walk in the forest?"

Obviously pleased and relieved at Becky's intervention, a broad smile crossed Bill's face and he nodded his agreement. "For now," Becky turned to Mrs. Bates, "how about a look at the famous view of the forest from the back porch that you spoke about. I'll bet the sunset this evening is just marvelous!"

Mrs. Bates smiled as she nodded her assent. I couldn't help but grin, too, in admiration at my older sister's skillful handling of the situation. Becky obviously had her own idea as to how best to introduce Bill to the Brotherhood of Light, and I, for one, was not going to argue with her.

"Okay, let's go," Becky said, with the schoolgirl charm that had never left her. She immediately rose and helped Mrs. Bates to her feet. Bill's mother, grinning all the way, led us through the kitchen to a spacious covered porch running the length of the rear of the house. Here, we sat in old rockers in silence, bathing in the pink and vermilion rays of the setting sun that now surrounded the farm from the treetops of the forest to the west, to the farmlands to the north and south.

Sitting there, my thoughts wandered to nights like this in Vietnam. There, too, the sun set in spectacular colors illuminating the jungle trees and sky. The feeling of peace that I felt now contrasted sharply with the tension and turmoil that filled me then.

I had had four close friends there who sat together with me in silence on nights like this. We all admired the sunsets, equal in magnificence to this one, but not one of them had survived. Tears filled my eyes in recognition of their lives lost in a war that more and more Americans called wrong. What were we to do, those of us who went and fought for our country? Were we wrong because the war might be wrong? Did those who died there, die for a wrong reason? And what did that matter to them, to their families, their friends?

This war was crazy, and upon coming home I had resolved to forget about it as best as I could. But something in what was happening here in my own hometown with my family and the farm made me think that the forces that had created the mess, as I had come to think of the war, also had something to do with the terror that seemed to be seeping into and beginning to surround our town. Something inside told me that the darkness here on Earth kept people from knowing more of their Light by creating havoc and confusion so that even good people fought each other, serving, without knowing it, not their own highest Light and good, but the confusing manipulation of the darkness.

I looked at those who sat with me here at the edge of this forest at the Bates farmhouse, a forest that in my own mind I was beginning to call sacred. Becky, tall and proud, sat with Bill in rockers at the end of the porch. Next to them, sat Mrs. Bates, and I sat next to her. Nobody could have told me when I left for the war that within a few months of my return to the States I would feel closer than I ever had with my sister. We'd played together as children, but now we were serious partners in serving the Light. She and I both knew that maintaining the forest in its pure state represented more than just salvaging the land. It represented an ongoing victory of good in the world!

Mrs. Bates' story had touched us both, and though Becky didn't yet know that I, too, had met Sakya, I knew that one day she would also meet him and we'd have this to share. I also knew that Mrs. Bates had taken quite a risk with her son in telling the story. For though his lawyer's mind could very well figure out how to help ensure that the land stayed with those it needed to stay with, I wasn't at all certain that he would believe the story that his mother told, no matter how true.

Something about him seemed rigid, stiff, as if in both his physical movements and his thoughts he was scared to be fluid and free. "Like a penguin," I thought to myself that first time we met.

And yet, I respected him. It took courage for someone like him to listen to a story like the one his mother just told and not simply stand up and leave, calling the whole thing crazy. I smiled to myself now as I went over the scene that had happened in the house just a few moments before our coming outside. Well, I thought, my smile broadening, he almost did just that, the only difference was that he stayed to listen to the whole story before calling it all crazy! I smiled again, now, as I thought of Becky's way of handling Bill, and I wondered what it would be like when he visited us the next day. These thoughts were soon interrupted, however, as Mrs. Bates again began to speak about the farm. As she spoke, she looked directly into the forest, not at us, as if she were speaking to the trees themselves.

"You know," she said, "on that first visit, we did spend quite a bit of time with your grandparents, Bill. For just as Sakya finished his story of the farm's history, we heard your grandparents coming up the driveway in their old red truck. You know, the one that you used to like so much."

"Yes, I remember it," said Bill.

"Well, we heard the truck and so your father got up to look to see that it was them who were arriving. I turned my head to follow his movement through the dining room and out the French doors to the front of the house. In a minute he was back. But during that minute that I watched and waited, this tall, strange man, Sakya, simply disappeared. To this day I don't know how. But without a sound, he was gone.

When I turned my head back towards his chair, it was empty! I've not seen Sakya since, but have had, in my own way, meetings with others from the Brotherhood."

And then, abruptly, almost as if a muse had overtaken her, she said, "The light we see here tonight is a reflection of the beauty of Earth, isn't it? I've sat rocking in this chair every night for years and the gift of this place never changes. You know," she went on, "I've never even been in the forest, nor have I ever had the privilege of attending one of those classes in our grand dining room that Sakya spoke of, but I'd like one day to do so. I'd like one day to dedicate myself, my life, to the Light." And then, almost as if musing to herself "Perhaps one day I'll have the chance," she said, "perhaps one day, one day."

She said no more, but I know all three of us we were touched by her words. There was something special about this place and its sunset view, and this made her words even more powerful. We sat for several minutes in silence before Bill suggested that it might be time for his mother to go in and rest. Mrs. Bates didn't protest. She only smiled at her son in recognition of his suggestion. I could see that telling her story had tired her.

Back inside the dining room, Mrs. Bates turned to us and thanked us for coming. But as Bill began to lead Becky and me to the front door, Mrs. Bates stopped us and asked that Becky stay behind for a moment. She wanted, she said, to speak with her privately. I waited with Bill at the front door for only a few moments before Becky followed, a big smile on her face. On the way home, I asked her what it was that Mrs. Bates had said to her, but she only looked at me, smiled that same big smile, and said nothing.

CHAPTER TWENTY-THREE
BILL'S MEETING WITH ANGELS

In the love of self, one finds self ... and then one can love another

Next day was Saturday. As children, we'd often help Mom and Dad load the farm's produce onto our truck and take it to the local farmer's market in Columbus, twenty miles away. We didn't know then that the farmer's market was a place for all the farm families to meet. They were always there, all families, and though they never seemed to spend time together at each other's farms, on farmer's market day, as Dad's booming voice used to announce to Becky and me every Saturday morning with his usual, "Get up you two, it's farmer's market day!" They would spend the day selling produce and chatting together.

Becky and I went every Saturday when we were very young, but by the time we reached our teens, we stopped going. This Saturday morning Becky and I rose early and had breakfast together, something we'd not done that often since my arrival back home. It felt a little like the old days when we were young. Dad and Mom would be out with the truck loading produce, and Becky and I would be here, at this very table, eating our morning breakfast. As we ate, we spoke again of the evening before. Becky had been quite taken with Mrs. Bates. They obviously liked each other. Then she spoke of Bill, whose visit we soon expected.

"Harry," she said, "I don't know, I like Bill a lot, but he seems so, well, stiff to me. Maybe it's his lawyer's background, but I really don't know how to speak with him about the Brotherhood. Do you have any ideas?"

I admitted that I couldn't see how it would be very easy to talk to Bill after his outburst the evening before. Just then, I heard the familiar voice of the Guardian, and I could tell that somehow, Becky heard it, too.

"You both need to understand," he said, "that Bill Bates had a childhood of great laughter and fluidity. But his father died when he was a young boy and at that time he became sad and introverted. Today, he will visit with you and we must ask the two of you a favor."

Almost comically, Becky and I nodded our heads in agreement at precisely the same moment, as if we were listening to a physical being sitting in the room with us. We both smiled across the table for we both knew that it would have looked very funny to someone watching from the outside.

The Guardian went on. "The favor we ask is for you, Harry, to take Bill on his walk in the woods prior to any discussions of the Brotherhood. For you Becky, we ask that you allow Bill to be who he is today without wanting to change him. His current style, we know, can be very frustrating, bullish, and, even at times unfriendly when he doesn't understand something. Perhaps, as he walks on the earth of this special place, he will soften a bit.

"Yes, we know that you both are wondering how we will get through to that one. Believe us, we have only to follow his own soul's destiny. Were it not for that, we'd not be here with you, or with him.

"Nowhere is it written that those of us in the Brotherhood who've made the journey home have the right to force any being into doing what isn't in their own soul's design to do. This is why each being is offered choices that they themselves have called forth in order to enhance their knowledge of their own Light. In this way, the Brotherhood serves as servant to the soul of each rather than in any way as master.

"Each truly has their own Light, their own unique vibration and frequency in the universal Oneness, including members of the Brotherhood. No one can take that away from an individual, except that the individual can live in such a way as to forget the Light, usually by rejecting its very existence. Sadly, this is the state of being of most living on Earth and it's our job to help beings who are ready to listen, to come to know that they're indeed worthy of knowing and loving their own essence. In this way, we do our best to help them remember who they are and their soul's purpose.

"For you," he said to me, "your soul's design of knowing your own Light afforded us the opportunity to support you in the war. For you Becky, a chance mishap on a snowy road brought forth the help you needed. In each of your cases, you both have been spoken to before these times, as youths, in your dreams, as instinct. The Light is always available to all, but only some listen to it. And even for those that do listen, circumstances in their life have to be such that they wish to continue to listen.

"Every so often, those of us from the Brotherhood will speak to a being, even in some cases appear in some form before a person, but the being needs to be ready to hear the message or see our presence. For most, the concept that Spirit is alive and well beyond the physical is too much, even though their soul may have called forth for knowledge of this truth. For others like yourselves the wisdom that is offered is heard and then, and only then, when the being is ready to consciously continue to learn, can we of the Brotherhood share our knowledge. This is the case with this one Bill Bates, as it was with the two of you and with the rest of humanity."

Referring to Bill, then, almost as if in an afterthought, the Guardian said, "He will be given his choice."

Becky said nothing, but I knew somewhere that she was disappointed that she wasn't going to have the opportunity to "explain it all" to him. After all, it was she who'd invited him over for that purpose. The Guardian asked then if Becky or I had any questions about his explanation. I had none, but I looked over at Becky, expecting her to say something. But I was wrong. She looked back at me, somehow aware that I knew what she was feeling, and without saying a word about it, said, "No, I have no questions." Then, she thanked the Guardian for coming.

My respect for her grew daily because of such incidents. Yes, I knew that she wished circumstances were different, but she had taken the truth of what the Guardian had said to heart and made a choice within herself to listen.

***

Bill arrived a little after ten. We both greeted him at his car and walked to the front door of the farm. Per our plan, as we walked I suggested we visit the forest together. Bill looked at me, and then at Becky, obviously disappointed.

"Aren't you coming with us?" he said to Becky, almost pleadingly. "I was hoping you'd be there to help me understand some of the things we spoke about last night."

Becky responded that she would be here to talk about those things when he and I returned from our walk. Even though he expressed disappointment, somehow I knew that his concern came not just from a man disappointed that the woman he's attracted to won't be spending time with him, but rather from a man afraid. Of what I couldn't say, but I suspected Bill's fear came directly from the thought of entering the forest itself.

From what his mother had said, to her knowledge none of the Bates family had ever been in the forest. For whatever reason, and unlike our own situation, Bill's grandparents had kept the forest off limits to his family. Bill had spent his teen years on the farm, but the forest must have seemed like a great mystery to him. Perhaps, I thought, he had grown afraid of the forest and now that he faced going into it, Becky's presence would have made him feel more secure.

As it turned out, what I had guessed wasn't far from the truth. As we left Becky behind and began the quarter mile hike down the back lane to the forest gate, he began speaking in such a rapid fire, nervous manner that it was all I could do to slow him down, and at the same time, try to understand what was panicking him.

Finally, calmer now, he spoke about how as a lawyer, trained to look objectively at facts, he was embarrassed to tell me the incredible fright he felt at the idea of going into the forest. "The truth is," he muttered almost incomprehensibly, "that thinking about going into this forest scares the heck out of me!"

We walked a few more steps in silence, both of us falling into silence after what he had just shared with me. Then, stopping on the path, he explained, "I've never told this story to anyone before because I was certain they wouldn't believe me." Then, thinking to himself for a moment, he said, "You know, after awhile, I wasn't sure I could believe myself. So, I've just been quiet about it. Now, that we own the farm and Mom and I need to decide what we're doing with it, I feel more responsible for the farm, and the forest. But I tell you," he sighed, "if I didn't have to deal with all of this, I'd feel a lot happier."

I nodded, not knowing what exactly to say that could help. But Bill didn't need more encouragement. Whatever was troubling him had obviously been dammed up inside for a long, long time. Now that he began to speak, the story seemed waiting to be poured out. He went on.

"As a boy, when we'd visit my grandparents, we would always sit out on that back porch in the evening and if the weather was good, watch the sunset over the forest, just as we did last night. My father and mother both loved it here, so whenever they could take the time off, we'd come for a visit. Well, one night, I guess I was about thirteen, Mom and Dad left me at the farm and went for an overnight trip to visit one of Dad's old school friends who lived north of here. I didn't feel like going so we all agreed it would be okay if I stayed home alone with Grandma and Grandpa."

He stopped walking and looked directly at me. "Harry," he said, "I'll never forget that night. I remember what happened just like yesterday." Bill resumed walking, slowly, along the path to the forest as he continued his story.

"Grandpa and grandma and I ate dinner in the grand dining room that night as usual, and then went out to watch the sunset on the back porch. It was a beautiful night like last night, all purple, blue, and orange. I loved being with them. I felt relaxed all the time in their presence. I remember we sat for a long time together. After awhile, though, I started feeling a little dizzy and queasy in my stomach. We all guessed that I had eaten something that upset my stomach. So grandma made me a hot cup of tea and put me to bed. The tea felt great and grandma's presence comforted me, so I fell asleep right away.

"Well, all of that was fine—that is, until I woke up. I don't know what time it was, but it must have been pretty late. Something woke me, but what it could've been, I don't know. What I did know is that I felt much better and hungry, so I decided to go downstairs to the kitchen to see if I could find something to eat.

"I got near the bottom of the stairs on the second landing, expecting to see grandpa and grandma in the living room, but they weren't there. Instead, the French doors to the dining room were open and I could see that the room was filled with people—I don't know, maybe ten or twelve.

"I was surprised, since my grandparents didn't have visitors too often, and never, to my knowledge at night. I didn't want to be seen, so I watched from the stairs as the group of men and women spoke together. I had never seen any of them before. I couldn't hear what they said, but they all seemed excited to be there. At the end of the table sat a strange, giant of a man with a turban wrapped around his head, with dark, golden-bronze skin. He spoke most of the time. After a few minutes, the tall man got up and the others followed."

Turning to me as we walked, Bill said, "I remember it ever so vividly. He was tall, like one of those really big basketball players, and wore a long white robe. I didn't know where he came from, but he looked like he was from an eastern country, maybe India. Well, the group followed him out onto the back porch and then started on down the trail that led to the forest gate. I'd never really seen anyone on that trail before. As far as I knew the gate was always locked. But now this entire group followed the tall man to the gate."

Bill stopped walking again. I could see the sweat on his brow as he related the story. "I didn't think much about what I would do, I just followed. I sneaked down the stairs and crossed the dining room and kitchen to the porch. But by the time I'd gotten to the porch, the group had moved all the way down the path and was passing through the open gate. I watched for a while longer. Even though I had my pajamas on, I decided to put on the old pair of sneakers that I always left by the porch door, and follow."

Bill became more animated now, as he spoke, his arms beginning to wave in excitement, as if telling a story that had just happened yesterday.

"I remember, I remember everything!" he said. It was amazing! The forest was lit that night by the rising moon and I could see it all, the whole ceremony!" At this point, I too began to feel Bill's excitement, for though I had been in the forest with both the Guardian and Sakya, I had no idea what Bill could have seen that night. He continued. "I walked down the path in the direction the group had gone. I could feel the soft dirt under my feet, and I tried to walk very silently, like the Indians used to do. I wasn't afraid. I was just excited.

"As I walked, I heard sounds ahead of the others talking in the forest, but I didn't know exactly where they were. At one point, the small path from our farm led on to a larger path heading west. I realize now," he said, nodding his head my way, "towards your farm. I followed the path, making sure that I knew where the small trail began so I could get back."

Bill paused for a moment, and looked directly into my eyes and said, "You may not believe this, but I was pretty savvy then, even at that age. I may seem stiff and maybe even a little fearful to you and Becky now, but then I was all gung ho." I nodded, again not knowing exactly what to say. Bill didn't seem to want me to respond, only to listen, as he went on with his story.

"Well, I went a ways down the path into the forest and there, to my left, was a small trail. The light was pretty good. At the end of the trail I saw a light, but it glowed from farther on into the forest. So, I followed it for a bit, and then, as I came closer to the clearing where the light came from, I decided not to go any farther, but to hide in the bushes. I found a good spot from which I could see the clearing and those in it. Those who were in the house were now all sitting in a circle around a large fire, built in a pit surrounded by stones. I didn't see the tall man, but I did see, to my surprise, my own grandparents sitting in the center of the circle, near the fire.

"They sat cross-legged holding hands together. The others in the circle also sat with eyes closed, hands on their laps." Bill turned to me, "At the time, the whole thing seemed spooky to me. But now, I guess they were meditating … then, I just didn't know. As they sat there, I heard my grandmother speak to the group. She didn't want them to move, but she needed them to know that they would have to focus their attention very clearly on their work that evening, making sure that their energies were held tightly within the circle.

"No one around the circle said a thing, but I could feel it that they'd heard my grandma's words. I mean, it felt like a steel wall went up around them. I don't know a better way to describe it than that. Suddenly, I felt myself far away from the group. Oh, they were still there, and so was I, but I had the feeling that they'd somehow cut me off from their reality, from what they were doing, as if they knew me to be there and they needed to ensure that I didn't get mixed up or involved in their ritual or ceremony, or whatever it was, I wasn't sure at the time. It's hard to describe with words," he said, "but that's the best I can do right now."

Bill took a deep breath, as if the telling of the story after so many years relieved him of something, a burden that had weighed him down all this time. "Well, I felt pretty scared and I wasn't sure whether to stay or just run," he continued. "I can tell you, after feeling that wall go up, running was the thing most on my mind. But something told me to stay. I don't know what it was, instinct perhaps. So I did, and what I saw that night in this very forest to this day still brings a knotting fear in my belly when I think about it. I'm not sure you'll believe me, " Bill said, "but I've got no one else to talk to about this and if I'm going to go into that forest again after all these years, I might as well get it off my chest."

I encouraged him to continue. Somehow I knew that Bill's story had importance and meaning beyond his own healing of his fear of the forest. What that meaning could be, I didn't know, but I did know it was important that he continue.

"At first, I just felt this pressure coming from the circle," he went on, "like I said, like a wall. I didn't see anything that could physically stop me, but I sensed that even if I wanted to go closer to my grandparents and the others in that circle, I wouldn't be able to. So, I stayed quiet and watched.

"At first they all sat silent and nothing happened. Then as I watched, to my utter amazement a large gold tinted white light began to appear in the center of the circle, right to the left of my grandparents. I'd say it was about six or seven feet high and two or three feet wide. I mean, a real live ball of light, like fire, but more gaseous," Bill struggled for the right word, then said "more … more etheric, yes, that's it, more etheric.

"My eyes couldn't believe what I saw as two more of these lights appeared right next to my grandparents. I felt really scared and I also wanted to warn them. I mean their eyes were closed and these balls of light just appeared right out of nowhere right next to them. But before I could do or say anything, the lights started taking on a form, and, you know what? They had wings. I swear it. I mean the beings that I saw that night had big white wings. They must have been angels or something," he said, now getting more and more agitated as he spoke. "I mean what happened was," Bill repeated, "that those three lights took shape!

"They were all white, but each had a different hue. The first was more gold or yellow, the second more blue, and the third was pinkish. I'd never seen anything like it. They took form, but they didn't really. I'm mean," and he stuttered, "they-they-they stayed kinda like light, but through the light they took human shape, with wings!"

At this point, I put my hand on Bill's shoulder, thinking that this would help calm him, and it did. He continued, speaking more slowly and clearly. "I don't know how to describe it any better, but that's what I saw. The strange thing was that the people in the circle seemed to know, even though their eyes were still closed, instinctively that these white light beings were there and began to stand up. And as the people stood and greeted these light beings, each of those around the circle began to glow a bit themselves as they opened their eyes and came in touch with the three … uh … angels.

"Nobody touched anybody, and nobody spoke, but as the three shapes moved from person to person throughout the circle, each person's own body began to glow, just a little, as if the light of the three were rubbing off on them."

Even though I could feel Bill's fear as he related the story, I could also feel his excitement, for as he spoke his eyes brightened as if he, too, had received the gift of the angel's touch.

"Well," Bill continued, "after going around the outer circle, the three came to the center where my grandparents now stood. Grandpa said something to them that I didn't hear, and then they embraced. I mean, I think that's what happened. Instead of just greeting grandma and grandpa as they did the others, they went forward and created a circle around my grandpa and grandma, the three of them, and as they did, the entire circle began to glow, including my grandparents!

"As I said, I felt scared, but now I was more scared for grandpa and grandma's safety. I wanted to do something, say something, but I couldn't cause this wall kept me from doing anything, I just felt frozen. Just then," Bill went on, "something happened that felt just about too much for my young mind. My grandpa and grandma, far from being afraid, seemed to be happy as can be to be there. And do you know what, Harry? They began to lift. Yes, lift up. Full of light like they were. They lifted, and they—I know you're not going to believe this, Harry—they disappeared, right there in front of my own two eyes. My own grandparents just vanished, and, along with them, the angels disappeared, too.

"I never felt so scared in my life. What had happened to them, I didn't know. I just knew they were gone! I thought to run, either towards the group, or away. I was that confused. Just then, I heard movement on the path behind me. I ducked down into the bushes and watched as my grandparents, who'd only moments before been standing in the clearing, walked down the path past me and back into the circle.

"I felt, well, dumbfounded, and frightened beyond belief. I didn't know what was real and what was not anymore. My grandparents looked okay, even happy, glowing, but for me the whole thing seemed weird, strange, and well, as you can imagine, unbelievable. I just wanted to run! I remember my heart beating so fast. I didn't understand any of it, it was all so illogical. Finally, I just decided to get out of there.

"At first, I walked along the small trail quietly so that I wouldn't be heard. But when I got to the larger path, I just ran, and ran until I got back to the farm. I went up to my room, but I couldn't sleep, so I sat in the rocking chair by the window in my room and looked out my bedroom window at the rising moon over the forest. Eventually, I did fall asleep. When I awoke in the morning, I wasn't sure whether I'd dreamed the whole thing or not. It all seemed so, well, fantastic. I really wondered if I had maybe just dreamed it up.

"Anyway, I dressed and went down to breakfast. Grandma and grandpa were there as always, and as usual they were loving and kind.

But nobody said a word about the night before. I thought about speaking about it, but I was just too scared. The whole thing seemed so unreal to me. Still, it happened and I just didn't know what to do."

Bill took a deep breath, as though he had been holding his breath the whole time. I watched as his face and shoulders relaxed as well, as if a huge weight had been lifted from his shoulders.

I took this opportunity to ask a question that had been on my mind. I wanted to know whether he had ever tried to share the story with his parents, or even his grandparents.

"I can tell you," he responded, spreading of his arms, "I thought about bringing it up every time I visited the farm. But the farther away from the event I got, the more I doubted my own sanity about it. After all, how could I tell my mother and father that I saw grandpa and grandma Bates disappear into thin air, surrounded by a group of angels, and then reappear again? In truth, I thought that maybe people would think I was crazy or something. So I decided not to tell about it," he concluded.

Then, looking down at the ground as we walked, he shook his head, as if deciding to make an important decision, and said with a sigh, "But now, I just had to speak. Mother's revelation last night about that same tall man and the how he disappeared brought it all back. That's why I had such a strong reaction to Mom's story. The whole thing's just been so confusing, and scary. Frankly, I wish none of it had happened and all this was just a dream. It would all make more sense to me that way."

At first I said nothing. By now, we'd reached the gate to the forest. The air immediately became cooler as the tall sycamores and cottonwoods shaded the forest floor below.

"This place is marvelous, so green and pretty," Bill said, as his head moved from side to side taking in every inch of the forest that he could. Like a child, I thought, finally visiting a magical storyland he could only imagine exists, but never really believing he would ever get to see it in reality.

I could feel his fear. He had been courageous to come today, and to speak about his grandparents and the circle of light in the forest. Now, after all these years, he had come to face the fright and panic that had overtaken him that night.

As we walked, I thought of my own reaction to the events of the past months. I, too, felt the excitement of the forest, its beauty and its mystery. My experience with the Brotherhood had taught me its significance and value. I trusted it all, the new information, the way Sakya appeared and disappeared, and the Guardian speaking to me. In that moment I felt thankful that I could share my trust with Bill as he came awake to his own destiny.

CHAPTER TWENTY-FOUR
FOREST SHARING WITH BILL

Seek knowledge and you'll find it, but it may change your life in ways beyond your current comprehension

As we went on walking into the forest I felt the gentle guiding voice of the Guardian. He wished for me to explain to Bill all that had happened to me with the Brotherhood: voices in the war-filled jungles in Southeast Asia, the visits with the Guardian in the forest, and my rendezvous with Sakya.

I was surprised at this request and struggled with the idea of revealing all I knew to Bill. After all, I reasoned, wouldn't he think my story a bit crazy—voices talking to me and seven-foot-tall men appearing and disappearing! A big smile came across my lips at the thought, for hadn't Bill's mother's story the night before been just like mine? Hadn't Bill just now revealed to me his story of so many years back with all the same attributes? Hadn't I believed them both without question?

Strange, I thought, how we bring our own experience, real live events of our life, into question if it isn't the experience most accepted by the norm. Telling *my story* was the right thing to do. It was real, just as Bill's story of his watching his grandparents disappear and then reappear was real!

"Bill," I said, as we walked further to the fallen oak trunk, "I want to share with you my own experience about all this and what's happened to me over the last few years. Maybe this will help you see where I am and, to some degree, where Becky is. Maybe then you won't feel so alone about what you saw as a young boy."

With that I told my own story of my meeting with what I called my guardian angel during the war, the continuation of the contact here in Ohio, my meeting with Sakya, and his explanation and demonstration of what Sakya called frequency adjustment. We walked slowly and I told him all I knew of the Brotherhood and what had happened to Becky and me since my return from the war. At times my voice trembled as I spoke of situations that brought up both the fear and wonder I felt about my relationship with that *voice* in my head.

I told him of the times the Guardian had saved me from making the wrong moves in tangled jungles, about my doubts about my sanity and about my final conclusion that the voice was real. I told him that I learned to listen out of choice, rather than out of necessity.

I surprised myself at my ardent description of all that I'd been involved in with the Brotherhood for the short time that I had been back.

It was almost as if I were a member of the Brotherhood. Yes, still here on Earth learning my lessons, but still one of them, dedicated to helping the Light prevail!

"I know," I continued, as we approached the oak log," that all of this sounds strange, even wacky, but it's true. Sakya is real, a real living being. I know because I sat with him right here on this log," I said, pointing to the spot where Sakya and I had first met.

"But," Bill interrupted, "how can it be? I've enough respect for you, Becky and Mom to know that all three of you aren't hallucinating. But how can it be? How can someone just appear and reappear? With my Grandma and Grandpa, after awhile I reasoned to myself that I really had been dreaming and that it never had happened. But now this whole situation has brought back my own incredible wonderings at the thought of it."

He looked at me earnestly now and said, "I do want to know more. Have you learned enough yourself to explain to me how it," and he struggled for words, "you know, how it all works? I've never believed in angels or things like that." He stopped himself, and smiled, thought for a moment, and said, "No, I guess that's just not true! Ever since the time I came into the forest that night and saw those three, uh, angels, I've been so freaked out that I just shut down and didn't want to know more. But now it's important that I know. I can't leave it alone any longer! Becky told me about her suspicion that those that want to get control of the forest had something to do with your parent's death, and that fire at the courthouse was no accident the other day. I just need to understand more about all this, even if it involves supernatural happenings."

I listened to Bill's request and wished greatly that the Guardian would come to help answer Bill about how the Brotherhood could even exist, and what role Sakya, Katran, and other Brotherhood messengers played as they came into, and out of physical form. But no matter how much I desired his presence, the Guardian didn't come.

"Bill, I can only tell you what I think about it, and I'm not certain how limited my view of the whole thing is or not." I said.

"Please do," Bill jumped in. "You have to understand that I have a lawyer's mind so I usually look for facts. But in this situation, all the facts are probably beyond both of us. Still, you know more about this than I. Even if it isn't the whole story, it's a good place for me to start."

Once again, I looked at Bill with admiration. Here was a man who'd seen angels, actually scene angels appear in front of his very eyes at the age of twelve or thirteen, but one who'd hid the truth of that situation, even from himself, for all these years and now he wanted to know. Yes, I thought, this is a courageous man, one worthy of my respect.

I turned my attention to answering his question as best as I could. "As I understand it from my teachers, we all are made of energy. Everything in the universe is made of energy, and energy is in the very highest form that we can conceive, is light. What this means is that, as I understand it, our bodies are made of light, but light that has been slowed down in frequency to shape itself into physical form.

"Now, I'm no scientist or anything, but I think the concept is that all that we see as matter is made of energy and that that energy exists at different vibrations or frequencies in the universe. Some of those frequencies can be seen, like planets and stars in the sky, or even our own surroundings right here in this forest, and some frequencies are vibrating at a higher speed and exist beyond human sight or ability to record in any way.

"So," I said, "can you see where I'm going, Bill? If matter exists at different vibrations outside the range of visibility that we can see, then, well, a whole host of things can exist in the universe that we know nothing about."

As I spoke, I started to get more and more excited. "I mean, imagine, a whole world, or even worlds or universes out there, right beyond our vision, that exist and we don't even know about them. To me it's mind boggling! Amazing! What if what's out there is so beyond our own mind's ability to comprehend that we can only trust that what's there is so, well, different, and beyond us. That its existence isn't at all a threat to us, but is focused on our visible world as a force for good wanting to help?

"Imagine further" I said, "that these invisible worlds vibrating at such different frequencies are as much a part of the One essence or Spirit that we call God as our own visible world.

"If that were the case, everybody and everything in the entire universe, whether we could see it or them or not would be related through a common parentage in this Great Spirit. And what's even more exciting for me to contemplate is the fact that it seems possible for those of us living in one frequency to somehow learn to raise our own vibration, I mean actually within our cells, to a higher level in order to interact with other, higher frequency planes, all under the auspices of God. Sounds crazy, doesn't it, but you know, I believe it's all possible, and all true!

"That's what the Brotherhood of Light is," I continued, "a focused effort on the part of those who've somehow succeeded in learning the secret of frequency adjustment, the actual frequency of their bodies, to such a place as to be able to ascend to a higher state, like Jesus did, and others, too, mentioned in the Bible, that it's in this process of raising one's frequency to a higher level that the nature of the Oneness of all things becomes so apparent to those of humanity who've found their path home that some of them decide to focus their attention on helping their brothers and sisters of Earth to achieve the same victory for themselves. This, I believe, is the journey of the Christ, and perhaps Buddha, and others. And I don't believe these were the first, nor will they be the last to make the voyage."

I took a deep breath and stopped speaking, letting the beauty of the forest and the gentle breeze wafting through the trees caress my face. We were sitting on the log now. The day was hot, and the sun shown bright through trees that were beginning to show signs of the arrival of an early autumn with their leaves turning sparkling gold, orange, and red. The sun's rays penetrated deep within the forest creating a mosaic effect of light that spread across the forest floor.

Bill remained silent. So did I.

I'd spoken my truth and now, I would wait for Bill's reaction. I leaned back a little on the log and let one of the rays of sunlight that streamed through the trees bathe me in its warmth. I relished the quiet and I thought that it wasn't often these days that I'd just come to the forest to rest and be nurtured in its stillness, even if for only a short time. I felt thankful to feel the forest's gentle healing nature as we sat together, Bill and me, in calm meditation.

For myself, telling Bill my understanding of the Brotherhood and of God had touched a place deep within. I had never spoken such words before, not even to myself, and I felt surprised and even a little awed at my ability to articulate an understanding that I didn't even know myself that I had. As I sat, quiet with the scents of the forest filling me, I knew without a doubt the truth of what it was that I had shared.

Bill's voice stirred my reverie. "I tell you," he said, looking directly into my eyes, "I don't know how I know it, but I know that what you just told me is true. There's a place inside me that knows this so well, and is so certain, that it can't be shaken!"

I looked at Bill in surprise. For his words echoed that same certainty that I myself felt.

He continued, "Ever since I was a boy I've known the truth of what you said about how all this works." He spread his arms and hands to take in the whole forest, sky and all, to emphasize his point. Yet the experience of actually seeing what could only have been real angels, and my grandparents disappearing in front of my very eyes, just shook me, deep to my core. I can't say I fully understand it, but it just scared me so deep that I didn't want to know any more of what it is I really do know. That's why, I guess, I've been so stiff. I didn't want to even breathe the wrong way for fear that somebody would call me crazy.

"But now, it's just been bottled up too, long," and he took a deep breath, "too, too, long. I do agree with you. I, too, am amazed at not only the prospect of what it is that you describe about the workings of the universe, but also about the real existence of this Brotherhood of Light. Wow," he said, looking at me with hands raised, "I don't know what else to say." And for the first time during the journey into the forest together, he seemed to relax.

At this point the Guardian came to me. He asked that Bill and I begin our journey back to our farm, saying that we'd done all that we needed to do for today and that we would return together to the forest soon.

***

Without mentioning what I had just received, I wondered aloud whether we would ever truly know all the workings of the Brotherhood. Then, turning to Bill, I suggested that it was time to head back. Bill agreed, and as we stood to begin our walk back I answered my own question. "I guess the most important thing we both share now is the knowledge within ourselves that the Brotherhood is real." Bill nodded his head, and we both walked the rest of the way back in silence. We found Becky working in the garden upon our return, and where Bill had been pensive on our walk back, now his eyes lit up at the sight of her.

"Hi, you two," she said with a smile and a wave, "how about some tea and cookies?" We sat together in the kitchen, Bill obviously happy to be with Becky. Though we didn't mention at all our conversation in the forest, I had the feeling that Becky somehow knew what it was that Bill and I had shared. This was a feeling I was beginning to have often with her as she spent more and more of her days with Katran and the other members of the Brotherhood. She didn't say much about those days, but she was changing, and so was I.

CHAPTER TWENTY-FIVE
HENRY THORPE AND FELIX BUTEZZ

Darkness takes one almost as a surprise, then courage brings one back to the Path of Light

Henry Thorpe squinted his silvery-blue eyes in the glare of the noonday sun as he and his best friends Ziggie and Blackjack John mounted their Harleys for the ride to town. As always, Henry knew that he would go first and be the lead bike on the road. This was the way it always was with the Alcaz Motorcycle Club. Henry was the undisputed club leader. Tall, blonde, with an angry look and equally angry red scar on his cheek, Henry's leadership had helped the club to gain its well earned reputation for meanness, cunning, and toughness, a reputation with which the other club members were proud to be associated.

Henry and two of the five other Alcaz club members who'd come to Placerville with him months before were heading to town for a meeting with the club's long time business associate, Felix Butezz. Butezz had invited the group to town to do what he called a "simple little job." But so far, they'd not found it simple at all. Not that Henry and the others minded hard work. In fact, they didn't mind at all what they had to do to get a job done, as long as they got paid well for it and could feel pretty well assured that they wouldn't get caught in the act of doing it.

For the most part, they'd been pretty successful. But this one was different. Henry and the others were used to following orders, finding out what it was they needed to do, and then doing it. But Felix wanted more from them than this and even as Henry had agreed to the deal, he wasn't at all sure that he could deliver on his promise to Felix.

Thorpe remembered back to the discussion they'd had. "Henry," Felix had said, "what I need from you is to get those people off their land, to get them to want to sell those farms. To put it plain and simple, you make life so much hell for them out there on their farms, that they'll be willing to take a reasonable offer on that land." This, Henry thought, he and the others might be able to do. But then Felix added, "And I want it all to look like a series of accidents. No one must suspect that anyone's trying to directly scare these people from their land."

This last part had bothered Thorpe, for though he and the others were known for their toughness, they'd not been known for the subtleness of their tactics. So, with some misgivings and Felix's offer of forty thousand dollars with a large chunk up front, Henry had agreed to the deal. So now, after six months of trying hard to create "accidents," Henry, Ziggie, and BJ were heading to town to give Felix a status report on their activities.

***

Felix Butezz ran his café with a rough hand, and to do so he had hired rough people who were used to working under less than friendly conditions. And yet, there was a certain charm about Felix. His eyebrows were always raised as in a look of questioning surprise, and when he met people, they seemed to think he was "friendly enough."

At five-feet-seven-inches he wasn't particularly tall. Nor was he particularly good looking with his too short nose, dark inset eyes, squarish face, and overhanging brow. In fact, Felix wouldn't have stood out in a crowd at all, except for one thing, his belly. At fifty-four inches around, its massive girth hung over his pants like a jelly bowl, swinging this way and that as he waddled across the floor of his café. For Felix, his belly was a thing of pride. He had no desire to lessen its size. In fact, he could be heard often commenting to confidants around the café that without his belly so full, he wouldn't have half the brains that he had.

In spite of his look and rough demeanor, Felix's café was working in this small town. It drew some of the town's most influential people for morning breakfasts and his evening dinner menu drew many of the younger crowd. Of course, some of his customers had commented on his roughness with his employees. Some even complained of the overall atmosphere being a bit dark, but they still came.

Felix's secret was that he entertained them. Each day he'd offer lavish specials for breakfast and lunch, and each evening he'd bring in the latest rock group to fill the little stage that he had had built at the end of his dining area. Free music and good prices for his food gave him all he wanted and needed for the café and his life in Placerville to be a success, except for one thing, and that one thing plagued and haunted Felix.

In spite of his success at positioning himself as a stellar citizen of Placerville, he had not been able to do what his father had sent him to this town to do: get control of the forest that sat in the middle of the five farms to the west of town. By this time, he'd expected that he'd be able to acquire control of at least one of the five. But so far, his efforts had failed. What his father wanted with the land, Felix didn't know. But one thing he did know. When his father wanted something, he usually got it.

So, about a year and a half back, with his father's money in hand, Felix set out to put together a strategy to get the land. He'd based his original plan on what he considered to be a natural human emotion — greed! Greed, he thought, would surely make the job easy. With this in mind, he'd sent Frosten and Freed to Placerville, checkbook in hand, to make the offers to five farms' owners—fully expecting at least several of the farmers to sell. But this didn't happen. Though significantly above market price, not one had taken them up on their offer, something about a farm compact, they'd said.

Felix wasn't sure what the farm compact was, nor did he care, but he was certain that he didn't want to fail his father. He'd never failed his father before, and he wouldn't fail him now! He'd seen how his father treated those who failed, and he didn't want to be one of them.

So, with his initial plan scuttled, Felix conceived a second phase of his campaign. He would come to town, buy the café, and establish himself as a respected member of the community. Then, when the time was ripe, he would position himself as the welcome savior, cash in hand, to those "poor farmers" having so much trouble on those old run down farms to the west of town. Felix conceived the trouble as a series of unhappy events, orchestrated by Felix and his old business associate, Henry Thorpe, and members of his Alcaz Motorcycle Club.

In the meantime, Freed and Frosten's offers of above market prices would continue, but only for a while longer. Eventually, these two would disappear from the scene, leaving Felix as a Good Samaritan, willing to buy the farms, in spite of troubles. As Felix saw it, the farmers would somehow associate Freed and Frosten with their difficulties, but would be more likely to sell to someone they knew and trusted, someone like Felix himself, who was building such a good and solid reputation in the town.

So, even though frustrated with the time it was taking, Felix considered his overall plan a good one. Just a matter of time, he thought, before it works, and when it did, Felix would be there to claim his victory. It was in this atmosphere that Felix called a meeting of his business associates to discuss their next steps.

CHAPTER TWENTY-SIX
JULIUS TRIES TO REMEMBER

Though a man wants wealth and glory, the soul's renewal ... that's the only victory to be had

At eighty years old, Julius Pond thought that he should feel calmer about life than he did. He wasn't sure how much longer he'd live, but he knew that before he died, he needed to straighten "something" out. His problem was that he didn't know exactly what that something was. Not that he hadn't tried to find out. He had tried, he really had, but so far he hadn't been successful. It's just, he'd think to himself, everything is all so confusing. And for Julius, it was.

For Julius' mind couldn't really cope with the particular events and actions of everyday life. Instead, he awoke each day with a strong sense of longing, for what, he didn't know. Yet in spite of his sense of missing something, he went ahead each day, acting out the events of his life as if in a dream. The dream itself caused him the greatest pain, for living it day to day was like sleepwalking in a nightmare. He knew that it wasn't he who did those deeds, acted that way, felt that anger, but he couldn't stop himself.

Now, as he sat in the rented room he called home in the old Harlan Inn, the small rooming house off the main road leading into Placerville, his mind wandered from this to that—as if by scanning the broad range of his experiences, his mind itself would find a path that Julius could finally follow, a path that would lead him out of the misty haze of emotions of anger, hatred, and confusion in which he found himself.

All at once, he remembered. It had all started after Lucy passed away. He'd been feeling pretty upset at something, something having to do with his brother, he couldn't remember what, and then, Lucy died. His loneliness at her loss created a sense of emptiness in him that was almost unbearable. But instead of throwing himself into work at the farm, or at the shop, as he had done always before during rough times, he found himself sitting day by day in front of his living room window staring out at the gray autumn sky overlooking mile upon of mile of fields that surrounded his farm.

Friends and relatives had come to be with him at first. Frank and his brother George had been his constant companions. But Julius couldn't find it within himself to even turn to them to speak. Yes, they gave him food and put him to bed, but after a time they just left him to stare at the vastness of the Ohio countryside.

Julius didn't know how many days he sat like this, just staring, but after awhile something inside told him it was time to move. That something soon became a persistent echo within him asking about his treasure. At first, Julius simply thought about other things, good times with Lucy, or his work, but each day it grew stronger. His treasure simply had to be found, he'd think. It belongs to me and I've the right to enjoy its powers and gifts!

Julius' memory blurred as he sat on his squeaky old bed at the Harlan Inn. A treasure? But the full memory soon filled him. Yes, he said to himself when it finally came, yes, my treasure, the beautiful chest that I made for that priest who came to see me from South America!

Images flooded through the haze of his mind, images of meeting a strange man, tall, a good man, at his shop. Yes, now he recalled, he was at the shop, it was August, very hot, very sticky and a man came in. Yes, he remembered, a man, maybe in his mid-sixties, with a white shock of hair and shiny eyes, yes, very shiny deep brown eyes. He saw him in his mind's eye, black robes down to the floor, a priest.

Julius struggled to recall it all as the scenes of his meeting the priest played in his mind, sometimes vivid, other times fading, blurring both vision and memory. Now, he remembered. The priest had come often that summer. Julius at first believed that he was just in need of companionship. They'd talked of many things, of life, of carpentry, of farming, and even of God. Julius remembered how easy he had found it to be with the man, to speak of things he had not spoken of for many, many years.

Eventually, they'd became friends, talking together for several hours each week, smiling, laughing, telling stories of their youth, and sharing dreams, fulfilled and unfulfilled. The summer months of the priest's visits rolled into early fall. Then, one day the priest arrived at his shop with a very serious look on his face. He said he needed to share something with Julius, to show him something that was very important, but that it was very personal, and private. He had asked Julius to swear an oath of secrecy. Julius hadn't known what it was the priest wanted to share, but they were friends, and Julius had agreed.

The priest hesitated for just a moment, and then from a pocket deep within his robes he pulled out a rumpled pouch made of what looked like very old and very rough peasant clothe. The vision of the meeting glowed clear in his mind; they were there, in his shop, the priest, Julius, and the pouch, that old, rumpled, yet somehow familiar pouch. Julius remembered the pull of it as the priest held it in his large hand. He stared at it as the tall man spoke of the long quest that had led him on, a spiritual quest to find the secrets of a mysterious order of men and women, a "Hierarchy Of Light," he called them.

Then, Julius had listened intently to the priest's story, but now, as he sat in the hotel, the memory came to him as if from a distant perch. The priest had been successful in his quest, and now had come back to this part of the United States to take the next step, the priest had said. Fog filled Julius' mind once more and he struggled to remember. Something about this area, the priest was saying, right here where Julius lived, and its importance. Apparently, there was a place, not far, that was a key to the priest's success. "Somewhere nearby." That was all Julius remembered: "somewhere nearby."

For the priest, the next step was to put to right a wrong that had been done long ago. Julius' mind flashed into focus and he remembered that as the priest spoke, he had looked directly into Julius' eyes and asked for his help in righting the wrong! Julius recalled how he had looked back at the priest, but only for a moment, for the pull of the pouch was more powerful than the look of his friend's gaze. He found himself transfixed by the presence of the cloth pouch still held in the priest's hand.

Yet, in the end, Julius had agreed to help. The priest had become his friend, and he wouldn't let him down. Julius' mind blurred for a moment, then focused again as he recalled the priest had stopped talking for a moment, lost in his own inner thoughts. Then, as if agreeing to something within himself, he began emptying the contents of the pouch, first into his huge hand and then into a small pile on the shop's workbench.

Julius remembered the excitement he felt at the time. Like butterflies in my belly, he recalled. For in front of him, on a clean corner of the bench sat a small pile of the most beautiful precious stones, gems of every imaginable shape and size, that he had ever seen. One hundred and eleven of them in all, the priest had said, a treasure long lost, but now found. Julius' heart pounded. Green emeralds, red rubies, blue sapphires, and more, all perfectly cut, in perfect proportion. Yes, he remembered the treasure! *His treasure!*

He marveled at their beauty. But there was something more, something special. The stones radiated an unexplainable light, a glow of magical light. Confused, Julius had looked out the window and then up at the ceiling lights of his shop in search of the source of their radiance. The priest had smiled. He would explain the shining light. No, the light wasn't an illusion, but part of the mystery of the gems. The gemstones, he'd said, were part of the treasure that he had uncovered in his search for the Hierarchy. Julius mind focused as he listened as the priest told his story.

CHAPTER TWENTY-SEVEN
THE PRIEST TELLS HIS STORY

Even though we seek the Light, it isn't always apparent where to look ... keep seeking anyway

The priest had gone to South America, he'd said, seeking a physical sign of the Hierarchy of Light, a group of supposedly advanced beings who'd learned the secrets of raising their physical bodies to higher frequencies or vibrations, into God Light itself.

Julius continued staring at the gems as the priest spoke, but he remembered his own question: into God Light? What did the priest mean? Yet, he never asked the question as he struggled to listen in the face of the pull of the gemstones and their ever-present yellow-gold light that surrounded them.

For the past ten years, the priest said, he'd been looking for a sign of this Hierarchy and some organized focus of its activity on Earth. Julius remembered the priest telling him that it had all started when the priest had read a small reference to the Hierarchy of Light in an old book lent to him at a meditation retreat outside of Athens, Greece. The book was written in Latin and was given to him by an old Spanish monk he'd met there. Julius' mind blurred, but cleared again, as he recalled how the tall, black robed priest had taken a deep sigh as he went on telling his story.

Ever since that time the priest told Julius he'd been looking for a sign of this Hierarchy. "You see, Julius," he had said, "my whole life I'd been seeking, searching for a hope of some kind of spiritual salvation that I had not found in my church. I had almost lost faith in the possibility of finding it, until I met that Spanish priest. He revived in me a real hope that what I sought, a more personal connection to the Divine, was possible." Julius had struggled to understand his newfound friend as he shared the story, but the gems and the radiance of their ever present glow, distracted him.

"We became friends, the Spanish monk and I," the priest went on, "at the month long retreat. In between meditation times, we would speak of our common search for spiritual meaning and salvation. Two days before the end of the retreat the old priest invited me to his cell, an unusual invitation for one attending this kind of almost silent gathering. He had something for me, he said. I visited him and when I got there he offered to loan me a book that he thought would be of value to me. I borrowed the book, promising to return it to him at the end of the retreat, but sadly the following day, the old priest passed away. No one knew where he was from, so, I kept the book."

The book the old priest had lent him filled him with hope as it spoke of a Hierarchy of Light, a group of advanced beings that worked on Earth to help enlighten humanity to its true connection with the Spirit of the One God. This had touched a place of deep recognition and desire within him, and the priest told Julius that he'd made it his life's quest since that time to find the Hierarchy, if it still existed on Earth, so that he could join and learn from them.

Julius remembered listening intently. But his interest, he recalled, became less and less focused on the priest's quest or with the Hierarchy. His only interest lay with the gems! His mind had whirled with anticipation, for he was convinced that they should be his. Why this should be, he didn't question. He only knew that from the moment he had set his eyes upon those beautiful stones, he'd wanted them more than ever he'd wanted anything before.

The priest continued his story, "The book had mentioned the Hierarchy and their work, but gave no reference to where those interested in learning from them could go." For several years, the priest traveled, visiting libraries and religious and spiritual centers around Earth searching for someone, or something, that could lead him to the Hierarchy. Finally, while visiting the library of an old monastery in northern Spain he found the trail that led him on his path to the Hierarchy. There, he told Julius, he found an ancient handwritten manuscript written in Latin with references to the Hierarchy of Light, now called the Brotherhood of Light. The manuscript, written sometime in the thirteenth century, spoke of a spiritual retreat, or Center of Light where the Brotherhood had lived and worked!

"At last," Julius recalled the priest's excitement as he exclaimed, "I found a reference to what I'd been searching for! The manuscript," the priest continued, "spoke of the Brotherhood's Center of Light and called it a special place where the Brotherhood met with students to teach those interested in pursuing the Path of Light the manuscript called it."

Julius' mind became hazy again and for a moment he lost the thread of the priest's story, and then, suddenly, he remembered—the priest's face had lit up in excitement as he continued telling his story about how he had spent many days at the monastery studying the manuscript, which described in some detail the focus and work of the Brotherhood of Light. But it wasn't until he'd nearly read the entire manuscript, the priest told Julius, that he noticed what the priest called the real treasure of the monastery. The priest had gone on to say that at the end of manuscript, tucked into a thin pouch-like envelope, rested two small pages of the manuscript that had either fallen out of the old binding, or been deliberately held away from the main body of text. The priest told Julius that he couldn't be certain of the intent, but as the priest pulled the first page out, Julius remembered that in his excitement at telling the story, the priest had almost dropped the book! On that page, he found a map that actually showed the location of the retreat of the Brotherhood of Light. Somewhere near a lake, the book had said, at the foot of the mountains. The priest, equally excited, told Julius that the second page showed an ink painting of the most beautiful chest the priest had ever seen. Gem encrusted with a bright light all around it, the painting radiated a light, the priest told Julius, so bright and compelling that he could hardly keep his eyes from it. "It was so, well, unbelievable," Julius remembered him saying. "I didn't know how the artist did it, but the painting of the chest had a glow about it, as if filled with a special light." The priest continued, "The chest was studded with inlaid gemstones, and from the painting it appeared that the gems themselves radiated the light!" At first, the priest believed the it to be an artist's trick, but later, he told Julius, he had found out differently—and that the glow had come directly from the gems themselves.

"You see it yourself, don't you, Julius?" the priest had asked him excitedly, "They really do glow!" And Julius, confused as he was both at that time and in now in remembering, recalled vaguely that he had agreed. The priest had said he'd found the map, but when he looked closely at it, the place names that identified the location of the retreat of the Brotherhood of Light were unfamiliar to him. Dejected at first, he told Julius that he had studied the map further and soon realized that the map represented a very rough view of the South American continent.

Julius remembered the priest saying that when he realized the map's connection to South America, his spirits had lifted, but that he couldn't take the manuscript from the library. So instead, he'd asked the Abbot if he could stay at the monastery and make a hand copy of it. He told Julius, "No one at the monastery seemed very much interested in my research as the manuscript had lain on the shelf for many, many decades without anyone touching it. So the Abbot agreed, and I spent the next three weeks, very carefully hand copying the manuscript, page by page." Julius remembered now the priest getting very excited again, as he told the rest of the story. "I also made a copy of the map, Julius," he'd said, "but for the drawing of the chest, I did something special. I made what I thought was an exact duplicate of it with colored inks that monks had lent me. Of course," Julius remembered the priest saying with a twinkle in his eye, "I'm no artist, so I don't believe I really captured all of its glow."

The chest held special interest, the priest told Julius, in that the manuscript had described it as being imbued by the teachers of the hierarchy with powers that could help students find the wealth and riches of their being. About how the chest was used, or the nature of its power, the priest said, nothing was mentioned, only that it could help students find their way on the path."

Julius' mind had wandered as the priest spoke, filled one moment with images of what he thought the chest might look like, and the next with his attention drawn back to the glowing gemstones resting in a pile on his workbench.

"The day I left the monastery," the priest had continued, "all the monks gathered in the great hall to wish me well. Word had gotten around that I had found a clue to help me on my spiritual path, and without really saying anything directly about it, they all let me know that their best wishes would be with me on my search, except for one monk. A man I had guessed to be about seventy-five or so years old, called Brother Ferdinand. He stayed off to the side of the celebration for the better part of an hour before he spoke to me. At first, I admit, I wasn't very interested in talking with him as his dour look, and sad, sad eyes made me feel a bit uneasy. But something, Julius, told me to agree to his request, made in almost perfect English, to spend a few private moments with me.

"We left the hall and he led me into the beautiful rose garden tended to by the monks of the monastery. In bloom at that time of year, and surrounded by luscious green hedges standing about ten feet tall, the perfume of the roses filled my senses as Brother Ferdinand directed me to one of the marble benches at the end of a path of red roses.

"We sat for a few moments in silence, our eyes resting on the beauty of the row and rows of roses, when the monk turned to me and told me he wanted to share a story that he'd heard many years back. It was about the Brotherhood of Light," he said. "I almost fell off the bench, my friend, my surprise was so great. While the monks of the monastery had wished me well, none before had expressed any interest in or even knowledge of my quest!

"Well, Julius, Brother Ferdinand went on to tell me that at the time that he heard the story of the Brotherhood, he doubted the truth or reality of all that was told to him. But he had grown older now and had realized that he had made a great mistake in not taking the storyteller seriously.

"Indeed," Brother Ferdinand said, as his sad eyes looked beyond mine to a vision only he could truly understand, 'I was visited by a Messenger, and I denied him.' He'd regretted his decision, and now wanted to personally encourage me to pursue the *great dream*, as he called it, of becoming a student of the Spiritual Hierarchy of the Planet.

"As a young man," Brother Ferdinand said, "he had been seeking a spiritual path for himself through the study of many different spiritual traditions. But none of these had helped him achieve a place of spiritual peace and wholeness. So, after many years of searching, Brother Ferdinand had decided to enter the monastic life.

"One day, after the monk had been cloistered at the monastery for several years, a man came to visit. He was a young man, but Brother Ferdinand had said that there was something in his eyes, a certain look, that made him feel that he was very old."

Julius mind again blurred for a moment and then he recalled how the priest went on to say that Brother Ferdinand had ignored the man's presence for the several weeks he was at the monastery, then one day the man came to Ferdinand's cell to speak with him. The man was getting ready to leave the monastery, but he had come to share a message with Brother Ferdinand. The young man didn't say where the message had come from, but only that the message was definitely for Ferdinand and for no one else.

Though surprised, Brother Ferdinand had listened with interest as the man described a place he had heard about in the America, "Where a group of spiritually advanced teachers taught students of the Light the ways of mastery, a place where seekers truly interested in the path of Light might go to be taught."

The priest went on to tell Julius that what was even more remarkable was how specific the messenger was as to the location of the place in America where such teaching could be learned. Julius remembered pulling himself away from his focus on the stone enough to ask the priest where the school might be located, and to his surprise, the priest had recounted that the messenger had told Brother Ferdinand the school was, "In a place called Merced County, Ohio, near a small town called Placerville." He had spelled it out to the priest: "P-l-a-c-e-r-v-i-l-l-e."

Julius' memory came back sharply, as he remembered his surprise at the priest's words and that he had blurted out his own amazement by saying, "Why that's right here!"

Julius looked around the room curiously. As if somehow it all didn't make sense to him. The priest had nodded his head in agreement, and then, Julius remembered, the priest had become quiet, thoughtful for a moment, as if Julius' interruption had brought him back to a great truth that he had almost forgotten. Almost in a whisper the priest said to Julius, "Yes, Julius, that's right, it's right here."

Then, without saying more, the priest continued his story. "The visitor couldn't tell Brother Ferdinand any more, except to say that if he were to make the journey to the United States, he would find help there to assist him on his spiritual path."

Julius remembered how the priest had gotten quiet, then went on to say how Brother Ferdinand had told him that as the messenger got up to go from his cell, the young man had looked deeply into the monk's eyes,

as if looking into the very depth of my soul," the priest recounted
Ferdinand's words, "and said, 'I've come a long way to share this
message with you, but it's you who've come a long way to allow it to be
heard! I thank you for the opportunity to share,' and then the strange
young man turned and left. After his meeting with the messenger, Julius,
Brother Ferdinand told me he fell into a deep, deep, depression."

Julius' recall stayed sharp as the priest told the rest of Brother
Ferdinand's story. Over the years, Ferdinand had become comfortable in
the monastic life, and he knew that he no longer had whatever it would
take to make the journey to the United States. He'd come to terms with
his decision not to go to America, but had thought often about the
visitor's message as the years went by and felt a deep sadness for not
having acted on the extraordinary message that had come to him, always
wondering whether he had made a grave, grave error in not seeking the
retreat of the Brotherhood. The priest told Julius that it was very sad and
that he could feel the man's pain. "It felt very old, and deep," the priest
had said, "but I could do nothing."

Julius remembered the priest looked away then, as if recalling events
that had happened just the day before and then continued. "Brother
Ferdinand looked at me, Julius, with his very old and very tired eyes and
said, almost in a whisper 'At least someone has a chance. Please, be
careful and may the Light of God accompany you on your search.'" The
priest went on to say that Brother Ferdinand had sighed a deep sigh, got
up, and blessed the priest in Spanish before leaving the rose garden.

The priest turned once again to Julius. "As you can image, for me this
meeting was like a prayer answered. Here I had found reference to the
Brotherhood and even a map to one of their retreats in South America.
This was already a great blessing, but now I'd been told about a place
right here in America that might be a place of training! After the monk
left, I sat in the garden for a long time, wondering what I should do next.
Should I seek the retreat in South America, or come directly to the United
States to search for the place here in Ohio?

"I couldn't tell you why, Julius, but though my logic kept saying that
I should come to search in America immediately, something inside, like a
little voice, kept telling me that I needed to seek the Brotherhood of Light
in South America before coming here. So I did. That was more than four
years ago."

As the late morning sun began to pour into Julius' room, he struggled
to remember what had happened next, but his attention, and memory,
faded again and then returned as he was able to recall the priest's story of
having followed the map and with the help of members of the local
Indian tribe he had searched for, and finally found the hierarchy's retreat
deep in the jungles at the foot of the Andes. "There was nothing there,"

the priest told Julius, "but a series of two room adobe ruins, six in all, as if a small colony of people had lived there for a time when studying with the Brotherhood. But now, only parts of the walls stood.

"I asked the tribes people to leave me there," the priest said, "and with supplies that could last me several months I stayed on alone at the ruins hoping that somehow the advanced beings of the Brotherhood of Light would know that I had come and send a messenger for me, or contact me in some other miraculous way."

But none had come, the priest told Julius. Days turned to weeks, and still the priest found himself alone, day after day roaming in the midst of the ruins. With supplies dwindling he was about to give up, but decided to survey the area a last time for any sign that might help him on his continued search. It was then that he had discovered the gems.

"I'd almost forgotten about them and the chest," the priest had said. "After the years of looking for the retreat, and my disappointment at finding only an empty ruin, the gems and the chest had simply slipped my mind. As I walk through the jungle that day around the perimeter of the retreat, I literally fell into a room that I'd not known existed before. I walked, or should say, tripped into it because although the walls had almost entirely eroded, the part of the room that lay under ground level still held in tact, and it was this part of the old wall that I tripped on. The ruin was overgrown with colorful plants and flowers of every kind imaginable, like a jungle flower garden. Vines and orchids intertwined with palm trees growing in the middle of the room which was different than the others. It must have been the meeting place for the retreat, for when I finally was able to get a sense of it size, its measure was much larger than the other rooms, perhaps sixty to sixty-five feet square. I counted myself very lucky to have found that room, because it was there that I found the gems!"

Even as the heat of the day began to pour into his room, Julius' mind became clearer as he picked up the thread of the priest's story. The priest had gone about the tedious task of beginning the clearing of the undergrowth when he had discovered the entrance to another, subterranean room. "I can't tell you how my mind swirled with anticipation when I discovered that room," he'd said. "I wasn't sure why, but I *knew* that I'd find something important in there." It was dark as he'd entered the room and it took a long time for the priest's eyes to adjust, but when he finally could see, the first thing he saw was a mud-brick alter in the corner of the room. At first, the priest said he didn't see anything else. Then, to the side of the alter he saw the pouch, the very pouch that he and Julius had just looked at.

"You can imagine how excited I felt," the priest said, "I start for the altar, but something, no, not just something, but a voice, a very distinct voice inside me, very real and very strong, but kind, came to me and told me to stay put, to not to go to the alter yet.

"I remember breaking out in a sweat. I can tell you, it scared me. Here I was in the middle of the jungle and hearing voices. I thought I might be going crazy. But the voice had spoken calmly to me, as if the words came from a friend standing in front of me, rather than from someone, or something, inside my head! My heart pounded as if electrical charges were running through it, but after a while I calmed down enough to listen. The voice continued very clearly. It told me that I had indeed found a past retreat of the Brotherhood of Light, and that they were very happy that I had pursued my dream of creating a closer relationship with the Great Creator.

"The voice went on to say that the Brotherhood would help me in whatever way they could to realize my dream. For now, they would lead me, if I wished to follow their guidance. I felt startled, but very excited. Perhaps, I thought this is the way the Brotherhood works with their students. So, even though it felt so very strange to speak aloud with nobody physically present, I told the voice that I wanted to follow the guidance."

Julius got up to lower the blinds at the south facing Harlan Inn window as the sun heated up his small room. Sitting down on the bed, he thought to himself that even though he'd listened to the priest's story, he did so only half-heartedly. His real attention, he recalled, focused on the glowing gems that sat on his workbench only a foot and half away from his reach. As the priest spoke of the voice speaking to him in his head, Julius' own memory wandered back, only for a moment, to a time when as a youngster growing up in Pennsylvania he, too, had heard voices and even spoken to them as if they were real. But that was so far back, he thought, so very far back. He'd forgotten it these many years—but now, as he remembered the priest speaking in the shop, he also remembered that he'd wondered about it.

The priest continued his story, "The voice now led me to go to the altar and to take the pouch in my hands. As I picked it up, I felt a tingle of energy like I had never felt before. My whole body felt lighter, honestly, as if I was going to float. Oddly, the pouch had the feeling of being both light, and heavy at the same time. I can't describe it any better than that.

"The voice asked me to go out to the sun to a clearing I'd made near the center of the meeting room. As I carried it outside, my mind soared, as my body felt like it was walking on air. The voice laughed gently inside my head as it informed me that the feeling of being lighter than air was a quality of the contents of the small bag that I carried.

"The voice told me that the pouch and its contents had been left inside the underground room with a protective energy around it more than five hundred years ago. 'The contents are very sacred,' it had said, 'and hold special blessings and energies that can help those who come in contact with them become closer to their Source.' But, the voice went on to say that it 'takes a person dedicated to the Light *in all of his or her being* to work with these energies.'

"I can't tell you how I felt, to be there at an ancient retreat of the Brotherhood, being guided by, I guessed, a member or members of the Brotherhood! When I followed the voice's guidance and took the pouch outside, the sun was high in sky. At first I could hardly see with the glare, but my eyes soon adjusted to lush beauty of jungle all around. I walked to the center of the clearing. When I arrived the voice instructed me to empty the contents of the pouch onto the ground. I listened and poured the gems, a small handful at a time, onto a large flat stone I'd found, and as I did I marveled at their radiance as they sparkled in the sunlight.

"I'd never seen anything like it before. There in the sunlight of the South American jungle I could see a bright, bright yellow-gold glow around them. Right away I *knew* that these were the gems that I'd seen with the golden glow radiating from them on the ink drawing of the chest that I'd copied from the manuscript at the monastery.

"The moment I had the thought I got immediate confirmation that I was right. It was as if something or someone told me so, but not in my mind. Instead, my body tingled all over with a kind of *knowingness* ... and nothing more needed to be said.

"Then I heard the voice again. It said that I had come to this place with a clear heart and that that was cause for great celebration amongst the Brotherhood. My personal determination to continue my quest to work directly with the Spiritual Hierarchy of Earth was well known to them. It said that the Brotherhood was pleased to help me on my path.

"The words came that the Brotherhood wished for me, if I so chose, to undertake a 'mission of Light,' as they called it. They wanted me to take the pouch and its contents where it would be of most value to the planetary hierarchy, a place in the United States called Merced County, Ohio, the same place Brother Ferdinand had spoken to me about."

Julius remembered how he'd perked up at the name as the priest spoke it and how he had wondered, even as he felt pulled by the glorious stones sitting on his workbench, at how anyone could find anything at all important about Merced County, Ohio.

"The voice told me," continued the priest, "that while the Brotherhood could provide spiritual help and guidance to humanity, it needed to work through those in the physical who, by their own free will, chose to do the work of Light.

"He said that my quest to find the Brotherhood had led me to discover the location of the gemstones after all this time. Because of my faith and perseverance the voice told me the gemstones' special qualities can now be used again on Earth to help guide students of the Light along on their journey. He told me that the Brotherhood would help me by providing guidance along the way on my return to the United States.

"Then the voice spoke more directly of my own spiritual journey. It said that my bringing the gemstones to America helped fulfill my own journey, even though this activity would also help others, and that I wouldn't be involved in it unless it related in some way to my own spiritual evolution. Then the voice said something that has stuck with me to this day. It told me that each moment in the day, each activity of thought or action that I undertook always related directly to the awakening of self knowledge and the evolution of my own life and life stream."

The priest stopped his story, and Julius recalled the priest telling him that he'd never heard this term life stream before and that the voice didn't elaborate on it, but somehow that term had just struck him as important. He still didn't know that he truly understood what the word might mean, but he thought it had something to do with his soul, not just in the present, but with him and his eternal soul and his journey in life.

***

At this point Julius got up from his creaky old bed and walked to the window. He felt agitated, but didn't know why. He looked out the window at the cars passing by on the road that stretched in front of the Harlan Inn. His mind felt clearer now, as if recalling the priest's story itself had helped him somehow remember something about himself that he'd forgotten.

As he looked out, he remembered how his ears had perked up when the priest spoke of the guidance that would be given when he came back to America, more than they had to the other parts of the priest's story. Something about a voice talking, giving guidance. Somehow it seemed all so familiar to him, and again he wondered about his own experience as a boy. What was it that had happened then, he reached in his memory, but couldn't find the levers that would bring it back, and then, as if a movie had been on hold or intermission and now starting up again, the priest's story rushed back into his memory.

***

"Julius," he recalled the priest saying, "it felt odd, this talking in my head, but the entire time I heard the voice I experienced the most exquisite sensation of being, well, calm and content. I'd never felt this way before in my life. In the past, I struggled even with being able to spend time quietly alone and in my meditations. The kindness and calmness of the voice brought with it a very real sense of quiet within me, and also a sense of safety.

"What happened next," he had said, "surprised me, for without really thinking about it I found myself saying out loud, 'Thank you' for the stillness I felt inside, and for the Brotherhood's accepting me as a student.

"Overwhelmed with gratitude as I was, my eyes filled with tears. I'm not one who usually cries, but at that moment I felt that I'd come in contact with a part of me that had been hidden for a long, very long time. I began to weep like a baby. When I finally stopped, the voice came to me and simply said, 'It's we, Master, who are grateful to you for your love and dedication to finding your way home.'

"Then it asked whether I wished to continue the journey with the chest. I knew what they meant, at least in part. With the reference to the journey with the chest came a picture in my mind of the gemstone-laden chest, the one I had drawn the picture of in Spain. I didn't hesitate a moment. I nodded my head and said I was willing, even though I didn't know exactly what would be asked of me. It was then, that I was asked to bring the pouch to this area, 'a place in the state of Ohio in the United States,' the voice said. When I got here I would be led to the right place and I would find one who could rebuild the chest and return the gems to their proper place."

Julius became agitated as he walked around the increasing hot room as he remembered the priest stopping then, and looking at him with a curious look on his face and saying that his own intuition or guidance had led him to visit. The priest had said that he didn't know why, but when he arrived at the Columbus airport, he felt the need to come to this town and he knew his guidance would help him find the maker of the chest. The priest told Julius that he wasn't sure how that would happen, but on the way to the hotel from the airport his taxi passed by Julius' shop and as he turned to look at it, the priest said that he knew that this was the right place.

Julius' mind lost the thread of his thought, and then he remembered the priest as he spoke to him. "That's why I've come, Julius," the priest had said. "I don't know exactly why you've been chosen, but I've learned to trust the feeling that came that told me that your shop would be the place where the chest would be rebuilt. That's why I first came last June, to get to know you, and then to ask for your help."

Julius remembered the priest had looked at him then again in a curious fashion, as if he wasn't entirely certain that Julius would agree to help. But Julius had had no hesitation. As hazy as his mind had become, he recalled feeling honored that the priest had come to him. He liked the man and he wanted to help. For somewhere inside himself Julius, too, knew that it was right for the priest to have come to him. Still, something else nagged at him, for his agreement to help came in the midst of a rising sense of anger, an anger Julius had rarely experienced before in his life. He remembered reasoning to himself at the time, even as he had agreed to rebuild the chest, these gems are mine! Why should I help anyone have them? But these thoughts soon faded into the background of his mind, as his affection for the priest, and his own inclination to help the man came to the fore.

CHAPTER TWENTY-EIGHT
JULIUS BUILDS THE CHEST OF LIGHT

No one knows when the challenge will come, but it will come, and will say "will you return home now … to the Light?"

Julius had made a deal with the priest. He would help. Julius' mind struggled to recall more as the scenes faded in his confused mind, and then returned once again.

The priest had taken a deep sigh at Julius' positive response, but had hesitated as well, turning his head and ear slightly upward and to the right as if he were talking to himself, or listening. After a moment the priest nodded, as if agreeing to a silent, but important dialogue that went on inside his head. He then turned back to Julius, more relaxed than before, and smiled his own assent to the agreement.

Very calmly, the priest reached into the inner pocket of his black habit and removed a large, square envelope. He didn't open it right away and Julius remembered both the priest's excitement and his own. At the time, he'd not been sure why he'd been so excited, but now as he paced around his room in the Harlan Inn he remembered that day and knew why the envelope had brought such excitement within—even before it was opened.

He muttered to himself, "I knew what was in that darn envelope, and I knew *it was mine!*"

His mind brought him back to the scene. The priest opened the envelope and removed a piece of yellow parchment paper with a colored-ink drawing of a chest sketched in very fine detail on it. Placing it gently alongside the gemstones on the workbench he said, "Isn't it marvelous? I don't know who the original maker was, or how it was made, but it's the most marvelous piece of workmanship I've ever seen. Don't you agree?" and Julius had nodded his head in agreement.

When the priest spoke of the care he had taken in painting every detail of the chest, from the picture he'd found in the book in Spain, Julius didn't understand why he'd taken such time rather than just making a rough drawing of the chest and it dimensions. But now he understood! The priest had captured in his ink painting every nuance, every detail, of a small chest that was, Julius thought to himself then, simply extraordinary in every way. "Yes, the most beautiful piece of work I've ever seen!" he told the priest. Even to Julius' skilled cabinetmaker's eye, he had to wonder how the maker of the chest had been able to craft such an elegant and seamless piece of work.

Indeed, Julius couldn't see how the chest held together, so perfect was the workmanship. Each corner looked as if carved from a single block of wood, although he knew that this was not the case. Even in the priest's painting, the bejeweled chest shined like the blackest of black nights, as if lacquered with the night sky itself. From every side of the chest the painting radiated the light emanating from the very same gemstones that sat glowing on the workbench. Inlaid insignias and lettering of white ivory and nacre-like stones scrolled across the top and bottom edges of the chest. Exquisitely carved designs of encrusted gemstones and ivory interwove on the chest's remaining surfaces.

The priest told him something about the thirteenth century, and then spoke of Julius creating a chest exactly like the one in the painting, asking if he thought he could duplicate the chest, and Julius had remembered he had eagerly said that he could. He had no doubt his skills were up to it. In his mind, Julius *knew* that the chest and the gemstones rightfully belonged to him.

His heart pounded with excitement. "That chest," Julius found himself saying aloud, "it really belongs to me. I should've never given it to him. This time, when I get my hands on it, nobody's goin' to steal it from me again!"

CHAPTER TWENTY-NINE
BECKY JOURNEYS WITH EGEDINE

Dancing in heaven's fields is closer than we think!

Becky ran to the forest for her lesson. Six-thirty in the morning was not too early for a woman raised on the farm. She'd been used to getting up at sunrise, but over these past several months of her lessons, she'd never enjoyed the early morning as much as now.

The lesson lasted only an hour or so, but their impact heightened a sense of exhilaration in Becky that seemed to last for days. Katran came more and more often, at first, one time a week, but soon after that, almost every day. They would walk together for the time of their lesson, sometimes alone, and other times they would meet with the family of deer that Becky had come to know and love. They gave no names, but Becky's affection for these kind creatures grew as she ran with them through the intricate web of trails that endlessly wove through the forest.

Today, she felt especially excited, for she *knew* that her friend Egedine would be waiting for her. Egedine had not visited with her since the first time she'd come to the forest for her lessons with Katran. But over this summer of almost daily meetings with Katran, Becky had begun to recognize within herself a growing sense of *knowing* beforehand that an event would occur, and then the event would happen just as she felt it would.

On this day, as she sometimes ran, sometimes skipped down the path to the meeting log, her heart beat with anticipation. She was not disappointed, for as she turned the corner of the last curve in the trail, she saw the magnificent stature of the white Unicorn. She rushed to him, and without thinking about it, through her arms around the Unicorn's neck, and gave Egedine a huge hug.

She could feel that Egedine was surprised, but pleased at her show of affection. She smiled at Egedine as she spoke to him in her head. "Old friend, I don't remember all of what we have done together, but the love I feel for you tells me we have spent much wonderful time together. Please tell me about our past, I would so like to hear."

The Unicorn's eyes glowed with warmth that ran through Becky's veins as the pleasant caress of the hot sun on a July day. "I can't tell you now, Little One," the Unicorn responded. "We have much to do and my time here is limited. But I will tell you that as you learn more, you'll know our past together, for it's only the clouding of your mind that keeps you from remembering."

With that, Egedine sent Becky a vision of her climbing onto his back. As she did, Becky felt that same sense of exhilaration and lightness that she felt whenever Katran came to her. She never tired of the sense of power and well being that came over her at these times, nor did she ever think she would get used to it. It felt like soaring above the clouds, and yet it also felt like she *knew herself* at these times better than she ever had before.

Atop Egedine, Becky stroked his silver mane and felt how familiar it felt to sit astride his wide white flanks. "We'll be leaving the forest as you know it for this journey," he said. "You'll find where we're going very familiar, but still very different. Don't be surprised at what you see or hear. The energies of this place are quite different than those that you're used to, so please stay with me and we will see what it is we can see."

Egedine began a slow walk with Becky atop him through the forest, at first on the main path and then on a small side trail, one that Becky knew well for she had been on it many times before. But this time, all seemed different and Becky felt it as though this were her first visit to this part of the forest. Things seem changed, she thought. Is it the light? She wasn't sure, and yet the colors appeared richer and deeper than she had ever experienced before. Shades of green seemed to radiate a deep and golden glow that made the forest feel like a tropical heaven, and the earth itself seemed transformed from mere dirt to a mossy brown loam.

All moved in slow motion as Egedine and Becky traveled upon the forest floor. Soon, Egedine moved off the trail into the woods itself. To her astonishment, and at first, disbelief, Egedine led them directly toward the trunk of a giant old oak tree, and then, right on into and through the tree! She could feel the cells of her body gently whisper as they came in contact with the molecules of the tree. Time lost its shape in Becky's mind as all seemed slower than ever she had seen or believed possible before.

The journey took only seconds, but to her it was like entering a timeless world of magic. Each second became an hour of kaleidoscopic color and sounds as the forest world around her that she'd known became a place of infinitesimal whispers and motion. Oak leaves became fibrous patterns of finely woven lace, as Becky's skin melted in and through them. For a moment, Becky felt confused as her human form merged with the infinitesimally minute patterns of the leaf. Was she human or the leaf? The answer came immediately and her confusion ceased as she *knew* the leaf and she as part of a unified "field of Light" where *being* replaced separated consciousness.

Egedine spoke of the unity of all things in the Light of the One, and Becky knew his words as reality as her flesh and being became one with her surroundings. She felt the Unicorn's strong body beneath her, but was no longer riding atop him, but instead a part of *his* being. She was

Becky, but now more than that, a part of Egedine's life, and the life of the trees, and the earth and even the air, there was no separation. She was alone, yet totally one with all that was or ever could be.

Egedine's kind voice came to her. "Becky, we're home now. I have brought us to a time-of-before that you'll remember. But stay with me, for what you'll see will bring energies within you that will make you want to stay here, and this isn't our purpose. Remember, stay with me."

Becky nodded her head in assent as her senses bathed in the lush greens, browns, yellows, and ochres of her surroundings. This was her forest, yet it was different. Everything, the branches of the trees, the forest floor, and even the brilliant whiteness of Egedine's flanks emitted a glow that she'd never seen before. It's as though everything's got a halo around it, she thought to herself.

Everywhere she turned, the land radiated the warmth of the golden glow blending with the almost dreamlike quality of the forest colors. A bird began a song she'd never heard before. Becky looked up to the trees, but couldn't see it. Heightened senses tingled as the bird's song touched a place deeply in her heart. She felt lifted, lightheaded, and free.

She took a deep breath as Egedine spoke within her mind, "My beloved friend, we have come to this place I call home to show you a very important part of life on Earth. Yes, we did go through the tree, but we have not left the forest. You see, the forest is sacred, not just in the dimension in which you live, but in this one as well, the one in which I live."

"Oh, Egedine, please tell me more," said Becky. "This place is so wonderful, I feel so, so … happy here, light and airy, as if all the weight of the world has lifted from me."

"In a sense, it has," the Unicorn replied, "for we have traveled no distance in space and time as you know it, but we have traveled at a higher vibration, a higher frequency that has enabled us to move from a lower level of existence to a higher one. What this means is that we have raised the frequency at which the molecules of our bodies abide, and this makes us able to move from a lower vibration existence to a higher one.

"It's no surprise, then, that you feel lighter, for the weight of the world has really been lifted from you. The frequency at which we needed to raise our vibration to come here is so high that those heavier lower frequency emotions, thoughts, feelings, and even memories that you held within you only a few moments ago, were unable to follow."

Becky's thoughts raced, trying to understand. Yes, Katran had instructed her on her own ability to raise her physical body's vibration. But she hadn't even begun to imagine at the time what Katran's words really meant! To be here now, in her forest, but a place so different than what she was used to, made her feel dizzy, beyond reality, and for a moment she questioned her sanity. *How can this be real? I must be going mad!*

But she knew that she was not. Her journeys with the deer, and even Katran's appearance and disappearance in the forest, had somehow registered within her as mysterious events, unexplainable, something that *others* knew about, but not her. She was Becky, born and raised in Placerville, and so even though she and Harry were learning from these kind and mysterious masters in the forest, she was still the same person she had always been. But now something had changed, and she knew that it would change her view of life and reality forever!

"Let's walk for a while," Egedine said, as he instructed her to dismount from his back. Becky landed gently on the ground as she and the white Unicorn walked on soft forest soil. Together, they journeyed through the forest on trails new and different from the ones familiar to Becky. Her senses heightened at each turn as a new tree, flower, or plant that she'd never seen before showed its glowing face to her. A gentle, sweet breeze carried the scents of the joyous forest to her as they walked. Egedine said nothing, but Becky felt him strong and confident by her side.

"Who comes to this forest, Egedine?"

"This is the place of the Brotherhood of Light. Just as in the dimension in which you live, it is a special place used by the Brotherhood to aid those of us who've made the journey from the level of vibration in which we live to the next. Yet, we, too, must learn about the next step, and part of the Brotherhood's work is to help each of us go on from here to even higher levels of God reality."

"I don't understand," Becky said. "What do you mean, 'go on to higher levels of reality?' I thought you and Katran spoke of the highest level we could reach, the same one Jesus and other masters reached, the one in which we learn to raise the vibration of our being to a higher level. You're telling me that even here learning is necessary to go on even further?"

Becky could feel the smile and warmth radiating from the Unicorn as his answer resonated through her. "You're an astute student. I'll do my best to answer you. Many frequencies of existence resonate through the universes. At the level at which you live, you 'see' what you can see, and so you think that this is the only reality. You're learning that others exist. And just as you learn about heightened levels of reality, we of this dimension must learn about even higher levels.

"Many masters of Earth have ascended to this level and have learned to go on to new heights. But those who wished to stay and help our friends on Earth to make the journey remain in this dimension. Here, Masters have the ability to travel through time and space, to see the past, present, and future, and to transport their physicality from one dimension to another.

In essence, here, we have learned to know the energies of the universe as our own, and we're able to practice use of these energies. But many go on from here to higher levels of spiritual consciousness. Those of us who stay use our powers to help Earth.

"We Unicorns were once plentiful on Earth, but the deepening of thoughts and feelings hostile to the Light caused us to leave that plane." Egedine stopped and Becky could feel her friend's pain about the exodus of Unicorns from her plane of existence. "Our departure was not voluntary, and many did not make the journey, leaving their bodies behind. But that's a story for another time, Becky," Egedine said.

"This forest, in particular, is a place of retreat and training for the Brotherhood," he continued. "It's here that elements of the plan of Light and Love for Earth are discussed and worked out. It's also from here, that the Brotherhood makes decisions about which ones of us will do what to help Earth, and in what ways. All here are self-chosen members of the Brotherhood, so we work together to fulfill our pledge to help Earth."

Becky listened as they walked. Then she found herself suddenly reminiscing about her parents. She wasn't certain why. After all, she reasoned, here I am in this most unusual situation being taught about mastering the different frequencies of life, and my heart is feeling all the deep pain of missing them as if they were still alive, back on the farm, waiting for me to come back for lunch. She simply didn't understand. Beside her, Egedine continued his gentle pace through the forest. Down a narrow trail just large enough for the Unicorn and Becky to walk side by side. They soon came to a fork in the trail.

Egedine spoke without any acknowledgement of her missing her parents, "We will be leaving the boundaries of the forest as you know it. We will enter a part of the larger forest that was turned to farmland long ago in your realm of existence before your parents and the other farm families arrived to protect the remaining land. The forest as you know it," he said, "is a part of this once greater expanse of forestland."

They took the path to the right, which widened considerably, running alongside a small creek adjacent to the path. Becky's eyes took in everything, the creek, the trees, and even two squirrels chasing each other round and round a tree. And still, all things of this forest held that golden glow about them. Becky's sadness about her parents gave way to the excitement she felt at being here in the forest with Egedine. She was about to ask Egedine about the golden light when the path turned slightly again to the right where they came abruptly into a large clearing. In it, next to a small pond, stood three very tall men, each wearing a different colored robe, one of gold, one of blue, and one of green. They're magnificent, Becky thought, and immediately she was filled with a sense of embarrassment, as she realized that these men knew exactly what she was thinking.

The forest floor here lay covered with a moss green grass that felt like soft cushions under Becky's feet. As she and Egedine approached the robed men, a smile as broad as her own crossed each of their faces and, in unison, they all began to laugh. Becky, the three men, and even Egedine laughed a laugh so full, so heartfelt, so pure, and so *connected* to each other that Becky could hardly tell whether she laughed as a separate being, or laughed with the three men and Egedine as one being, sharing in joyous unity and Oneness. As they laughed together the glow of golden light grew brighter around them and for the first time since she and Egedine arrived in this forest, Becky noticed an ever so gentle glow of that same light beginning to glow around her.

Her heart felt full now, as they all came to a quiet place together of calm and love. Her feeling of unity with these men and Egedine was much more than any such feeling she could remember experiencing. A gentle thought came to her mind, Perhaps it's because we're sharing through thought, rather than words, that I feel such a strong feeling of oneness with them. She let the thought pass as it didn't matter to her why she felt the way she did. It only mattered that she *knew* that she was with friends, content, and that the unity she felt with them was real. The three stood with her for a moment in silence, and though they'd not met before, Becky felt the same warmth towards them that she felt towards those she'd known and loved her whole life. Indeed, these men were family.

The golden robed Master spoke to her. "We're here" he said, "to show you parts of your own history that are necessary for you to understand. We, too, acknowledge the love your presence inspires in us all, its warmth and its glow. It is not the everyday journey for one in your position to come to be with us here at this time, and in this place. We thank you for your courage, grace, and good will. We've much to do together, for the journey you're on," he continued, "will bring you to understand much about the workings of Great Spirit's higher thoughts and consciousness in the Light and of the lower thoughts and consciousness of what is experienced as light and darkness on your plane of existence. We admire those who choose the Path of Mastery—working to understand and unfold their own forgotten inner Light. The temptations to remain unconscious to one's origins and source in the One God Light are great, and many great souls have fallen into the darkness on this plane."

Becky listened, but found herself bathed in the *feeling* of what was being said rather than the words themselves. She knew that she was being spoken to, but what she received in her being were images and feelings. The word "Light" invoked within her a deepening smile, a state that held her as if in the arms of eternity. And the words about great souls gone astray, brought such a deep pain to her heart, a sadness so great that she felt she wouldn't be able to bear it.

Egedine spoke to her, "Be aware that your pain is all of our pain. The unity of Light encompasses all that's shadowy within it, and even though the darkness may appear to prevail at any one time in the course of humanity's evolution on Earth, it is the Light that's all and ever, for it's the base of all. All else is illusion, and eventually gives way to the truth of Light's reality."

The others said nothing, for Becky could feel that all in this reality lived the truth of Egedine's words. "We've come to enter into a time long past," he continued, "a time when the Brotherhood worked more directly on Earth to heal the wounds of humanity. I myself roamed on that beautiful plane at that time. But regrettably it was a time when the Light lost ground in the ebb and flow of life on Earth. You'll see much, and the Masters here will accompany us."

With that, Egedine asked Becky to once again mount upon his back. She nodded. Becky couldn't help but feeling how much easier and lighter she felt now than she did the first time Egedine invited her to join him in this way. She remembered his words about the lightness that comes when the weight of the earth is lifted. She felt that way now, weightless, happy to be alive. Stepping lightly, she moved to mount Egedine, and suddenly found herself atop him. How did that happen? she thought. A smile came to her face as she understood that she was not in her own forest, but one like hers, somehow similar, yet, another place, another time, another vibration.

She felt Egedine's smile as they walked, she upon his back and the three robed Masters of Light alongside. Everywhere, the forest glowed with its bright golden light surrounding the richness of the colors of the trees, the sky, and the earth beneath their feet. And as they walked Becky couldn't help but know that the three walking alongside her were somehow different than all that surrounded her. Yes, they, too, held such a glow, but unlike the trees of the forest, the earth, Egedine's and the one that now began to surround her, theirs' seemed somehow deeper, as if they *were* the glow themselves, rather than having the Light all around them. Walking along the path next to Egedine, she could almost see through them. It's as if, she thought to herself, they're made more of that Light than they're made of the physical elements of their bodies.

She could see the smile on the face of the Master of the Blue Light as he was the closest of the three walking alongside her and Egedine. Immediately, she realized that the Master knew her thoughts. Becky had forgotten, smiled, shook her head and spoke directly in her mind to the Blue Light Master, a bit complaining and a bit in recognition of the fact of his being able to hear her thoughts. "I feel like a child in a world of adults…a bit small and embarrassed before the mighty truth of this place and the One Mind that you and I and *all* seem to share."

The Blue Light Master smiled in acknowledgement of the wisdom of the truth of what Becky had just shared, and with a sparkle in his eye, said, "Yes, we all feel a bit that way."

"It all seems so strange and wondrous," she said aloud. Then something inside of her surrendered to the truth of it all. A broad smile crossed her face and a then a heartfelt laugh came from deep from within her and rang out across the forest. She felt happy here, and not even the shadow of concern that showed in her blushing would make her doubt that she was loved, and that those around her could, indeed, be trusted with her innermost thoughts.

She continued, "I feel so much love here. Is this the way it always is?"

"Yes, the Master of the Blue Light answered, "It's always like this in the higher realms. But let's save this discussion for later, for now, we wish you to know that we're taking you to a place of great value to you. You'll see much but you must stay, as Egedine said, with him, for the danger is such that we may not be able to rescue you should you leave him. We will call, if the need arises. Heed our call and all will be well."

Again, Becky felt her emotions swinging back and forth from adult to child. She knew that she could trust the Masters and Egedine, but a part of her wanted to tell them that she could take care of herself, that of course she knew not to leave Egedine, hadn't he already told her that, and that they didn't need to treat her like a little girl, that—" She stopped herself and again a big smiled crossed her face, and she simply nodded her head in final agreement with the Master's words. The other two Masters came closer to Egedine's side and they smiled along with Becky. She was amidst friends, and she *knew* it.

The group walked on a few steps further before they came to a place to the right of the trail where the forest leaves and trees began to shimmer in a way that made their outline seem to fade in and out. One moment the greens, lavenders, pinks, and browns of the forest trees and flowers radiated strong and full in their brilliance, and the next they faded and merged into the gentle shimmering light, like a rainbow of pearly nacre shining brightly in the midday sun.

Egedine, with Becky on his back, turned off the path and walked on down the small deer trail into the area of radiating forest light. The three Masters followed along behind, as the trail led a little further into the underbrush towards an even more brightly lit area of the forest, about seventy-five feet or so down the trail, a place Becky immediately thought of as an door in the forest. With each step, the path narrowed as birch and alder trees pushed in on the trail, as if there to create a narrow entryway to reach the door of this magical place. Becky and the others said nothing as the five of them approached the shimmering doorway, Becky atop Egedine, and the three Masters in single file behind them. Then, without discussion, the entourage walked through the forest's portal of Light.

CHAPTER THIRTY
VARNESS "CHEST OF LIGHT"
AND BECKY'S MEETING

Never before has man/woman had so much opportunity to come home. Yet too often the people of Earth have passed on the decision to follow the Light

For Becky, nothing changed. The magical forest seemed the same with its glowing gold radiance as Egedine returned them to the path that they'd been on only a few moments before. Egedine assured Becky that all was well through images and words that appeared in her mind, and through a gentle rocking of his head as Becky stroked his beautiful white mane. But something had changed; the Masters were different!

As Becky looked behind her, the three were no longer there in the form in which she had known them. Instead, she saw three tall and shimmering lights, each one magnificent in the radiating glow coming from them, yet each still maintained a slightly different color and tone from the other, one with a golden tint, another blue-white tint, and the third with a greenish tint.

"Yes, Becky," the Green Light Master said, "we've passed into a different realm here, one that's slightly higher in frequency than the one where either you live, or the one from which we've just come — where Egedine lives. Here you see us in a form closer to our pure essence. You and Egedine have not changed, as we're holding the energies around you for protection in this sometimes volatile realm. What you will see in this new realm are events ideas and images that have been placed in time and space by those who've lived on Earth throughout all the millennia of existence. Here you will find the memory, in all its completeness, of all things that have ever been thought or actually become manifest on Earth.

"Remember, *vibration and frequency create the form and essence of life in the physical world* as you know it. Our passage just now through the Gateway of Light brought us to this frequency where the past becomes more readily accessible to us." Just then, Egedine, who'd continued on the trail, rounded a corner and the group came to the edge of what seemed to Becky the exact clearing where Egedine had first brought her to meet the Masters a short time before. But now, within the clearing stood a group of men and women, and in their midst stood three, very tall angels, who vibrated that same Light as the three Masters.

The Master of the Golden Light said, "While this is the same place that you have been before, this isn't the same time. Those who are here in this grove can't see or speak to us. For in time, this has been completed. It isn't for us to disrupt or change the course of events that happen to or on Earth. So we watch, and we ask you to watch along with us."

In her mind, Becky agreed, though she had many, many questions. Immediately, the Gold Light Master spoke in response to her thought, "We know, Becky," she heard, "that you wish answers to your questions, but watch, then we may talk," he said. As he spoke, Becky's entire being vibrated with the gentle kindness of his words.

She turned her attention to the scene unfolding in the clearing just twenty-feet before her. Three men and two women stood in an arc in the center of the clearing with their backs to her, Egedine, and the Masters from the Brotherhood of Light. Becky's eyes fixed on the angels. As much as she'd heard of angels and had always believed in them, she'd never seen one before, and now, here in the clearing, right in front of her, stood three of them, with enormous, sparkling wings. The angels, and others gathered in the clearing, focused their attention on something on the ground before them. She couldn't see what it was that they were looking at, but couldn't help noticing the intensity of the group's concentration. At the same time, she began to feel a great sense of warmth in her heart emanating from the circle. Even though she knew that this scene had taken place in the past, Becky felt every detail of it as if it were very much happening in her present.

She felt the angel's kindness as their radiating light encircled the men and women of the group. The light glowed so bright around their winged bodies that Becky found it difficult to discern physical differences between them, but she knew them by the extraordinary colors of each, one a little more yellow, another more lavender, and the third glowing more pink than the others.

Egedine moved still closer in to the clearing and as the men and women reached down closer to the object before them, Becky saw what it was that attracted their attention. Before them, on a large flat stone, sat a chest illuminated with a brilliant golden light around it, inlaid with the most magnificent gems of every color imaginable. The angels instructed the five to touch the chest, and as they did, Becky remembered that she had seen this chest before. Yes, she thought to herself, this is the same chest I saw the very first time I met Katran the same day I met my beloved deer friends!

"You're right," spoke the Master in blue, "it's the same chest, but watch now, Becky." And she did.

As the five touched the chest, they seemed to take on the energies of the chest, each beginning to glow a golden light. The angels instructed the five to release their hold, stand up and join hands together in a circle around the chest. As the group moved to do this, Becky's mind whirled in astonishment as standing directly facing her on the other side of the circle stood both her mother and father; much younger than she'd last seen them, but still her parents.

Becky gasped out loud and could hardly contain herself as she began to leave Egedine's back to run to be with them. She'd missed them so much, so very, very much, and now here they were. Her whole being reached out to join them, to touch them, to be with them! But, as she placed a foot on the ground, in an effort to be with them, the blue light Master's strong, but gentle words came to her, "Becky! Heed the call of the Masters!" and she stopped. Rather than leaving the Unicorn's back, she made the choice to stay. Using the leverage of the earth beneath her foot she vaulted back up upon Egedine's back. Instead of running toward those she loved, she watched with tears streaming down her cheeks.

The five moved slowly in a circle around the chest, and Becky recognized Mr. and Mrs. Blakely, who owned the farm directly north of hers. She didn't know the other person, a man of about fifty, who was the fifth person in the circle, but the others didn't matter to her. For Becky, all her attention rested on her parents and their every movement, even as Egedine beneath her moved closer to the circle.

Becky, Egedine, and the Masters stood now within feet of the group, as the lavender angel spoke aloud to them. Becky *knew* that several of the group couldn't hear the angel in their minds, and that this was the reason for the angel's choice to speak out loud.

She'd made the choice to stay atop Egedine, but as they moved closer to the group Becky could hardly keep from leaping from Egedine's back. So close were they to her parents that she could have reached out and touched them. Still, she heeded the call, knowing that it was safer for her to watch and listen, even though her heart ached.

The lavender-colored angel spoke to the group. "This chest is the chest of Golden Light, called Varness," he said. "Its origin is of the Light, made in higher realms of the Consciousness of the One Light. Those who made the chest lived long before Earth knew of tragedy, separation, and the sad victories won by the darkness. In those times, angels and other beings such as we lived in higher frequency realms around Earth, rarely descending to the planet. As the influence of darkness began to penetrate deeper and deeper into the physical environment of Earth, these entities strove to find ways to assist seekers to remember and maintain their connection to the beauty and power of the Light. These are the ones who created this chest and brought it to Earth's surface.

"For millennia, the chest moved from one mystery school of Earth to another, all part of the great teaching works of what became known as the Hierarchy, or Brotherhood of Light, whose members chose to serve Earth and her destiny in this way."

Becky cleared the tears from her eyes and watched as her parents and the others listened intently to the story of Varness. A tender smile crossed her lips as the thought came to her that her parents, along with the others, looked like angels with the gentle glow of Light that surrounded them after touching the chest. The lavender angel moved to the center of the circle and continued. "In the beginning, the angels taught the mysteries of the Light to those living on Earth. But as the energies on Earth became denser, they retreated to the realms of Light surrounding Earth.

"Advanced students of the Brotherhood became the teachers of the *Path of the Light*. Each of those attending these schools studied consciousness and its roots in the One Great Spirit, the source of all things. In time, more and more students flocked to the schools. The most advanced of the students, as teachers, still had much to learn. To accelerate the opportunities for them to know their own Light, and thus be able to convey the knowledge better to their students, these teachers were brought to the realms of Light by the angels to study with them, much as you've been brought here today.

"Eventually, the students became Masters, and thus came to learn the consciousness of the One. But the process was not always an easy one. So, the angels sought for a way to help the students and teachers to experience and know their light in a more direct fashion. It was then that they decided to create the chest Varness. Its purpose is to help those who are interested in higher knowledge touch their own energies and the energies of these higher realms.

"The Angels of the Brotherhood conceived and held the image of the chest in their One consciousness until its form took physical shape. As is the case with all things in creation, the golden chest came into being with her own name, Varness, which means Passage to the Heavens. Once created in these realms, those working with the Brotherhood on the planet focused their own energies together to precipitate an identical copy of the chest on Earth. For many centuries Varness served as a gift to sincere seekers, helping them know and feel the experience of their own higher vibrational frequencies. But the strength of the darkness grew on Earth and school after school came under attack by brigands and other's whose consciousness served the dark. The chest, always protected, now became an object of desire for those who thought that it would give them great power. Legends grew around it, and band after band of those working for the dark sought it.

"Eventually, to save the chest, the Brotherhood instructed the students of a remote school in the jungles of South America to destroy the outer shell and to hide her gems that carried the essence of the Golden Light. The students made a record of the location of the school and the existence of the chest and its powers. The record became part of the then secret holdings of a monastery in Europe, and later became part of the monastery's library. Until recently, the Brotherhood has been content to let the existence of the chest remain a secret. But Light is growing on Earth at this time and it needs all the help we can lend to it to overcome the misinformation and confusion of darkness and move into a time of humanity's universal awakening. So, within the next few years, in your time, the chest will be found, reconstructed and once again will be put into service on Earth."

Moving closer to Becky's parents and the others, the angel continued, "You've come here to learn of Varness, and this is good. It will be your task in the time ahead to receive the chest and, as in days of old, use it in the Forest Mystery School, of which you are caretakers, to teach sincere seekers. As Masters yourselves, you'll know how best to use the gift of Varness, but be aware, the forces of darkness know of the existence of the Golden Chest. Once reconstructed, they will react as they did in the past to find it, and try to use it in the service of darkness. We of the Brotherhood will work with you to ensure that this doesn't happen, for in the hands of one of ill intent, Varness has the power to destroy them. Those who work in the darkness don't know this. They seek the chest for its legendary Light, which they believe will enhance their own power. But only seekers of pure Light may receive the gift of Varness, all others will perish."

As the angel spoke, Becky watched a phenomenon that she was to see often in the years ahead. As her parents and the others accepted their charge, the Light around them glowed even brighter than before. It's as if, Becky thought, acceptance of their service to the Light expanded their own personal illumination.

Egedine's gentle voice came to her. "We must go now. We've much to do, and must return. As you know, Varness has been reconstructed and is held within the forest. There she'll be used as in days of old to aid those seeking knowledge. You, Bill, Harry and others have a role to play in this, in protecting Varness, and we will help in the ways we can." Though Egedine spoke directly to her within her mind, her attention rested elsewhere. Yes, she had heard the words, but her heart reached out to her parents, still ever present in the scene before her, and once again the urge to join them pulled at her, and then they were gone! They all disappeared, and Becky found herself transported on Egedine's back to the meeting log where she'd met him only a short time before, and she began to cry. Like a child lost in the forest after dark, she wailed as one injured so deeply that the entire forest could hear. She'd found her lost parents, though only for a few minutes. Her pain at losing them again added to the pain in her heart that she'd felt all these months since their passing.

Egedine and Becky stood alone in the clearing where the meeting log sat alongside the creek. Egedine's gentle voice instructed her to come down from his back to the soft earth of the forest floor. As she did, she reached and locked her arms tightly around his neck, for she felt that she couldn't go on. Even as the journey to meet the Masters and learn the story of the chest of Golden Light had lifted her to fantastic heights, now, the return home without her beloved parents catapulted her into the depth of despair.

"Surely," her little girl's voice spoke to Egedine through her tears, "the journey of becoming a Master isn't supposed to hurt so much?"

Egedine said nothing at first, and for a moment Becky relaxed, breathing more easily as she felt the strength and kindness of his mystical presence. The familiar smells and sounds of the forest filled her as the sweet scent of the Unicorn's mane brought comfort to her being. She stayed like that for some time, how long she didn't know, resting against his side. The sun shined brightly through the tall sycamore trees and a gentle breeze caressed her face. Finally, Egedine spoke gently in a way that she could hardly tell the difference between his calming words and the forest breeze, so alike were they.

"We're home now, to the home that you know so well. "But," he went on, "you've changed. The path of self awakening is a path that takes one back to the beginnings of all things ever created by the one who's on that path, and it's this part of the journey that causes the pain.

"Your lessons with Katran have taught you much about trusting yourself and your relationship to the forces of nature and other creatures on Earth. Our journey with the Masters just now has taught another lesson. To understand this, you'll need to better understand the nature of your own energy and the energies of the world in which you live. We traveled far, yet not far at all. Just as those who don't believe that members of my race exist, they, too, wouldn't believe that we could travel together to other frequencies of life.

"This may be the hardest thing you'll have to learn: to *be* yourself and listen to your own inner wisdom, no matter what the daily life on Earth tells you is normal and right. Earth life does yet not recognize the true reality of God's presence on Earth and beyond. *In my Father's house there are many mansions* is a phrase yet to be understood." Becky looked quizzically at Egedine, trying to understand. Egedine's body shook a bit as Becky felt the Unicorn's laughter. "Indeed," Egedine continued, "my presence in the forest here with you and our journey just now isn't that which most people would call normal or right! Despite that, I *am* very real! This will be your challenge, my beloved friend. As you go further along your path to self mastery, you'll need to still and control your sensitivity to your surroundings and those in it, so that you can hear your own true voice within."

Becky continued to rest her head on the Unicorn's mane as he spoke. But now, somehow, she knew that he would be going. She stepped back as the Unicorn gently moved its massive white head near her own, placing his cheek next to hers. Their eyes met then and they shared in that look all the affection they felt for each other.

"Remember Becky," Egedine said, "this is the time of the return of Varness. You'll go to the forest soon to seek it out so that you and Harry and the others may begin to bathe in its Light and experience its essence. Without another word Egedine turned and walked into the forest, and, as he did so, gently disappeared, as a wisp of ocean fog disappears with coming of the morning sunlight.

CHAPTER THIRTY-ONE
TELEPATHY AND LESSON ON
MAN AND WOMAN

Nowhere is it written that one must come home, yet it's still the destiny of all should they choose to follow it

Becky and I had been close before I left for Vietnam, but now that we shared the teachings of the forest, we became closer in a way that neither of us could have predicted. Our experience of telepathically receiving our teachings, each from our own unique set of teachers, had begun to have an impact on our relationship. We found ourselves beginning to speak about the same things almost at the same time. Becky would begin a sentence, and I would, without thinking about it, complete it. It was as if she and I knew the sentence before it was even present in our conscious minds.

It came as a shock to me when Becky and Bill began dating. Of course, I'd seen the way they looked at each other from the beginning. However, I hadn't realized the deep commitment they would come to make to each other and how that commitment would become part of not only Becky and Bill's relationship, but also my own connection to the two of them. Their new relationship set in motion a new and rich telepathic connection between the three of us, even though Bill had not yet begun studying in the forest with the Brotherhood—an event the Guardian had recently told me would happen soon.

Bill and I had begun to meet regularly to research the roots of the farm family compact. As a lawyer, he wanted to know how ownership in the land of five distinct properties came into the hands of five different families all dedicated to preserving the forest.

Our telepathic unity began displaying itself at one of our meetings at Bill's office in Placerville. As we looked over the available land deeds for the properties dating back to the eighteen hundreds, Bill began speaking about his own farm and the unique circumstances by which his family came to own the land.

"You remember what my mom said about our land. We came into control of it after my Grandma and Grandpa disappeared in that boating accident. Grandpa and grandma had been there a long time. As I looked at their farm papers, it seems like they bought the place in the early 1930's, during the Great Depression. It's not clear where they got the money, but it's common knowledge in the family that they came from somewhere in upstate Pennsylvania. It's strange," Bill said, "from what I know about it now, the other farm families also seemed to come from somewhere in Pennsylvania, but these came, it seems later on in the 1940's."

Just as I was about to say what I knew about the families from what little my father had shared with me, Bill said, "I know you've a lot to share about what your father told you about the families."

I looked at him a little strangely, then shared some of what I knew about the fact that the four remaining families came from the Pennsylvania Dutch area of that state. A little later in our meeting, the same kind of thing happened. I was about to tell Bill about the Blakely farm and about the close relationship that developed between Mr. Blakely and my parents when they would meet at the farmer's market each week. Then Bill chimed in, "Now, tell me about the close friendship between Mr. Blakely and your mother and father." He then explained that his mother mentioned that she knew that they'd been close.

This kind of thing happened more and more often in our meetings, and I began to feel a bit disconcerted about it. Finally, I asked the Guardian about it on one of my visits to the forest for my lesson at the meeting log. As I walked along the main path the Guardian came to answer my question about Bill's psychic abilities. "You must remember that there are no accidents along the path of Mastery that you and Becky have embarked upon. For Bill, his mother has been deeply committed to the Brotherhood for most of her life. He's no stranger to the concept that God expresses in many ways, but because of his fright in the forest as a young man, he has stayed away from the Brotherhood and his own journey as a seeker of self knowledge and wisdom. But now that has changed. You might say it's because he is working with you on the legal aspects of farm ownership and it's this that has sparked his interest, but this would be wrong. This one, Bill Bates, is opening to his own destiny of Light, and as I've told you before, he, too, will join us soon in the forest for his lessons. For now," he continued, "he has come to you and your sister as a vehicle for his own opening to his memories as a youth and to his own soul's journey of discovery. Help him for he has much to offer."

I felt a sense of growing warmth within as the Guardian continued to speak about the special destiny of Bill and Becky's coming together, and, in particular, of Bill's awakening and its relationship to Becky. He went on to say, "We won't say much more for now about this, but we do wish to answer your question about Bill's psychic abilities beginning to show themselves."

I felt a smile ripple through my being, a feeling of sparkling, gentle light as the Guardian continued, "This will seem like a story out of fairytales at first, but we wish you to know that it's the destiny of every man and every woman to one day meet their mate, either in the body or in higher realms of Light. In this case, Bill and Becky have chosen to meet again after many lifetimes of not being with each other. They are what might be called, old souls.

"We've taught you much, Harry. But we have yet to speak about the journey of man and woman on Earth, about the way that they were whole at one point, a single point, a Spark of Light together merged as a unity, a wholeness that surpassed anything that's currently understood as love.

"Each half existed at a higher vibration as part of the whole entity, knowing no distinction between its male self and its female self. It existed as a Unified Whole—thoroughly balanced and one within the Unity of All Creation. The ever expanding consciousness of the Great Spirit creates the possibility for existence in many planes of reality, all existing together simultaneously at different frequencies or vibrations within the Oneness.

"And so it came to pass that the Unified Whole that encompassed both man and woman voyaged in many planes of existence learning the mysteries of life within the Consciousness of the Great Spirit, the Oneness itself.

"As these sparks of Light traveled into different and denser areas of the Great Spirit's creation, the differing vibratory frequencies began to affect the essence of the spark that contained the Unified Wholes. As frequencies lowered, eventually to manifest the material worlds of the universe such as stars and planets, so, too, did the vibrations and frequencies of the Unified Whole. Now, rather than a single consciousness, the elements of the consciousness of the spark began to break up, to see itself not as a wholeness, but as separate parts of the whole, as separate parts of Light. As the voyage continued into denser and denser frequencies, the duality within the whole grew and could no longer hold together. The electrically charged male and female parts of consciousness came to play a growing role in the existence of the spark and eventually, the density of material existence became such that the spark of Light, originally a whole part of the Oneness of Great Spirit, separated into two smaller sparks, each possessing the unique elements of their own electrical charge—male and female, each remaining a part of the Oneness, yet each separate. "The Guardian paused for a moment and then continued. "It's these smaller parts of the once Unified Wholeness, now separate and unique in their identities as man and woman, that descended to Earth. As I said in the beginning, it's the destiny of every man and woman to meet their mate, either here on this plane, or in higher realms, before choosing to move to even higher frequencies of Light. This meeting of *twins* is the completion of their Earth journeys and the healing of the duality of the soul."

151

I listened to the Guardian, but didn't know what to say. It all seemed so foreign to me. Sparks of Light of the Oneness existing together in higher frequencies, splitting into man and woman on Earth! Did that mean that I was part of a whole, a spark that had also separated? Would I one day meet my other half, either in the physical or beyond? I felt excited, and a little confused. The Guardian's explanation had touched a place of truth within me.

That day Sakya and I only spent a short time together, so I didn't have the time to ask him about the Guardian's explanation. The Guardian's account of the journey of men and women together, originally one with each other in perfect unity, did give me an inkling of what might be happening with Bill and Becky. If they are mates, part of the same once unified whole, meeting again on Earth, then it's likely that whatever Becky underwent in opening to her own telepathic abilities, Bill would share as well. This could begin to explain the unusual situation of Bill becoming telepathic with me in the same manner as Becky and I did. My mind reeled at the prospect of the truth of this realization and I yearned to know more of my own mate and life before the time of man's *descent to Earth.*

CHAPTER THIRTY-TWO
FELIX DISCOVERS THE CHEST

No one can choose for another; the darkness holds one as long as one chooses to be held

Standing in a clearing in the woods near the old park service road off Ohio Route 64, Felix waited for the rest of his team to arrive. He found the place perfect for the meeting that would lay out the plan that would lead to the achievement of his ultimate success. He was enough away from town to not be seen, he thought, and off a rarely if ever used park service road leading to a once proposed, state park.

"Yes," Felix congratulated himself, "this place is perfect." Other, not so pleasant thoughts crossed his mind, too. He'd been upset initially at the prospect of dealing again with that old madman, Julius and his ravings about a magic box, but Felix's' recent meeting with his father had changed all that.

He'd mentioned the old man and his crazy box to his father. But instead of laughing about it, as Felix presumed he would, his father remained quiet for a moment and then rose up and slapped Felix across the face, almost knocking him off his chair. He called him an idiot for not telling him sooner of the existence of the chest.

Since that meeting, his father had been obsessed with the chest, its whereabouts, and how it came to be rediscovered. Felix hated his father at times like these. He knew that his father blamed him for missing what was perhaps the most important part of his assignment. Felix hated being thought of as stupid by the man he most admired, looked up to, and feared. So Felix had spent his time since the meeting trying to figure out how to get his hands on the chest, though he didn't know where it was, or even why his father gave it such importance.

***

Felix visited the old man, Julius, and had gotten a rambling monologue about how Julius' had remade the magic box from plans given to him by a mysterious priest, and about how Julius' own brother had stolen it from him. Julius couldn't say more than two sentences in a row without his attention wandering, so Felix had worked hard to get the story out of him, something about precious gemstones and a priest who listened to mysterious voices who commissioned the old man to make the chest. He added how the priest had brought the gems and box design with him from South America, and something about this area of Ohio being home to a sacred place where the priest would bring the chest when it was completed. The priest didn't know where that sacred place was, but he would find it and deliver the chest.

It seemed from Julius' ramblings to Felix that Julius had made the magic box with an eye towards keeping it for himself, telling the priest that it had been stolen. But to Julius' dismay, the priest must have known his plan, because within minutes of the completion of the chest, the priest showed up to take it, telling Julius that he'd found the place he'd been looking for and would take the chest there.

Felix flinched as he recalled how the old man had become wild in telling his story, ranting about how that priest had stolen *his* chest. What was even worse, Julius said, was that he'd found out that the priest had brought the box right here to Placerville, to his brother's farm. Julius' face had turned blood red in telling Felix how he'd shown the chest to his brother on the same day as the priest's visit, and how he was certain that his own brother had schemed with the priest to steal the chest from him all the time and hide it. When Felix asked about the whereabouts of the chest, Julius had said, "Inside that damn mysterious forest that they're all trying so hard to protect. That's the so-called sacred place the priest talked about. They've hidden it from me there. I know it, and I'm going to get it back!"

Felix left Julius, but since that visit his own mind had begun to dwell more and more on the chest, and the stones, those precious gemstones Julius had described, hidden in the forest. From what the old man had said, Felix thought they'd be worth a fortune. He wondered, just for a moment, what he would do with such a treasure if he could get his hands on it. But his mind turned immediately away from the thought, for he knew his father, and he knew very well how his father dealt with those who crossed him!

They waited, the old ones, for the right time and then they left for home...but some stayed behind and these are the helpers who are called upon at times of need

I watched with joy as Becky and Bill met at our farm or in town each morning for breakfast, except for those mornings when Becky's appointments with the Brotherhood of Light in the forest kept her away. On those days she'd come up with some excuse for Bill about how she was needed at the farm or was doing some errand with me. But this morning was different. Even though Becky had no appointment with the Brotherhood, she'd asked Bill to stay away.

She wanted to talk to me about her concern that the more she was getting involved with Bill, the less time she was spending with me. She wanted reassurance that I was okay without her around all the time. "After all," she said, "we're the only family we have, what with Uncle Julius being so crazy and no real relationship with the rest of the family. I want to make sure that we stay close and that you're okay with me spending so much time with Bill."

I was going to laugh and make some off the cuff remark to Becky, assuring her that everything's okay with me, but something stopped me. I felt her inside me and I felt her worry and pain, so I stopped. This wasn't usual for me. I'd never thought of myself as a particularly sensitive kind of person, but I was changing. My own visits to the forest, my meetings with Sakya and the others, had brought me closer to Becky in a way different than I ever could have imaged. And now, I thought, it's one thing to care for your sister, it's another to care about what she cares about and why! "Becky," I said, as I walked over and put my hand on her shoulder, "I want you to know that it's very much okay with me with what you and Bill are doing. I know you feel protective towards me, but I'm really doing okay. As you know, I've been reading a lot, and I started to write down some of the things that Sakya and the others have been teaching me. It's, well, a journal of my forest visits and it has really filled my time, so please don't worry, I'm not lonely, and I've got plenty to do."

She looked at me then for a while, and said nothing. And in her look I saw both awe and amazement, and I read in her mind the words, my little brother has grown up. We looked at each other a little longer without saying anything, and then Becky told me something that will always stay with me, no matter where I go or what I do.

"I want you know," she said, "I'm certain that Mom and Dad would have wanted us to know the Brotherhood of Light in the same way that they did, and I *know* that they would have loved to share that with us, if they could've. They weren't very talkative, but they gave us a lot. Now that we're on our own, I want you to remember them fondly. I know that you didn't feel that close with them, but I think it was because they had their own spiritual journey and it took a lot of their attention. Now that we've embarked on our own journey, I'm sure that we'd all be friends."

Her words struck a deep cord within me. Indeed, I was not so certain that Dad or Mom would be our friends now, any more than they were close with us when we grew up. I responded, "Yes, I did feel hurt as a boy when Dad treated me more like a farmhand than a son. But you know he gave me a lot, too. He made me feel like he respected me. Even though he wasn't that affectionate, I felt his respect. It was basic. He had a way of seeing the world that saw each person for who he or she was. He never judged anyone overtly, but I had the feeling that he respected people based on another set of criteria than most. He wanted people to be responsible for their own doings.

"I remember him talking about that once, 'Each man has a right to be who they want to be,' he said, 'but each man has a responsibility to create what they want to create. Too often, men and women don't see who they are and what they're responsible for creating. You, Harry, must always be responsible for what you create.'

"He never said anything more about that, but I know that while he was alive and we were growing up, I tried my very best to be aware of what I was thinking and doing, and creating. I guess, now that I'm talking about it, I did care more about pleasing him than I even realized. He was quiet, but boy, did he have strength and a moral conviction that always led him to do what he called the right thing. Maybe, he and Mom got that from their meditating. Now that I know that they literally raised us—the whole family—in the light of the Brotherhood, with all the listening that entails, I understand better what he meant. I think he meant that we all need to be aware of what it is that we think and do, and say and feel, so we don't create consequences in the world that go against what our highest nature would want to create. As I grew up, I really tried to understand what was the best way to do the right thing, and you know, the only times an answer came to me, a really right and true answer, were the times when I listened to that voice inside me."

Becky smiled as she listened. I could see that she respected what I said. Yet I knew that she still wasn't quite sure how to be with me, and I smiled inside myself as the thought crossed my mind. "Yes, Becky, little brothers do grow up," I said with a sheepish grin on my face. Becky smiled. We spoke more of Mom and Dad and how they must have worked hard at being on their own path, yet at the same time finding a way to prepare us for our own sacred journey with the Brotherhood and our role as protectors of the forest. Becky and I both agreed that they had a faith about them that all things were in their right order. I think they knew that if Becky or I didn't take the path of working with the Brotherhood, then others who were on the path would come to help protect the forest and its secrets.

We sat around the farm's large kitchen table for some time. As the sun poured in from the south, golden rays filled the room and I knew we felt more comfortable together than we ever had before. We reminisced about our youth, and spoke in amazement about our life now with the Brotherhood. By now it was mid-morning, and Becky went off to call Bill to arrange to have lunch with him. As it turned out, this worked fine for me, for as she went to the phone the Guardian's familiar voice came to invite me to a meeting in the forest. When Becky got back, I told her about this, and so we went our ways, she to get ready for her luncheon with Bill, and I to my meeting with the Brotherhood.

CHAPTER THIRTY-FOUR
A SPECIAL FOREST MEETING

Days pass, nights go by, but love of life itself still reigns as the key to returning home ... to you!

Without knowing why, I felt a great sense of anticipation as I walked through the forest heading for a meeting at the oak log with the Guardian. The Guardian had invited me this morning and I wondered what it was all about. The Guardian's voice came to me as I hurried to our meeting place. He said, "Today we asked you to come to the forest for a special meeting with someone you've not seen for a long, long time." I didn't know what to think, but inside me I felt a gentle excitement, like a wisp of wind on a summer day, a kind breeze dusting my skin, my face, my eyes.

The forest whispers songs of yore
Songs of winter summer and the fall
All in the springtime of days gone by
Yes we see
The trees we are
... see
We see the love gone by...
We see the recapturing of Light
like a bird landing on a gentle lake
the surface calm until arrive the dove
the eagle, the egret, the seagull

Not all land on the water
Not all know the essence of Light life
But all know that the return of love is a joy
... to all life
All in the universe
All in the heart of the One

The forest sings to you today, Harry Pond
We sing to your courage
And hail the Master you
Become
Receive her well ...
Receive her well ...
Receive eternal Light "I AM"

I was about to ask more when I rounded the corner and there at the meeting place stood Sakya, and with him stood the most beautiful woman I had ever seen. I stopped in my tracks and stared. Almost as tall as me, with brown hair that shone bright in the early fall midday sun, she wore a loose fitting gown that flowed over her body like a veil down to the ground. I couldn't tell the material, only that it glowed like a milky white opal gem imbued with pale pastel accents of pink and blue, giving it the appearance of being almost transparent. But that was not all! For though the gown was almost see-through, behind it, instead of seeing the body of the woman, I saw only shining light, as if her whole being were made not of flesh and bones, but of light itself!

Sakya waved a kind greeting to me, but I couldn't answer. Astonished, I found myself speechless. My thoughts raced. I know her, I told myself, it's because I know her that I can't speak. But it was more than that. Her familiarity stirred a place deep within and a certain sort of fear arose within me. My body shook as I approached the two, Sakya in his seven foot tall eminence, and beside him, this strangely familiar woman.

Sakya smiled again, and I knew his smile was an effort to comfort me. Still, when I arrived before him and the woman, I almost collapsed. She was so beautiful, so pure and sure of herself, so different, and yet so familiar. I felt a deep pain in my chest, the exact place that Sakya had called the seat of the soul, where the heart and memories of the Divine meet. The woman smiled. Her eyes blue, like mine, sparkled bright in the midday sun and her smile lit up her face as her cheeks turned a rosy red. I looked at her with what must have been a troubled look on my face. She said, "It's all right to smile back, it's been a very long time. You can relax now, Sakya and I will explain all to you."

I took a deep breath. I hadn't realized it, but I'd been holding my breath, and now as I began to relax, I managed a small, boyish smile. I felt shy and confused. For a moment, all around us became silent, as if the woods, the trees, the bird and the animals of the forest disappeared and we, the three us, stood alone on a vast sea of timeless life. I heard the woman speak, this time her words came from deep within me.

"Your shock at seeing me is understandable. We've not been together for a long, long time. But, I've come now to remind you, and to tell you," she said, as her voice resonated softly within me, "that we will indeed be together again. The journey on Earth is a hard one for every soul, but in the completion comes the remembrance, and with the remembrance comes the joining together of the twin elements of the soul, male and female."

As she spoke I could hardly stand it. So deep was the pain I felt in my soul that the world around me had no substance. I saw visions of lives gone by, first in this one, then in others. Different forms, different names, different places, but all me, and she was there. But, all was not ideal. I saw us together, parting, together again, and again. My pain was hers, hers mine. We were the same, yet so different here on Earth. She in her woman's form and thoughts, I in my maleness, with my own set of ideas. We simply didn't understand.

My mind swirled as her words continued, "Yes, we've been together countless times, and not always in the most wonderful of circumstances." Different visions came, visions of us loving each other deeply. Calmer ones now passed through my mind. It all happened so fast, this meeting in the forest, my introduction to her, and now the intimate viewing of so many times, so many lives, me and the woman standing before me, looking different, but the same, a beautiful woman, this very woman, the very same energy, the very same eyes! My mind spun as my logical brain tried to step in to make sense of what was happening. As instructed by the woman, I tried my best to remain calm. I breathed deeply as I watched and listened to the story.

"Harry," she said, "long before you brought yourself here to the realms of Earth, you lived for many, many lives in another place, at another frequency, and I lived there with you." With her words came images of a place that looked like it existed in a sea of clouds, white-gray clouds. A place, a building of sorts, with Greek-like columns and an endlessly tall cupola-like roof above, without doors, or windows, just the columns and the open sky full of clouds all around. A balcony with railings of shorter columns surrounded the building. From this place, she and I viewed the world around us, a world aglow with billowy clouds, ever moving, never ending. These clouds, I knew, never changed, never went away, never turned from day to night, never from gray to blue, never from fall to winter, spring to summer. No, they were always there. As I watched I felt it all, so alive, so familiar. I knew this place and excitement began to well within me.

I saw myself there, very tall, close to Sakya's height, and her there with me, much taller than now, with light golden orange hair, and eyes that sparkled blue as now. We laughed together as we looked outside to a land of fallen rocks, gentle breezes and a river of a water-like substance that radiated a pall orange light as it meandered over the land. No, this was not Earth, yet our smile came from our sense of contentment at being together in this very special place.

The scene shifted then, dramatically. Something had happened. No longer in our idyllic temple, we were amongst crowds of people here on Earth after a great tragedy. We were lost from each other. I saw scene after scene of each of us, living our lives—different clothing, different faces, different times; always attracted to each other, always coming together, life after life, each time never staying together. I saw the tragedy—a catastrophe in the heavens, many had perished, and yes, I'd been involved, been a leader, and been wrong! Very wrong! I saw her then, struggling to convince me not to participate, not to leave our life together, but I had, and it had caused us to fall. I'd followed others. They'd told me of the power that I could get by lending my energies to the expedition, and I had gone, hungry for I knew not what. I'd been naïve, had followed, become one of those who lead the expedition, and, sadly, I saw that many had perished ... a whole world—a planet, Maldek—exploded into the heavens.

Now, the vision shifted back to Earth. I saw me, lifetime after lifetime, wanting to hide, wanting never to remember, never to remind myself of being involved, or my role in the horror, or even my true name. And it had worked, for a time, in a way, I became asleep, and it was okay, because I didn't want to know, to remember. I saw her choice: to follow me here, even after the horror, to bring me back home, to our world, that other place, that other time, but she couldn't. So strong was my own desire to never remember, never know myself that I pushed her away, lifetime, after lifetime, after lifetime.

I watched it all as tears filled my eyes, and I knew that I wouldn't be able to hide from myself ever again. Sakya came to me then, his strong, assured voice resonating in my head. "We're here to continue the learning and Celuin's presence is helping you remember. We must go now, we have another to meet. We will return here soon and you'll have more time together. But for now, please follow me." Reluctantly, I agreed, and I followed Sakya down the main path, my head still spinning from my meeting with the woman Sakya called Celuin. We walked on a smaller forest path leading directly north into a denser part of the forest that I couldn't remember ever having visited before. I couldn't help but look back to assure myself that Celuin was still there.

My meeting with Celuin had shaken my sense of myself. Uncertainty filled me—I no longer felt certain that the "Harry Pond," the "me," that I had known myself to be since my childhood, was really who I was. Surely, my own memories were real. But now, after my visit with her and the dimensions of existence I saw us together in, they felt expanded, stretched in all directions, in all dimensions, as if the sky had opened up and rayed forth rainbows of new insights, thoughts, and feelings about my identity, my life, and myself, and not all of them positive!

CHAPTER THIRTY-FIVE
THE LIGHT OF GOD ALWAYS PREVAILS

We struggle, we fight, we ask ourselves how we will ever "arrive" at our destination, yet we know; deep within we know that we are all One and that all is well

I spoke to Sakya as we stopped for a moment along the path, "Please, Sakya, tell me what's going on? I feel so very confused. You've taught me about my past, and I've even seen visions of lives lived before this one. But now, my meeting with Celuin has opened my inner vision beyond where I've been before. Frankly, Sakya, I feel scared."

"You feel the awakening," he said, "and you fear it. This is natural for one that comes in touch with that which he has most wanted to avoid knowing about himself. You've not wanted to remember, and, like many others who are awakening at this time, you feel shaken and afraid to be reminded. But, you cannot turn back. That which Celuin showed you *is* your own history. Every master must learn to be with, see, and accept that which he or she brings forth in memory about their own unique journey, to be with it, to own it as the truth of his or her own lives lived, his or her own life stream.

"No one can do this for you, this owning. None of us of the Brotherhood can magically make this past go away. Were we to try, we wouldn't be able. The life of each being in the universe is recorded on the records of time. And in time, each comes home to those records to own the events of the life stream that they've lived. It's the path of the Master. A path followed by only those who've come to a place in their own evolution where they wish to know themselves, their true nature and identity, more than they wish to stay asleep."

White billowy clouds passed overhead as we stood in the forest. Sakya looked down at me from his seven foot height with a broad smile of friendship and compassion, as he continued to speak to me in my mind.

"When you come to that place, Harry," he said, "as you have, you realize that you can never turn back. That knowledge that you've asked to be given to you in your own soul, now comes forth. And if you wished to turn back the pages and not remember that which you've so tried to forget, you could not.

"Remembering *you* is *the* path of Mastery, for to remember yourself, to remember *all* of you, to know *all* of you including the memory of your roots, your *birth* in the Light of the One, and to forgive yourself when necessary for those actions that you judged yourself as not being of Light,

IS the only way forward. Then, and only then, can you forget again the things that had so pained you from your past and be reborn in the Light of your own true nature. In fact, it's then that you have your *own* Mastery of life that can be consciously accepted, Harry Pond, and go on to merge with the greater self, a greater self with only One consciousness, the consciousness of the Unity of all things with the One."

I struggled to understand. Sakya's smile made me know that he knew my difficulties. Who was I? Who was listening to Sakya? Was I Harry Pond the person I'd known myself all this time to be, or was I something grander than that, a part of a greater self, whose consciousness was merged within a greater reality—one that I was just now beginning to touch?

As we continued to walk further along the path, I realized that the path had been created fairly recently, with the dense brush that grew at the base of the tall sycamores gently swept to the side. I say "swept" because unlike other forest paths that I'd seen or been involved in creating with my father as a youngster, this one felt like it had been made, not by humans wielding a machete, but rather by a gentle breeze intent on moving the underbrush.

We walked on and soon came to a circular clearing, where sycamores and ancient white oaks joined to create an amphitheatre like opening in the forest. It was here that Sakya had me wait for my meeting. He didn't tell what it was all about. Instead, as he walked away into the forest, the outlines of his massive body already beginning to fade, he turned and smiled. Speaking to me in my mind, he said, "Have faith. Though you may not understand all that's happening in your conscious mind, the higher part of you, the part that has called forth for full knowledge of your own true essence and self, is in charge and is able to ensure that all is in right order."

And with that, Sakya was gone. I sat down on a fallen log that reached into almost the center of the small clearing, baffled. Having met Celuin, all I wanted to do was to go back to be with her. But here I sat, alone in the forest as the afternoon sun began to fade behind the tallest sycamores. What was I doing there? Why had Sakya taken me away from my meeting with Celuin? What could be so important?

I didn't have to wait long for my answer. Within minutes of Sakya's departure, I heard a ringing in my ear—a sound that had been with me now for several months—and I knew what it meant. It meant that I would be receiving a message, a short one, from the Angels of Light who worked with me. Of course, I'd known about angels before, and I even called the Guardian my *guardian angel*, but somewhere within me I hadn't quite believed, really believed, that angels, lots of angels, existed.

Despite the fact of the Brotherhood's training these past months, that I'd actually seen the invisible become visible, that I felt the deepest of love in my heart for the Brotherhood and the "path of Mastery" that I was learning, I still had doubts, doubts about the reality of it all. Yes, Becky and I were in this together and even Bill's mother confirmed the reality of the Brotherhood and of the world of Light that existed everywhere. But the day to day reality of living in America, talking with my neighbors about the crops and how we all hoped the Ohio State Buckeye's would do well this coming season, competed with this new reality. I still doubted the truth of the world of Light altogether, but I couldn't deny my own experience of working with Sakya and the others, and the truth of the Light world all around!

I sat, my head slightly tilted to the side, listening as if for a far away sound, a sound once heard, but lost, and now again returned. The words came now, as always, short and to the point. "Celuin will not stay. She came to aide you in remembering. Humankind has forgotten a past filled with both hope and tragedy. You've seen this, and now you heal, for you're neither the hope that was lost so many times, nor the tragedy of events in which you participated. Instead, you are the real *you* who's called forth within your soul a call to remember and know your true self. Remember, as your heart opens to the truth, *you are the Light on the path that you must follow*. With or without Celuin you are that Light that will lead you on."

As the words faded in my mind, I felt tears fill my eyes and I began to cry; a cry so deep and uncontrollable that I thought in the midst of it that I would never be able to stop. It all seemed too much for me. Meeting Celuin, then losing her, then being told that I had all I needed to find my true nature, when I felt nowhere near being able to lead myself on such a journey. So the tears came, and I let them flow. I stayed there, alone in the forest for I don't know how long, my arms crossed on my knees, my head nestled in the crook of my arms, sobbing. I felt exhausted and drained in a way that I'd rarely felt before.

A new sound in the forest aroused me, a sound that rippled through the clearing as if a fresh breeze stirred the trees awake from a long and deep sleep. But as I looked up, no breeze touched my face, no wind brushed my hair, and the forest remained still. I sat curious for a moment, then, across the clearing from where I sat, a most glorious orange glow began to take form. Cloudy at first, it came more and more into focus.

I watched with awe as the orange light, initially opaque and foggy around the edges, began to take on the shape of a very large man with whitish hair, glowing deep blue-violet eyes, attired in flowing robes of orange and gold. Over these months, I'd seen Sakya appear and disappear before and I had gotten used to it, at least somewhat. For Sakya seemed to me to be, even in his heightened state of consciousness, still somewhat of a "man," one who'd lived on Earth, yet one who'd sought and found the secret to higher states of existence. Yes, a very extraordinary man, but nonetheless still somewhat recognizable to me. But now something more was happening. My heart beat wildly in my chest at the presence of this being. My thoughts calmed and my being relaxed into a state of pure ecstasy. Without thought of doing so, I stood to greet this visitor, and at that moment, I knew that I knew him, and that my love for him was very old, and very deep. My heart smiled.

The rippling sound continued around him, as if this being brought with him waves of energy from a distant place, a place that I personally didn't know, but one that I knew must be of great power. And now, as the sound stopped, I found myself moving from the log towards him. As I did so, I felt each of my steps, one by one, somehow merging with the orange and gold wisps of cloud-like energy still emanating from the robed stranger. Aware only of the pure beauty of the one before me, and of the incredible feelings of love that I possessed for him, I couldn't tell how I actually traversed the distance between us. As I found myself facing him, looking up into the eyes of one so very, very, old, I knew that it didn't matter how I had gotten there. Words seemed unnecessary. For life felt full and content simply to be in the presence of one so grand.

He smiled as I moved now only a foot or two from him, and as he did, a deep purple blue radiance shone forth from his eyes, a radiance as deep as the deepest ocean, and as vast as the starriest of nights. My whole being relaxed as I felt rush through me a sense of compassion and care for not just the entity before me, but for the whole world. My entire body seemed to lighten, and for a moment, just a moment, I actually thought myself beginning to float, so light did I feel. As I stood looking deep into the eyes of this glorious being before me, I knew that this was the Guardian, the very one who'd been with me all this time, and I, too, smiled a smile of pure love and joy.

The Guardian's words resonated within me as they'd done so many, many times before. "Harry," he said, "the time is urgent and though I'm greatly privileged to spend time with you in this way, great danger looms near and we must act!" The Guardian's words resounded with a sense of urgency, yet I experienced only a feeling of the ecstasy. It was as though he brought great wealth with him, not of money, but of pure joyfulness. He moved closer to me, his form still within the orange and gold mist.

"We have much to do, so please listen well," he said. But I couldn't. I stood frozen before him. His was not the strong and solid presence of a Sakya, who brought forth great wisdom and kindness and, indeed, always amazed me at his ability to appear and disappear before me at will. Sakya was a great teacher, a teacher of old committed to helping those who seek the answers of heaven and earth, and helping them to find those answers. But, before me stood not a teacher, but a God! The Guardian seemed to come from a place and carry energies that were far removed from Earth and its solidity. His being continued to glow a misty orange gold light about him, and the words he spoke in my head, although spoken from the same voice that I had heard so many times before, came to me as if he stood within my very being, filling my cells with his essence. I felt I was in heaven on Earth, and even though the Guardian's words resonated of urgency and need, I had no place for them in such a reality.

He seemed to know this, for in the very next moment he moved forward and embraced my shoulder and gently led me to sit on the fallen log at the edge of the clearing where I'd been crying only a few moments before. His touch felt as a wisp of wind, not like a touch at all, as if the air itself were moving me. It gave me ground, as if saying, "It's all right to feel what you feel, but it's also a time of great urgency on Earth, and so earthly actions are needed, even as you feel the heavenly vibrations of your own true nature."

Despite feeling so filled with the heavenly Light only a moment before, I could once again feel the familiar earth beneath my feet. Even as I sat there, I knew, almost as if waking from a dream, that the Guardian had come to tell me something important, something I needed to hear, and something upon which I must act ... and soon.

"Harry," his voice resonated within me, "life on Earth is a challenge of light and darkness. As we've taught, upon descent to the vibrations of the physical plane of Earth, God-Man's and God-Woman's vision of their own true Source became clouded as *survival* mind replaced God Mind. At the extremes, humanity developed thoughts and ways to be on Earth that incorporated activities, feelings, beliefs and actions that focused on the duality of earthly light and darkness, on good and bad. At one extreme, special mystery schools sponsored by higher forces of the One were created across Earth to help those wanting to maintain their memory and connection to their Source. At the other, parts of humanity, obsessed with surviving the Earth experience with power, created concepts of logical mind and survival mind to control what was seen by them as an animal-like existence on Earth, rather than one directly connected to God Mind. This element of humankind focused on controlling its destiny on Earth by seeking and gaining control of life, including having control and power over other human beings and the resources of Earth.

"Where what we call the forces of Light developed schools, religions, churches and even cultures to focus on humanity's source in God Mind, the forces of the dark created structures of power that rejected or minimized the influence of the Light as the source of all—choosing instead to focus on the logic of survival, power, force and corruption. Some *sleeping gods*, as we call them, rejected the existence of the One entirely, while others of these sleeping ones sought to control the religious orders and institutions that were originally based on the true existence of a higher Light in all. Because of this, doctrines arose within religions that limited God-Man's and God-Woman's view of themselves. Humanity lost its direct connection to the One and to the purer qualities of its own *Beingness*. Instead, humankind became a creation separate from its Source—unaware of it in day to day, moment to moment existence—unable to connect with the essence of its own true nature.

"With these corrupting doctrines in place, the forces of darkness began to exercise control over every aspect of institutional life on Earth. But as it's seen this will change in the years ahead as circumstances within the universe are making it possible for more consciousness of the truth of the One to come forth on Earth.

"In this place, we've come to a crossroad. Those with ill intent toward the *Light* have formulated a plan to destroy the forest. This must not happen. You must return to the farm and consult with Becky and Bill. Becky will know what to do." By instinct I stood, ready to move to action as I had been trained to do and done so many times before, but the gentle voice of the Guardian spoke again of calm and of faith.

"This isn't a war of man against man. In a sense, no war is of man against man. This is a challenge of Light to still the confusion and pain caused by those who still work within the consciousness of earthly darkness. It is, as it has always been here on Earth, the job of Light to confront darkness, to embrace the Oneness and expand the consciousness of One Great Spirit. So," he continued, "go with calm and peace in your being, for the Light of God always prevails, and the one who knows this, knows that all is and ever has been safe in the hands of the Oneness."

I began to ask one of the many questions that swirled in my head, but the Guardian's words, so clear and direct, rang within me and quieted my questioning mind. Indeed, I thought, I have no questions to ask, and no place to go, and I knew in that very moment that my life would ever be one of service to that Light that Always Prevails.

Buoyed by this knowledge of my own commitment, I stood and stepped forward directly into the cloud of orange and gold energy surrounding the Guardian, seeking to embrace him, to thank him for all. As I crossed into the orange field, I found nothing to touch as the Guardian's body, which I naturally thought to be solid, simply disappeared. I found myself filled with a glorious ecstatic feeling, a feeling too grand for words as his energies blended with mine. I knew then that this was the life of the Masters of Brotherhood of Light, men and women who lived once as solid beings on Earth, and now lived instead as Beings of Light, filled with the grace of the Great Light of the Oneness.

I felt embraced in the field of orange energy, but not by a man, but by the Light itself. The Guardian spoke to me, and his voice felt like my own as it rang out like a clear bell within every cell of my being. "Be proud, to follow your own path home. Your own voice will never fail you. We love you, and thank you. Without your commitment and the commitment of others on Earth to help the Light, all our efforts would come to naught. In the true sense of the word, you, Becky, Bill, his mother, your mother and father, and so many, many others are now and have ever been the life force, the hands of the Light here on Earth. Be proud!

A feeling of contentment washed over me, a slow and steady sense of the rightness of things in my world, that whatever happened and whatever I did or didn't do in the future would all be well. Being in unity with the Guardian in this way gave me the feeling that I was living above Earth and not on it. I reveled in this feeling as I stood within the midst of his Light.

But all too soon, my reverie came to an end as I felt the Guardian begin to fade. I wanted to yell "Stop, don't go, I love you, I need you," but I couldn't. Even in my feeling of despair at his leaving I knew that my plea came not from a place of self awareness and mastery, nor from that place within me that knew what it needed to do to help the Light in this time of danger, but from the little boy inside who wanted to stay protected in the arms of the Light forever. I wanted to nurture that little boy, take care of him, hold him to me, but I knew I couldn't, at least not now, for the danger seemed too great!

CHAPTER THIRTY-SIX
MEETING VARNESS "PASSAGE TO THE HEAVENS"

Seek your own essence of Light and you will find it in the everyday reality of existence

I found myself alone in the forest, this place in which I had spent so many, many, hours as a boy, and knew and loved so very well. Instinctively, I wrapped my arms around myself. I stood for a moment with my eyes closed bathing in the remaining glow of my encounter with the Guardian. The morning sun's rays poured through the leaves of the trees to fully bath my face and body. I stayed like this for only a little while, reveling in the warmth of the sun, my eyes closed. Suddenly, I sensed a presence with me in the clearing. I opened my eyes and quickly looked around, wondering who or what it was. Then, I saw it! There on the ground across the clearing at precisely the spot where the Guardian had originally appeared, stood a brilliant, shiny bejeweled chest, radiating such a strong light that I needed to squint my eyes to look directly at it. Cloud-like wisps of the Guardian's orange and gold Light swirled around the chest, and then they were gone.

I stood there for a moment, frozen. My experience with the Guardian still filled me, but the appearance of the chest brought me back to earthly reality with a shock. I wanted to stay in the warmth of the Guardian's presence, but I couldn't. I wanted to ignore the chest, but I knew better. Inside me, I felt the pull of my own inner instinct, my own inner voice, and I knew that I must go to the chest and, beyond all logic, "know it" and even "love it!"

As I approached the chest across the clearing, I wondered what it meant to love it and know it. This was a box, about a foot and a half wide, two-and-a-half feet long, and a foot-and-a-half-high, an inanimate object. My inner voice argued against my own logic. "This isn't just a box," it said. From every side it radiated rays of rainbow colors. Glowing gemstones embedded in the outer walls of the chest—red ruby-like stones, blue-violet sapphires, and radiant green emeralds—combined with other colored stones, merged with the morning sunlight and created a fireworks of blossoming color!

I squinted my eyes again as I approached the chest. Even with my eyes half shut, an inkling of memory skirted the corners of my mind. I remembered this chest from somewhere. I'd seen it before! It was different than I remembered, glowing but less brilliant, less, full of Light! Flashes of those memories came, Dad and me, yes, the workshop, Uncle

Julius' workshop! Then I remembered all, this chest, Uncle Julius' pride in making it, and my father's equal pride in him. Indeed, here sat before me the very same bejeweled chest that Uncle Julius had shown us that time before I left for the war. This was that very one, I had no doubt about it!

But something about it had changed. As I stood before it, the chest pulsated with energy, an energy that began to fill me as I came closer to it. I wanted to laugh, I wanted to cry. I felt so alive, so full of life. The closer I came, the more I felt the actual *presence* of the chest, as if it were a living being. This chest was alive! I could feel it! My heart raced with excitement.

This was not the chest I'd seen at my Uncle Julius' that day. Exquisite as it was, as wonderful a piece of work as it was, as incredibly beautiful in its glowing essence as it was, it was not the same as now. Now, it was imbued with an essence of life and I fell in love with that life. I wanted to live forever, and I couldn't imagine being happier than in that moment. The Guardian's voice came to me then, so different from my physical merging with him, yet so full of that familiar vibration.

"This is Varness, whose name means Passage to the Heavens. Both you and Becky have had introductions to the chest before, and now the both of you and others will get to know Varness more intimately, for her powers are many as you'll find in the days ahead. For now, it's best to know that Varness is an ally who will help you protect the forest. Varness is no ordinary chest. It's sacred, and has been impregnated with the blessings, desires, energies, and even the consciousness of many entities of the Light for the sole purpose of helping those who seek to find their way. Working with Varness, you'll find that her only rule is that her powers may be used to only serve the Light!"

I listened intently to the Guardians words as a rushing of images flooded my mind. I saw myself standing beside a woman on a high hill that was covered with the greenest of green grasses. We'd just climbed the long distance to the top and looked down into a lush valley of golden light. Her face seemed familiar, but from where, I didn't know. We stood, quiet, atop the hill. Together we knew that we'd achieved a great victory in reaching its heights, and knew as well that the pathway down into the golden valley would be easier, than the journey this far. The sun warmed our faces, and we smiled at each other, a smile at life and at the joy we felt. We were in love with it all. But, the vision lasted only a moment before the Guardian's words continued. Deep down *I knew* in that moment that one day this vision would come to pass.

"We begin your lessons with Varness," the Guardian said, and for the next four hours the Guardian and Varness communicated information to me about the forest, its place on Earth, in the universe, and beyond and about those who oppose the knowledge of the Light. During this time I became more than a student learning from the masters, but a companion on their journey as they showed me vision after vision of the Brotherhood's efforts on Earth. Each vision came alive with gemstones vibrating with color even more brilliant than before. The chest literally pulsated with energy as it radiated the *feelings* and *emotions* of the Guardian's stories. I became not a viewer, but a participant, fully alive to the possibilities of each moment.

I saw the forest in days of old with secret societies of seekers who worked with the Brotherhood to discover their true nature. I felt what it was like to be side by side along the journey of those who sought. I saw other schools, in forests, caves, deserts, plains, mountains, islands, and on boats on the sea, in places throughout the world where the Brotherhood taught those who were willing to learn. From sacred places in the Gobi desert to those in the deepest jungles of Africa and South America, I saw schools filled with different faces, teachers and students from different times throughout the history of humanity's stay on Earth. *I felt* each time what it was like to be there. Along with the schools came the great sadness of the Brotherhood. With every school, with each group of seekers, came often the threat of destruction. No matter what the time in history, no matter where the place, the forces of darkness inevitably came to challenge the expansion of knowledge of the Light on Earth.

All the while, the Guardian and Varness led me on as a team, working together to take me deep within each teaching, each experience. In this way, I came to understand the workings of Varness and the Brotherhood, and indeed, how Varness' unique powers and role helped seekers experience the *feelings* of their own awakening, their own enlightenment, and help them to know the reality of the world of Light and their relationship to it. In one instance, I heard the Guardian's voice and saw a scene of students in what seemed like this very forest, long ago, learning with the Brotherhood and Varness about the healing ways of the Brotherhood. While that was happening I could actual *feel* the experience of what was being taught through Varness as waves of feelings and knowledge and wisdom poured through me as the gems on the chest, pulsating pure Light and energy, embraced me with their radiant beauty. I felt myself to be both student and lesson all at the same time in a wild play of vision, depth of emotion, and joyful sense of completion in knowing the full wisdom of a thing, from question to answer, to the knowledge of the source of both.

I learned of the concept of living holograms, of the complete knowledge we hold within us of emotionally charged life events from this and from past life experiences, held in single, internalized pictures of the event. I learned that we hold these events within not just as pictures.

They're held as full holographic remembrances of entire scenes that no matter when they actually occurred, feel just as real now as then, as if these living events have just happened, along with all the feelings, emotions, physical sensations, sounds, smells, and even deep soul connection to them.

I learned that positive emotions and feelings associated with the Light come with us from lifetime to lifetime and help us build remembrance of the One within us, while negative emotions carry with them fear, hurt, anger, pain and other emotions that confuse us and keep us from focusing and knowing our Light.

I learned that without healing these negatively charged holograms, including the needed healing of our feelings and remembrances of the people relationships we had or still have with those who participated in them with us, they remain within us, carried within what the Guardian called our soul vehicle, until we address and heal them. From lifetime to lifetime these many pictures, or holograms of fear, attachment, hurt and other such negative emotional charges lead us on, influencing our life choices, creating relationships with others as they hold us to replay the same set of emotional charges that existed in the original holograms, until they're healed!

So powerful are these negative holograms and the emotions they contain, the Guardian said, that they keep us from opening our eyes to *see* who we truly are. Without healing, we find ourselves plagued in every lifetime with the same untouchable fear as we encounter situations similar to the one that brought forth the emotion in the first place, or find these fears triggered by other seemingly unconnected circumstances — like a visit to a new place that suddenly feels familiar, a sound that stirs, or even a smell that reminds us of the original emotion.

The Guardian and Varness taught me that it's the nature of these negative emotional charges that, like a magnet, calls them forth to us for healing. The emotional charge draws to us a situation in this life that may free us from the negative experience. Without our conscious focus on healing, we tend to structure our lives from one to the next trying to avoid the fears, never really knowing what it is that's "wrong with us." We continue to run into similar situations time and time again until one day, we finally decide to seek out and find the path to healing.

"The soul remembers its origins and wants its freedom!" the Guardian said. "So rather than being able to run away from these situations, the soul is drawn time and again back to similar situations to allow each of us the opportunity to release the painful memory that's holding back the soul's freedom."

***

I wondered about my own holograms of fear, wondering if I would have the courage to face them as did the students I watched. Varness' presence would help, I knew, for that was one of her great gifts, the ability to help one see the root source of one's hidden fears, and then nurture the student, smoothing the way for the healing to happen.

The radiating gemstones embedded within Varness' walls seemed to be the key to the healing power of the chest. Their beautiful rays penetrated deep within each cell of the body of each student, seeking out those places within the cell that held the most powerful of the negative emotional charges. I watched as these magical rays of Light helped warm each student's heart to give them the courage to face their most powerfully charged emotional traumas. Then, with the help of the Master from the Brotherhood of Light, I watched as each student stood in the midst of those emotional traumas and released them from the depth of their being forever.

In all this, Varness played an active role as partner in the healing, as if the chest were endowed with its own wisdom and knowledge about how best to assist a student in becoming a Master. I didn't understand it all, but my heart raced with excitement at the thought of working with the Guardian and Varness on my own charged holograms to help me learn to do what I'd seen other student from the past do: confirm the existence of these painful memories, and then enlighten their soul by releasing them forever.

***

The Guardian came to me. "Yes, Harry, the truth is that you and other seekers need to have an abundance of courage to outweigh the fears you've gathered within yourself. This is what life is made up of on Earth, the duality of each individuals own soul journey, and the inability of one to truly find one's enlightenment on that journey without looking at what it is that keeps one in fear. These untouchables, as we call them, relate to events or situations that have happened to one on Earth, or things one has done that a person judges within themselves as too painful or frightening to remember. It is fear of coming in conscious contact with these untouchables that keeps humanity from knowing its true essence within the Consciousness of Oneness!

"Fear keeps the individual from seeking their own true nature. In seeking this nature, countless searchers have been rewarded with quiet moments within. When one goes beyond fear, one finds his or her true place in the universe, or should we say, one remembers one's true place in the universe! It's this remembrance that each and every soul on Earth has within, if they choose to look.

CHAPTER THIRTY-SEVEN
FELIX'S DECISION

Know your name ... Know your life ... Forget your true name ... Forget to live your true life

Waiting for the others in the woods by the old forest service road, Felix Butezz nodded his head in confirmation of his decision. Yes, he had made a good choice. Rather than follow the original plan to secure the forest and the chest for his father, he would implement his own plan. He'd struggled hard now for two weeks with his own desire to find the chest, his desire to keep it for himself, and the sure knowledge of his father's wrath should he pursue such a path. His resentment at his father's abuse had grown over these past few weeks since his last visit with him, a resentment that had expanded in proportion to his desire to have the chest for his own. At times he'd thought himself crazy to even think such a thought, but the pull of the chest led him more and more to view the idea of keeping it for himself as a realistic one.

He had thought it all out and to him the simplicity of his plan bordered on genius. Standing in the clearing alone, minutes before the others arrived, he congratulated himself on it. In broad outline, his plan called for nothing less than the destruction of the forest, but not before, he got his hands on the treasure chest. His father would be upset, but that didn't bother him, since the plan called for Felix to disappear after the event and never be seen or heard of again, especially not by his father. He would never let his father intimidate or abuse him again.

Felix reasoned that this time, he'd be the one that would get the better of his Daddy and he wouldn't be able to do a thing to him. Felix surmised that he might miss his father, but the thought of living a life of luxury far away from Daddy seemed well worth it. He knew that in taking the path that he planned, his father's wrath would make it impossible for him to ever return. All this he contemplated as the others began to arrive.

CHAPTER THIRTY-EIGHT
A ROOM OVERLOOKING THE FOREST

Others did their part, you do yours; now enjoy the gifts of the knowledge of the Light

I stayed in the forest only a while longer that day. My life would never be the same. But as I walked home late in the afternoon, I knew that this was not yet my time. The Guardian's warning about the danger to the forest echoed strongly within me, but my meetings with Celuin and the Guardian, and my experience with Varness had filled me with a sense of hope, wonder, and anticipation about the future. My focus now must be, I knew, on the safety of the forest. It needed to be protected, and I remembered the Guardian's words, "Becky will know what to do."

Becky wasn't there when I arrived. She'd left me a note on the kitchen table saying that she and Bill had decided to take a short trip to the mountains in neighboring Pennsylvania and that they'd be back in a few days. I didn't know exactly what to do next, as I was certain, as the Guardian had said that Becky held the key to ensuring the safety of the forest. As I could do nothing about her and Bill's departure, I decided that the best thing to do was to stay around the farm for the next few days to be there in case they decided to call.

***

The next morning I got up filled with energy. The rising sun poured through the windows of my bedroom providing much needed warmth after a cooler than usual night. The events of the previous day still filled me as I dressed and went down for breakfast. With no word from Becky, I decided that staying around the farm doing some handyman work was the best way to ensure that I'd be there if Becky and Bill called. My plan was to work first on the old warped doors that hardly fit the openings of the upstairs bedrooms. The farm was nearly one hundred years old, and besides the ever-present squeaky stairs, the foundations of the main farmhouse had settled over the years causing what Dad used to call, the door problem. So, with some degree of commitment and a touch of nostalgia, I decided that my first handyman project would be to fix the door to my parents' bedroom. I'd not spent much time in that bedroom even as a child. They were, well, secretive, and as a child when we did anything at all together indoors, it was mostly downstairs in the living room.

As I stood before their bedroom door with tools ready in hand, my mind wondered to all the times when I had curiously looked into their bedroom, wanting to go in, rummage about, and see what I could find. In my private reverie, I imagined that I'd find all sorts of magical objects with miraculous and special powers, able to transform the world around me. But I never did go in.

The room stayed empty since there passing. Except for Becky's weekly dusting, neither she nor I had spent any time exploring Mom and Dad's possessions. Yes, we'd talked about what we might do with their clothing and other things, but for now, we'd decided to leave everything the way it was when they were alive, at least for a little while longer.

But now, as I began the door project, my curiosity, and even a vague sense of need to find completion with them, led me into their space, a space that had once been off limits, but now opened to me, as if the room itself had been awaiting my presence. Words and impressions filled my senses as I passed through the room's narrow entryway that led into the bedroom's main sitting area. "Harry," the room seemed to whisper to me, "this is a sacred space, their sanctuary, walk with reverence here."

The bedroom was really two rooms in one, a bedroom and a French style salon or sitting room. Originally a second story addition to the old farmhouse's one story kitchen, Mom and Dad had had the walls of these two upstairs rooms broken down to create their large bedroom. Now combined into one, these rooms came together in the northeastern corner of the house, which during the morning hours, became a sun-filled oasis as the Ohio sun rose across the verdant, ready-to-harvest fields to the east and south. Floor to ceiling picture windows at this corner of the house on both the north and eastern walls gave the room a sense of being part of the outside landscape, rather than a separate bedroom in a separate farmhouse. In fact, this is what I remembered most about the room the few times I was allowed into it as a boy, that it felt like its own world, a bit like a spaceship ready for launch at the just the right moment.

Mom and Dad's ever present armchairs sat at the foot of the picture windows facing outward to the north looking directly onto the lush green forest. From here, the forest spread north and east with individual branching arms leading off along the way to access paths to the other four farm families. Besides access through these paths, the forest protected its secrets with a dense ring of underbrush around its outer edges, blocking access to the curious bicyclist, or others, seeking to discover its secrets.

From their vantage point in their armchairs, Mom and Dad could see a painting that hung on the bedroom wall; the very same purple *fleur-de-lys* symbol of the Brotherhood of Light, embedded in a background of pink within a heart that I had seen in my vision-journey with the

Guardian. During the winter, when they could rest from the work of the farm, I'd often see them sitting for many hours here by their window, looking out over to our fields to the east. Becky and I would come home from school, and there they would be. We knew what to do, come in the house, take off our cold clothing, and partake in the wonderful pot of hot chocolate that Mom would have ready for us on the stove along with the snack she would leave in the refrigerator. This was our ritual every day, and every day when the weather allowed, Becky and I would go back out to play for a while until it got dark or was time to come in and do our homework. We'd see them there from our place in the front yard or in the fields where we'd play, sitting in their armchairs, sometimes eyes open, other times eyes closed, meditating. They'd wave at us at times and smile. Mom would even signal when it might be time to come in. But once they sat in those chairs, we knew that they'd be there for awhile.

Now, in their room, I walked slowly across the worn oriental carpet that spread from the narrow hallway entrance all the way to their armchairs by the windows. I rested my hands on the back of each chair; tears came to my eyes. I stood for a moment, quiet within myself, feeling the fabric of the worn chairs under my hands as I looked out the windows to the forest path that I'd return home on just the day before. I thought, they knew, my parents knew the Brotherhood of Light very well.

It had been a long, very long time since I'd last been in this room, yet nothing of the surroundings seemed to have changed. I looked to the *fleur-de-lys* symbol and reminded myself of the homework the Guardian had given to me to meditate with the symbol, a homework still to be done. My gaze stayed with the Brotherhood's symbol for a moment before passing around the room to the brass standing lamp with its fringed lampshade alongside the armchairs and to the tattered Oriental rug with its ragged edges—signs of the years of wear. The old rug stretched across the room all the way to Dad and Mom's four poster bed adorned with a once brilliant, but now faded, white covered down duvet with matching embroidered white pillows. Dad's large oak roll top desk and swivel chair sat against the western wall of the bedroom, directly next to two large windows that looked out to majestic sunsets over miles of Ohio farmland to the west. Opened now and covered with neatly stacked piles of papers, it was here at this desk that Dad would spend many hours reviewing farm accounts and paying bills.

Finally, on the north wall of the bedroom, sat Mom's special, long and low to the ground antique powder table and stool that she loved so much. The cherry wood table was adorned with three attached mirrors, two of which almost faced each other. Multiple light bulbs strategically placed around the frames of the mirrors gave Mom all the light she needed. This was her special place. She called it her boudoir, and she would always make room in her day to come here, to be alone with her own thoughts, leaving me, Becky, and Dad to care for ourselves.

I breathed deeply. The bedroom brought back deep and not always comfortable memories about those I loved so much. Each piece of furniture, each light, all of it remained as I had remembered it, each in its place, and each in its own unique way a monument to my youthful memory of it. Perhaps, I mused, it would be different now, if they were both alive. Perhaps, we'd all feel closer, perhaps ....

I looked out the windows towards the forest one last time before heading back to the hallway to my door-fixing project. The sun stood high in the sky and I could feel its Indian summer heat begin to radiate through the roof of the farmhouse. I reasoned that starting the job of fixing the bedroom door now would ensure that I'd be done before the farmhouse's non-air-conditioned upstairs became unbearably hot in the midday sun. I turned to go, but something held me. Perhaps it was instinct, or intuition, whichever, I knew that I needed to stay. There was something more here for me—something important. I was not sure what it was, but I did know that I needed to find out before I could leave Mom and Dad's bedroom.

My eyes scanned the room once more. The sun's rays had made their way from the windows near where I stood across the room to Dad's roll top desk. Instinctively, I moved from my place by the armchairs into the center of the room. What was it? What was I looking for? I walked to Dad's desk. All seemed normal: a few bills marked paid in full, stapler, pens, pencils and a few scattered miscellaneous farm documents. Becky, I knew, had taken the important farm documents and the bulk of farm related records and accounts to the living room to pay bills and work on the books down there. With these gone, the drawers stood barren. I stayed by the desk a moment longer in case I should notice anything unusual. I found nothing and turned to go back across the room.

Perhaps, I thought, it's Mom's special place. I walked the few steps to her boudoir, wondering whether I'd find the "treasure" there. The room was growing hotter as the morning sun rose higher in the sky to its midday arch. Whatever I was to find I'd have to find it soon, I thought, or put off the search until later when the sun wasn't so hot. Cosmetics jars sat neatly arranged on the top of Mom's powder table alongside her nacre shell hairbrush, comb, bottles of oil essences, hairpins and other such paraphernalia. Across from these, on a little shelf at the right end of the table, sat a small jewelry box and next to that Mom's reading glasses.

At first I noticed nothing unusual. Then I saw something! A faint glimmer of light radiated from beneath the shelf holding the jewelry box! At first I thought the light might be a reflection from the sun hitting a piece of jewelry that had fallen from the box, but it couldn't be because the angle of the sun's rays actually created a shadow in that area. Besides, I thought, this glimmering light seemed to be too bright to be a reflection of a piece of Mom's jewelry. It glows differently, and even, I thought, in a way somewhat familiar.

The shelf stood on small pegs, perhaps three-quarters of an inch high, that lifted it above the powder table just high enough to give it its own identity. With such a small space beneath the shelf, I couldn't have imagined that anything could have been placed there. But I was wrong, for the light seemed to be coming from underneath the shelf. I bent down to look, and I could see that a square object that might be a small book or box had been pushed to the farthest corner beneath the shelf. Excited by my find, I reached into the narrow space, but could hardly maneuver my fingers deep beneath the opening to touch the object. After some struggle, I finally touched what felt like the back spine of a small notebook or diary of some sort. I manipulated it into a position that allowed me to edge it out from it secret place. The moment I lifted it into my hands I felt a warmth flow through my entire body, as if I were being filled with a special kind of love or care. My eyes rested on the treasure in my hands. This was the reason, I knew, for my staying in the bedroom!

Not very large, perhaps five inches wide by six inches tall, and only a quarter of an inch or so thick, the notebook had a handmade cover of golden-yellow fabric, a fabric I recognized as the one Mom had used to make the curtains in the downstairs dining room. The book itself looked homemade, as if someone—Mom, I thought—had pasted together several pages to make a notebook and then glued a cover onto it. But this was no ordinary diary! Set in a perfect circle at the center of the front cover were six tiny glowing gemstones of exactly the same sort that I had seen embedded into the sides of the Varness just the day before!

I blinked at their brightness. These stones were very, very small, almost chips, but they radiated their light directly to me as did the stones of Varness. At first, I felt confused at the presence of these stones. But my confusion gave way to a broad smile, a smile that turned unexplainably into an ecstatic burst of laughter as the warmth of the light continued to penetrate my being. I felt buoyant, in awe, as if I'd just come in contact with an old, old friend I'd not seen for a long time. Without thinking about it, I found myself, book in hand walking to Mom's armchair and sitting down. The heat blasted through the slightly opened windows. I opened them farther and decided that the small breeze coming off the forest would just have to do, as I turned the book to its cover page and read, "A Very Small Diary for A Very Big Subject." And then on the next line, Mom's name, Margaret Pond, and the year the little book was written, 1964. Tears came to my eyes again as I read her name, and I wondered whether I shouldn't just put the book back and leave the room out of respect. But I knew I needed to stay so I read on.

Dear Diary,   *September 4, 1964*

A strange and wondrous thing happened to us last night. Daniel and I were sitting on our porch admiring the pretty sunsets. What a wonder! The sky shot full of pink and purple and orange everywhere. I'll tell you a secret, diary, my heart felt so full at seeing the beauty that I almost cried. We were there just enjoying the beauty of the night coming. It all felt so relaxing, just talking and rocking. Becky was out somewhere or other, and Harry, bless his soul, just left for Vietnam last week. We were alone.

Then something very unusual happened. A man came to visit us, a priest all dressed in black with a white collar. Daniel and I haven't been to any church in ages, so you can imagine what a surprise it was. He said he wanted to share something with us he'd been doing with Julius. Seems like Daniel and Harry had met the man at Julius' shop that day they'd visited, the day Harry left. At first I wasn't that interested, thinkin it was mostly men's talk. But Daniel knew better and made sure I stayed and listened. So, we invited him to set a spell and enjoy the sunset and a glass of my homemade lemonade. Well, am I glad I stayed to hear his story, cause after a bit he started tellin about the box that he'd asked Julius to rebuild for him. The one that Harry and Daniel saw at Julius' shop that day and were impressed with.

Daniel'd told me right away that he'd knew that the piece that Julius was working on was very, very, special as it had magical jewels that glowed of pure light all around its sides. Daniel said he felt a kind of kinship with it, even a sense that he had a destiny with it. But didn't know why, only that seeing it caused chills to run all up and down his spine. After working with the Brotherhood all these years I guess I shouldn't have been surprised that his intuition about the piece wouldn't be just a passing thing. As it turned out that chest was the reason for the priest's visit.

I paused for a moment, putting the small book down as I remembered the meeting that day. I had just seen the chest with Dad for the first time and I remember feeling a tingle of excitement as we left Uncle Julius's shop. I remembered the priest, but I hadn't really participated in the meeting with him as I was getting ready to leave for Nam. I just wanted to be alone a bit and not have contact with anyone else but Dad. Besides, I recalled now, the priest had seemed very much more interested in talking to Dad rather than to me.

***

I began reading again and as I did I could feel the power of the stones imbedded in the cover of Mom's diary affecting me. Mom's writing was pretty sparse. But to my amazement, I found myself able to see in my mind's eye the actual scene Mom wrote about as it unfolded in its full detail—as if I were an invisible participant in the story, able to hear and see it all, but not able to be seen nor heard by the others.

I watched in my mind's eye as Mom, Dad and the priest—a big man with a shock of the whitest, white hair—sat on the porch talking as if they were the best of old friends, chit chatting about this and that as they looked on at the glorious sunset.

Mom wrote in her diary,

... the priest said he wanted to talk about why he'd come, and began to tell us a story about how he'd been a seeker all his life and that he'd now found what he felt was the secret of happiness, and it involved him listening to God within him all the time. He went on to say that he'd come to speak to Daniel and me because he'd been guided to share something special, and that he'd come because of his connection over the past many years to the Brotherhood of Light.

Well, I was already shocked to hear a perfect stranger talkin to us about listening to God the same way that we talk with each other and with the Ascended Masters. But when he mentioned the Brotherhood, I just about fell out of my chair, and I could see Daniel, who's usually pretty calm, squirm a bit in his rocker, too It's just not a usual thing for us to meet anyone at all who's involved with the Masters like us, so we just don't talk about it much.

I put the diary down in my lap and looked up at the *fleur-de-lys* painting on the wall. How true a statement that was, I thought, as the reality began sinking into my head that the symbol right there on my parents' bedroom wall was of the Brotherhood of Light and that they, too, had a connection, like Becky and me, to the Brotherhood. I read on.

... and was I surprised when Daniel told the priest that he had heard of the Brotherhood. The priest became pretty excited about that and went on tellin us about how he'd been searching for this "mysterious order" for many years and how his search had taken him all over the world until he finally found a trail that led him to the Brotherhood.

I watched with a touch of warmth in my heart as Dad and Mom listened to the rest of the priest's story. He told them he'd found an old manuscript and in the manuscript a drawing of a chest with many sacred stones inlaid into it. From the manuscript he'd learned that the Brotherhood had used the chest long, long ago, but he wasn't sure how. The priest said he'd searched for the chest for many years and then finally found where it had been stored. The chest itself had been destroyed. What he did find was a pouch with the sacred stones in it.

As the priest talked, I saw Dad getting more and more interested. Eventually, he sat up at the edge of his rocker and interrupted the priest right as he was about to go on and asked him what all this had to do with Julius and what he was building at the shop. The priest seemed startled at Dad's straightforward question. But then paused and closed his eyes, as if he were asking inside himself for the answer, and smiled as he told Dad the whole story about how he'd been led in magical ways to bring the sacred chest and the drawing of the chest here to Mercer County. Once here, he said, he knew he would be know where to go, who to talk to and what to do.

Mom' diary continued,

The priest told us the story of how he'd come to town with his sacred treasures and said he felt guided to take the stones and his drawing to Julius who rebuild the Brotherhood's chest for him. As for the next steps he should take, he said he'd been guided about that, too, and this is why he had come to visit right now with Dad and Mom. Well, when the priest was done his story, I watch Daniel do what he usually does when he's trying to figure out what's goin on, he lowered his head, closed his eyes and listened within him and then lifted his head and smiled at the priest, thanked him for answering his question, and asked him to please continue his story.

The priest paused as if deciding whether it was okay or not to share what he was going to say next, nodded his head as if he was agreeing with himself that it was okay and leaned forward a bit in his rockin chair, lowered his voice almost into a whisper as if he were afraid that others would hear his secret, and told Daniel and me about how he'd told Julius the first part of his story about coming to Mercer County and having the chest rebuilt, but not the second part of the story. 'Cause that part, he said, he'd seen in a dream. And the dream showed the chest sitting on the ground in a lush green forest clearing. The forest colors and the colors of the chest itself were more vibrant than anything he'd ever saw, like as if they'd glowed in the dark. Around the chest he saw a group of people that he didn't recognize, but he knew that what they were doing was the work of the Brotherhood.

He stopped for a moment after telling Mom and Dad about his dream. Then, his voice choked up as if he were almost about to cry and he looked directly at Dad and told him that in the dream a man broke from the circle around the chest and walked up to him and placed his hand on the priest's shoulder and thanked him for bringing the chest back to its rightful place. The priest told Dad that in the dream, he'd just nodded, but that he'd felt a great sense of kinship with that man, as if they both were on the same journey in life. I watched as the priest sat back in his rocker, seemingly more relaxed that he'd gotten this part of the story out. Still looking directly at Dad, the priest told him that he hadn't known what to make of the dream until the day he'd met me and my father outside of Julius' shop. And then he said, to Dad, the moment he'd seen him there he had recognized Dad as the man in the dream who'd come out of the group to speak to him.

As the priest spoke to Dad, a calm expression came over his face, as if he'd been waiting for a long time to share his dream with the right people. I watched as he turned to Mom and with a smile in his eyes told her that she too was in his dream, one of those around the circle. He paused and with a quiet softness in his voice, as if the weight of the world had been lifted from him, he thanked both Dad and Mom for helping him fulfill his role of being the one who brought the chest back to the Brotherhood. I watched as the three sat quietly for a time, just rocking on the porch in the early evening light. Then in the quiet of the moment, the priest turned to Mom and Dad and said he'd known from that day at the shop what he was supposed to do with the chest—to bring it to Dad as soon as Julius finished building it. Once he did that, he told them, he didn't know what he would do—maybe go back to South America.

Mom wrote,

We heard the priest's story about how he'd knowd to bring the chest to Daniel after meeting him that day at Julius' shop. After he was done, neither me nor Daniel spoke a word. We both were shocked, I think, at what was happening. Daniel and I've worked for many years with the Brotherhood and many magical and wonderful things have happened to us, but the priest's story was something different, very different.

I could tell the priest was telling the truth 'cause chills ran up and down my spine as he spoke.

***

The heat of the day was beginning to get to me as I put the little diary down on my lap. Still, something about the stones made it bearable. Their light radiated a gentle cool glow of energy that seemed to amplify the occasional burst of air that came into the room from the forest. I wiped my brow with my handkerchief. The priest's story revealed another part of my parent's life than the one I had known, one that connected me to them in a way that I had not been when they were alive. I felt a swell of pride in them. I knew the trust the Brotherhood must have placed in them to have Varness delivered to them. I went on reading the rest of Mom's diary. It was short and concise. But as I read, I continued seeing visions in my mind of the events Mom wrote about as they blossomed and unfolded.

Mom's writing continued,

With Daniel knowing beforehand that he had special destiny with the chest, the priest knowing of us from his dream, and my knowing the truth of what he was saying by the chills I felt, we were all pretty comfortable with each other. So comfortable we were that none of us mentioned the chest at all, and I might of just forgotten about it had the priest not brought it up. Finally, he told us that he'd meditated and knew that once he gave the chest to us it was up to us to decide what to do with it. From that point on, he was goin to continue his own journey. He got up and went to his car to retrieve the chest, brought it back to the porch all wrapped up in a blanket and gave it to Daniel. I wanted to see it right away, but Daniel thought that it was best if we waited, so I said okay, even though I was mightily curious to see it. The priest sat down for a spell more and the three of us quietly rocked together enjoying the night air. After a bit, he got up and said it was his time to leave.

I watched as Mom and Dad walked the priest to his car to say goodbye. Once settled, instead of starting it and driving away, he looked up directly into Mom's eyes, took her hand in his and told her that he'd been guided to give her something, and that she would know exactly how best to use the gift he had. As he spoke he placed a small, colorful cloth bag into Mom's hand. Mom thanked him for the gift and went to put it in her pocket, but the priest insisted that she open it right there. So, she slowly poured out the contents of the bag into the palm of her hand. The diary continued,

As he was leaving he gave me something in my hand, and was I ever so surprised. 'Cause glowing in my hand were six very small chips of colored stone. They were glowing just as the stones that Daniel and Harry had described that day after coming back from visiting Julius at his shop. There was one orange, and two blue stones and three others that were sort of reddish in color—but they all glowed and gave me such a warm feeling inside! I put them away and thanked him again as he drove off down the driveway and onto the county road.

Daniel and I waved goodbye.

I turned to the next page. On it, dated September 5th 1964, I found Mom's final diary entry,

One more thing, last night after the priest left, me and Daniel meditated on it and received that we should take the chest into the forest, and that's just what

we did this morning. Took it to the place where Daniel used to take Harry camping, and left it there in good hands.

***

I sat for quite a while in the room. A tear rolled down my cheek. The sparkle of the glowing chips of sacred stones radiated their warmth from the diary cover, and with them came a feeling within me of being cared for—as if I were a baby gently wrapped in a blanket. My eyes closed in a dreamy sort of reverie in acceptance of the warm caress of the light from the stones. The heat of the day blasted through the windows, adding its warmth. I took it all in as a child would who'd not been protected or nurtured for a long time.

The phone rang and jarred me from my reverie. I must have dozed off for some time. I ran to get the phone in the upstairs corridor. It was Becky telling me that she and Bill were about an hour away and would be home soon. They'd planned on a full three-day vacation, but Becky told me that just as they arrived at their destination, the Guardian had come to her to tell her that it was urgent that the two of them return. I told her of the message that I'd received in the forest about the urgency of our acting to save the forest and that the Guardian had pointed to her as the one who would know what best for the three of us to do. She seemed to know this and told me that we would talk when she got back.

I was relieved to know that she and Bill were on their way. In my hand, I still clutched the diary that I'd been reading. In a way, discovering the revelations about my parents over these past days gave me a new view of my life, a new sense of what it had meant to grow up in this house. Pieces began fitting together, pieces that had never made sense before: Mom and Dad's excessively long times away in the forest; their forbidding us from coming after them; the times when the entire forest was off limits to us; the late night visits of "friends" whom Becky and I never really got to meet; and their intense faith in the Oneness in all life. All of this and more began to fall into place in my mind. The smile grew as the outline of our life together—the family Pond growing up in this house—began to fill in with the details of the life with the Brotherhood of Light that my parents had led.

The diary, I knew, needed to be returned to the place where I found it. Becky and I would have to decide what to do with it and the sacred stones embedded in its cover at a later time. For now, putting it back under the shelf in Mom's boudoir would be the safest place for it. I returned it and then left the room. As I did, I said a little prayer of thanks to the spirit of Light within me. My visit gave me a new look at the people who'd raised me, and I was thankful that I'd had the opportunity to read the diary in their room.

In the hall, I gathered my tools to put them away. No, I thought to myself, today won't be the day I fix these doors. Just for a moment, I wondered if I'd ever really have the time to fix them.

CHAPTER THIRTY-NINE
BECKY WILL KNOW THE WAY

We choose the path of magic and magic chooses us

Becky and Bill arrived back about noon. We sat together in the living room to figure out what to do next. They both looked rested, even though they'd had to cut their journey short. Becky spoke first. "We all know that the darkness that has been trying to get control of the farms and the forest is getting more frantic each day. I don't know about you, but I've been feeling it these past weeks as kind of a mounting tension. Those that want the forest, for whatever reason, seem to be getting desperate. These are the same forces that may have been responsible for Dad and Mom's death, even the capturing of Uncle Julius' consciousness, making him somehow a pawn in their plans."

She turned to Bill and said, "Bill, I haven't spoken that much with you about the Brotherhood of Light. I chose instead to leave that to Harry. But now it's very important that you join us in the listening process and tell me or Harry any advice you might hear from the Brotherhood as we go on. Both Harry and I have had messages from the one called the Guardian, that the forest is in great danger. Neither of us knows exactly what that danger is, but both of us do know that if the Brotherhood thinks that the forest is in danger, then we'd better do something about it. We need your help now because you've had experiences in the forest that may be invaluable to us to help save it."

Bill looked quizzically at Becky and then at me. Their relationship, up to this point, had been one of staying on the surface of issues related to the threat to the five farm families and the forest. Though Bill had learned a great deal about the Brotherhood from his mother and from our conversation, Becky and Bill had never really spoken about the Brotherhood. Now, Becky's reference to information that he had shared with me privately must have made him wonder whether I'd shared his secrets with Becky. And, from the look on his face, he didn't seem happy about it.

For my part, I felt uncomfortable and somewhat astonished that Becky had mentioned Bill's childhood experiences. I hadn't mentioned a word to her about what Bill had shared with me that day.

Becky smiled as she watched both Bill's and my face express the consternation we felt over what she'd just said. Then, looking more directly at Bill than at me, she said, "No, Bill, Harry didn't tell me about what you and he spoke of in the forest that day. I have no knowledge at all about what exactly you shared with Harry about your experiences in the forest. All I know is that you've had certain experiences that may help us in the time to come. I know this because the Guardian came to tell me this just before we arrived back at the farm today.

"Bill, if you ever want to share with me what those experiences were," she went on, "that would be great. But for now, the Guardian simply asked me to state the fact that because you've had certain happenings in the forest and you have certain knowledge that could help us. I would like to spend some time together with you in a more leisurely way, but we don't have the time right now, the danger is too near."

I could feel the tension mount in Becky as she spoke. She knew the reality of the danger, but she didn't want to offend or hurt Bill's or my feelings. "For now," she continued, "please believe me that Harry has not betrayed your trust. It's just that," and at this point, Becky almost cried, "well, it's just that," and she paused again, "you'll have to trust that the information we receive is real and trustworthy."

Becky stopped. I felt her anguish at having to speak to Bill this way, so directly about things they'd not really addressed together before. But the messages from the Guardian were quite clear, and though Becky had seemed to be relaxed when she came home, underneath it all, she felt the stress of the danger.

I put my hand to her shoulder to reassure her. At the same time, Bill reached for her other shoulder to do the same. Becky looked at me, and then to Bill with a look of gratitude in her eyes and said, "Oh, I so thank you. I'm not used to leading any charges or anything like that, but the Guardian told me that I would know what to do, and that I shouldn't be afraid to tell you both what needs to be done."

Bill spoke, "Please, please know that I do trust what it is that you said. I did feel upset for a moment, but I realize that you meant no harm, and that Harry," he looked at me now, "has not betrayed my trust, either. I admit, the whole situation still shakes my nerves, but I'll do whatever I can to help. I promise to listen for whatever information that I can give to help out."

As Bill spoke, I could feel the tension disappear from Becky's shoulders. I knew her well enough to know that she would be able to handle leading us on our mission, but the decisions she felt she needed to make weighed on her. "Becky will know what to do," the Guardian had said, and now was the time to "do" something, and Becky was feeling the pressure!

I resolved to support her all the way as we went forward. After all, I reasoned, in Nam I'd followed a lot of people less able than she. As I thought about Becky a warm feeling, a knowingness, came over me that all would be well, and I knew not to worry, that Becky really would "know what to do."

"Okay, then," she said, her confidence coming back into sharp focus, "we've no time to spare, we must contact the other farm families and warn them, from there I'll let you know what to do next."

CHAPTER FORTY
THE MEETING

Never before has the darkness been so confronted with Light. Never before has Light been so strong

Felix smiled to himself as he thought one last time of the plan. He'd thought of everything and put all things in place, the bank transfers, airline tickets; all elements were ready. All that was needed now was the chest. Yes, the chest that would be his victory and his pathway to everything he had ever wanted. Felix felt sure that from his father's reaction when he heard about the existence of the chest, and from what he could glean from the old man, the chest would likely be worth a fortune. Daddy wouldn't have reacted like that, he mused as he touched the still remembered painful spot on his cheek where his father had struck him, unless the chest is worth a lot.

As he stood in the clearing, Felix relished the thought of holding the chest in his hands that evening, for he was certain of the success of his plan. The deafening sound of motorcycle engines filled the clearing, announcing the arrival of Henry Thorpe and the rest of the Alcaz Motorcycle Club, and interrupted his delight at the wonder of his plan.

Though annoyed with the noise, Felix did his best to ignore it, choosing instead to continue his reverie, at least for a moment or two longer, about his coming good fortune. The magical glowing gemstones embedded in that chest, they're my ticket, he concluded, as the last motorcycle engine shut down. With them I'll have all the fortune I need to escape Daddy and never again to be seen in this part of the world. Felix smiled to himself. By his own will he was destined, and even deserving, of living the life of luxury he envisioned for himself on the far away tropical island he'd chosen. The chest would provide him the right opportunity to make his destiny come true!

***

Julius came next in his pickup truck. Then John Freed and Robert Frosten, separately in their cars as late afternoon clouds brought welcome relief from the sweltering heat of this early September Indian summer day.

Felix knew he would need Julius' help in finding the chest. The old man had told him about his visits to the forest many years back. From Julius, Felix learned of the central path running the length of the woods, the trails leading from the five farms to the central path, the two minor trails fanning off the main path leading to clearings in the woods and a host of deer trails that may or may not be there now. Felix's interest focused mostly on the smaller paths.

The old man had become extremely excited when he talked about them, telling Felix of his certainty that he'd find the chest in the clearing at the end of one of these two trails. "Somewhere off that main path. That's what the priest told me," the old man had spat out with great venom. "He told me he gave the chest to that traitor brother of mine, that the chest would be hidden in the forest for some ritual or other, sitting in a clearing." Felix remembered that Julius had stopped talking then, as if lost in his own world for a few moments, and Felix had waited. Then, as if awakening from his stupor and remembering Felix's presence with him, Julius said, "It's not in the farmhouse, I looked, it's in the forest, *I know it is!*" The old man's own plan called for him to look for the chest in those clearings until he found it.

Now, as his group congregated for the meeting that would set the stage for what Felix called "the assault on the forest," he thought of his own plan. He knew that he would have to use all of his wiles to keep the chest for himself once he got Julius to lead him to it. The old man certainly would want it, but Felix had no fear of him. He would do what he had to do to get the chest for himself, and he touched the thirty-two-caliber pistol he'd brought along with him, kept now in the front pocket of his pants. No, the old man didn't worry him, but Henry Thorpe and the members of the Alcaz Motorcycle Club did. Once they saw the chest or found out about it, they would know its value and want it for themselves, Felix surmised, or at least want their share of its value.

Thorpe may be rough, Felix thought, but he's not dumb. Felix had racked his brain to figure into his plan a way that would ensure that he kept the chest once he got his hands on it. The idea of brute force against the likes of the Alcaz gang had no appeal for him. Frankly, he was certain that they'd find some way of overpowering him and then take the chest for themselves. Finally, he'd come up with a plan. He would have Thorpe and his crew enter the forest from the north on the trails farthest away from the central path, and most importantly, farthest away from the trail that he planned to use with the old man to enter the forest and find the magic chest. While they were diverted with their work of putting fire to the forest, he and the old man would have the time to find the chest, and then, once found, he would get out while he could, counting on the chaos of the fire as cover for his leaving.

His plan for Thorpe and the other members of the Alcaz Motorcycle Club had unique advantages. He smiled once again to himself at his own brilliance as he thought through it again. For one thing, the road to the northeastern-most farm had been blocked off and closed for several weeks now. Rumor had it that old man Henley had tried to stay on the property after the fire in some shed or other, but recently had to move in with relatives over in the next county. As for the other northern farm trail that he planned to use, the Blakely trail, Felix had had Frost and Freed scout it for him just this past week. They'd discovered to Felix's glee that the layout of the farm allowed for access to the forest without ever being seen from the Blakely farmhouse.

These trails would provide perfect access for the Alcaz gang; remote from the main highway, but still able to provide Thorpe's crew access to the heart of the forest to ensure that their work of destroying it proved successful. Most important for Felix, Thorpe and the others would be far enough away from the main trail to give Felix the time he needed to find the chest, secure it from the old man, and leave the forest.

Felix waited with a broad grin on his face as the others gathered in the clearing. He'd even thought to buy the cans that the Alcaz gang would use, and have them filled with gasoline. He was proud of himself. Yes, he thought, my plan is perfect and bound to succeed!

As for the rest, finding the chest for Felix presented the only real challenge to his "perfect" plan. The old man felt certain he knew its location, and from what the old man had told him about the forest's layout, Felix had decided that they would do best to enter the forest from the Pond family trail, which the old man had said could be gotten to without being seen. And then, having taken care of the old man along the way, leave the forest at the other end that led to the Bates family farm. He'd checked out each of the five farm's proximity to the road and this one presented the easiest access to the old jeep he'd already parked on the road near the trailhead several days back.

Yes, brilliant, he thought, smiling to himself, just brilliant! Comfortable with his direction, Felix approached the group, but it was not he who spoke first, but Henry Thorpe.

"I don't know about you, Butezz, but my guys and me are getting pretty tired of hanging out around here. So if this meeting you called is to do something, then we're for it. But, even the little bit of money you pay us isn't enough for us to just sit and do nothing. So," he said, pointing a threatening finger at Felix, "if we're not going to do anything, then me and my guys have talked about it and, we'll be cuttin' out of here this evening to go back home."

Felix had anticipated Thorpe's unhappiness. For several weeks he'd seen Thorpe and the others in town at the local bar, and had heard them shouting their discontent about being prisoners of this one-horse town. Still, Felix knew not to be concerned. Instead, he would offer Thorpe two things he knew he wanted, money, and the possibility of more power! Thorpe had, for some time, asked Felix to help him and his club get into what he considered the big time by working with Felix's father. In the underworld that Thorpe and members of his Alcaz Motorcycle Club inhabited, Felix's father's name held almost legendary sway. Known and feared far and wide as the controller of a multitude of dark and illegal activities both in the U.S. and abroad, Felix's father was someone Thorpe and his gang would do well to serve. "A step up in the world," Butezz overheard Thorpe say one time to his men. "Yes, a step up!"

For this reason, Thorpe had agreed to stick around and wait these past months to help Felix in his plans. Now, not even the prospect of meeting Felix's father would hold Thorpe and the others much longer. Henry Thorpe's icy blue eyes blazed fire at Felix as he finished his tirade with his final remark, "We know you've got influence, Butezz, with your father and other important people, but we're not afraid. We've done a good job for you so far, but this is your botched job, Butezz, not ours and you can tell your father that the Alcaz Motorcycle Club stands behind its work, and anytime he needs real help in getting a job planned and done, he can call on us!"

Felix smarted at the insult. As smug as he felt about the success of his plan, and even his next offer to Thorpe, he hurt at the mention of his father and Thorpe's slight that his father might be better served to hire Thorpe and the others. Even though Felix planned on crossing his father, he remained sensitive to the issue of pleasing him, and Thorpe's words struck home, throwing him off balance.

Felix responded with the words he'd planned on using, but because of Thorpe's attack, they didn't come out with the authority Felix would have liked. "I know what it is that you and your men want and I'm prepared," he tried to say in his most businesslike voice, "to give you all you want." He went on, but as he spoke, Thorpe's glaring eyes stared straight in to his, continuing to show the disdain he felt for Felix. Felix couldn't help but falter. "I've a-a-action to offer you," he stuttered, "and money, and s-s-s-something e-e-e-else you want." At Felix's last words, Thorpe's ears perked up and his angry gaze at Felix softened. "What else are talking about?" he said, with a softer, but still wary voice.

Thorpe's response gave Felix a moment to recover. Instead of bringing back the embarrassing childhood stutter he'd just displayed, Felix got control of himself and his confidence. "I'm talking about work with my father," he lied. "Do this job well, Thorpe, and my father and me will want to talk with you about working for us in other capacities."

In truth, Felix had never spoken of Thorpe or the others to his father, nor was it his intent to ever do so. In Felix's mind, his success in this venture would end forever his relationship with his father, so Felix had no second thoughts about winning Thorpe and the others loyalty with a lie about his father's future intentions. At least for the moment, it worked.

Thorpe took a deep breath and his attitude noticeably changed. From aggressive attacker only a moment before, he became more like a scolded child as he went on the defensive, explaining to Felix that he didn't really mean what he'd just said, but that he and the others were getting antsy and wanted to get this job done and move on. Of course, he and the Club were ready to do whatever Felix wanted them to do to get the job done.

Felix smiled. He'd used his father's name as a trump card at other times, and it never failed to work like a charm. He said, "Okay, Henry," in his most conciliatory voice, "here's what we need to do." As Felix spoke, he led the group to the center of the clearing where he'd made a rough sketch in the dirt to show them what he wanted them to do.

***

Julius and others listened as Felix laid out his plan. Thorpe and the others would go to the two farms north of the forest immediately after dark. Part of the Alcaz Motorcycle Club would enter the forest through the now fenced off road to the Henley farm, and the others would quietly sneak their way past the Blakely farmhouse to that forest entrance. Thorpe would lead the first group, and Ziggie and Blackjack John would lead the second. Once on the trails, the teams would scout the paths for the best places to light the fires in a way that would destroy the entire woods. Thorpe and the rest of the Alcaz Motorcycle Club crew were to get out of the forest as soon as they could, after being certain that the fires were hardy enough to spread. The rest of the Alcaz Motorcycle Club members would leave the area, but Thorpe would stay around the next day to meet Felix to get his final payment for the job, after Felix assured himself that the job had been properly done.

Thorpe argued at this last point. "It's too damned dangerous, Butezz." He scowled. "I've got to get our money and get out of this area as soon as I can after the fire. You need to come up with something better than this." In the end, they agreed to meet early the next morning, just before dawn, at Felix's café. Of course, for Felix it hardly mattered what he promised Thorpe and the others, for he planned to be comfortably on a plane headed for South America at precisely the time of his proposed meeting with Thorpe.

As for his stalwart salesmen, Freed and Frosten, Felix would have them drop him and the old man off on the road near the Pond farm. There, he and Julius would use a small deer path that Julius knew about that led from the road directly to the Pond trail to the forest. Once they were on their way, Freed and Frosten would stand guard along the road between the Pond farm and the place where Felix had parked the jeep down the road near the Bates farm—far enough away from the Jeep so as not to interfere with his departure after getting his hands on the chest, but close enough to warn him of any dangers. Felix had some affection for these two, and had agreed to give them their final payment for their work before the group descended upon the forest, "For a job well done," he told them, "a job well done!"

Beyond all else, woman knows her name ... but the Earth experience continually throws her out of balance

Becky knew what to do. Inside herself she found constant solace for the decisions she was making with the Guardian and Katran right by her side. She always considered herself brave, but raised as a woman on an Ohio farm, she'd learned to keep her place. Not that Dad or Mom had meant it that way. It just was the way it was. Now there was no "keeping in place." The forest and the farms seemed in great danger and she knew that she had the answers to the puzzle of what to do, to save the situation to ensure that the Light would be served.

Men like Harry went to war and the result, she'd often felt, was that only by killing and death does someone win. Surely, she'd thought to herself, there has got to be a better way. Dying may be a solution, but not one that she felt was needed. There simply had to be a better way! So, she approached this task of protecting the forest and the farm with this in mind, along with the support and guidance of the Guardian and others of the Brotherhood.

She'd had Bill contact the Henley and Hayes families to tell them of the potential danger to the forest. Harry was to call the Blakely family and warn them. Together, they would be on the lookout for a potential danger. Exactly what it was, Becky was not certain. The Guardian had certainly warned them about the danger, but when it was to come and in what form, she didn't know. So she just acted and trusted her instincts as to what to do next.

She felt troubled. Why would anyone want to hurt the forest, or even stop the activities of Light that were taking place there? Yes, she understood the danger, for Mom and Dad were gone, and nothing could bring them back, but still, she couldn't really understand the minds that wanted to hurt the Light. Where did they come from? Why would anyone want to destroy the most precious thing anyone could have, which in her view meant direct contact within oneself, with the love and creative forces of God and nature. She simply couldn't understand.

As she pondered these questions, Katran's familiar voice came to speak to her. "We of the Brotherhood have long asked the same questions. The forces of darkness are not ones that are well understood by those on the path of Light. Even if in the past, the students of the Light have had contact with the dark forces. The reason for this is that it's impossible to live on this beautiful Earth without being influenced by these forces that seek to create chaos and destroy awakened consciousness.

"With you," she said, "because we've been on a learning path so close, ever so close to the elementals of the forest and therefore the direct forces of nature themselves, the thoughts that go on in the minds of those who serve the dark have become more and more foreign to your own way of thinking. As you'll attest yourself, if you think several months back before you began your own studies in the forest, you had a much better idea of what these others might be thinking."

To this, Becky nodded her head. She did have a better idea of what she thought those who were on the wrong side of the right had in mind. She thought of her attitude towards Uncle Julius. Surely, he had fallen into a sort of pit that served the "wrong side," and no matter how much she loved him, several months back when Harry had just arrived back home, she thought she had a pretty good idea of the kind of thoughts her Uncle might be having, of jealously, greed, or envy that might lead him to his actions. Now, she wasn't at all sure she really knew what she felt about Uncle Julius and what might be going on in his head.

She just couldn't be that clear about it anymore, and the more she studied the Light with Katran and others, the farther away became the thoughts she used to have about feeling certain of Uncle Julius' bad thoughts.

"Yes," said Katran, interrupting her, "you have come onto the path of Light, and so it's becoming increasing difficult for you to conceive of what the dark forces might be thinking, or even feeling. The truth is that we of the Brotherhood and those who work with us on Earth don't need to know what they believe. No, we need only know that we know what's right by the direct contact with the Oneness with us. So, we *do*, as you're asked to *do* now, exactly what comes to us to do in the service of the Light. And as you know already, the Light of God Goddess always prevails, always knows what to do next.

"We say this," Katran continued, "for you to know that trusting yourself in this matter is trusting All That Is. You're part of the Oneness, the whole, and you've learned to listen well, so trust that you know the right place to listen to and the right thing to do."

With that, Becky knew that Katran had left. She always did, and it always shocked her that that special feeling of nurturance that came with Katran's presence, whether Becky was with her in the physical or Katran communicated with her in her mind, left when Katran left. At that moment, Becky vowed to pursue the evolution of her own Light as far she could to create her own special energy that would sustain and nurture her in the future.

That's truly what my journey is all about, she thought; to know my own Light so well that I touch that place of divine love energy within me, bring it forth and know the truth of my being.

***

At that moment, Bill and I went into the kitchen to report to Becky that though we'd each tried to contact the farm families that Becky had assigned to us, neither of us could reach anyone at the other farms.

"They're not there," I said. "So, we will have to do whatever it is we're going to do on our own. We don't know exactly when an attack on the forest could happen, or when the other farm family members will be back, so what should we do next?" I asked this last question with full trust that Becky would know what to do! I waited in anticipation for her answer as my concern was growing that we needed to act, and soon!

Becky said nothing at first, and then did something I had never seen her do before. She closed her eyes and tilted her head for just a moment, as if listening to something or someone. Afterwards, what came from her mouth rivaled any strategic plan from any battlefield commander that I'd ever heard. Becky told me later that from the moment she closed her eyes to the moment she gave Bill and me our last marching orders, she found herself in what she could only describe to me as a state of grace as the words flowed from her lips.

We both listened intently to her plan, and without hesitation agreed to follow the instructions she gave. Neither of us said a word about the strength, force, and certainty of Becky's words, but I knew that Bill felt their power as I did, and I could feel the tremendous respect we both had for her as we left to follow her direction!

***

Becky stood alone in the kitchen for several minutes after Harry and Bill departed. In truth, the experience of knowing what to do still resonated within her in a way that she hadn't experienced before. She felt, she thought, exactly the same way as she felt when she had been with Katran or the Guardian or others of the Brotherhood. But, instead of being bathed in the higher vibration of *their* aura, she found herself *enfolded within her own* higher energies. And, though she felt a bit off of center at the experience, she couldn't help but feel grateful to that part of her that allowed the Oneness to express through her.

CHAPTER FORTY-TWO
ASSAULT ON THE FOREST

Darkness tries hard to create nothingness where there's life, but life ... true and real, ever sustains and grows

Felix's plan went into motion that very same evening of the meeting. After dark, the Alcaz Motorcycle Club headed for their appointed entry places at the Henley and Blakely farms. The challenge, as Henry Thorpe saw it, was not to have the motorcycles heard close to the farmhouses or forest, so as not to associate the fire with the Club. Therefore, he instructed Blackjack John and Ziggie and the one other Alcaz Club member who went with them to park their bikes in a place that couldn't be seen about a half mile away from the place at the Blakely farm where they would eventually enter the forest.

He and the other two Alcaz Motorcycle Club members with him had less of challenge at the Henley farm as no one was living there. Still, Henry planned on taking no chances, so he and his team parked their bikes about a half mile away from the Henley farm in a field along the road. From these two launch pads, he and his men would sneak their way along the road to the respective farms and, carrying their recently filled cans of gasoline, enter the woods along the assigned trails and do the job they came to do. Henry felt confident that he and the rest of his gang would be successful and that Felix Butezz would pay them well for it. He felt even more certain of this after this afternoon's planning meeting with Felix, when that little twit, Butezz, showed how frightened he was of him when confronted by his angry glare.

In truth, Henry had used that glare and the fact that it tended to make the scar on his face turn an angry bright red when he expressed his rage at someone or something to his advantage numerous times. He'd noticed many years back the fear that others had of him at those times, and in his own way, Henry felt proud of himself that his actions brought others to fear him. He liked the feeling of power it gave to have others feel that fear when he was around, and he smiled now as he remembered the scene from the meeting earlier in the day when Felix had stuttered. Yes, he thought, I let the twit off the hook, but only because of his father, not him.

Henry arrived at the appointed spot to park the bikes and, with the others, headed quietly along the edge of the Henley farm road towards the forest trail entrance. Blackjack John, Ziggie, and John, the third Alcaz Club member making up their team were in the process of doing the same, sneaking past the Blakely farm to quietly enter the forest along the Blakely trail. As fortune had it, the moon shone nearly full, so no flashlights were needed. Henry liked that, thinking it gave the whole operation a sense of destiny, with the moon's light on the Alcaz Club's side to make the job of destroying the forest a little easier.

Nothing could stop the plan from succeeding, Henry thought, and allow him and his men to leave this one-horse town forever!

**

At the appointed hour, Felix accompanied by John Freed and Robert Frosten arrived at Julius' hotel room to pick him up. They would go together, the four of them, and then Freed and Frosten would be there along the southern road to pick them up after they did their work. In describing his plan that afternoon, Felix had not exactly described to the others the kind of work that he and the old man would do when they entered the forest. He had just said, "Julius and I will do our destructive work along the main path of the forest after entering the wood on the Pond family trail. Julius knows of a way we can get onto the trail without being seen."

Indeed, this last part was true, the old man did know of a way onto the trail along a deer path that would bypass the Pond farmhouse. For the rest, Felix had a made a deal with the old man; they would go into the forest together and Felix would help him find the chest. But after that, Julius would help Felix set fire to the southern end of the forest along the main path. As far as Jack Freed or Bob Frosten were concerned, their job was to be there when Felix and Julius came out of the forest along the same trail that they'd used to enter.

Felix smiled to himself as Julius entered the car. Though Frost and Freed, and even the old man, believed the outlines of his plan, everything was ready for *him* to leave the forest with the jeweled chest at the other end of the main path and then continue on to the road where his jeep awaited him for his escape. Nothing could be simpler, Felix had said to the others, "We simply torch the forest and then go about doing what we've been doing as if nothing has happened."

They were on their way and the four of them arrived at their appointed place well after dark. The moon's position in the sky gave Julius and Felix all the light they needed to make their way along the deer path towards the Pond family trail. Julius carried a bulky, newly filled gasoline can with him along the path that made it difficult for the two to be as quiet as Felix would have liked. The can bumped into brush and got stuck here and there in the brambles of berry bushes that lined the narrow deer path.

Walking on, Felix considered once again how he would get the chest from the Julius. Doing away with the old man had little appeal for Felix, but he felt he had no choice. Somehow subduing Julius and leaving him there alive, with the possibility that he might survive the fire, made little sense to him. Felix concluded that for his plan to be successful, the old man must not be around to tell what had happened. So, even though Felix had never been involved in anything like this before, and in fact got nauseous at the first sight of blood, he decided that this was something he would just have to do in order for the plan, and his future life to work out.

A little further along, the deer path opened onto the Pond farm trail that led directly east towards the forest's main path. Julius' large frame and age made his movements awkward, and though this trail was larger than the trail they'd just left, Julius kept bumping into trees and bushes. "Quiet," Felix hissed at Julius. "Be quiet!" Julius didn't hear. For him, he was on a journey to get back the most important thing in his life: his chest! It belonged to him, had been stolen three years back, and now he was closer than ever to getting it back. The fact that they were to sneak into the forest didn't even cross his mind. Julius' focus was on his quest and this was nearly over. The chest would soon be his!

CHAPTER FORTY-THREE
HARRY AND BILL AT HENLEY'S FARM

Men have choices always, some choose the Light, some the darkness, but the choice of Light is open to all

I knew, somehow, that the threat to the forest would come from many different directions. Now, as I drove with Bill towards the Henley farm I could feel the danger in the air. In Nam, I'd had this same kind of intuition about events that were about to happen, and now I felt the same. Becky's right in sending us to the northern farms, I thought, I can feel it. We need to protect the forest from all directions.

The other farm families weren't home when we had called, so other than our farm and Bill's mother at his farm, the northern farms seemed most vulnerable. "We need to especially look to the Henley farm," Becky had said, "because from all that we've heard, it's vacant right now, and most accessible." So, at Becky's direction, Bill and I had set off to patrol and at least warn the Hayes and Blakely families about the danger should they return home this evening."

Driving along the road in Bill's late model sedan, we came to the locked gate that blocked us and others who might wish to go farther down the Henley farm road. I admit, I felt a kind a comfort in the No Trespassing sign hanging prominently from the center of the fence, but my comfort didn't last long as Bill's lawyer's mind came in to shake me awake. "You know," he said, "if I wanted to attack the forest that sign wouldn't do much to deter me." I had to agree. So, instead of recommending that we just turn around, thinking that the gate and sign were enough, we parked the car, got out and headed down the road towards the farm. Even with the bright moonlight, the dark night sky displayed its grandeur with millions of stars as we walked the quarter mile to the Henley farm. When we arrived, what we saw brought sadness to my heart, and I know Bill felt the same, as the light of the moon showed the burnt remains of the Henley farmhouse.

Bill and I both stopped for a moment as we gazed at the ruin, saying nothing. Then Bill said, "I'd heard about the fire, but I hadn't really understood that it had been so devastating." I said nothing, just nodded, but I knew that the burnt ruin of the farm brought a sharp reminder to the two of us of the reality of the potential danger we all faced.

To the right of the farmhouse, down a short path, we could see the old log cabin, the one, I guessed, where old man Henley had stayed after the fire. We decided to check around the property and especially look to see where the trail to the forest began. Bill took off down the path that led to the cabin, thinking that this might be the start of the trail into the forest, and I circled around the farmhouse ruins a little further to the south to seek the beginning of the trailhead that would lead into the forest.

As I came around the house, I saw in the moonlight what looked to be a trail. This would be the right location for the trailhead, I thought, heading south to southwest towards the main path. I loved this forest and the thought of exploring its northeastern most reaches on this trail brought a feeling of lightness to my heart. As I came closer to the trailhead something else much more important and much more urgent alerted my senses—the smell of fresh gasoline! I bent down seeking the source of the odor, and almost retched. The ground beneath me was saturated with freshly spilled gasoline. There was no mistaking this smell. I turned immediately to get Bill, but didn't have to go far for the trail he'd followed ended at the cabin, and he came around the side of the ruined farmhouse to find me just as I turned to find him.

Bill said nothing as he, too, bent to seek the source of the smell. We looked at each other and knew immediately what this meant. Without thinking further, we turned our attention to the trail. Whoever spilled this gasoline likely carried more with them with the intent of destroying the whole forest. How many were ahead on the trail, we didn't know, nor whether they were armed or not. We spoke about it, and we decided that we didn't have time to call Becky or the police, but needed instead to follow those ahead of us. "They simply have to be stopped," said Bill, "at all costs!" I agreed.

My military training had prepared me for occasions such as this. With or without a weapon, decisions needed to be made and risks needed to be taken. I wondered about Bill, who had no such background. "Don't worry about me," Bill said, as if reading my thoughts, "I may not have the background, but I'll do all that I can to stop these criminals."

Okay," I said," but you'll have to let me take the lead on this." Bill agreed and we decided that I would go first, decide the best course of action and let Bill know, as best as I could, what he could do to help out. He agreed to follow my every instruction.

The smell of gasoline increased as we went along and crossed the small bridge across Olden Creek. The further we went, the stronger the stench of gasoline filled our nostrils. We said nothing as we moved on further along the narrow path. We needed to stop them from lighting the fire, and, unless they planned on leaving the forest the long way around on the main path, then those spilling the gasoline would have to come back along this very trail before starting the fire.

As I thought about it, I made a plan to be prepared for their return. Bill and I stopped and spoke in whispers as I explained my plan. He would wait in a small clearing we'd found along the path just to the northeast of the bridge. His job was to do whatever he could as a backup to my activities to ensure that the fire never got started. If those ahead got past me back along the trail to where Bill hid, then he would know that I was not successful in my plan and Bill would need to do all he could to stop them. I had faith in Bill's ability to handle himself. He had been an athlete in high school and college and was still in pretty good shape. Still, I thought, it had been a long time since high school and this situation was very dangerous, more like the ones that I faced in the war, and not at all like the occasional fist fights that broke out in a high school or college sports stadium.

For me, I planned on picking off those ahead one at a time. I wasn't sure how many there were, or how I would do that, but my military training and experience in Vietnam had given me confidence that I could be successful, if there were only a few. I left Bill and walked further on, a handkerchief over my mouth and nose to keep the smell of freshly spilled gas from overpowering me. I moved slowly through the forest bush, doing my best to stay quiet, as I'd done those many, many nights on patrol in Nam. About an eighth of a mile further I heard loud voices.

I approached cautiously. A little way further, the moon's light let me see a break in the path where I saw three men, all dressed in the familiar black leathers of the motorcycle club that had been hanging out in town. I ducked behind a tree to consider what I should do next. As I listened, I understood that two of the men where in heated argument with the third about money and not being paid yet. As I wondered what I would do, when the Guardian's familiar voice came to me.

"Harry," he said, "you're very brave, but we need you to be cautious around these three. Fear makes men volatile, more volatile than they would otherwise be. The calm and peaceful feeling in the forest causes these three to feel uncomfortable. They argue over money and the best way of doing the job they've come to do. They'll fail, but you must still maintain care." I nodded in assent.

Heeding the Guardian's words, I moved a little closer to the clearing where the three stood. From my new vantage point and with the help of the full moon, I could see into the clearing without obstruction. Immediately, I recognized the man facing in the direction where I hid as the blonde man with the scar on his cheek who'd stood in front of his motorcycle that day in town, glaring at me. His look made me know that he was no friend. Now, his hand in a fist, his rage pouring like fire from every bit of his being at the two men dressed alike, I knew with every ounce of my being that this man had been an enemy of the Light for a very, very long time. The Guardian came again, to confirm my own knowingness. "Yes, Harry," he said, "that one has long ago left the influence of the Light to serve the darkness. As it is seen, Light will eventually return to him, but now, he must be stopped."

I nodded in silent assent, wondering what course of action I would take next, when a remarkable thing happened! Next to the taller of the two motorcycles appeared a small globe of golden light floating in the air, only a dot, which then, in a magical instant, turned into the full golden light of Sakya in all his giant splendor. I gasped, and was certain that the blonde man heard me as he looked my way. Whether he heard or not didn't matter, for things changed rapidly from then on. In one moment, the tall man stood arguing with the scar faced man, and in the next, he turned his head and saw next to him a godlike giant aglow in golden light. His mouth dropped in disbelief. His head turned away once, and then, he turned it away a second time before turning back, only to stare in disbelief at this apparition standing alongside him. He stood like this for only a short time, and then let out a scream that curled the hair on the back of my neck before he turned and ran as fast he could back along the path I had just come down.

I watched in astonishment as the second man looked to Sakya, hesitated for only a moment, and then, without speaking a word he, too, turned and ran after the other along the path passing me, just a foot or so from where I hid. The blond man stood his ground, watching first the others as they ran back along the trail before turning his attention to Sakya's golden presence. An ugly smile crossed his scared face, a smile that seemed to say, "So you think you can scare me? Well, you can't!"

The look on his face, his stance, ready to attack, made me know that rather than feeling fear, as the others had, this man felt only joy at this meeting with a being of pure Light, a pleasure, *the* pleasure of taking on the Light. And, if he could, destroying it!

He moved quickly as he picked up a thick branch from the ground and, heavy as it was, with great force swung it, aiming to deliver a deadly blow to the midsection of Sakya's body. But before the blow could reach its destination, Sakya presence simply faded back into pure Light. Instead of a great victory coming from his act, the man was left standing there by himself, starring in disbelief as the ball of Light disappeared before him.

I could see the anger in his eyes. Regaining his composure, he reached for the pocket of his black leather jacket and soon pulled out a cigarette lighter he'd found there. Once again, that dark smile crossed his lips, as he knelt down near the gasoline cans that the three had emptied onto the soft earth of the forest floor. I knew, in that moment that he intended to set the forest ablaze, not only to finish the job he'd started, but to show the Beings of Light they couldn't stop him from doing his foul deed.

I couldn't let him set fire to the forest. I left my place behind the tree and ran as fast as I could towards him! Hearing my footfalls, the scarfaced man looked up and, as he recognized me, his eyes lit up and that twisted smile once again returned to his face. I felt the hatred, and the glee that he felt at meeting me here in this darkened forest, as if this, too, had been a long held desire and one that he could now fulfill.

With the practiced air of one skilled in his trade, he reached into his pants pocket and emerged with a very large, very ugly switchblade. At the edge of the clearing, I stopped short, remembering the Guardian's admonition to approach this man with extreme caution. The malevolent look I'd seen on his face that first time in town appeared even more deadly this night in the forest. I faced an enemy who knew what he wanted to do, and was well versed in doing it. My heart pounded as I went into a warrior crouch and began my slow approach to his position in the center of the clearing. He crouched, too, but as I began moving closer to him, rather than move onto the attack as I expected, he uncoiled out of his crouch and stood tall, and, taking the knife by its tip, threw it directly at the center of my heart.

Even with the moon shining bright, I found it hard to see the knife's trajectory. By instinct, I lunged into the bushes to my right as the knife passed by the left side of my body, barely missing its mark. As I hit the ground, I struggled to get up, but found myself in the midst of a blackberry patch. I struggled to free myself from the cutting edges of the vines. Thorns ripped my skin as I moved. Fortunately, I saw nothing of my enemy. Rather than pursuing the attack, I heard his footsteps moving away from me to the south. When I finally got myself out of the blackberry patch several minutes later, the scar faced man was gone, escaped down the trail towards the forest's main path.

I faced the choice of following the blonde man or going back to help Bill with the other two who needed to pass his way to leave the forest. Would they set the forest ablaze? Would Bill be able to stop them? I wavered for a moment. We had to stop them from doing the damage that they'd come to do. And then, mercifully, the Guardian's familiar voice came to me. "Please, Harry, trust that you're on the right path and that Bill and the forest are well taken care of to the north. This one must be stopped, for it is he, and he alone who presents the greatest danger."

Looking one last time to the north, I sent a prayer of protection to Bill, and then headed to the south after the man in the black leathers, the leader of the Alcaz Motorcycle Club.

CHAPTER FORTY-FOUR
BECKY SEEKS HELP

Opportunities to know the fullness of oneself abound ... take them often, for passing on them leaves one feeling hollow ... and alone ...

Becky knew that time was of the essence. The fact that the other farm families weren't at home to watch and protect the land meant that she, Harry and Bill would have to take the lead. Hence, she'd sent Harry and Bill to check out the northern farm family trails to protect them as best they could.

Now, she sought help from others, and it came to her to call first her cousin Frank, Uncle Julius' son. She had no other choice, she thought, we need help and Frank can be trusted. As she was about to call him, the Guardian came to her, confirming her choice. "Yes," he said, "this one has waited a long time to help you and your brother. In his own being he has a great guilt that he feels for the fact that his father may have been responsible for your parent's death. He has great wisdom that can only help you if he goes beyond his guilt. If you can, cultivate that within him. You will be well served by this one."

Becky called and Frank agreed immediately to come over to the farm. When he arrived, Becky told him as much as she could about her knowing of the danger to the forest, and asked him to go with her along their trail to patrol the forest's main path. Before they left, at Frank's suggestion, Becky called Sergeant Gerhig, who wasn't in, and left her a message about what was happening. They headed out for the forest.

CHAPTER FORTY-FIVE
FOREST ESSENCE

Nothing of Light truly disappears ... it changes shape ... raises in vibration and frequency ... but never disappears

Blackjack John, Ziggie and a third Alcaz Motorcycle Club member successfully found their way to the Blakely farm trail. Together, they'd been quite successful and had crossed the Blakely bridge over the creek without incident. A little way farther along the trail they found a place they felt ideal for setting the fire. Blackjack John liked his work, liked working with Ziggie and especially with Henry Thorpe. Henry was his hero, so he felt especially proud to be leading this part of the job and he knew that Henry would pay him well for it, in money and in compliments.

Together, his team had distributed their payload of gasoline up and down the trail from the bridge into the forest along several very narrow deer paths and was ready to put light to match and head out. The three laughed together as they walked gingerly back along the path toward the bridge. They felt confident in their work. They'd done an excellent job. All that was needed was to light the match, and safely leave.

It wasn't until they reached the bridge that they realized that all was not as they'd thought. Standing on the bridge, with guns drawn, were three state troopers who decidedly were not at all happy with the excellent job they'd done.

***

Julius knew that the chest would help him in some way. Inside him a small voice had recently begun to nag at him. It said, "You need not *steal* the chest. It is here to help you regain something that you've lost. You need not take it away. *Go to it* for your own healing!" He didn't know where that new voice came from, but he did know that it competed greatly with other voices in his head that had repeatedly told him, over and over again during these past years, that the chest belonged to him and that he had a right to it!

For Julius, this new message only made life more confusing than before and he did his best to shut it out. He kept thinking that at his age he should be more grounded, more on top of things. Surely, he'd think amidst the general confusion of his life, he should just have it all together by now.

These new thoughts wouldn't go away, and soon they were joined by other, even more uncomfortable ones. Julius found himself remembering his brother Daniel and Daniel's wife, Margaret, as if they weren't gone at all, and even planned at one point to visit them on their farm before he finally remembered who he was, and what they'd done to him! Now, as Julius and Felix walked down the forest's main path nearing the small trail to the clearing where Julius felt certain he would find *his* chest, Julius' thoughts turned again to his brother, Daniel. He'd been away from home when Daniel was conceived and born, yet when he did return, Julius remembered feeling proud of his little brother. He liked his small hands and his giggling laughter when Julius tickled his small feet. Scenes flashed in his head of him and Daniel over the years. A tear came to his eye, and then, suddenly, Julius' anger returned, whipping it away. He shouldn't have stolen it, he thought. He really shouldn't have. First the farm, and then the chest.

This dialogue played back and forth like a small concert in his head. He wanted his chest, but the closer he came to going into the forest with Felix to finally get it back, the more these thoughts of the past invaded his mind. That was precisely how Julius thought of these new thoughts, as an invasion. It's like someone is trying to throw me off with all these memories, he thought, to keep me from getting back my chest! For Julius, these thoughts played like a bad melody inside him, making his life even more confusing than before. "It all should be easier than this," he said out loud.

The night stars sparkled clear alongside the moon this evening, clear enough for him to see every step as he and Felix came closer to their destination. It had been many years since Julius had been in the forest and to him, everything seemed somehow different. The path they walked on should have been only five or six feet wide, according to his memory, but now it seemed closer to a dozen, and the trees seemed taller. What he remembered as a straight path that had some twist and turns, even sharp bends along the way. In all ways the forest had changed from how Julius had remembered it, except for one, the forest's smell. This remained the same, and as Julius walked deeper into it, his mottled memory began to clear as the familiar forest scents penetrated deep inside his being.

***

He remembered his stay at the farm and the pleasant times he had had with his brother before they'd argued and he had left. He remembered the times he'd taken walks into this very forest to experience the peace of this land, and he remembered how, when he and his Lucy were first married, they would visit Daniel and Margaret. The four of them would walk down this same forest lane that he walked on now, talking and laughing. Each step took Julius deeper into memory and with each memory, his mind cleared a little more. But, with each bit of clarity an equally strong pull to remember only one thing came as a cloud across his mind: his chest. His anger returned, as he assured himself that he was right on track in getting back his treasure.

With his anger came certainty, and with that certainty came affirmation that despite those voices in his head that argued against his original plan, raising questions within him, he was correct in doing what he was doing. Surely, he thought, as he walked on, I'm doing the right thing to get back what's mine! But his conviction was beginning to waiver, for with each passing moment in the forest, each step along the path, each whiff of a familiar forest aroma, came more memories of a quieter and more peaceful past. With these came doubts about his mission, and his goal! "I know it's right," he said again to convince himself. "I know it's right!"

***

Felix's gruff voice interrupted his thoughts. "Well, are we nearly there?" Felix was getting impatient, the further he went into the forest the more uncomfortable he felt. "Something about this place gives me the creeps," he said. "The sooner I can get out of here the better." In fact, Felix's own feelings at double crossing his father were starting to get to him. It wasn't that he felt guilty at not following his father's orders, no, it was that he felt afraid, afraid of what his father would do to him if he found out. The further he walked the greater his fear became.

As he talked with Julius, his fear, frustration, and anger at even feeling these childish emotions, all came out. "Listen, old man," he said, "I've been following you now for some time and you haven't said a thing. Either you know where we're going or you don't, but I tell you, if that story about the chest is bull, I'll have you pay for it, you'll be sorry!"

Julius said nothing; his thoughts were once again on the times when he, Lucy, and Daniel and Margaret would walk in the forest. He remembered a time when they walked together up a side trail to a large clearing. The clearing was surrounded by trees awash with fall colors of red, orange, vermilion, and yellow, and he wondered now whether the clearing would look the same in the moonlight at as it did that other time. He looked around for signs that he might find familiar, but saw none. The sound of Felix's voice speaking next to him touched him not at all, for his thoughts were focused solely on finding his treasure. Where was that trail? He struggled hard to remember how far it could be down the main path. Then, in the moonlight, he saw it, unmistakably, a trail leading off to the right of the path. Yes, he thought, his heart beginning to soar at the thought of finally getting his treasure back, that's it. I know it's it!

Felix continued his banter at Julius even though Julius seemed lost in his own world, refusing to answer. "I tell you, old man," he said, "if you don't find me that chest you're in big trouble. I didn't go to all this trouble and put up with all your crazy jabber all this time for nothing. It's the chest that I want!" Even as Felix uttered these words, he stopped himself short. He didn't want the old man to suspect his true intent. Quickly he said, "Oh, I know that the chest belongs to you, Julius, but I'm just excited about seeing it, your beautiful work and all, and those magical stones. As soon as we find it, we'll get it back for you and then do what we came to do with that gasoline can."

Once again, Julius didn't answer, he simply turned, still holding the gasoline can, and walked up the trail leading to what Julius knew in his heart would be the path to his treasure. Felix could say nothing, and so he followed. By this time, the narrow path with its overhanging trees made it difficult to see ahead. Felix turned on his flashlight and showed its light in front of Julius, who continued to walk on, as if he didn't even notice the darkness, the heaviness of the gasoline can he carried, or even Felix's presence alongside him.

While Felix followed Julius up the path, his mind worked furiously going over his plan to get the chest from the old man. He reached in his pocket and touched the thirty-two-caliber handgun he carried. Felix knew that even though he didn't like the idea of doing it, he had to make sure the old man was not around to tell the tale of his taking the chest and his escape. Yes, he thought, I'll have to be brave and do it, but in the end I'll be off with the treasure and no one will ever find me.

They continued on down the path, with Julius in the lead and Felix shining his flashlight from behind. Suddenly, they were in a clearing and to Felix's surprise, his flashlight was no longer needed. There, across the clearing about seventy yards on an old log stump sat the most magnificent thing Felix had ever seen. Standing in awe, his heart pounding, words came out of Felix's mouth in a whisper without his realizing that he had even spoken. "The magic chest," he said softly, "it's here and it *is* real." Then, as realization set in, he said, "Old man, it's real, you didn't lie, it's real!"

Felix stood motionless, mouth open, hands dropped to his sides, and his eyes wide open. "It's real," he repeated softly, "it is real." The glow of the chest radiated a light into the rest of the clearing in a way that illuminated the whole area. Without thinking about it, the flashlight Felix held in his simply slid from his hand and dropped to the ground. The old man told the truth, and even Felix's father knew the value of this magnificent thing all along. That's why Daddy wanted it, Felix thought, that's why, to cheat me out of what's mine. This chest is mine! I did all this work, stayed in the lousy town all these months while Daddy had all the luxury at home. No, he won't take it from me. No, sir, he won't. The chest is mine. I deserve it, and will have it.

CHAPTER FORTY-SIX
JULIUS AND FELIX MEET VARNESS

Knowing self means knowing the goodness of self ... and of life itself!

Julius stayed quiet all the time he led Felix Butezz on the trail that eventually led to the clearing. The path, its smells, the feel of the earth, and even the touch of the branches of the trees brought back memories, clear memories of the times he had been in the forest before. With these his mind cleared for what seemed like Julius like the first time in years. He remembered the chest, the priest, his brother Daniel, Harry; most of all, he remembered something he had forgotten long, long ago, something about those voices he'd spoken with as a youngster. He remembered them now, and he remembered what they'd said!

"Julius," they'd said to him, "Julius, remember, your greatness. One day, you'll do a great deed for humankind and it will pay back to you in your time of need. Remember Julius, don't forget, it's your destiny." When *had* he heard those words? He recalled trying to remember them when the priest spoke of his own inner communication, about *his* journey to find the chest and then to bring it back to Merced County to be rebuilt.

At the time, Julius, had had a vague memory that he, too, had such communication, as a young teenager, but it had been so long ago. He had forgotten what those voices had said to him, so many years back. Now, in this clearing, it all came back, the words spoken, the friendship formed with the friendly voice that felt like his, but was not. He remembered how, as the years passed, he'd spoken less and less with the voices as he went about seeking his own way of survival in a world that he didn't understand, a world that frightened him greatly.

Now, standing in this clearing and facing his treasure, the magnificent chest that he'd built with so much love, that very same voice came back to him. "Julius," it said, "it's good to remember the time before life took you away, far away from yourself and your heart. This chest that you've reconstructed from the plans of old is here in this sacred forest to remind you of those truths we spoke of so long back. "Do you remember what else was said?" the voice asked. "Can you recall?"

Julius shook his head, and by instinct turned to run away, like a lion caught in a cage needing to get out. Hearing this voice brought a jolt of memory that made him break out in a sweat, and the only thing he could think to do was to run. He didn't want to remember. His life had been one of seeking out pathways that best allowed him to survive, to overcome his fear. Now, this voice brought back memories of an earlier time, a gentler time in his life, when hope seemed more the watchword

Harry Pond Looks Homeward

than fear, when his inner relationship with himself led him to explore different ways of being as he grew up. Then, one day, he recalled that he realized that he needed to grow up, that he needed to take care of himself in the world, and that he would need to be a big man in the world. But he didn't at all feel prepared to take care of himself, and a deep fear of not being able to survive entered his world.

All this came to him in a flash, and his response was only to go away, far away, but he couldn't. The chest, his chest, glowed in front of him just across the forest clearing and he had come too far now to turn back. So, instead of running, Julius moved forward, in his mind, closer and closer to the wonderful magnificent magical box he'd created to take it back home, to a place where he could just be with what he was a treasure he was certain really belonged to him.

But now, as his steps brought him nearer to his goal, the warm glow emanating from the chest, which had dimly lit the forest's clearing, began to expand. As he approached within feet of it, the chest greeted him, with a burst of glowing radiant light from each of the stones. They bathed Julius' entire body and, for the first time in a very long time, Julius smiled. It was a smile of recognition, like meeting an old and dear friend who one has not seen for a long time. In that moment, his mind now clear, Julius realized that he wouldn't take the chest, it didn't belong to him!

It has its own life, and its own destiny, he thought, and he understood then that the voice within him that had spoken these past weeks the words, "the chest will heal you," had been right. The chest would heal him, and in that instant, Julius knew, without a doubt, that the chest must stay in the forest where the priest had seen that it belonged!

***

But as Julius' mind cleared, Felix's became more possessive. Rousing himself from his initial shock at seeing the chest, with its marvelously radiating gemstones, Felix spoke to Julius, "Okay, old man," he said, relishing the beauty of the object he knew would soon be his, "so this is the chest that you told me about. It's pretty, all right!" Felix knew that the chest's beauty went far beyond his expression of pretty, but he calculated that if he showed Julius his excitement at seeing the chest, the old man might suspect that he wanted it for himself. He didn't want that to happen, at least not until he was ready for it to happen. As best as he could, Felix wanted to stay neutral for the moment in the old man's eyes, even in the face of his own excitement at coveting the chest for himself.

As Felix walked a few steps closer to Julius, and to the chest, he could hardly keep himself from running to it, grabbing it, and running out of the forest with it. He wanted the chest so badly he could barely contain himself. The urge surged within him, and only his desire to stick to his perfect plan kept him from following through on that urge. But something about the chest, beyond the wealth and freedom it represented, drew him to it. It felt to him that the magical box called him to come to it, to bath in its light, but Felix dismissed this thought as nonsense. For now, he would stick to *his* plan, wait for the ideal moment, and then the chest would be his.

Felix had not expected Julius to reply to what he said, for no matter what Felix said, Julius had stayed silent, as if in a trance. Now, though, Julius turned towards Felix and said, "You will not have the chest," he said, "it's not mine, and it isn't yours. I was wrong. The chest has got stay in the forest where it belongs!"

Felix looked at Julius in surprise. The old man had not spoken since they'd entered the forest, and now, speaking for the first time, he stood tall in his six-foot-five-inch frame and spoke with a strength in his voice, a certainty in his manner, and a look of determination in his eye that Felix had not seen in him before. This caught Felix off guard. Felix didn't know what to say, but his hand went instinctively to his pocket to touch the weapon that he felt certain would keep him in charge of the situation.

More confident now, Felix spat back at Julius his own ultimatum, "Now you listen to me, Julius, we had a deal, I help you get the chest out of the woods and you help me put fire to this horrible forest! You'd better keep your deal, or e-e-e-else." Felix stuttered, as the firmness of the Julius's words and manner began to affect him.

"We won't be doing either!" Julius said, with a voice so strong that Felix took a step back. "I won't let you! The chest doesn't belong to me and it doesn't belong to you. This forest *is* sacred and nobody, nobody has the right to destroy it."

"What do you mean we won't be doing either, we came to do a j-j-job," Felix spat out, becoming more and more flustered by the moment at the old man's insistence, "and we're gonna do it," he said, his voice rising now in frustration and anger.

Julius stood taller than he had in years, as he simply repeated the words he'd just spoken, "The chest," he said firmly, "belongs here, and I won't let you have it!"

***

But as the two men spoke, something else began to happen. The stones on the Varness began to emanate a brilliant light that illuminated the entire clearing. Along with the light came a gentle humming sound, a tone of great beauty, a song. Yes, I know that sound, Julius thought, standing mesmerized by its purity and beauty. It stirred a place deep within him and his heart opened and softened as he listened.

What Julius felt as sweet harmonies, Felix experienced as excruciating pain. The harmonies created within him a longing he could hardly stand, a longing for something of beauty, even kindness that he had rejected long ago. As he stood close to Julius in the clearing, bathed in the light and sounds of the chest, he rejected again this inner calling that would align him with the beauty and harmony of the world. "No!" he yelled, "I won't be fooled by some sentimental trickery played on me by an old man. This chest is my passport to freedom and I shall have it."

Ignoring Julius' demands, Felix rushed passed Julius and lifted the chest from its place on the tree stump and at the same time pulled the thirty-two from his pocket.

"Now, you listen to me, old man," he said, pointing the gun at Julius as he struggled to hold the chest under his arm with his other hand, "I'm taking this chest and not you, not anybody is going stop me!" As Felix held the chest, the sounds emanating from it halted and its light dimmed, giving off a gentle glow now that lit only the area around Felix and a few feet out from him.

Julius stood still saying nothing at first, seemingly mesmerized by the harmonies and the light coming from the marvelous chest that he had crafted. But, as the light dimmed from Varness, and the harmonies ceased, Julius reacted to Felix's action. Feeling clearer now than he could ever remember feeling, he looked directly at Felix and calmly, simply, restated his earlier words, "You will not have it. It doesn't belong to us, and I won't let you have it!" As he spoke, Julius moved his six-foot-five-inch frame a step closer to Felix.

His gun pointed at Julius, Felix began circling to his left around the outer edge of the clearing with a goal of reaching the trailhead. Even with the gun, Felix's hand began to shake as the old man took a second small step toward him. Though he'd planned on ensuring that Julius wouldn't be alive to tell the story of his taking the chest, the sweat of fear poured from his brow, burning his eyes as the imposing frame of the old man moved slowly towards him, seemingly unafraid.

He'd never killed anyone before and even at the expense of his father's ridicule, he had once refused an assignment from Daddy to do away with a man who'd crossed his father. But now, he could see no other choice. His own plan led him to it. He simply couldn't leave the old man alive to tell what had happened. So, as he moved slowly towards the path that would lead to his freedom, he felt his finger tighten on the trigger of the small gun held in his hand.

"You'd better not come closer, old man, or you're th-thr-through!" he stuttered to Julius. But Julius continued his steady pace towards him, uttering the same words over, as if lines from a story he'd memorized long ago, "It's not ours and you can't take it away. I won't let you."

Felix continued inching his way towards the trailhead, as Julius continued his relentless, almost slow motion march towards him. Felix knew now that he must do what he had planned, to end the threat of the old man's relentless advance towards him. He felt the gun in his hand, as sweat formed to moisten his grip on the gun. I must do it, he thought, I can't wait any longer. He was nearly home. He needed only take care of this bothersome old man, and get out of the forest and his plan would be nearly complete. Felix moved now to within a dozen feet of the deer path. He raised the gun a little to steady his aim at Julius.

CHAPTER FORTY-SEVEN
THORPE ARRIVES

Standing at the Gate, some will choose to go in, and others will chose to try to close the door once again so they will not have to look at the Light inside

Just then, from the area directly to his right, Felix heard loud footsteps. Instinctively, he turned towards the sound, and entering the clearing was Henry Thorpe. The full moon reflected brightly against his black leather jacket, his blonde hair, and the bright red scar on his face. Breathing fast at first from his escape from his meeting with Harry, Thorpe said nothing. Then, gaining his composure, he looked at Felix first, and then at the still glowing bejeweled chest under his arm and at the gun in Felix's hand and said, "Well, well, Felix, what've we here? Looks like you found yourself a treasure."

Felix didn't respond at first, but he felt his knees begin to shake. Nothing and no one had ever scared him more than Henry Thorpe, but the gun he held in his hand gave him some sense of confidence. Thinking quickly, he said, "Yes, Henry, I-I-I found this treasure just as we were about to put fire to this part of the forest. I was just bringing it back so we could figure out how much it was worth and split it up, but this old man tried to take it from me, so I had to hold him off with the gun."

Julius stood still and waited for Felix to finish what he was saying, and then, looking at Felix and then to Henry Thorpe, he repeated what had now become almost a repetitive chant to him, "It doesn't belong to us, it must stay in the forest." Henry Thorpe said nothing. He knew Felix was lying, and that had he not stumbled upon them along this path that he thought would lead him out of the forest, he wouldn't have ever heard of, nor seen the treasure.

"Okay," he said, "but what about the old man, what're you gonna do with him?"

"I guess," said Felix, "we'll have to get rid of him."

At that point Julius reached his huge hands up to the sky and with agility unexpected in a man of his years, leapt from where he was and in a few steps knocked Felix over with a football block that sent him flying to the ground. In the process, he grabbed the chest from Felix as he went down and then suddenly, as if his own impetus for action had somehow been satisfied, Julius just stood there, all six-feet-five-inches of him, hugging the chest with both hands close to his heart. He was swaying back and forth as if he were holding his own baby in his arms. Then, carefully, very carefully he placed the chest back on the log stump where it had been when he and Felix entered the clearing.

Henry Thorpe didn't hesitate. At Julius' attack on Felix, he followed and instead of going after the chest, as did the old man, he reached for the gun that fell from Felix's hand as he went down. Now, he thought, he would have the treasure that the old man held and the pleasure of being done with this little twit, all at the same time. Of course, he would split the bounty with the rest of the Alcaz Motorcycle Club members, but from the looks of the glowing jewels on the chest, this would well be able to pay them, and more, for the work they'd been doing in this town.

"So this is what this has all been about, Felix," Henry Thorpe said, standing over Felix, "You planned on getting this jeweled treasure all along and then leaving us holding the bag if we got caught burning down the forest."

Felix, still stunned from the blow that Julius had delivered, shook himself off slowly as he stood up. "Listen, Henry," he lied, "I didn't know about that chest before, but now that we've found it, why don't we split the profit and I'll still pay you and your men for the job done tonight in the forest."

Thorpe said nothing. He knew not to trust Felix, and was now just trying to figure out what to do with this situation, when he heard rustling in the bushes along the forest path behind him. He stepped to the side of the path, gun in hand, still pointed at Felix. The moon and the glow of the chest that was now beginning to brighten after Julius had placed it back on its tree stump gave enough light to see clearly across the clearing. All three men stood still, silent, a tableau in the moonlit night as the noise from the path came closer and closer to the trailhead. Then, as if in a dream, the action in the clearing began again as Becky entered, followed by Julius' son Frank, who held a flashlight to guide his and Becky's way.

Henry Thorpe wasted no time. In a flash he saw his opportunity to have the chest and a pathway to safety all at the same time. He moved quickly behind Frank, and standing at the trailhead entrance to cut off any possibility of escape, immediately commanded Frank and Becky to move over towards where Julius stood at the far end of the clearing.

"Okay," he said, "so this is what this forest has been all about," pointing to the chest. "You've all been hiding this treasure here. Well," he said, "I'll do just fine with it, thank you!"

Waving the gun at Felix, he said, "Butezz, go over and get that box for me, and bring it back here."

"Henry," Butezz said, "I tell you it's great you came before that old man attacked me again so we could take that old box, sell it and split the money." Then, looking at Henry Thorpe in a kind of knowing way, "And you know, Henry, my father will be real happy that you saved the treasure chest so that we could all share in the wealth."

"We're not sharing anything, Butezz. I've had enough of your lies. Get that chest and bring it over here, now!" he said, pointing the gun directly at the short fat man.

"B-b-but, I, we're partners, "Felix stuttered, "I-I-I thought—"

"Shut up, you little fool. How long did you think you could take us for a ride like this? We'll put fire to this forest all right, but you and the rest will be here to enjoy the blaze. Now, get me that chest, Felix, or else."

Felix, head drooping down and looking like a little boy who'd been scolded, obeyed Henry Thorpe's order. But as he walked nearer to the chest, Julius stepped in front of him.

"I told you, Felix," he said, standing tall, his white hair and beard reflecting the light of the moonlight and the increasing glow of Varness, "it doesn't belong to us and it must stay here. You can't have it." And looking directly into Henry Thorpe's eyes, said firmly, "Neither can you!"

Thorpe stood for a moment saying nothing, his gun still pointed at Felix and Julius. Rage flared in his eyes and then, without a word, he held Julius' gaze as he slowly, very slowly moved the gun from Julius' and Felix's direction to point it directly at Becky. "Do as I say," he said, and a smile came over his scarred face, "or else she'll be the one that pays!"

For a moment, this exchange with Thorpe launched Julius back into his old state of confusion. His eyes clouded over, his shoulders sagged, and his head dropped as conflicting thoughts entered his mind. What should I do? Whose side am I on, anyway? Then, in the midst of these tortured thoughts, Julius felt the Light of Varness embrace him, and with that Light came the ringing of an old and familiar voice within, one he had not heard since his teenage years.

"Julius," it said, "you're doing the right thing, but you must let him go. He will take the chest, but do not fear. All is well."

As the voice spoke to him, Julius' head raised and his back straightened, and now he starred directly once again into the eyes of Henry Thorpe with the same confidence he'd felt only a few moments before, and said, "You can have the chest, Thorpe, but if you hurt Becky, I'll hunt you down and find you no matter where you go, and you'll pay for it!"

Thorpe only sneered at Julius' words. Then, he said, waving the gun at Felix, "Pick up that chest, you're coming with me." Then, to Becky he said, "You too, you're coming, just in case this old man has more crazy ideas."

Becky opened her mouth to protest, and then thought better of it. She'd been startled at the events in the clearing. The forest, for her, had always been a special place, a sacred one, never a place of violence. But, now, violent men, with violent thoughts and actions were here in her sacred forest. A voice inside her told her to be calm, that all would be well. Despite her initial fear of seeing this man with the gun, she knew in her heart that she would be safe. As for the man's orders to go with him, she wondered whether she should resist. The chest, she knew, belonged to the forest and that Uncle Julius was right, it must stay here. But inside herself she also knew not to fight this man with the gun, at least not now. She'd seen him several times in town, and each time she couldn't help but think how dangerous a person she felt him to be. So, as directed by Thorpe, she took the few steps she needed to take towards the entrance to the trailhead. She now stood only a few feet from this man, who waved his gun back and forth, pointing it alternately at her, Felix and Uncle Julius and Frank.

***

Felix also followed Thorpe's orders as he walked to the now fully glowing chest, and grabbed it off the tree stump. Even now, as he lifted the chest with both hands, Felix's mind worked overtime trying to figure out how he would overcome Thorpe's advantage and still have the chest. I can still get it," he thought, "if I play my cards right! But now, in the midst of Felix's musings, Thorpe abruptly ordered him to put the chest down. Puzzled, Felix looked back over his shoulder at Thorpe who'd taken off his black leather jacket and threw it to Felix's feet. "Wrap it the jacket, Butezz," he said, "we can't have the light from that thing tellin' the world exactly where we are!"

Felix obeyed. All the better, he thought, in the dark I'll find my chance!

Thorpe pointed his gun now at Julius and Frank and said, "You will not follow, or else!" Frank nodded his head, but Julius just stood there, a strange look in his eye, and he repeated his earlier warning to Thorpe. "You'd better not harm her!" Thorpe ignored the old man's warning and as Felix passed him with the chest held in his arms, Henry moved over towards where Becky stood and roughly grabbed her arm and pushed her in line behind Felix. He turned then to depart on the trail, but out the corner of his eye, he saw the Julius coming at him.

"I told you not to harm her," Julius shouted, and within an instant he was nearly upon Thorpe. Thorpe turned to ward off the old man's attack. He'd seen how Julius had knocked Felix over, and he wouldn't have this happen to him. He stepped to the side and, with the arm not holding the gun, he pushed Julius away to the right, deflecting for a moment the old man's charge, nearly falling over himself at the impact of interchange.

But Julius wouldn't stop, "I told you not to touch her," he shouted, and now he was on Thorpe again, nearly knocking him down. Thorpe, as he struggled to stay on his feet and in control of the situation, fired one shot at Julius. Julius fell to the ground, holding his right leg as the bullet entered into and then passed through his upper thigh.

Frank moved towards his father and was about to make his own charge, but Henry Thorpe, regaining his ground, pointed the gun directly at Julius' head, who lay at his feet holding his leg in pain, and said to Frank, "Don't move or he's a dead man!" Frank stopped, and then to Julius, "If you try to follow, old man, the next time, it won't be your leg." Then, turning to Becky and Felix, he said, "Okay, we're going!"

As the three started their journey back down the trail to the forest's main path, Thorpe quietly leaned down picked up the flashlight that Felix had dropped nearby and put it in his pocket. Before leaving the clearing entirely, he went to where Julius had put down the still full gas can, picked it up and carried it with him down the trail!

***

Moonlight showed the way as the three walked down the narrow trail, leaving Frank Pond behind in the clearing tending to his father's injured leg. As Becky followed behind Butezz, the voice of her Uncle reached to her like a dream, as if he called out to her through the years and his pain, "It'll be okay, Becky, hold on, we won't let them hurt you!"

Tears came to Becky's eyes. "Why, that's Uncle Julius's voice!" she murmured softly, almost speaking to herself as though she were the teenager who remembered her favorite Uncle and the many times he had been there for her in her youth, protecting and supporting her. Tonight in the forest, her Uncle Julius was back. It felt like a dream, a ghost of the past, returned to her after a very long absence. Once again he was there, protecting her as best he could. He'd even risked his life for her, and once again, just as the voice within her had done, he'd reassured her that all would be well.

Walking a few paces further down the trail, Becky now remembered her parents and her suspicion that Uncle Julius had been somehow been involved with their death. How could she reconcile this suspicion with her Uncle's actions tonight? Harry had said that he thought it possible to save Uncle Julius, but what could she do with her feeling of loss, her grief and the hurt of missing her mother and father. What if her suspicions were right? Becky shook her head in confusion as she walked down the trail behind the short fat man carrying the chest in his arms. How could she, she thought, ever trust this man again, her Uncle? How could she ever open her heart to him again?

In answer, the voice of the Guardian came to her. "Be patient Becky," the Guardian said. "This one did lend his energies to try to get the forest and the farm away from your parents, but he did not knowingly participate in their death!

As she walked on, a scene in town flashed across her mind. Her father and mother were driving to town on a dark and rainy late afternoon. In an instant, the vision showed her Uncle driving by the same street in his pickup truck just as her parents had left their car. With him in the front seat of the truck was the very same short fat man who now walked ahead of her on the trail. She saw Uncle Julius pointing to her parent's car, telling the fat man that his brother and his wife must be in town. Then she saw Uncle Julius drive his truck through town, down the main street, and drop the man off in front of a café, and then drive on out of town.

The vision lasted only a moment, yet Becky found herself awash with emotion as the vision unfolded. The Guardian said nothing as the scene continued. She saw the short fat man leave Uncle Julius' truck and go around to the back of the café to meet with three men on motorcycles. The leader of the group, dressed in the black leather outfit of a motorcycle club, seemed to be the very same tall blonde man with a scar on his face who now walked directly behind Becky on the deer trail. Two black-leather-clad members of the same club sat astride their motorcycles alongside the blonde man listening, as if waiting for their orders. The short fat man didn't spend much time meeting with the riders, but what he said sent a shiver of fear through Becky and then a surge of rage as he told the men of her parent's presence in town, and where their car could be found. She watched as the short man told the three motorcycle riders to "Put a scare into those two, maybe they'll sell after that!"

The scar faced blonde man smiled as he nodded his assent. Becky watched the scene unfold as the three men drove their motorcycles to where her parent's car was parked. While one looked around to see that no one was coming, another got off his motorcycle and scurried beneath her parent's old model sedan with a wire clipper in hand. In a moment he emerged from under the car, a smile on his face, leaving unnoticed, on that wet and rainy day, a stream of fluid pouring out from beneath the engine of her parent's car.

To her ultimate horror, Becky found herself walking behind the one in the scene who'd ordered the action that led to her parent's death, and in front of the one who'd carried out the deadly order. Whatever fear she'd had of the scar faced man, or for that matter, of the little fat man in front of her, disappeared as her anger grew at the scene she'd just witnessed. For her, she could do nothing else but confront them. They were the murderers of her parents, and gun or no, Becky needed to do something. She simply stopped in her tracks along the trail, ready to face them both.

"Keep moving," the scar faced man said behind her. But Becky didn't. The moon was at its highest now and she turned and looked directly into the man's eyes, anger building within her, and said, "You murdered my parents and maybe you think you can murder me, too, but you won't be able to. Your dark ways can't win, they'll simply fail."

For just a moment, Becky thought she saw a flicker of fear in the man's eyes, then recovering, a twisted smile came across his scarred faced as he lifted his gun and pointed it directly at Becky's heart. "Move" he said, "or you'll be the next." But Becky had no intention of doing that. She knew deep in her heart that she was safe, and without knowing exactly why, she knew that Harry was nearby and would help.

"You killed my parents and you and this little swine here," she said, pointing to Felix, whose brow poured sweat, "will pay for it."

In spite of her decision to stand firm with these two villains, something shifted within her, a subtle sense that told her not to fight now, to follow the man's order to move on. She didn't know why this was so, but over these months with the Brotherhood she'd learned to trust that sense, and she knew now that this was the best thing to do. She turned from Thorpe and started walking down the deer trail. She said nothing as she moved forward at a strong pace, passing Felix, but Thorpe, slowed by carrying the gas can, would have nothing of her going forward. "Stop," he shouted, "you'll stay right here in front of me, just in case one of those others has ideas about saving you."

Becky slowed her pace in response and waited for Felix, who uncomfortably, took the lead carrying the chest still covered with the black leather jacket in his stubby arms as he walked past her. They continued on and soon came to the forest's main path.

Felix turned to Henry and said, "Listen, Henry, I've checked this place out and the best way to get out of this damned forest is to the east over towards the Bates place." As he spoke Felix put the chest down gently on the ground and pointed to his right. "From there we can get out onto the road where Freed and Frosten are waiting with a car," Felix lied, never mentioning the jeep he'd left there for his own planned getaway.

Henry said nothing. He didn't like Felix and certainly didn't trust him, but he had not planned at all on being in this part of the forest and so had not designed his own escape route. Whatever Butezz had in mind, Thorpe felt confident that he could keep control of the situation and get away with the chest. Reluctantly, he agreed and the little group of three turned right on the main forest path and began their walk towards the Bates family farm entrance to the forest.

CHAPTER FORTY-EIGHT
BILL MEETS AN OLD "FRIEND"

The Spirit sees what the mind only hopes for ...

Upon Harry's leaving, Bill regretted staying behind at the clearing by the bridge. For one thing, he was not a man who liked to wait for things to happen, nor was he afraid to be in the action, or to act when action was needed. He wanted to move, to do something, but here he was, alone in the forest on this moonlit night, waiting. He walked to the bridge and looked down at the waters flowing beneath. The quiet ripple of Olden Creek comforted him. The scents of the forest, combined with the dance of the moonlight on the creek and the gentle hoot of an owl atop a nearby sycamore, put him into what he later described to Becky as a magical state, despite the danger of the situation.

"What a night," he said aloud, "just like that night in the forest at grandpa's and grandma's house." As the words left his lips, a shock wave of emotion passed through him. With the words came the sudden realization that, indeed, he was standing in *The Forest*, the one of his youthful fright, and he was *alone!* For just a moment, Bill's legs grew weak and that old panicky feeling in his belly came back, just as he had felt that night in the forest so many years back. Then, in an instant, as if by magic, it was gone. The panic rushed out of him as a wave leaving the shore to be replaced with a true sense of calm.

He wasn't certain why, but he felt more relaxed and at peace with himself than he could ever remember feeling before. Words couldn't describe it, he thought later. It was a feeling of having been transported to a land of ultimate quiet. The hoot owl's gentle song disappeared, though it still graced the forest night with its calls, as did any other of the myriad sounds reverberating throughout the forest. Bill heard only the silence, a quiet, a peace beyond words. He looked around, first to the north, the direction from which he and Harry had entered the forest only a few moments before. Then to the south, where those bent on destroying the forest had laid their deadly path. Bill stayed alert, even in the midst of the calm, for he knew that Harry might need him at any moment. He saw nothing unusual, but felt only the stillness of the night.

The quiet astounded him, so still, so calm, so comforting. He let his eyes wander upward as he looked into the brilliance of the night sky, lit by the yellow-orange glow of the full moon and the sparkle of millions of stars. He thought, what a wonderful place this is, and for a moment, just a moment, he regretted having stayed away all these years.

Then, he remembered that night so many, many years before. He wondered what might have happened that night had he stayed and continued to watch, or even dared to join his grandparents and the others around the circle. The stillness surrounded him as he thought of that evening, and what *could* have been.

Then, in an instant, Bill's senses came alive as he heard the sound of movement at the south end of the bridge. Instinctively, he squatted down, ready to act. But a broad smile crossed his face, for instead of the danger he was expecting to appear, the full moon showed only on a mother deer and her fawn as they gently moved past the far end of the bridge. Then, as if in a dream, at the far end of the bridge, a ball of light, of golden-white light, began to appear. At first a small circular globe, it made its way through the stillness of the night, illuminating the south end of the Olden Creek bridge, about five or six feet above the ground. The ball grew larger and larger. Bill watched intently. Then he saw in the midst of the golden light, the shape of a man, a very tall man begin to appear.

Bill legs began to tremble, beginning a dance he knew well as a high school football player, as his body readied itself to run. The quiet of the night and the calm in his heart kept him still on the spot on the bridge. Unexpectedly, he felt not fear, but an excitement that stirred deep within him. As the shape of the man came clear, he understood why. Standing less than ten feet away appeared a man he recognized as the very same one that had seen in his youth, the same tall man who'd led his grandparents and the others into the forest that night, and the very same one, he was sure, greeted so long ago his soon-to-be-married mother and father at his grandfather's farm.

A tall, massive man, nearly seven feet tall with bronze skin, sparkling brown eyes, a robe of pure white, and wearing an Indian style headdress; yes, this was him. What was his name? Bill struggled to remember, the one his mother had given. "Sakya." Yes, that was it. And in that instant, Bill heard, in a pronounced accent of India, the words, "Yes, Sakya, that is my name, and I am at your service. But before we talk further," the tall man said, "I must advise you that very shortly we will be seeing two rather frightened, and rather upset men coming along this path. For us, this isn't a problem, and I would advise that we simply move ourselves over there behind those tall trees. They won't harm the forest, but will leave directly. Please do not concern yourself about this. They'll be dealt with later at the appropriate time."

Sakya moved slowly, then, onto the bridge to where Bill stood, stopped and bowed slightly, and with palms held together in front of his forehead, he said, "Namaste, William." Without thinking, or even knowing the meaning of Sakya's greeting, Bill mimicked his gesture and said quietly back, "Namaste, to you Sakya, Namaste."

Sakya nodded back and then, without further word, continued across the bridge to the stand of trees at the edge of the clearing. As he passed, Bill heard Sakya's voice in his mind, "William, it's time for us to know each other, but for now, please follow me, we don't have much time." Bill stood for a moment, hesitating in silence before following. Had he really just heard Sakya talk to him without using words? It all seemed so unreal. He didn't know why he'd responded the way he had just now, but he couldn't deny how comfortable he'd felt in echoing Sakya's greeting back to him. It was as if a long ago memory had returned to whisper the familiar, Namaste, in his ear. But wasn't Sakya part of that nightmare in the forest that had happened to him so long ago?

As the confusion in his mind mounted, Bill felt no fear. For in his heart he knew all was well. Sakya *had* been the one Bill watched lead his grandparents and the others into the forest that night. But now, as Sakya walked by him on the bridge, rather than being a nightmare to repress as he'd tried to do all these years, Bill found himself excited and wanting to know more.

A thousand questions for Sakya came rushing into his mind, and still, Sakya's warning about the need for haste came back to him. So he followed the tall man to the clearing to the north of the bridge and there stood alongside him behind the sycamore grove near the clearing's edge.

Neither Bill nor Sakya spoke, although with Sakya speaking to him telepathically just a moment before, Bill had the sense that Sakya could read his thoughts. Bill looked up to see if Sakya had a reaction to his revelation about being listened to, but Sakya just stood there, silent, waiting, his eyes closed, with a look of utter calm on his face. Bill said nothing. The sound of men's voices in the forest to the south stirred Bill to attention. As he turned to see what might be happening, the moonlight revealed two men, dressed in the telltale black leathers of the motorcycle club that had been hanging around town these past months, coming out of the forest into the clearing.

"That bastard," Bill heard the taller of two say as they began crossing the bridge, "that bastard Thorpe! He got us into this crazy situation and then, just when we can finish the job and get our money out of this, this happens. Giants, ghosts, or whatever that was back there. The whole thing's nuts." The man began coughing and Bill heard him mutter under his breath, "damn gasoline smell!" The other, a short stocky man with a bald head with a dark beard, grimaced and nodded as they crossed the bridge, "You're right," he said. "Thorpe's a liar. He said this would all be so easy. I know one thing, I'm not letting Thorpe off the hook, even if I have to track him down all over the country to get my money." Then, as the two reached the north side of the bridge, the man continued, "Hurry up, let's keep moving. Whoever or whatever that giant of a thing was back there might be just right behind us."

Standing next to Sakya, Bill couldn't help but smile at the mention of that giant back there. As much as he was ready for action to stop these two from damaging the forest, he also felt no fear and no need to do anything but watch and let the situation unfold as it would. His only concern now was for Harry. Harry had gone down the same path that these two had used to come to the bridge. Where was he? Was he okay? Even with these questions, Bill continued to have the feeling that all was well and that nothing needed to concern him about Harry's welfare or about these two gang members. Standing next to the giant somehow put him into a place of *knowing* that all was in right order and that he didn't need to do more than just watch.

And watch he did, for as the two ran past the sycamore grove, neither he nor Sakya moved to stop them. Bill looked to Sakya several times to get a sign as what they should do, but Sakya remained still next to him, eyes closed, with no expression of care or concern on his face. On the contrary, rather than concern, Bill felt the peaceful presence of the man next to him. He even thought he saw a faint glow of golden Light emanate from the Sakya's body as the two motorcycle club members passed the grove on their way out of the forest.

Soon, Bill heard the sound of motorcycles roaring down the road of the Henley farm as the two Alcaz gang members headed towards the county road to the south. Bill turned to Sakya with a questioning look on his face. Calm as he had been while the two men passed, now that they were gone, Bill felt that somehow justice had been denied by the two getting away unhindered. He wanted assurances, too, that Harry was okay. He was just about to speak when Sakya turned to him, a broad smile on his face, and bowed. Sakya's brown eyes radiated a calm and shining beauty beneath the white of his headdress. Bill was about to ask about Harry and also confront Sakya about letting those two bandits get away, but before he could speak, Bill heard the words inside his mind, "Harry is all right, and the others will be caught, do not fear!"

Sakya smiled again, speaking aloud this time, and said "William, yes, it's new for you to communicate this way. We may see each other again, and if we do, you'll learn more. For now, if you'd like, we will speak aloud, about things that have bothered you for some time about that night in the forest, your grandparents and more. This we can do. You've waited a long time. We've other work to do as well that argues for our postponing our discussion of that night. As I said, those two won't go unpunished, but others still threaten the forest. As it is seen now, the best course of action is for you to return to your farm and go to the forest gate and wait there. We will be with you and you'll learn more as we go." Sakya paused for a moment and then added, "Conveniently, your mother's friend from town has come to take her to town for an evening of bridge at her house. She has left a note telling you that she won't be home, so don't concern yourself about her welfare."

Bill thought for a moment about Sakya's offer and what he'd said about the two being caught. As attractive as it was to talk about that night, and his hope that talking about it might help clear his heart from those painful and scary memories that had plagued him since his youth, he knew that time was of the essence in saving the forest. If Sakya thought it best that he should go home to his farm, he would go there. Bill felt relieved at the news about his mother visiting her friend in town. But the fact that those two had gotten away, and even with Sakya's assurances, the fact that his farm was now empty and vulnerable to attack stirred his desire to get back home.

"Sakya," he said. "I agree that putting off our conversation about that evening for now would be best. I know that talking about it would help, and I'd love to do that, but I as you said, the greater need is to do whatever I can to help save the forest. I must go to the farm now." Then, looking away from Sakya's steady gaze, almost as an afterthought, Bill mumbled, "I only hope that I don't end up just standing around again and can be of some real help!"

Sakya's smile grew and as his smile broadened, Bill felt it as a gentle wind of warmth and affection washing over him in an 'all is well' way. Sakya said, "Yes, Bill, the desire to be helpful is noble. Even your wish to get into the action is noble, but do not mistake action for success, or even for supporting that which you're setting out to do. Your role in the victory of the Light in this matter is most important. Please don't prejudge it as unimportant or as one of being only a bystander. This could not be further from the truth. The Brotherhood of Light works with students in many ways, and though the student may not at all be aware of how valuable his or her help is, each and every person who commits time and energy to supporting the work is most important to the overall success of the Light on Earth! The darkness has come way too far, William, to be left alone, and Earth needs all the assistance it can get. Those with the desire to help add the tremendous force of their own energy to the efforts of the whole realm of Light, and this can only make a difference. For this, we thank you and honor your courage for participating with us.

"Your grandparents participated in these tasks as well. The work of assisting the Light takes many forms. That night, your grandparents participated in a ritual of initiation on their own journey of learning to raise the physical vibration of their bodies, but they'd given many years before that to the task of protecting the forest. Now, you're participating in the same activity. Never think that it's nothing!"

Sakya stopped speaking, then. For a moment, Bill thought he would continue on with what he was saying, but Sakya didn't. Instead, he closed his eyes slightly and tilted his head, as if his ear were listening to something up in the sky, and then, just as quickly, opened his eyes and said, "Indeed, William, time is of the essence! You must hurry, for time is getting shorter, and you must be at the gate at the appointed time."

Bill turned to ask Sakya one last question. He wanted to know if he would ever see him again. Bill turned back to where Sakya had stood and found himself staring in amazement, eyes wide open, mouth agape at an empty forest, for where Sakya had stood only a moment before now stood only the quiet of the forest in the moonlit night, and the tall sycamore trees swaying in the gentle breeze that was beginning to rise from the northwest.

CHAPTER FORTY-NINE
HARRY FOLLOWS/AT THE GATE

Sometimes we learn to dance, even though we've not knowingly signed up for the lesson ...

As I went down the path following the scar-faced blonde man, I realized how important the forest was to me and to my life. I'd grown up here and it was here that Dad and I spent many hours together. Yes, I thought, he was tough on me and I can't say that we exactly understood each other, but the time in this forest together were high points of my memory of him. Mom, too, came to me, as she dried me off after coming in all muddy from an adventure in the forest, or put honey on a bee sting I'd gotten in the forest that swelled my leg like a small balloon. And now, this forest, which had been so much a part of me, was in real danger.

I cautiously went forward, aware that that the blonde man could be waiting for me around any bend as the trail wove its wave towards the main path. Within minutes, I reached the main path. Which direction had that one taken? To the right would take him to my own farm, to the left his path would lead to Bill's place. Immediately, Becky came to mind. Was she safe? What to do? And now I called on my own inner wisdom that had served me so well during the war. "To the left it told me, to the left."

Without hesitation, I headed down the path to towards the Bates farm. Once again, I moved cautiously along, expecting an attack at any moment, but none came. Soon, I came to the path that led to the little clearing where Dad and I had camped out those many nights. My instinct was to pass by it, to continue my pursuit of the blonde man along the main trail. Something, though, pulled me to it. And then to the right of the main trail I saw a smaller trail leading south deeper into the forest. For a moment I felt confused. My instinct told me to go straight to pursue the one I was after, but I knew something important also needed to be dealt with on that path. At that moment, Cousin Frank emerged from the trail with Uncle Julius right alongside him, being held up by Frank, blood running down the makeshift bandage that had obviously been hurriedly wrapped around his leg.

"What happened?" I asked. Uncle Julius said nothing as Frank told me what had happened and that we needed to hurry, that the scar faced man had taken Becky and the chest, and was heading out of the forest. Through which gate, he didn't know. I listened intently to Frank, but my eyes were on Uncle Julius the whole time. This man had so been a part of my early years and been so off these later ones, and now, as our eyes met,

I knew that something had changed in him. At first I didn't know what it was I saw there.

He looked weary and full of his eighty years. Then, something subtle shifted and without saying a word, we both *knew* each other as we did then, when I was growing up and he my beloved Uncle. In that moment I knew that my Uncle Julius was back! A smile of recognition crossed both our faces and he spoke. "Yes, Harry" he said, in a painful whisper, "I'm here. Hell can be visited in many forms and at many times, and I've had my visits. I'm back!" Then the pain in his leg surged and he bent over in agony but for only a moment. Then looked up and said, stronger this time, "We must save, Becky. The plan was to leave by the Bates family farm entrance. You and Frank must leave me here. Go!" he said. "Go quickly, time is short!" Then, all at once the weariness and pain seemed to envelope him, and he collapsed into Frank's arms, unable to hold himself up. "Go!" he managed to say, "go!"

Each moment, we knew, meant more danger for Becky. So, Frank and I quickly looked around and found a comfortable place for Julius near a log by the trail. Immediately, as we helped him down to the ground, Uncle Julius' eyes closed fully and a big sigh came from him as if this were the first time he had truly rested in many, many years. Half conscious, he could hardly speak. But, in a murmur, so quiet I needed to bend over to hear, he muttered under his breath the words, "Go, save Becky!"

With Frank by my side, we quickly headed down the trail. I lead us on the path sticking to the shadows of the large trees all the way. Still, as we went, I wondered about Frank. Something told me that it was right for him to come along. But without knowing why, I felt protective of him even though I knew he'd had the same training as I had had in marines. Still, I didn't want him getting hurt like his dad, but mostly, I realized now that I wasn't at all certain I knew how I would manage to get Becky free and at the same time keep us safe.

I thought of a plan. "Frank, we need to be real careful, now. We know those guys are dangerous, so what I suggest is that I go forward and you back me up. I think it would be best if you'd drop behind me and stay about fifty yards back in the shadows, then if I get into trouble, you'll be there to help in whatever way you think best." Frank nodded his head in agreement, "Okay, Harry," he said, and in a few steps more we parted, and I continued on alone.

It wasn't too far to the Bates farm entrance from the point where Frank left me, about a third of a mile, so I slowed down my pace to make sure that I didn't blunder onto the group by accident. The need for silence slowed my movements. This approach ran smack up against my growing feeling that I needed to get to Becky quickly. The Guardian came then to calm my fears about her safety. "Becky is well," he said, "Varness protects her even at this moment. Still, there's a need for you to hurry."

I nodded, saying, "Thank you," to the Guardian for his help and walked on, guided by the light of the moon.

***

With Felix in the lead, still clumsily holding onto the covered chest, Felix, Becky, and Henry came closer by the step to the Bates entrance to the forest. Since leaving the deer trail Thorpe had become increasingly impatient and tired of carrying the gas can. Repeatedly, he asked Felix when they would arrive. Having never been in the forest before, and having only that old man Julius' description to go by, Felix could only say in frustration and in fear at the rising anger he heard in Henry Thorpe's voice, "Soon, Henry, soon. I know it's just around the corner."

Becky said nothing. She knew that she would need to do something, even though she didn't know what that would be. And she somehow *knew* that Harry would play a role in whatever it was that she did. Two things, though, she was sure of: that she wouldn't leave the forest with Henry Thorpe; and, that she would do all she could to make sure that the forest stayed safe and the chest remained here, where it belonged.

A little further along, the main forest path came almost to a halt as the path widened into an open area that faced a wall of impenetrable blackberry bushes wrapped around the base of tall sycamore trees. Here, the three turned south to follow the path as it moved sharply to the right on its southward trajectory towards the Bates Family gate. As they walked, the path narrowed for some distance to the width of a small deer trail. The trail wove its way through a stand of old white oaks for about an eighth of a mile, only then to emerge onto a section of trail with what seemed to Becky like never-ending bushes of tall blackberry and mulberry bramble. It ended in a large grotto-like clearing surrounded by dense undergrowth on three sides and overhanging foliage above.

The path came to a dead end at the far end of the clearing. Thorpe ordered the group to stop as he put down the gas can and came forward waving the gun menacingly at both Becky and the fat man, ordering the both of them to move to the side of the clearing. The group found themselves in a semicircular clearing about seventy-five feet in diameter. At the far end of the clearing, the tree cover gave way to more open moonlit skies and here the group saw the outlines of a huge rusty old wrought iron gate rising about nine feet or so above the ground, the forest entrance from the Bates farm that Butezz had promised, only minutes before, would be there.

Framed by metal posts to the side and a thick metal lintel running across the top, the gate stood entirely overgrown with ivy vines amidst tall stands of blackberry thickets. The thickets spread across the far end of the semicircular area on both sides of the gate creating a formidable barrier separating the Bates farm to the east from the forest and the roadway beyond that, making it impossible to enter or leave the forest here, except through the narrow farm-gate entrance.

Felix almost jumped for joy in relief upon seeing the gate, so much so that he forgot for a moment the seriousness of his situation with Henry Thorpe and his own plan to steal the chest for himself. "Here it is, Henry," he shouted. "Just as I said it would be! eeh! eeh! eeh!" he squealed, as a child would do, excited to have pleased his parents and expecting to be offered the prospect of a long awaited candy treat as a reward. "This is it, Henry," he said. "See I told you it was close!" Then, catching himself, he muttered under his breath, "Damn!" for he knew that in Thorpe's eyes his excitement showed him to be weak.

Even with his anticipation of Thorpe's ridicule, Felix didn't feel afraid as his mind turned quickly on how to get the chest from Thorpe, and safely leave the area. I need to do it now, he thought. Get that chest for myself. But how? How?

Thorpe's smiled twisted with distain as he ordered Felix to go forward and open the rusty old gateway. Felix, quietly, did as he was ordered, but still had the chest in his hands as he moved forward. Yes, he thought, now I might have my chance! But his excitement soon faded as Thorpe said, "And Butezz, put the chest down first, over there," pointing with his gun to a tree stump about ten feet to the right of the gate. Felix's spirit sank once again as a sigh of despair emanated from his pudgy body. Still, he did as ordered and moved to the stump to put chest on it, and then moved forward to open the rusty old gate.

Becky said nothing. She had never been at this end of the forest before, but something inside told her that she knew more about this gate than she was remembering. What was it? And then in a flash she recalled, *That's it, I've got it!* A smile crossed her face as she remembered Bill's mother's story that night of the Bates farm, the forest, how this gate was used as the entryway into the forest for trainings of the Brotherhood, and finally, that it was always locked!

A sigh of relief welled up in her chest at the remembrance, and without thinking, she placed her right hand over her heart. Yes, she thought to herself, her smile gently broadening as the words "There is a God," silently rolled from her lips. In the next moment, what Becky remembered Mrs. Bates saying proved true as she watched Felix, under orders from the scar-faced man, Henry Thorpe, moved to the fence to open it.

At first, Becky wasn't sure what Butezz was doing as he arrived at the gate, his back to her and Thorpe, seemingly struggling to free something. Then he turned and complained, "I can't find the handle, Henry. "There's too much overgrowth here."

"Just keep looking," the blonde man muttered, waving his gun again at Butezz, obviously impatient with the whole process. Felix turned back to the task of uncovering the gate's secret of entry and exit. At first, he found nothing but the ever present ivy vines and remnants of the summer's offering of blackberry branches and thorns. Felix pulled them away as best he could, being careful not to prick himself on blackberry thorns, and then, in the midst of the vines, he saw the gate's huge, heavy metal handle "I found it, Henry, I found the handle!" he shouted, excited like a child finding a long lost toy. Then his heart sank as the moon showed the handle as part of a very sturdy keyed lock. Not just any lock, he thought, but one of those old strong ones made of steel that looks like it was meant to last a thousand years. Felix tried the handle, but it wouldn't move. It was locked tight!

In that moment, Felix almost collapsed as his head dropped to his chest and he fell into a deep, deep despair. Without the key to the lock, his planned route to exit was blocked. His heart sank, his already sallow skin became pasty white, and his body began to shake. Beyond his fear of his plan's failure, the fear of what Thorpe might do plagued him. Felix had no doubt that Thorpe was capable of doing away with both him and the woman, and then leaving the forest another way, if he could, along with the chest. Somehow this last thought sobered him. Though terrified of Thorpe's reaction, owning the chest, having it near him, he realized, was even more important than his fear.

Calming himself, he began figuring ways to deal with the situation. The gun! Yes, the gun, he thought. If I could get that gun from him. Then, just as quickly, he dismissed this idea. Thorpe would never let that happen!" In spite of Felix's past prowess at figuring ways out of difficult situations, in the micro-seconds that passed between the time he discovered the gate impassable and the time he would have to turn to tell Thorpe this news, he could think of no good way to get himself out of the situation. Like a wave, his fear of what Thorpe would do when he found the way out blocked, again washed over him.

"Henn-rrry," he said, with a slight stutter as he turned to face the blonde man with the gun "we can't get out this way, the gate's locked tight." With every word, Felix's fear of Thorpe's reaction grew stronger; he could see the man's rage mount, the scar on his face growing redder and redder. Hoping one last time to cut off Thorpe's violent reaction, Felix muttered, without much conviction, "B-b-ut, Henn-henrrr-rry, maybe there's annn-other way out nee-ee-ear here."

Thorpe said nothing, but his actions showed all as he lifted the gun in his hand to the level of Felix's heart, threatening to fire. Felix gasped, not knowing what Thorpe would do. Just then, both men froze in a macabre tableau of rage, fear, and reaction as they heard the sound of footfalls shuffling through fallen autumn leaves across the ground on the other side of the gate, coming closer and closer to them and to the gate with each step. As the sound approached, so, too, came the unmistakable light of a flashlight moving from side to side, top to bottom on the gate, creating a tapestry of rays showing through the small spaces left by the interweaving of ivy leaves, vines, and the still berry laden branches of blackberry bushes.

Thorpe was the first to react. As if awakening from a dream, he motioned a threatening gesture of silence with the gun, first to the fat man in front of him, and then to Becky standing to the left of the gate opening. Silently he waved the gun at Felix, ordering him to the side of the gate, not far from where the chest rested on the tree stump, still wrapped in Thorpe's black leather jacket.

Soon, the rustling of leaves ceased as the footsteps stopped on the other side of the gate. A moment later, they heard a gentle shaking of the gate, and then leaves and vines being pulled aside, as the person on the other side sought, like Butezz had an instant before, to find the secret of the gate's entrance, and to set the doorway free.

They heard a man's low whisper. "Yes!" it said in satisfaction as the mystery of the forest's gateway gave way to the searcher's probing and pulling hands. Becky stood silent, watching, waiting, wondering who it was on the other side, knowing that whoever it was, she needed to warn them away. Then, through the silence, came the sound of someone hurt, "Ouch!" Then, a little louder, the man's voice said, "Damn, damn those prickles!" And Becky knew that voice as Bill's and she could restrain herself no longer, "Bill," she shouted, "it's me, Becky, don't open the gate, they're here, the murderers, they're here, and they've got a gun!"

"Becky," Bill's startled voice came back, "it's you." But before either one of them could say more, Thorpe acted. Leaping quickly to Becky's side, he grabbed her from the rear, one strong hand roughly clasped over Becky's mouth and the other holding the gun to her head. "Now you listen, here" he said to Bill, "you open that damn gate right now or you'll never see her alive again!"

"Are you okay?" Bill asked Becky. But no matter how hard she struggled to free herself from Thorpe's iron grip, the scar-faced man held her, making it impossible for her to speak. She wanted to shout, "Get out of here, Bill, don't do it," but she couldn't. She twisted and turned, but Thorpe only held her tighter, with each movement of her body, and then he whispered in her ear, "If you don't stop struggling, I'll shoot right through the gate." With a quiet laugh, he said, "And maybe, just maybe, I'll get him."

Becky stopped her struggle. An eerie silence filled the night as they waited for Bill's reply. Crickets sang their evening song, trees rustled in the evening breeze, but nothing came. Then Bill's voice broke the silence, "All right," he said, "I'll open it, just don't hurt her."

"Okay," muttered Thorpe, "just do it fast!"

In a moment, the checkered rays of the flashlight's beam showed once more on to the grotto floor through the gate, creating a dancing play of light as Bill found the opening to the gate's lock, put the key in, and unlocked it. Then, with some effort, he began pushing it open, breaking through the tangle of vines that told of the many years that the Bates family farm entrance to the forest had gone unopened.

Becky could stand it no more, and as Thorpe's attention and focus moved to what was happening at the gate, she broke the grip of the hand that held her silent and shouted, "Bill, stop, don't open it, get out of here, they must not leave the forest, they must not have the chest, it's just too important." Her words were stopped in mid-sentence as Thorpe tightened his grip once again, forcing her to silence.

"You, open that gate or else. Come in, with your hands up and the key in your hands," he roared. "Do it, now," he shouted, "I mean it, do it *now*!"

***

As I continued down the main forest path my apprehension grew. I knew that Becky was okay, but I still had that feeling in my gut that I'd known so well in Nam, that something big was about to happen and I needed to be very, very alert. The main path widened considerably as I came nearer to what I felt must be the end of the forest. As I came around a sharp bend in the path the trail narrowed, moving now from east to dead south, I knew that this must mean that I'd come to the eastern edge of the forest. I walked on, slowly, as silently as I could with an increased awareness of each step, each leaf that I stepped upon, and the need to avoid stepping on another, and each branch along the way that I must evade. My belly told me something big was up, and I felt thankful to that feeling in me that urged me forward, but with caution.

Soon enough I found my movements constricted in the narrow trail passageway, with the need for even more care in moving along without being heard. I measured my steps along the path under the now canopy of overgrown brambles and blackberry bushes. The high moon still showed the way through a myriad of shadows that played through the thinning overgrowth.

About fifty yards along, I heard voices and most distinctly, Becky shouting something, a warning to Bill. "... not open it." And then came the loud voice of a man, snapping orders, angry, mean. I couldn't hear what was said, but I knew that I needed to hurry. I came closer, caution accompanied my every breath. Even with the anger of the man's voice, a sigh of relief rippled through my body, for just as the Guardian had said, Becky was okay. I'd heard her voice, but what about Bill, how did he get to be with Becky in the group ahead? I let go of the thought for now, for I heard the danger in Becky's voice, the fear for herself, and for Bill.

I wanted to rush forward, but I knew that every step brought me closer along the path to the group. Going on, I would end up in the heart of it, and at the mercy of the man with the gun. I slowed down. I needed to see what was going on before acting. I looked to my left and then to my right for an opening, a place that I could get close enough to see without being seen or heard. To my left the thickets of bramble and blackberry thorn bushes made passage through them impossible. To my right, the forest seemed more friendly as the brier patches above gave way to large sycamores and ancient oaks, but once again, I could see no way through the thick underbrush beneath the towering trees. I decided that I would simply have to take a chance and crawl on my belly along the path to get closer. But only a moment later my heart dropped as I realized the folly in this with fallen autumn leaves beginning to spread along the floor of the forest path.

The Guardian came to me then, "Harry," he said, "move quickly down the path. Be silent, to your left you'll find a passageway used by the deer through the thicket. No leaves have fallen there and you'll be able to come close enough to see what it is you need to see." I obeyed immediately, and soon enough the trail appeared on the left. A small, low opening that would require me to bend down beneath the overhanging blackberry bushes as I moved along. I wasted no time. I had no time to speculate as Becky and Bill's safety were at the top of my mind!

I moved quietly along the deer path, my body bent over to avoid the stickers above. Soon enough I reached a place through the blackberry bushes from where I could see. Still hidden from sight, from here the deer trail led directly into a clearing. From this place I had a clear view to the clearing's end to the south where I could see a continuation of the wall of overgrown ivy, brambles, and low undergrowth wrapping around tall trees that formed an impenetrable wall to the east and south end of the forest at the Bates family farm. In some places over ten feet tall, this wall of thicket and undergrowth made casual passage into the forest impossible.

From where I stood, I could only see one person, the short fat man with the round belly who owned the new café in town where the

Jay Allan Luboff

motorcycle gang hung out and who'd recently made an offer to Bill to buy the Bates farm. The fat man stood to the right of the wall of the clearing where the south forest wall began its journey across to the west. The forest stood protected from unwanted entrants by a natural barrier of impenetrable undergrowth and tall trees that ran all the way from this spot across the southern edge of the forest to our farm at the forest's southwest corner.

I watched the man as he seemed alternatively excited, jumping up and down with knuckles in his mouth like a little boy about to receive a birthday present, and then looking scared with his head turning to and fro, once again like a little boy, but this time one who isn't sure whether he was about to be scolded or not. All the while, the man's eyes and head continued to dart back and forth. One moment he looked to the forest clearing to the left, and the next moment he'd dart his head back to the south wall looking intensely at something on the wall.

I looked around at the clearing and noticed something odd on the stump of a tree to the left of where the café keeper stood. There, I saw a slight glow of light, and looking more closely, I recognized the now muted radiance of Varness emanating from beneath what appeared to be a black leather coat. I gasped silently under my breath, for even though I had a strong sense in my heart that Varness was safe, I felt the same protective instinct towards it that I felt towards Becky and Bill. In that moment I knew Varness not as an inanimate object, but a living force serving the Light. I knew that I must find a way to help protect it.

My thoughts raced? What should I do? The Bates farm entrance to the forest must be near. I thought, perhaps I could—but my thoughts were suddenly interrupted as I watched the unfolding events in the clearing. Through the tangle of thorns and berry vines on the south wall of the forest, I watched as the focus of the fat man's wild attention became clear. Amidst the undergrowth a portion of the overgrown wall slowly moved inward as leaves, brambles, and berry vines gave way revealing a hidden gate in the forest wall.

The short man froze at the movement in the wall. A grotesque smile played across his face in the as the gate continued to be opened, not without difficulty, by someone entering from the other side. I watched in anticipation, and soon saw the familiar face of Bill coming through the arched gateway, his hands raised above his head with something shiny, a key, dangling from his right hand.

"Damn" I thought, "what on Earth is Bill doing here?" I didn't have much time to think about it, for just then I saw the blond man push Becky before him into the center of the clearing. He held a gun to her back as he moved forward, his other hand tightly held her around the neck.

"Okay," the man said, talking to Bill, "you stand over there," motioning Bill to move alongside the fat man, near Varness, "and throw me that key, here, on the ground in front of me." As he said this, he released his hold around Becky's neck and pointed the gun to a place in the middle of the clearing where he wanted the key tossed. Becky waited not one moment. She raced immediately from the man towards Bill, but stopped suddenly as the man fired a shot over both Bill and Becky's head.

"Now, listen," he said, "toss me that key, or else."

Becky stood several feet from Bill. "Bill," Becky said, her back to me now, "don't do it! He and his hoods killed my parents; we can't let them get away.

At first Bill said nothing. I wasn't sure what he would do. The man continued to snarl orders to Bill. "Toss it right there," he said, pointing again with his gun to where he wanted it to go.

Tension mounted as Bill didn't respond. Then, without saying a word, as if he'd know all along what he would do, Bill quietly tossed the key, not to where the man with the scar had ordered, but, instead, over his head, over the south wall gate and out onto the other side of the forest wall! In a flash, Bill moved backwards and pressed the gate with his back and buttocks. The sound of the gate locking made a loud click that echoed through the small clearing as Bill's weight closed the opening, effectively sealing the passage out of the forest through the farm entrance.

The little fat man was the first to react. Instead of the smile on his face that I'd seen only moments before, a grimace of pure anguish twisted his mouth as a low, hiss-like sound of pain came from his lips "Nooooo!" he squealed. "No!" And in the next moment, he collapsed to the ground and began weeping, like someone who'd just lost his most cherished dream. He pounded the earth with his right hand, yelling "No! No! No!"

Bill said nothing, but swiftly moved to Becky's side once the gate door locked in place. Then, as if choreographed and without a word spoken between them, they turned in perfect unison to face the blonde man, not with defiance, but with an incredibly calm strength!

I prepared to act, but heard the voice of the Guardian say, "Wait, they're fine," so I didn't move. The whole thing happened so quickly that the blonde man seemed stunned for a moment, not knowing how to react. But soon enough he got his composure back.

"Okay," he snarled, "you think you've won, eh, well, I can kill you now or later, it doesn't matter to me. Butezz, get your ass off the ground and grab that box!" And then, "Do you know another way out of here?" "Only," murmured, the short man, "the way I came in with the old man, and I'm not sure I could find my way back."

Pointing the gun to Bill, he said to Becky, "You'll show me another way out of this forest, or I promise you both, I won't hesitate to pull the trigger, and it won't be over your boyfriend's head or yours."

Becky's voice seemed frightened not so much for herself, but for Bill. "All right," she answered, "we'll need to go back along the path to the forest entrance to the west. The path isn't always so straight, but I'll show you the way."

Bill stood alongside Becky saying nothing. As I looked at them both, I had the strange experience of not really seeing any difference between them. Their strength in the face of this madman was equal, but something else, something about Bill and Becky seemed, well, more like brother and sister, almost twins. As she spoke, the tone, the inclination of her voice sounded so much like his that I almost couldn't tell which one of the two had spoken, and I wondered whether Becky and Bill were "Sparks of Light" as the Guardian had explained, as both of them had such similar energy and even appearance.

The short man, the one the other called Butezz, didn't respond immediately to the blonde man's order. Instead, he stayed on his knees, and in pure frustration, mumbled something over and over again as he continued to weakly pound the ground. Then, as if hearing the order for the first time, he looked up at the blonde man with an air of one resolved to a situation that seemed almost impossible to him and said in a voice so low that I could hardly hear it, "Okay, Henry, okay."

I waited and watched. Even though a chilling wind was beginning to blow through the forest, sweat formed on my brow. The situation differed so greatly from anything I'd encountered before. What should I do? I wanted to act, but knew to listen to the Guardian. I must not take any action that would result in Bill or Becky getting hurt. I had to rethink my training, my approach, and I decided to trust that at the right time I would know what to do. In the meantime, I would wait for further guidance to come.

I could hear in the scar-faced man's voice that as his frustration mounted his nerves were being pressed to their limits. In this state, he felt especially dangerous to me and I knew not to take any unnecessary risks. The only thing that holds that man back, I thought, is that he needs Becky and Bill to show him the way out of the forest. I would continue my vigil. I would wait.

For a moment, time seemed to slow as things in the clearing took on a dreamlike quality as the group began forming itself for the journey back through the forest. Then, in an instant, all came clearly again into focus as the blonde man barked orders for the group to begin moving back along the path. I stood silent, not moving a muscle as the procession passed just feet from my hiding place. The short man led the way, still carrying the chest in its covering, with Becky behind, Bill behind her, and then the blonde man following with his gun pushed into the small of Bill's back. Before they left, the blonde man took off his belt and made Becky tie it through a loop of her jeans in the back and then to a loop in Bills own belt. In this way, both Bill and Becky were effectively hobbled. Though this would take the group longer to get through the forest, it ensured that neither would risk jumping off the trail and disappearing into the forest without the other awkwardly tumbling after.

The sound of the autumn leaves on the forest floor brought back memories of my youth, with the same autumn sounds, the same autumn chill, and for a moment, I wanted to be back at home in my warm bed, reading a good book. I'd felt this often in my boyhood at the time of the falling leaves, a precursor to winter's cold nights, but this memory disappeared now as the group passed by my hiding place.

I felt the urge to act, but knew not to, at least not here on this narrow part of the path. I could feel the desperation growing in the man with the gun. I must wait for the right moment. My thoughts turned to Frank. I knew that he was out there in the forest somewhere and I only hoped that he would keep himself out of harm's way as the group moved on. Except for a hoot-owl calling its special call, silence filled the night, the wind had stopped. I looked up. A sparkle of stars blanketed the sky. Quiet and still, the forest seemed, as I, to be waiting and watching. I moved onto the path, far enough behind not to be seen, nor heard, but close enough to act when the chance would arise.

The sound of the footfalls of the group joined nature's chorus as the small path turned sharply from its north-south trajectory and widened as it turned east at this end of the forest and meandered westward across the forest toward our farm. I wondered what I should do as I followed, making sure to hide my presence in the forest shadows. From my place on the path I could see the scar-faced man with his gun pressed firmly into Bill's back, shoving him forward as Bill struggled with Becky to keep an even pace, so as not to fall.

As I followed, the wind began to rise again from the west sweeping its way through the tall trees sending autumn leaves falling to the forest's floor. Together, the sounds of the crickets, owls and falling leaves combined to create the illusion of a choreographed forest dance, written by an unknown composer from another time, and another place. In the midst of this dance, I noticed something changing: the path seemed to be getting brighter! A few steps further brought the group to an even wider part of the path where several deer trails from the north crossed the main path. The scar-faced man stopped the group and shouted to the short man, "Keep that coat over that box, we don't want the whole world to see us when we leave this damn forest."

Yes, "I thought to myself, that's it. It's the glow coming from Varness that's getting brighter. That's what's causing the increased light. I watched from my place far back on the road as the short fat man struggled to contain the chest's expanding light. But no matter which way he tried to cover Varness with the jacket, the illuminating radiance increased. The blonde man shouted again to cover the chest, but the short man only looked back at him with a despairing look on his face and said, in a whimper, "I can't, Henry, I can't, the thing seems to have a life of its own."

"No, excuses," the blonde man shouted again, "just do it!"

With every moment I could feel the tension of violence-about-to-happen, filling the air as the man with the gun stopped the group, moved the gun away from Bill's back and pointed it directly at Butezz. "You stop that thing from glowing right now, or you've had it, Butezz. And you know what, I wouldn't mind doin' it at all, you've been nothing but a pain since this whole job began. Worthless, no, even less than that. So figure out how to cover that chest, and just do it, right now," he shouted.

But the short man could do nothing to still Varness. As much as he struggled to wrap the jacket this way or that, the chest increased its radiance. I watched the Light begin to glow through the jacket itself! The blonde man, his face turning red in fury, moved away from Becky and Bill and advanced on the short man, coming within only a foot of him. As he did, I watched Bill and Becky, still hobbled by the belt, move to the side of the path hoping to keep out of the raging man's way.

From my place in the darkness, I moved to the center of the path nearer to the group, hoping for an opening. The blonde man moved still closer to the chest, his frustration continuing to mount as the man called Butezz frantically struggled to cover the glowing Light of Varness, now so bright that it shinned directly through the Motorcycle Club black leather jacket, as if the jacket weren't even there at all! Butezz looked around and stuttered, "It's not my f-f-fauu-u-u-lt, Henry, I can't he-he-elp it. Then he screamed, "It's getting hotter, Henry, I can't hold it!" And in that moment the blonde man's black Motorcycle Club jacket burst into flames! As the fat man released the chest, I prayed that Varness would not be damaged in its fall to the ground!

CHAPTER FIFTY
VARNESS RETURNS

Many watch and wait, but only those with an open heart SEE the Truth of the Great Spirit when it comes

Rather than crashing to the ground as I imagined it would, the chest simply, slowly and gently floated to the earth, landing perfectly upright! Not one trace of the once flaming jacket remained, and not a single sign that the flames ever existed showed on the brilliant black wood of Varness. Instead, the chest seemed to pulsate with a sense of quiet and calm, immune from any flames. For a moment all the forest stood still, embraced by the chest's energy, quiet and serene, as if encapsulated in a magical mist of silence. Not a sound could be heard, a silent moment, I thought, in the field of time.

Then, as quickly as it came, the silence lifted and the forest came alive again, but not in the same way as it had before. Something in the forest had changed. It's moved, I thought, into a different wavelength, a different timeframe, a different zone of existence. Even the gentle evening breeze slowed to match the rhythm and pace of the chest's dreamlike fall. Trees slowed their motion, and the pace and tone of the once loud clicking chorus of crickets softened, quieted its melody as they, too, came into attunement with the gentle vibration of the bejeweled chest.

I knew now that something in the forest had shifted and would never be the same. The light, the brilliance of colors, the trees, the foliage, and even the sounds of the forest came to my ears in tones so vibrant, so beautiful, so full as to bring tears to my eyes. In that moment I understood that as dire as the situation might seem, the chest Varness, the *Passage to the Heavens* had now fully returned to Earth to share the gifts of Light embodied in Her creation.

***

In seconds, Varness' glow, now unhindered by the jacket, began to fill the forest and sky a with a rich orange-like color reminiscent of the many sun rises that Dad, Mom, Becky and I had watched morning after morning on the farm. So radiant was Varness' Light that I needed to turn my eyes away, just for a moment, as they adjusted to its brilliance.

I looked over at Bill and Becky who stood illuminated, and even frozen, at the edge of the forest path. And, on the other side of the path, I saw cousin Frank revealed beneath a stand of oaks, no longer clothed in protection of the darkness. The fat man seemed not to notice the change as he bent down one last time in a frenzied attempt to recapture his grip on the chest, as if the loss of Varness from his hands meant somehow the end of life itself.

Although I didn't know how it could happen, in the midst of the Light I found myself able to feel, truly experience and feel the fat man's every wish, his every emotion, his every desire as if they were my own. He wanted that chest so badly, he would have died for it or, I realized, killed for it! He struggled to regain a grip, but the heat of fiery Light radiating from the chest's marvelous array of stones made it impossible for him to come even a little bit close to it. Still, he wanted to possess Varness so badly he would have done almost anything to get it. I heard his thoughts, "It's that bastard Thorpe's fault. I'll kill him!" Now emboldened by his obsession, he thought to attack the blonde man who stood only a few steps away from him, "Gun or no gun!"But he found himself unable to move, frozen amidst the brilliant forest tableau created by the majestic Light. No matter how feeble his attempt to hurt the blonde man might be, he couldn't even try, for the power of Varness held his every movement in check.

The man called Thorpe raged all the while, and I could also feel *his* every emotion within my own mind and hear every word of his own inner voice. I flinched at feeling the hatred and darkness that permeated this man's every thought and action. Should I kill the fat little bastard and the others now, grab the chest and run, he thought, or just get the hell out of this forest and leave that stinking' chest? As he pondered his choice, he, too, found himself frozen where he stood as the sunlight like glow of Varness continued to grow stronger, ever brighter, lighting up not only the path, but also the evening sky.

My thoughts turned to Becky and Bill. I wanted to move to be with them as the ever brighter Light moved closer and closer to reveal my own position in the middle of the trail. But I, too, couldn't move. I heard both Becky and Bill's voices in unison in my mind as they spoke. "We're okay, Harry." And then Becky added, "but we can't move, we're stuck right here." From his place on the other side of the trail, Frank added his voice to theirs, "Me, too. Me too! I can hear your thoughts, and the others, but I'm frozen to the spot."

My heart pounded. My own position would soon be revealed in and I would be powerless to help the others or myself. I spoke within my mind to the others. "Try to move, try to get back into the forest out of sight of the Light." They each answered that they couldn't.

To my dismay the Light expanded, showing my place in the middle of the path. And, as it did, it bathed us all, Thorpe, Butezz, Bill, Becky, Frank and me in a circle of pure orange radiance. My position revealed, I looked over at the man with the gun. I could feel his emotions, hear his thoughts, but curiously he couldn't hear mine, or even feel, I knew, what it was that I was feeling.

We locked eyes. He wanted to lift the gun and fire. He had no place in him that still questioned what action he would take if he could. He knew now what he *wanted* to do. He would survive. He would kill us all, and try to take the chest with him. With or without the chest he would leave the forest by the way he had come in, setting the forest ablaze as he left. His eyes dropped down for a moment to check the position of the gasoline can that rested on the earth by his feet, and then they lifted again back to meet mine. "Yes," he thought, "that's the best way out of here."

Intimidation and threat spilled through his eyes towards me, and then I heard him say within his mind, "But before I go I'd love to make this one beg me for his life." And still, he couldn't move, couldn't lift the gun to threaten me. And now, only now did he really become aware of the power of Varness. Though he felt the power that froze him to the spot when first the orange Light touched him, somewhere he had not really believed it and blocked it from his consciousness. It was as if the Light itself were some kind of mirage and the whole situation a dream that he need not acknowledge or recognize as something that could or would affect him, that it would somehow fade away. For the first time, Henry Thorpe began to worry about his situation and his thoughts began to turn from his strategy of attack to one of figuring out what he could do to get the hell out of this forest. Even as he thought this, the Light bathed us all, including Thorpe and Butezz, holding us in place as in a still life painting.

The Guardian's voice rang out in the forest. "Listen well, Children of Light" it said, "each is given a choice and each must choose well." Nothing more was spoken, yet as his words faded in my mind, I felt the orange glow penetrate deeper and deeper within every cell of my being, so strong and brilliant that I felt that it actually had the ability to change my body from solid matter into pure vibration, pure frequency of Light. In spite of the danger of the situation, I closed my eyes to be with the feelings of pure love and contentment pulsating through me. I felt myself all aglow. Strangely, it felt as if I were becoming a bright light. I forgot about the danger for a moment and all fear left me. I stood bathing in these feelings, and just for a moment turned my thoughts to Bill, Becky and Frank to see how they were doing. I knew right away that they were also feeling the same power.

I felt, too, the tremendous resistance from both Butezz and Thorpe to the deepening penetration of the Light. Butezz, who stood closest to the chest, simply shut down. Over and over he spoke the words, "No, No, don't do that to me." Then, because he didn't have the strength to fight the powerful feelings generated by Varness, he simply collapsed on the ground and continued to mutter, "No, no, don't do that to me … Daddy will hate me, Daddy will hate me, Daddy will hurt me."The man called Henry Thorpe had a very different response. Instead of collapsing as Butezz had, I felt him focus all his strength on keeping the ray from penetrating his being. I met his eyes and they no longer looked with their menacing energies at me, but were turned inward to a place within himself from which he drew energies—from the darkest forces of the universe.

Within myself I could feel him reach out to these forces of darkness, calling for their help. I could no longer look on. I had to withdraw and block my own attention from his inner space as his call brought forth such vile images and energies, such distorted feelings of malice loathing and hatred that I could no longer remain, or even listen any longer to the man's inner dialogue.

Still, I kept my gaze on him. I couldn't move and he had the gun and intended to use it. I looked on as his face contorted and transformed, as if it were matching the foul energies of darkness. He seemed to be turning into a less than human-like being and more like a creature that I could only imagine coming from an underworld nightmare of the foulest sort. The scar on his face turned livid red and the color of his skin turned from its pasty-white hue to an ugly, off-shade of green.

In response to Thorpe's dark plea, something changed. The forces he called seemed to answer him back, for the Light of Varness dimmed slightly, became a little less clear, a little less sharp, as if a slight mist or fog were setting in. A chill ran through me as I sensed shadowy energies in the forest that I had never experienced before. They were attempting with all their might to stifle the pure spirit of the orange Light. Thorpe's eyes changed as they refocused on me to one of disdainful glee. A shriek of laughter came from his lips to let me know that he *knew* himself to be successful in his call, that he was not alone and the forces of darkness had headed his plea.

For a moment, fear gripped me, for I also felt the power of these forces. Then, without warning, came a ripping sound of thunder that shook the earth beneath my feet, and with it a strike of lightning so brilliant that it was all I could do to bear the sound and watch the light with blinking eyes as it raced across the night sky. It was as if heaven and earth were combining in this very moment to create something new, something strange and different right here in the air above the forest floor. And yet something old, like an ancient roadway, was opening to a distant place, long ago forgotten.

I watched as a part of the sky above the forest turned brighter than the rest as if cut out from the fullness of the glorious night sky. It moved ever downward through the orange Light of Varness toward where we stood. In the richness of that patch of lightened sky I could see sparkles of Light glimmering all through it, and for a moment I thought that the stars themselves were descending to Earth, to the very spot on the forest floor where I stood.

Varness' orange Light continued to expand around the sparkling filled sky, framing it, as if making room for it as a glittering jewel might be framed on a background of pure black velvet. It was as if Varness knew the purpose of this descending sky. Then, in an instant, all in the forest became quiet again. But something changed. The forest's silence resonated with an almost inaudible humming sound that had not been there before. Instinctively, my hand went to my heart, for the sound touched a place so deep within me as to almost bring tears to my eyes, as if my heart were being touched by memories of love so old, yet so familiar, full, and deep, that I almost cried with anticipation and joy.

I heard Becky's voice in my head. "Harry," she said, "What is it? Do you see it? Can you feel it?"

"Yes, I do, I do." I answered back in my mind, as I marveled not only at the humming sound, but also at the magnificence of the sparkling Lights all around that had descended to the forest floor right in front of where I stood.

"I see it, too," Bill's voice echoed in my mind.

Frank remained silent and I knew that he had not seen the thundering Lighting, the sparkling sky, nor could he hear the sweet humming sound that filled the three of our hearts and ears. I knew as well, that neither Butezz nor Thorpe could hear the sounds or see the Lights on the forest floor. Then, as if waking me from a dream, I heard Becky's loud warning ring out through the trees of the forest's night. "Watch out, Harry!" she shouted, "We can move again, and so can they!"

Her warning came too late. I couldn't move quickly enough away from my place in the middle of the path. A smile crossed Henry Thorpe's face as he realized that he could move. For just a moment we locked eyes again, and I saw the malice, the hatred, the dark force of his ill intent. The smile grew darker and more twisted as he bathed in his moment of victory. He had me, and we both knew it. Without a moment's hesitation, he lifted the gun, aimed at me and fired. I saw the sparks fly off his gun as he fired twice and the bullets raced towards me. I felt certain that I would die. But the bullets never reached me. Standing before me in the same instant as Thorpe pulled the trigger, I saw a huge blue-white colored angel, with rainbow colored wings. In his hand he held a sword so brilliant that I needed to raise my arm to partially shield my eyes. Still, I watched as the two bullets, in a slow motion, never reached their destination, but instead were dissolved into thin air as the blue-white angel swept his shinning sword across their path with miraculous speed, first to the left and then to the right, stopping their momentum and turning them into nothing.

Everything began to move quickly. The angel didn't arrive alone. Three other angels appeared: an orange one in front of Becky, a gold one in front of Bill, and a rose-colored one in front of the place where Cousin Frank hid.

Henry Thorpe stood in shock. Where had the bullets gone? How could he have missed the mark? Despite his consternation, the dark smile remained on his face. Although he couldn't see the blue-white angel, or the other Angels of Light that had come to protect Becky, Bill, Frank, and me, he could feel *the others* that had come, the dark ones who'd come to support him, to stand by him, dark angels, twisted and contorted in their aspect, with grey black wings, greenish skin, and malevolent eyes.

Undaunted, Thorpe turned his attention to Becky and Bill, pointing the gun at them. He couldn't fire, even with the presence and support that the dark ones gave him. He tried to fire the gun, even called on their dark help, but couldn't. Before our eyes, in our own forest, the forest that Becky and I had played in as children, a battle of Light and darkness took place. The Angels of Light stood in the face of darkness, holding Becky, Bill, Frank and me as if in a mantel of protective energy, *a ring-no-pass*, from the hatred of the dark ones.

The Light Angels combined their own power with the Light of Varness to surround each of us in a sphere of glowing Light. Still, a shiver of pure fear and disgust ran through me as I felt the ill will of the dark angels toward us. They wanted to destroy each of us, they wanted the chest, and they wanted the Light to perish from Earth forever.

They were not without strength, for their power seemed to come from Thorpe himself. Though I could "see" that Thorpe *couldn't* see the Light angels, I saw the streams of dark energies pouring through him to the Light Ones in an attempt to destroy them, or at least to weaken their power, and I understood, then, that Thorpe's hatred and malice fed the powers of the dark forces of the universe, that through this man, and those like him, these forces continued their presence on Earth.

Thorpe's smile became uglier and more distorted as he continued to sense the dark presence. Other dark ones used what power they could gain from Butezz, although the force of darkness they gathered from them didn't equal that of the energies of hatred of Thorpe. The dark angels gathered around Butezz and Thorpe. Six tall ones, three around each man, each I thought, uglier and creepier than the next. But something about them told me that they'd not always looked this way. As soon as I had that thought, scenes of places I didn't recognize passed before my mind's eye. Other planets, other times, when each one of these dark ones themselves, younger in looks, less twisted and ugly than now, were given choices to turn back to the Light. None had taken those choices. In one vision, one of the dark ones, still looking young in age and not yet twisted, had helped a young native child of some land long forgotten keep from falling off a cliff. The child was crawling near the edge and this dark one had come to help the child fall to its death. Instead, the dark angel chose to scare the child *away* from the cliff, and it had survived.

I saw an Angel of Light descend alongside the dark one, and offer that one a choice to "come back home." The dark one could have returned to the Light, but instead scoffed at the Angel of Light, and attacked the Light Angel with its wings, and the choice was made.

Now, as I regarded this same one, its face full of contorted hatred, I saw what working for the darkness really means: the poison of it, the never-ending commitment to destroy beauty, grace, love and dignity. In my heart I knew that I would oppose these dark ones and others like them. I also felt sorry for them, for it seemed to me that they were prisoners of choices they'd made oh so long ago and somehow could not, or would not now reverse. Nor could they even contemplate at this point turning back to Light, from where they'd originally come.

All this flashed across my mind in just an instant, and I *knew* that Becky and Bill had also seen all that I'd seen, but that Cousin Frank had not. Still, I thought, Frank knows what's happening. I don't know how he knows, but he knows. And I knew as well that neither Henry Thorpe nor Felix Butezz could see the Angels of Light, or the dark ones. Thorpe could feel their presence here in the forest, ready to aid him and encourage him on, and it gave him confidence.

"So," he shouted across the clearing at me, "you think you've won, but you haven't." Emboldened by the forces of darkness surrounding him, and with his gun still pointed at Becky and Bill, Thorpe's face twisted with a disdainful smirk, as he struggled to fire. I couldn't tell when he might be able to move again, as the struggle of the Light and dark continued. I dared not move for I still feared what might happen to Becky or Bill, in spite of the miracle that I had just witnessed.

We stood there for several seconds like this, me frozen in the middle of the path, Becky and Bill held captive at the edge of the forest path, Thorpe's gun pointed at them. Then something shifted in the forest even as Thorpe spoke, the powers of the Angels of Light grew stronger and stronger as the Light of Varness continued to grow in its radiance across the forest and the sky. The dark ones felt the impact of that power!

The six dark angels tried to radiate their own dark energies in support of Thorpe's actions and to protect Butezz, who'd now gathered strength from their presence and was able to stand. But as much as they tried to stifle the Light, the strength of the Light grew and Thorpe remained in check, unable, at least for the moment, to harm Bill and Becky. And now, as the Light in the forest grew the outlines of the shapes of each of the dark ones and their wings began to blur, become less defined, more ethereal. As I watched, I understood for the first time that the true power and force of the Light comes directly from the Light itself, which is all and everywhere. But the force and power of the darkness draws its strength from its ability to enlist souls in its dark efforts to always confuse, distort, stifle, harm, cast a shadow, and otherwise hide the existence of the Light. Its goal is to extinguish it from its own sight, and the sight of the universe.

I saw Thorpe redouble his efforts to maintain his position as he willed with all his might that the darkness prevail. I watched as waves of supporting energy passed from him to the dark angels as their own energies now grew stronger and their color returned along with their renewed strength.

"Okay," he said, looking at me "maybe you think you'll get lucky a second time. There are still three bullets left," he said "pointing the gun directly at Becky, "but maybe you won't!" And with that he ordered Butezz to grab the can of gasoline and then ordered Becky, at the point of the gun, to come to him as he was taking her with him out of the forest.

I stood my ground as my doubts set in. Yes, a miracle had saved me, but would the Angels of Light be able to save Becky and perform that same miracle a second time. My faith was challenged. I heard the Guardian speak to me in my mind, "Do nothing, all will work out!"

Becky and Bill seemed to hear that as well, for as the Guardian's voice faded from my mind, she left Bill's side, walked across the path and moved to join Thorpe and Butezz with no protest from Bill. With gun still in hand, Thorpe ordered Becky and Butezz to walk down the path in the direction of our farm. Butezz, with the heavy gas can, went first, and then Becky, and then Thorpe, walking half backward, half forward, followed with his gun pointed at Becky. He looked alternatively forward at his steps ahead and then back at me, as the angels of darkness, strengthened by Thorpe's dark will alone, surrounded the three of them.

The Angels of Light stood in their place, guarding each of us, except for the orange one who stood next to Becky. This Light Angel followed her, floating gently in the air as she crossed the path to join Thorpe and the other. As they walked, the orange angel floated just above Becky, creating a space around her that the dark ones couldn't penetrate.

My heart pounded and several times I began to move forward, to take action to help. I simply could not and would not let her be hurt. Still, the Guardian's words rang in my ear, "All will work out!"

The power of the orange Light of Varness continued to grow and I could feel that the presence of the Angels of Light grew with it. What also grew was my own faith that all would be well. Bill seemed to be in the same place as I and as the power and faith of the Light filled him as well. I heard him say to me in my mind, "Yes, we must wait, we must trust." And so we waited.

The three walked down the path which went straight ahead for several hundred yards before turning. Still illuminated by the Light of Varness, I could see clearly every step Thorpe and the others took. But that would change in just seconds. Only ten yards from where the group stood, the course of the path changed and would soon curve into a darkened area of the forest unlit by the Light. At this point, the three would disappear from view. I watched anxiously as they neared the turn. I knew beyond a doubt that I must not let them take Becky any farther.

Before moving any further, Thorpe suddenly stopped and called Butezz to his side. The dark angels still stood strong about him, as did the orange Angel of Light who stood vigil over Becky. Emboldened by his ability to help renew the strength and presence of the dark ones, Thorpe's thoughts turned to his unhindered escape from the forest. I could hear those thoughts as he ordered Butezz to empty the contents of the gasoline can a few feet from where they stood, and then set the fire that would, Thorpe hoped, destroy the forest. As he barked the order to Butezz, Thorpe looked directly at me with a dark look a certainty that I and the Light had lost.

Butezz moved to follow the order as he quickly came to the spot where Thorpe had indicated and without hesitation, poured the gasoline from his can out from one side of the path to the other making sure that he fully drenched the forest trees. All the while, Thorpe kept his gaze on me, but continued pointing the gun at Becky. Butezz, his work finished, threw the empty gas can aside, and then reached to his pocket to pull out a cigarette lighter.

I knew that I must act, for as soon as Butezz lit that fire I might not be able to get through the blaze to get to Becky. I had to take the chance. I needed to act now and pray that the Light Angels would protect Becky as I moved toward her and Thorpe. Thorpe turned his attention from me to Butezz, urging him on and then shoved Becky forward, continuing to move with her down the path. His gun was still aimed at her as I readied myself to act.

Then, without warning, from Frank came a huge cry. It echoed throughout the forest in a voice so loud, so strong, so different than any I'd ever heard before, as if it came from deep within the far reaches of the Universe, as if from within the heart of God.

"No!" it said, "You will not have her!"

Thorpe turned to the voice, but it was too late. Frank had already jumped from his place of hiding in the oak grove where he had gone unnoticed by Thorpe and now ran across the path. With all the speed and strength of the three-time All State linebacker, he tackled Thorpe at rib-height, hitting him with such force and power that the horrible sound of cracked ribs rang out throughout the forest. Thorpe screamed in agony as Frank, driven by the force of his two-hundred-and-twenty pounds, threw him down to the ground. It happened so quickly. I began to move forward to help Frank, but the force and power of Frank's tackle dislodged the gun from Thorpe's hand and sent it flying up the path about ten feet from where Butezz stood, and a good twenty-five yards from where I stood.

I heard Butezz's thought as he hesitated at first and then moved to where the gun landed. I must get it! It's my only chance, and with that thought I saw a vague image within Butezz's mind that somehow, with the gun in his hand, and Thorpe's help, he could still get the chest for himself. As Butezz moved to the gun, Becky stood over the struggling Thorpe, looking to see how she could help Cousin Frank. I realized that she had not seen the gun dislodge from Thorpe's hand and shouted, "Becky, the other one's going for the gun, run, get into the forest! Hide yourself!"

"You, too, Bill, get to safety. Now!"

Without hesitation, Becky, the orange angel still hovering over her, ran towards the oak grove that had served as the hiding place for Cousin Frank, and then on into the forest darkness beyond the grove. Bill heeded my call and, along with his gold angel protector, moved quickly up the little deer path that started from the main forest path into the shelter of the dense forest underbrush. In a moment, even though the forest glowed bright with the expanding Light of Varness, both he and Becky were impossible to see as they disappeared deeper into the forest.

With Henry Thorpe disabled on the ground, the angels of darkness began to lose their power and their forms again began to blur around the edges. Clearly, the strength of Thorpe's hatred and anger had not only filled the man with a strange dark power, but also filled the dark ones with that power. In spite of Frank's action against Thorpe, the dark angels retained some of their strength and the six dark ones left Thorpe's side and moved to surround Butezz, who had now gotten to the gun and picked it up. With a mad look in his eye he pointed it at Frank and stuttered, "G-g-et off hi-i-imm, le-let himmm up!"

The stench of fresh gasoline filled the forest. Frank's action had taken the fat man's mind off torching the forest and I began to move in this opening to help Frank, but stopped myself as quickly as I'd begun realizing that my movement at this point might do more to spook Butezz than help Frank. Strangely, something in me knew not to worry and that all would be okay.

I watched as Frank responded to Butezz. Frank was different and I didn't know at first what it was about him that had changed. Instead of being concerned about Felix Butezz and the gun, Frank seemed to have no fear at all as he broke his hold on the struggling man beneath him, and looked up directly into the eyes of the man with the gun and said, in a deep, but gentle voice, "No, little man, you put that gun down. It's time to quit!" Frank's words seemed to echo throughout the forest, "It's time to quit! It's time to quit!"

I felt a strength in Frank that I'd not felt before. From his eyes came a radiance of orange-gold light. A light that grew stronger in each moment and filled every part of his body, surrounding him with that same Light that filled the night sky, and the forest floor. Cousin Frank's very being was being transformed by his presence in the forest, and the influence on him of the Light of Varness, the *Passage to the Heavens*!

Felix Butezz felt it as well. The strength, resonance, and power of Frank's words ran through Butezz's body like a thunderclap within him, a shock that nearly knocked him off his feet. Having gotten hold of the gun, Butezz's strength had renewed itself for a short time, especially with the presence of the dark ones who surrounded him. But the power and the force of Frank's words hit him hard. Thorpe's downfall had seriously influenced the dark ones' ability to stay in the forest, and this combined with the growing strength of Varness was having its impact, draining what seemed to me to be the last of Butezz's already limited courage and will.

In this very moment, when I expected this man, Felix Butezz, to collapse, he reached to a place inside that helped strengthen the power of the dark angels around him. Where it came from, at first, I didn't understand. Rather than losing strength, Butezz seemed to be gathering it again, not so much from the dark ones, whose powers were indeed fading, but from another place, one incomprehensible to me.

The Guardian came to explain. "It's his fear" the Guardian said, "It is his fear that drives him on!" I turned my attention back to Butezz and I heard the words ring out, "I must not fail, I must not fail." And then, in the next instant, I saw in my mind's eye a vision of Butezz riding in the back seat of a long black limousine with a white-haired man with chiseled features. They were talking about the forest, and the chest. The older man, who countenance sent a shiver of fear up my spin, spoke with an icy voice to Butezz, demanding to know why the younger one had failed him. Felix started to explain and then, without warning, the older man began slapping the younger man, Felix, violently across the face— again and again calling him an idiot. In the image, Felix didn't even try to defend himself, he could only whimper, "Don't hit me, Daddy, don't hit me anymore, please Daddy, I tried my best."

The scene faded as Butezz repeated his threat to Frank, "Let him up, or I'll shoooot!" But Frank didn't budge. He only looked up from his hold atop Thorpe and again, with a voice of a power that filled the forest said to Butezz, "Stop now, little one. Stop!"

And Butezz, even with the strength of the fear that had driven him on, could no longer hold to the powers of darkness. As his will to resist the power of the Light collapsed, so, too, did the ability of the dark angels to stay in the forest, and the six dark ones flew away into the night sky creating a weak wisp of darkness across the stars as they passed.

Butezz screamed a cry of pain, as if the leaving of the dark ones brought physical pain to his being. He then wailed a second loud cry of despair. He could go on no longer, and he knew it. He couldn't threaten Frank further. He couldn't use the gun. A glazed look of madness filled his eyes. Frantically, he looked to the left and then to the right. What would he do? What could he do? He looked down at the unused cigarette lighter that he still held in his hand. Tears of frustration filled his eyes. Still pointing the gun at Frank, he moved towards the gasoline on the forest floor as if going to light it. Then, without warning he stopped, and madly turned the gun towards the empty forest to his right, then toward his left, as if enemies were pouring out of the Varness lit woods from every direction. Finally, in a last gesture of despair and frustration, he pointed the gun at me. And then, in his madness, he realized the "true" source of his torment, he turned the gun directly to Varness.

Butezz stood trembling, facing Varness. Tears filled his eyes. For just a moment his tears reflected the beautiful orange glow of Light radiating from the chest, and in that instant I could feel his heart soften. Unable to take the contradictory pulls of the Light and the darkness within him any longer, something in Felix broke. The softness in his eyes disappeared, and the mad rage of a man defeated crossed his face. He could stay in the forest no longer. He needed to be free. He turned to head for the darkened trail ahead and as he did, in one last gesture of despair, defiance, and frustration, the short fat man took the gun and threw it directly at Frank's head, missing him by only inches. Immediately, he disappeared around the curve of the path, out of the presence of the Light, into the darkness of the forest.

I ran to see if Frank needed help. Despite Thorpe's injury, he still weakly struggled to get out of the grasp of Cousin Frank. Frank looked up and said, "I'm okay, I can take care of this. What about Becky and Bill?"

I turned to look for them. Both were coming out of the woods from their hiding places and I knew they were okay. "Yes, they're fine, Frank," I said with an air of relief, "just fine." I took a deep breath and said, "I'll go after the other one now." I started to move to the darkened curve of the forest path to follow Butezz. The fading moon would only dimly light my way now, but enough to follow along fairly rapidly on this very familiar part of the forest path. But as I moved forward, the Guardian stopped me.

"Stay for a moment," he said, "there's more to learn here right now with that one." I wanted to make sure that Butezz didn't escape. I wanted to move to action, but I knew to listen to the Guardian. He had been right too many times in the past for me to doubt. I stayed and I waited. The Light of Varness continued to bathe Becky, Frank, Bill and me, and Henry Thorpe as well. But while I could see and sense the renewed life in the four of us that resulted from the Light, Thorpe continued to resist, keeping his eyes closed even as he struggled with Frank, as if seeing the Light were a plague that he must avoid at all costs.

Becky's radiance showed through in Varness's Light, and I saw a strength in her coming forth from a memory of herself so very long ago, before this time and place on Earth. The energies of a time when she knew herself full of love and power. A time when she felt no fear. She radiated this power and fearlessness, expressing a power and nobility in her almost royal in nature, and she, too, like Cousin Frank, took on the orange-golden glow of Varness as it radiated through her eyes and surrounded her body.

I looked over at Bill. He had a smile on his face and a sense of happiness coming from him that reminded me of a newly born child. The experience of seeing the Angels of Light and being with them and experiencing directly the power of the golden angel who'd been protecting him renewed Bill. I could read in him a feeling of peace and calm about what he'd seen in the forest as a youngster. For now he knew the truth of the path of his grandparents and the truth of their role with the Brotherhood of Light as leaders among the family farm holders.

As for Cousin Frank, his entire Being glowed. The power that had come forth from him as he spoke to the fat man and Thorpe came from a place deeper within him than I could know. "Yes, Harry," the Guardian said," your Cousin Frank opened himself entirely to the forces of Light from the beyond. Varness helped and what came forth in him is knowledge of the true power of the Light. Though Frank may never understand the workings of that force, he will call on that power often to help the Light in the days and years ahead.

"And you, Harry, what about you?" the Guardian asked. I closed my eyes and went within and a large smile crossed my face. "I learned that I *am* a child of Light. That all I need to do is to continue to show up in the right place at the right time to help in whatever way I can." I smiled again, "And I learned that I can depend on the fact that when I do, you'll be there, Guardian, to help me along the way!" I felt the Guardians own broad smile within me. "Yes, you're right," his voice said, and then I felt arise from deep within me an image I'd never seen before: an image of me, or a part of me, in a long blue robe standing in a temple of white columns full of Light. Next to me stood a woman dressed in a similar robe of deep burgundy, and we both were aglow with Light. In the vision, the woman and I looked outward, both with a smile on our face, and I realized that they were looking from their place in the white columned temple full of light, at *me,* where I now stood. Through their eyes I saw that I, too, the "me" here in the forest, radiated the orange-gold glow of Varness.

I didn't totally understand how I could be both watching me from the temple and being me here in the forest, but it didn't matter. The Light, indeed, filled me, and I felt an abounding joy at being alive and being me.

"Go now, Harry," the Guardian said. The path is short back to your farm and there's still a little light from the moon. The man Butezz won't have gone very far." I nodded my head as the image faded. I checked with Frank to see that all was well and that he didn't need my help with Thorpe, and headed for the curve of the darkened forest path where Felix had fled only moments before. As I did, I looked back and I saw the Light that radiated from the chest and the brilliant stones embedded within its walls slowly began to lose its glow. It's as if Varness is going to sleep, I thought. Then, as if by magic, the chest simply disappeared into the darkened forest. I *knew* that Varness had returned to its place of rest in the forest clearing where my dad and I used to go when I was a boy. I smiled again at the memory and at the comfort I felt in knowing Varness rested there, and headed out on my way to deal with Felix Butezz before he could get away.

***

The moon's dimming glow still provided a small measure of visibility to the path in this part of forest. I needed to go slow at first until my eyes adjusted. I felt at home here. I knew the trail very well. This area of the forest had provided Becky and me hours of fun as the backdrop for the wondrous games we'd play after school and during our summer vacations or on the weekends. From here we would here our mother's call telling us it was time for lunch or dinner.

Tonight, as I followed after Butezz, I felt something had changed in the forest. The presence of the dark angels, Thorpe, Butezz and the others, had somehow soiled the forest, left a stench that would need to be healed. The sacred quiet of the forest would need time, I thought, to cleanse and purify itself of their presence. My thoughts turned back to Felix Butezz. I would have to hurry to catch him. The few moments the

Guardian had me stay behind had given him a pretty good head start. I needed to get to him before he got out of the forest and had a chance to flee on to the road. My eyes adjusted to the darkness and I ran down the path as fast as I could.

As I rounded the last bend of the path before reaching the forest entrance to our farm, to my surprise, I nearly tripped over a scene that had me burst into laughter. I realized that what the Guardian had said about Butezz not getting very far was right. Here, in the middle of the path, about two hundred feet from our farm entrance and lit by the lights of our farmhouse beyond, I came upon a smiling Uncle Julius, all six-foot-five inches of him, white-bearded and all. His wounded leg was wrapped as Frank and I had left it, and he was sitting atop a squealing Felix Butezz, who squirmed beneath him whimpering, "Let me go, old man!"

The smile of triumph on Uncle Julius' face was a thing to behold, and that look in his eyes! Like a child who'd done his good deed for the day, he beamed all over, and I could only stand there in and marvel at the scene. That smile. That look. They were the smile of old and the same look that I had seen so many times throughout my life, and had known and loved all these years, and my heart melted in thankfulness at seeing them again.

"Hi Harry," Uncle Julius said, "I had a feeling you'd be coming along this way and I figured you'd want to me hold on to this one for you."

"Indeed, Uncle Julius" I said. "Indeed! I couldn't hold my laughter back as relief came from deep within my heart, and I knew that my laughter could be heard all the way across the forest to were Becky, Bill and Frank were. "Yes, indeed!" I said, one last time. "Yes, indeed!" as tears of laughter and joy filled my eyes.

***

As I approached Uncle Julius and Felix, two police cars, lights flashing, come up our farm driveway and stopped in front of the house. Sergeant Annie Gerhig was the first to arrive, followed by three other officers. I told her what had happened, where the others were and two officers immediately set out to arrest Thorpe. As they left, I heard one of them put a call for two ambulances, one for Uncle Julius and second for Thorpe. The third officer stayed behind and handcuffed a still whimpering Felix Butezz, and escorted him into the caged back seat of the police car.

We didn't have to wait long for the ambulances. In only minutes the flashing lights of two entered our driveway and two teams of paramedics came running onto the main forest path. The first team treated Uncle Julius, while the second went off to deal with Henry Thorpe. I didn't have time to say much to Uncle Julius before he was away to the hospital, but I made it a point to tell him that Becky and I would come to the hospital the next day to see how he was doing.

Soon enough, the team of paramedics and the two police officers that had gone into the forest emerged around the curve of the trail with a stretcher bearing the injured Thorpe. He seemed to be in serious pain and had an oxygen mask over his face to help him breathe. They passed where Sergeant Gerhig and I still stood at the gate. As the sound of the ambulance sirens faded down the road into town, Sergeant Gerhig got a call on her walkie-talkie. Her officers discovered two men sitting in a car on the main road who claimed they knew nothing of farm or the situation, but were there just relaxing on a country road on a nice fall night. The Sergeant wanted me to see if I recognized them and asked me to accompany her to the road.

On the walk down, she told me that the other members of the Alcaz Motorcycle Club were all under arrest, two of them having been caught trying to set fire to the forest near the Henley farm forest entrance, and the other two were caught by the state highway patrol as they drove their way out of town. These two had confessed to trying to burn down the forest, the sergeant said, but told some wild story about a giant with a turban on his head stopping them. "You know," one reportedly told the state trooper, "like a genie from a magic lantern."

Sergeant Gerhig didn't smile as she told the story, but only looked at me with a questioning look out of the corner of her eye as if she wanted me to say something about the seven foot tall magic genie of the forest. I only nodded and said nothing. I took a deep breath of the clear Ohio fall night air. The mixture of scents of farmland and the forest filled me, and the night sky filled with stars gave me a sense of peace and belonging.

"You know," Sergeant Gerhig said, "if it wasn't for your sister Becky's call, we would have never caught those motorcycle club gang members. Good thing she had the foresight to do it because they'd already broken camp where they were hold up these last months and were heading out of town. My guess is forever, after doing their dirty job of torching the forest. We got here just in time."

I nodded again, feeling a kind of quiet contentment that come over me. The policemen who took Thorpe away told me that Bill, Becky, and Frank were fine and where just behind them. My walk with Sergeant Gerhig allowed me to relax for the first time in what seemed like a long, long time. All was well and I took another deep breath of country air.

We arrived at the road and there in the back of a third police car sat John Freed and Robert Frosten. They made a funny pair, these two, in the back seat of the police car with Freed being short, small, and thin, and Frosten being tall, bulky, and overweight. They reminded me of a pair of funny looking cartoon characters I'd seen in the comics as a kid. As I identified them for Sergeant Gerhig, I thought again what I'd always thought about them: that they were more pawns in the game rather than key actors and I wondered what would happen to them when they faced their day in court. Sergeant Gerhig thanked me for the positive identification and asked me to bring Becky, Frank, and Bill with me to the police station the next day to get statements from us and then she left to talk with the other officers.

***

As I began my walk back up our road to the farm, that same feeling of contentment at the quiet, the beauty of the night sky, and the fresh farm country air filled me. But something disturbed that feeling and I wondered what it was. I walked only a couple of steps up our road before I felt the need to stop. I turned and looked back at the road at the last of the police cars, their lights flashing, driving away. The moon still shed some light onto the Ohio countryside and all seemed well. Still, I felt something eating at me. I shook my head, ignoring the feeling for the moment and turned back up the road. Just then, from the west, I heard the sound of a car coming at a pretty fast pace around the bend of the curve of the road. I waited and soon enough a small van carrying a noisy bunch of teenagers passed our road on their way into town. I smiled at my concern, sighed a sigh of relief. But before I could take another step back up the road to the farm, a second car slowly rounded the same bend, a long black limousine. I watched the limousine coming past our farm entrance and as it did the driver slowed down. I wondered who this could be, and then I saw a man looking out the open back window directly up our road as if looking for something, or someone. A chill ran through me. I recognized the white-haired man with the chiseled-faced profile looking out of the limo as the very same man that I'd seen slapping Felix Butezz in the vision I'd watched only minutes before. This was the man Butezz called Daddy, and I knew in that moment that even though we'd stopped the assault on the forest this time, this man and those like him who served the darkness would continue their efforts to stifle the Light wherever they found it. The limousine continued on its way then, speeding up at it went down the road, leaving the area of the five farm family homes, and the forest, I hoped, forever.

***

Becky and Bill waited for me at the farmhouse. Cousin Frank had headed to town to be with Uncle Julius at the hospital, so the three of us sat together around the farm's old oak kitchen table. As Becky and I had done with Mom and Dad on countless nights like this as we grew up, we turned off the electric kitchen light overhead, lit the kerosene lantern and put it in the middle of our large table and sat down for a quiet cup of tea. The three of us sat in silence for what seemed like a very long time, each of us holding a warm cup in hand as protection against the cooling fall night. My mind wondered. Yes, I knew we had much to share, but sitting like this together gave us all, I thought, a sense of belonging, of togetherness, of family.

Then, in the midst of my reverie, Becky quietly asked me, "Do you remember the time I told you about the vision I had of a horse? Remember, you'd just gotten back home?"

I nodded, "Yes, I remember," I said.

Then, she turned to Bill and quietly recounted her vision. "I saw this large horse, a beautiful horse, black as night, strong and powerful, but it was stuck in a bog somewhere and strange animals that I'd never seen before threatened it and it felt to me like a friend and one that I would do almost anything to help it out of that bog."

She continued, now speaking to us both, "Well, you know what?" she said. "I saw a vision of that horse again in the forest just now. It happened just as those dark beings fled the forest. But instead of the horse being stuck in the bog, I saw it had escaped and now ran wild and free on a grass covered plain, its tail and mane flying high like music in the wind, and the sun shined brightly on its brilliant black coat. It sparkled like diamonds, and my heart lifted in laughter and glee. I tell you," Becky went on, "it felt so good to see it free. For the first time in months I took a deep, deep breath. I knew somehow that the horse's freedom meant that the attack on the forest was over, and that the peaceful Spirit of the forest was restored."

Both Bill and I joined Becky in another deep sigh as she finished telling the story. Somehow, the fact that we'd been linked in one mind during our time in the forest gave us a sense of unity that we'd not had before. I could feel that as Becky recounted her story of the freedom of the black horse, not only did her heart lift, but so, too, did Bill's and mine.

CHAPTER FIFTY-ONE
SAKYA TEACHES HIS LESSON

Light Prevails Always and Those Who Follow It with their Hearts Open Full Cannot Help But Find Their Way Back Home!

The next morning I woke at the dawn of a brilliant sunny day, dressed, and following an inner urging walked into the forest. As I got to the place where the path met the trail to the clearing where I knew Varness sat, I knew also to pass it by and so I headed for the oak log by the creek runoff where I first met Sakya. When I arrived, Sakya was there waiting for me. As I approached and in the dawn's rising light, both of our smiles sparkled with the sun's golden rays reflected in our eyes.

"Greetings," he said, his smile growing broader each moment.

"Greetings Sakya," I said, "I thought I would find you here."

"You listen well," he said, and then again said, "You listen well. Please, sit down."

"We of the Brotherhood have called you here to speak of things gone by. The brilliance of the sun this morning reminds us of the Light that we so well defended last evening, but it isn't a broad battle that will win the day. It is the work of each of those on the path of Light that meets the needs of the whole. Yes, we fought a battle, but did you notice that it was the individuals in the forest who made the difference, each following their own path. Frank listened well and played his part as did Becky, Bill and you.

"But," Sakya went on, "it's through each of your own evolutions that we of the Light can work. You saw how the darkness takes its power from the angst and hatred of those who choose to refuse their own Light. Well, even those who wish to follow the *path* need to make strong choices to continue, for what they encounter along their journey is the face of their own history. There isn't one individual on Earth who doesn't have some deed, thought, attitude or belief they've held, or action they've done in the past that they do not regret. The lesson we come to teach this morning is one of forgiveness of self. Even though many on Earth believe that the darkness is prevailing, it is not, not now, nor could it ever. What is prevailing in the outer or survival mind of earthly man is the chaos caused by the darkness' ability to confuse humanity into believing that it has no longer a connection to the Light.

"But this can never be true. The Light is all and everywhere, and except for those who've specifically made a choice to reject the Light, we've a great faith in humankind's ability to awaken from the dream."

He stopped a moment and looked up at the sun. His seven foot body towered over me. He smiled again and took a deep stretch opening his heart to the rays of the sun. "So," he continued "what this means is that for you and others who choose the Master's Path, you must work to do the one thing humankind has not wanted to do: remember your own individual history, and in the case of humanity, its own species history. You must all remember your own past, and then forgive it, all of it, totally and freely with an open heart and joy and move on. And when you do, you'll feel the freedom of your own birth in the perfection of creation.

"We of the Brotherhood are quite aware that this isn't an easy task, but one that requires great diligence and self kindness to literally re-inhabit your own history, reprogram the body, and enfold your world in positive thoughts and feeling about who you are. It takes great effort and for those of you on the path, we thank and praise you.

"So, yes, you'll be involved greatly in serving the Light in the years ahead, but it is remembrance of *your* past and the freeing of the self judgments that grew out of that history that's the key. We of the Brotherhood are here to help. Call on us often and you won't fail to *know* who you really are. You'll discover your own true name, Sat Nam! It's a bright new day," he said, "One that brings with it another victory. Others will appear and here and there attempt to destroy the workings of the Light; they cannot prevail. What we, with your help, can do is strengthen your knowledge of your beauty, your gifts, and your open hearted love of *you*. That is the Path of the Master and the one that aligns perfectly with your own true destiny. And, in aligning with your destiny, you serve the Light of all on this blessed Earth. So seek loving *you*, the real you, the one that has no self judgment but only self love, and we guarantee that you'll prosper and in the end find your way back home." With that Sakya smiled again as we locked eyes in friendship and love.

As I looked up at him, the sun showed itself behind him as rays radiating from his body. For a moment I couldn't see the outline of his body, but only the golden Light of the sun spreading out behind him from every aspect of his Being. I couldn't tell whether I was seeing an illusion from the position in which Sakya stood in relation to the sun, or whether the Light itself radiated directly from him. My eyes blinked as I tried to focus on his body and not on the sun's rays. And, when I opened them again, Sakya was gone.

I stayed in the forest for some time, just sitting and pondering Sakya's words. I'd heard the term "self forgiveness" many times before, but somehow never did it hold the meaning that it did now. It seemed like such a large task, and I wondered whether I could do it, truly forgive everything. But, as I sat there in the forest, deep within me, I also knew that if I could really forgive all, I would come in touch with a part of me ever so much purer than even I could image.

Yes, I thought, this is the Path open to all and is *my* chosen Path that I walk upon, the *Master's Path of self forgiveness* to gather my own Light and know me and my *true* name, SAT NAM, as Sakya called it. Before I left the forest I took one last look up at the sun as it rose now even more brilliant in the sky, and for a moment, just one moment, I thought I saw Sakya's face in it, smiling back at me from the sun's place in the blue Ohio sky.

About the Author

 Jay Allan Luboff is an avid fan of "Great Spirit," "God," "Source Energy," the "Oneness"—or whatever else you may wish to call it. And while this is true about Jay, he also believes firmly that each and every one of us is a part of that larger God reality and that we are all moving into a time of Conscious knowing of this truth. And so in writing this book, and future ones to come, he explores both our common presence in the Oneness and the resistance to this concept as Earth, through the expanding consciousness of humanity, births itself anew.

Jay has been on his own dedicated spiritual path for over a quarter of a century and he knows that the journey "back home" to self awareness is not always a smooth one, but a road that has its bumps and potholes along the way. His writings address some of these issues of humanity's "growing pains," individually and collectively, from a time of asleep consciousness to a time of awakened consciousness on Earth; from a time of resistance to a time of *allowing* the Divine truth within each of us to unfold its perfection.

On his own journey of discovery over the years Jay has written journals and poetry, short stories, and even an illustrated children's book. *Harry Pond Looks Homeward, The Spiritual Adventures of an Ohio Farm Boy* is his first novel. Jay is a dedicated husband to Chantal Marie, his wife and spiritual partner of twenty-five years, and works in the world as a consultant to help "Green" the planet.

ALL THINGS THAT MATTER PRESS ™

FOR MORE INFORMATION ON TITLES AVAILABLE FROM
ALL THINGS THAT MATTER PRESS, GO TO
http://allthingsthatmatterpress.com
or contact us at
allthingsthatmatterpress@gmail.com

Made in the USA
San Bernardino, CA
23 September 2013